HER HUSBAND'S LOVER

Madelynne Ellis

mischief

Mischief
An imprint of HarperCollins*Publishers*
77–85 Fulham Palace Road,
Hammersmith, London W6 8JB

www.mischiefbooks.com

A Paperback Original 2013

First published in Great Britain in ebook format by
HarperCollins*Publishers* 2013

A catalogue record for this book is
available from the British Library

ISBN-13: 978 0 00 753333 6

Automatically produced by Atomik ePublisher from Easypress

CHAPTER ONE

June 1801, Field House, Staffordshire, England

He's a man ... Saints above. He's a man and I want to touch him.

Emma Langley, who never touched anyone if she could help it, wanted to touch *him*. More specifically, she wanted to comb her fingers through the fiery strands of his hair and trace a fingertip down the ridge of his rather sharp nose. There were other more startling thoughts tumbling around her head too, but Emma took no account of them. It was quite shocking enough that she wanted to reach out and touch a person's skin, without contemplating anything more daring.

Perhaps she'd drunk overmuch wine at dinner. The delightful Mr Aiken had never let her consume more than a sip before being ready to pour her another. But no, she didn't think the wine to blame. Heavens, if it were that simple, she'd have taken to frequent tippling years ago. Rather, there was something quite special about the man – being, as he was, Lord Darleston, the eldest son of the Earl of Onnerley. A man, if certain recent newspaper epithets were to be believed, known for his perverse tastes and unnatural practices.

1

Of course, she gave no truck to such libellous specula-
tion – well, maybe a little. Her father would never knowingly have invited such a wretch into his house. Rather,
she supposed Darleston had enemies and slurring a rival's
reputation required little wit or ingenuity. Although – a
smile stretched the corners of her lips – perhaps perversity
could be attributed to his choice of evening wear. In a room
of glorified dandies, Darleston alone wore brocade. Black
knee-breeches disappeared into gleaming top-boots. They
on their own invited only minor remark – they were in the
countryside – but his coat ... that was a triumph: ostenta-
tious but not in a vulgar fashion, being formed, as far as she
could tell through the glass, from black Florentine silk. It
sported huge lapels in contrasting red and every seam, every
buttonhole, was edged in gold filigree.

She wanted to rub up against him and trace every thread.

Emma looked at her fingers in suspicion; the notion of
desiring contact was so very strange to her. Then she curled
the digits over her lips to hide her smile.

'Well, sister, what say you? Will any of them do?'

Emma turned her head as her sister inched closer to the
dining-room window. The moment their skirts brushed,
Emma recoiled, leaving Amelia in possession of the ledge.

'I should think not, dear heart, for there are only Aiken,
Connelly and Bathhouse whom you might consider and none
of them to your tastes. The other gentlemen are already wed.'

'Surely, not all?' Amelia strained onto her toes for a better
look. She was a good few inches shorter than Emma, and
her view of the interior was largely restricted to the tops
of the gentlemen's heads. 'Why do you dismiss Bathhouse?
Connelly I can understand – he is always so bilious and red
about the nose – and I know Aiken is quite besotted with

that ninny from the Walshes' party, but Bathhouse seemed most attentive earlier. And he's young. That has to count for something, does it not? I shan't want an old man.'

'Gracious, Amelia! None of them is a day above forty. As for Bathhouse, why, he hasn't two farthings to his name. He takes work as a tutor. Father would never approve.'

'Well, I shouldn't mind. At least one might assume he has a brain unlike most of the horrid popinjays I've been paraded before.'

Emma clucked in disapproval, a habit that seemed unavoidable in her sister's company. Most would assume snobbery to be behind their father's determination to provide them both with decent matches, but Emma knew the truth was far more practical. He wanted them never to starve – a condition he was more closely familiar with than any of his gentleman companions would believe.

Amelia continued to bob up and down, trying to catch a proper glimpse of Mr Bathhouse. Emma shook her head in dismay. She would have to maintain a close watch upon her sister and perhaps steer her in another direction. She stepped out of the flowerbed and gave a stamp to remove the soil from her shoes. 'Come away now, dear heart, it's time we went in. Father has very nearly finished his brandy.' He only ever drank one glass and always left a dribble the size of a guinea in the bottom to appease the good-luck fairies, a practice that had apparently paid off. The Hill family fortunes had certainly improved since the days of Emma's childhood. Heavens, they were now entertaining an earl's son. In their threadbare past the only guest they'd had was the debt collector, from whom they'd unsuccessfully hidden.

After a little cajoling Amelia stepped away from the window.

The lawn of Field House lay in golden shadows, the last vestige of the late sun still streaking the evening sky. Swarms of midges hung beneath the hollyhocks and the other encroaching foliage as the two women climbed through an open sash window back into the homely comfort of the drawing room.

Field House was for the most part rather staid and masculine in design, but the drawing room had been decorated by their late mother and showed a more feminine touch. Colourful embroidered cushions nestled between the more recently acquired porcelains and elegant damask-covered chairs. Wildflowers arranged in jugs added bright flashes of colour to even the dimmest corner far from the hearth. It was the only room in the house Emma associated with joy.

'I didn't see Lyle,' Amelia commented, as Emma lifted the teapot to give it a hopeful shake. By the feel of it, only the dregs remained. 'Why wasn't he with the others?'

The question carved furrows in Emma's brow. Rather than answer, she calmly settled the teapot and filled the space in which an answer ought to have been by draining what remained of her cold tea. Truthfully, she didn't know where Lyle had got to. He had certainly remained at the dinner table with the other gentlemen when she and Amelia left. He ought to still be there now. However, Lyle often wasn't where he ought to be. As for where he would most likely be found – Emma's cheeks burned, leaving her distressingly rosy. She immediately took a seat by the fire and thrust the guard out of the way to account for her glow. She'd lost count of the times she'd had to cover for him.

'I expect he was there and you just didn't see him, Amelia. Or else Father asked him to attend to something. You know

4

he isn't so sound on his feet any more and Lyle does like to be helpful.'

More than likely, Lyle had slipped away during the fuss over Darleston's late arrival and was now below stairs or else secreted in some other cubby-hole engaged in practices it would take the ingenuity of a fence to explain away.

If her father ever found out – she shook her head sadly – heavens, if *anyone* discovered her husband's proclivities, then her entire world would crumble. Divorce was not a pleasant word but, by God, that's what it would likely come to, if only so that she might protect her dignity and not spoil Amelia's chances.

Emma's terror at the prospect wasn't new and soon wore off, as did the flames in her cheeks. She'd known precisely how Lyle was when she'd married him. In truth it had been what had endeared him to her most of all. Other women might seek fidelity; Emma had known that Lyle would stray. In fact, she'd counted upon it. It had been her one great bargaining tool.

'Drat and dandelions,' Amelia cursed, rousing Emma from her thoughts with their favourite childhood blasphemy. 'I'd so hoped that Lord Darleston had travelled with a companion. I mean, who does not these days? I'm quite put out by it. I don't want to stay here and turn into one of those simpering old maids. I knew I ought to have insisted on going to London instead of being stuck here in the wilds. I don't see why I can't have at least one London season.'

'Patience. I'm sure Father will arrange something. Give him time. You know this gathering is important to him.'

'He'll be too withered to take me, or I too old to be of interest if I'm forced to wait much longer. I'm nineteen. The Walsh girls have already had two seasons.'

'The Walsh girls have no choice but to take whatever offers they manage to grab. Your situation is a little different.'

'Not so very different,' Amelia grumbled. She retreated to the rear of the drawing room, where she drew a book from a shelf and faked a deep engagement with it.

Emma's gaze strayed to the mantel-clock. From the direction of the dining room there was a scraping of chairs followed by the sound of heavy footsteps. The gentlemen, headed by Mr Hill, squeezed through the parlour door two abreast and availed themselves of various chairs. Seven of them were soon draped over the furniture, chattering loudly. Amelia made a beeline towards Mr Bathhouse. Emma made to follow, only to be intercepted by her father and Lord Darleston.

Ada came up behind them bearing a second teapot. 'I thought you might be needing some more, miss, with so large a party.'

'Yes, we were. Thank you, Ada.'

'Could you, dear?' Mr Hill gestured towards the steaming vessel.

Perhaps Amelia would be fine for a moment or two. Emma poured for her father and offered a second cup to Lord Darleston. The wretched china trembled abysmally when she held out her hand. Close up, the urge to touch him grew infinitely stronger. The coat ... his coat, heavens, if it wasn't the most marvellously perverse thing she'd ever beheld. Each swirl in the fabric had a raised pile that gave it such texture and shape. Indeed, seeing it up close she realised it was not simple brocade, but formed an interweaving pattern of maenads engaged in rather lewd play. Yet it suited him perfectly, drawing attention to his big strong shoulders and the perfect narrowness of his hips.

For a moment, she thought it might be only his outfit that engaged her senses. Then his hand shot out and steadied the wobbling cup and he blessed her with a smile that made the very corners of his eyes crinkle. He had grey eyes, flecked with specks of lilac that were like slivers of rain-washed slate. Light flared in the depths of his pupils.

That one look told her everything she ever needed to know about Lord Darleston. He was handsome and dangerous, and if she had any sense of self-preservation she would avoid him, else those fanciful ideas she'd been entertaining earlier might very well get the better of her. At the same time, she knew she wouldn't. Still, the sense of loneliness that had grown over the winter had only increased with the coming of lighter nights. She longed for a companion who was more attuned to her needs, someone who was wicked and exciting and who would give her a reason to thrive instead of growing old and drab. Lyle saw that she was cared for and comfortable, but she knew he found it hard to relate to her.

'Emma, my eldest,' her father introduced her. 'It's so good to have you home again, dear. I do wish you and Langley would reconsider my offer. The old place is so cavernous with only Amelia and me in residence. Where is Langley, do you know? I do so want to speak with him before I retire.'

'I'm afraid I don't know, Father. I thought he was with you. Perhaps he'll be back in a moment.'

Mr Hill's sallow brows wrinkled. Emma's heartrate doubled. *He knows. He knows.* Lord Darleston was watching them. *Oh, God, please don't let everything fall apart now.*

Her father sipped his tea. 'Well, yes, I expect you're right. But I think I may just slip along right now.' He turned to Darleston and cuffed him companionably upon the arm. 'I haven't the stamina of you young bloods any more. I'll bid you goodnight, milord. Gentlemen. Emma will ensure that Grafton sees to your wishes. Do forgive my atrocious manners.'

'Don't worry, Father. I'll see everyone off.'

'Yes, yes, of course you will. Goodnight, Emma. Mind you don't go needling, Lord Darleston. She can be quite the prickly philosopher, but you mustn't take her too much to heart.'

No, she oughtn't to be taken at all seriously. Emma enfolded her fists around the fabric of her skirts, whilst she maintained a well-practised smile. Silly old fool didn't believe her capable of a single eloquent thought. And he really ought to have considered, before inviting them, the fact that his guests would go late to their beds. Now she and Lyle would have to play host and hostess, wherever Lyle happened to be.

Her father leaned towards her, meaning, she realised, to press a kiss to her cheek, but when Emma stiffened all the way from her toes to her lips, he straightened at once. 'Well, goodnight, dear.' He tottered away, yawning into his teacup, and looking strangely frail. Perhaps Amelia had a point about the London season. Mr Hill's deteriorating health would likely make it impossible before long.

'I'm sorry,' she said, recalling Lord Darleston. 'He never does stay up past ten o'clock.'

'No matter.' Darleston's soft drawl coiled around her pleasure centres. It was quite wrong that a man's voice could make one feel quite so tremulous, not to mention it being a new and not altogether comfortable experience.

'He does you a disservice, I think.'

'What!' Her throat grew tight all around the neckline of her gown, and another blush began crawling across her skin. It was the curse of being fair. 'He says only what he believes to be true.' The fact that she had run his household from the age of fourteen had entirely passed him by.

'And do you believe I should disregard your chatter as nonsense? Do you often speak thus, Mrs –?'

'Langley,' she supplied, growing hotter still. 'And no, milord, I do not. Although you are at liberty to reach your own conclusion about whether what I spout is twaddle.'

Darleston gave a deep throaty laugh that rolled like a purr and sent sparks of heat to her breasts. He was quite the most ... No, it was wrong to think like that and positively discourteous to her husband. Not that they had a conventional relationship. Oh, to hell with it. If she couldn't be honest in her own thoughts, then she would never hear any truth. Darleston was beautiful. Not in a dandified, fashionable sort of way, but in an animal way. Something about him yanked at her as if there were a knot tied in the centre of her chest and he kept tugging on the other end.

Emma focused on a point midway down his chest. She dared not glance any lower, nor look up into his face for too long for fear that he would recognise the heat in her gaze. She'd seen other women look at men in this way, but she'd never done so herself. Looking led to touching, and touching was something she could never do.

'How is it you happen to be with us?' she asked, eyes downcast, as she retreated into the safety of an armchair.

Darleston leaned against the mantel. 'I did intend to stay elsewhere. Alas, that didn't work out. He had ... other plans.' Darleston's lips quirked upwards but failed to form a smile. 'However, as your father had already kindly extended an invitation, and I was already quite nearby ...'

'And do you like it? What you've seen?'

'I've scarcely taken more than a passing glance. I understand you have a hundred and twenty or so acres, but I'm sure

I'll find it charming, much as I find the lady of the house.'

Butterflies fanned the flames in her chest. It was an easy compliment for him to bestow, but not one she heard very often. Few sought her acquaintance or pleasure, preferring Amelia's vivaciousness. 'Strictly speaking, that would be my sister, not I.'

He turned his head to spy her sister out. Amelia sat at the centre of a ring of gentlemen upon a tapestry-covered pouffe. The week was clearly to be one rife with trouble. Just as Emma was about to intrude upon her sister's admirers, the drawing-room door swung open, admitting a blond gentleman.

Emma's concern switched to her husband. His expression was one of wistful delight, which transformed in an instant to one of rapturous joy. Good heavens, Lyle, she thought. Must you advertise the wickedness you've been about? She quickly turned her head, praying that, from what she could descry of the other gentlemen's thoughts, they merely saw Lyle as merry and not licentious.

'Darleston! God in heavens, what the devil are you doing here?' Lyle crossed the room in several bounds. He stepped past her without so much as a glance in her direction and enfolded Lord Darleston in a fond embrace.

'Langley!' Darleston sounded equally surprised to find Lyle wrapped tightly around his person.

'Heavens, man. How long has it been? It must have been years. You've met my wife, I see.'

Lyle turned his head towards her and graced her with a nod. A fantastic smile lit his face. Emma frowned at him. She couldn't see why Lord Darleston's presence should make him quite so joyous. Then again, Emma sucked down an unsteady breath. No! No, it simply couldn't be. The first man she'd felt remotely ... No! Oh, but it was. She could

10

tell just from the way their arms stayed around one another and the embrace encompassed not only the brushing of chests but of thighs and hips too.

They knew each other, and not just in the platonic sense.

'Yes, I knew of the wedding.' Darleston pulled away first. He gave a swift glance around the room but the other occupants were still crowded around Amelia and seemingly uninterested in anything else. 'My father made certain to send me the newspaper cutting. Happy, I trust?' He raised his eyebrows and glanced first at Lyle and then at her as if he was seeing them quite anew. 'Mrs Langley.' His lips formed her name, but he didn't speak the words aloud. Lightning flashed in his eyes.

'Yes. Absolutely.' Lyle slapped him upon the back.

'Children?'

Emma bowed her head. She stared at her hands clasped tight around her teacup. Why did everyone have to pounce upon that particular subject as if breeding were the only possible purpose in taking a bride? Or one couldn't possibly be happy without a dozen pale-faced imps running about one's feet? She prayed they never had a child. Not a single blessed one. Her mother had carried fifteen of the little devils. See where it had got her – a cold box in a rat-infested cemetery, rained on and covered in moss.

Lyle, clearly noticing her distress, waved aside the question. 'None yet. What about you?' He cast her an encouraging smile. He might take ridiculous risks, but Lyle also worked hard to maintain at least the illusion of an affectionate marriage.

Darleston gave a vehement shake of his head. 'Much to the Earl's vexation.'

'But there is a Lady Darleston?' Emma ventured.

11

'There is.' His very abruptness explained all that was missing from his response. Likely he and his wife were not on intimate terms, assuming they tolerated each other's company at all. Perhaps they even lived apart, occupying one grand house apiece.

Lyle slapped Darleston across the back again, as he finally relinquished his embrace. 'I insist that we celebrate with something more spirited than over-stewed tea. You don't mind, Emma, if I snatch him away, do you? It's been ... gracious, how many years?'

'Nine,' Darleston remarked dryly.

Emma gave a polite nod. What could she say? Foolish displays had never been her forte; she left such nonsense to Amelia, who would have stamped her foot and demanded a place in their conversation. 'I'll see to our other guests.' She made to rise, but Lyle shooed her back into her seat.

'No need to move, my sweet. Stay by the fire. We'll walk. You don't mind an evening stroll, do you, Darleston? You're not afeared of the country vapours? I find it most beneficial to take a little wander before bed.'

'Indeed, that sounds delightful. I'd appreciate the opportunity to stretch my legs. I've been stuck in a carriage for days.'

'Where've you come from?'

'Only from Shropshire today, but from London before that.'

'Stopping in on the old family pile?'

The candlelight glowed bright copper among the fiery strands of Darleston's hair as he shook his head. Lyle guided him towards the door.

'I stayed the night at Pennerley. Do you know the marquis? I had intended a longer visit but he has business in Yorkshire to attend.'

'And so you washed up here. How marvellous. How wonderful indeed.'

The door swung closed behind them. Emma stared at the abandoned cups of tea and poured herself another. A moment later she rang for Ada. 'Could you ensure my sister's bed is warmed, please?' It was time she coaxed that little goose away from the ganders.

CHAPTER TWO

The proposed drink went forgotten. Darleston allowed Lyle to guide him across the hallway of Field House and down the front steps, eschewing overcoats and accoutrements. Twilight subsumed the last of the day as they crossed the lawn, stealing the colour from his vision. They didn't really speak until they stood upon the bank of the Trent, well out of sight of the house amongst a copse of ancient sycamore trees.

'I didn't ... I had no idea that you'd married Hill's daughter,' Darleston began. She'd told him her name and it hadn't sparked a flicker of recognition. He'd met other Mrs Langleys before, but ... 'I mean, I knew you'd wed, but I'd really no idea there was a connection.' Silence swallowed his words, which wasn't such a surprise. What the hell did you say to someone you hadn't seen for nine years and to whom you'd made promises you could never hope to keep? 'Lyle.' He put out his hand and touched the other man's arm, making the briefest of connections. 'If my presence is going to make things awkward, I can make my excuses.' Hell only knows where he'd go when he left. He was fast running out of friends with country estates. The last place he wanted to end up was home, where Lucy could find him. Increasingly it looked as if he'd have to take a long, slow tour of the Scottish Highlands and grow a beard so that he'd blend in with the locals and not drawn undue attention.

Not drawing attention would be a damned fine strategy at this point.

The trickle of fear slowly running down his spine made him look about as if he might find spies perched within the tree bowers.

Lyle's response acted as a burr upon his senses. 'Is that what you think – that I'm afraid of you exposing my past?' Lightly, tentatively, Lyle's fingers rested upon his shoulder. Darleston turned towards the touch, so that they stood face to face, far too close to be friends, not quite close enough for lovers.

They had been lovers – extraordinary lovers.

He wouldn't cause trouble. He refused to bring trouble.

Lyle's eyes gleamed in the darkness. The shadows and hopes writ within them were not so very different from those he'd seen years before. Yet Lyle had aged, as had he. Nine years didn't pass without scoring a few lines, even if the overall composition remained largely unchanged: same wide-set eyes and aquiline nose, the widow's peak – more prominent than it had once been – that drew the gaze. And that same wicked-as-sin grin he'd spent years trying to imitate.

It hardly seemed appropriate to stare, given that he'd just been enjoying a pleasant welcome from the fellow's wife. It wasn't often he was treated with grace and respect any more. Since February, comely hostesses magically vanished whenever he came within forty feet.

He risked a quick glance into Lyle's eyes. Desire so familiar he could almost taste it swam in the inky depths of those pupils. For a moment, it was as if no time had passed at all.

'You don't want your name sullied alongside mine,' he insisted, already recognising the brewing danger. The problem was that he didn't actually want to move away. Rather he wanted to press close and find himself entwined in Lyle's embrace. It took every ounce of self-restraint to take a single step backwards instead.

Lyle's lips quirked. 'I don't need you to sully my name. I'm capable of that all by myself.' He followed Darleston's retreat and extended his arm past Darleston's ear, neatly trapping him betwixt his body and the thick trunk of a tree.

Conflicted, Darleston froze. Their last parting had been untidy. It seemed wholly rational that this beginning would be messy and awkward too.

'By all means practise your excuses, Robert, but don't leave on my account. Of course, if you feel you need to run away –'

'Ought I?' Of course he ought. Given the current euphoria bubbling beneath his skin, he ought to call his carriage right now and not look back until he'd crossed the county border. In an act of further lunacy, he maintained the eye contact they'd already made.

That wicked gleam – damn! Lyle's ability, with barely more than a slight upturning of his lips, to reduce him to an irrational, seething ball of desire had ever been his downfall. The scent of port lingered on the other man's breath, mixed with a trace of aniseed.

'Christ, Robert! I can still hardly get over the fact that you're here. For the longest time I didn't know what they'd done to you. I wasn't sure ... I wasn't informed, merely packed off like a piece of baggage and told to toughen up. I spent the first eighteen months in that Indian hellhole living off the memory of you.'

Darleston almost imperceptibly shook his head, having no

17

comparable sentence to relate. 'Nothing happened to me.' It smarted a little to admit it. Lyle had taken the brunt of the punishment, though he was pleased to see the army hadn't broken him. Meanwhile, he had suffered little more than embarrassment and his mother's reproachful looks, both of which were quickly forgotten. No, his penalty hadn't come until much later, when he'd stupidly committed the same crime twice. Then his mother had found him 'a nice young bride' to keep him busy and 'out of the second footman's underthings'. Not that it had worked. It'd been rather naïve of the countess to think it would. But then, she'd never been quite as bright as she liked to believe.

'I sometimes imagined you'd write.' Lyle's words broke though his introspection.

Darleston gave a derisive little snort. '*I* sometimes imagined I'd write. But what the hell was there to say? What is there to say now?' He couldn't think of anything that would mend broken hearts and promises. Certainly nothing that would reverse the flow of time, or allow them to make that fateful day over.

'Maybe you don't need to say anything.'

His loins agreed, even if the rest of him didn't. Words wouldn't fix anything. Kisses might smooth away the awkward memories, but life had moved on from where they'd been. Nearly half his life had passed since then. He'd been married, acted the libertine and taken dozens of whores and other lovers to his bed. He'd been rejected by the one man he really wanted and laughed at by the only other that he admired. He really couldn't stomach any more pain.

Which wasn't to say that he wasn't tempted. Lord, he was sorely tempted.

Lyle leaned closer still, damn near pressing their foreheads together. His lips parted, revealing a tiny hint of moisture upon their surface.

'Wait!' Darleston covered the temptation with his raised fingers. 'Think. We're not boys any more. Do you really want to be caught in a compromising position in your father-in-law's house?'

'Promises, promises ...' Lyle mused, eyes ablaze with salacious intent.

Dear God! That wasn't the response he'd hoped to evoke. They needed to think seriously about this, about what they were doing and how drastically it could go wrong.

'You were never so cautious in the past, Robert. Grown timid in your dotage?'

'Look at what happened before. I can't afford to cock things up. Things are dicey enough already.'

'Give in to fear and they've got you anyway.'

That was true. And there really was comfort to be had in Lyle's embrace.

It wasn't really a kiss – not at all – being hesitant and whisper-light. Quite platonic really.

He wouldn't fool anyone else.

They both stood stock still after their lips had parted, barely daring to move. They stared at one another, chests rising and falling, breath bated. Darleston's heart hammered and hammered. It had been years and years and years. But he'd never forgotten. Hunger for everything he'd lost and for everything he needed gnawed beneath his skin. He couldn't shake off the need to lose himself in the fantasy of love again. One could only fake numbness so long. The cracks in his façade grew wider every season. Lucy hadn't driven him from London, he'd driven himself. That which he'd used for years to appease his appetites no longer sufficed as a balm.

He needed something solid and real. Stability. Something to hold on to, to fight for and trust.

The message hadn't entirely filtered down to his loins though. Lyle – incredible, beautiful, Lyle. The first man he'd swived; the first man he'd sucked. Lyle – who now had a pretty little wife and needed the stigma associated with sodomy like he needed toothache. He didn't want to destroy everything the man had built for himself.

He didn't want to pull back and walk away either.

'Don't brood, act,' Lyle enticed him.

It was damned hard to resist when the offer was being dangled before him like that. Darleston grabbed the open front of Lyle's dress coat and tugged him closer. He'd remained abstinent since the last time with Giles, save for the unmentionable mistake of the day before. Now his cock craved release like a drunkard longed for a bath of gin. He needed this. It was what he was. And it was easy. Oh, so very easy and real.

Why wouldn't he risk everything when it felt this good?

Memories, sparked by Lyle's scent, came flooding back as he reversed their positions and shoved Lyle hard up against the unforgiving bark of the tree. Good times and bad, the terrible pain of separation and the numbness that followed. Suddenly, he had to fill that empty void he'd been burdened with. He crushed Lyle to him, revelled in the hard press of muscle against his torso as they kissed again. Furious this time. He wanted to get closer, to rub up against the man's bare skin. He inhaled Lyle's scent like it was perfume; grew intoxicated on the musky aroma.

Dexterous fingers began to work open the buttons of his frontfall.

'You've a wife now. Are you sure about this?'

The tip of Lyle's tongue brushed the outer edge of Darleston's earlobe, causing a waterfall of bliss to shoot through his veins. 'I've a wife. You've a wife. Damn near entire population has a wife. And mine won't mind. I need to have you, Robert. Do you realise you never allowed me that pleasure before?'

Was that true? He guessed it was. Pretty much everything about their relationship had been lopsided in those days. As an Earl's son he'd taken precedence, and that had applied within the bedroom as well as without. Few men had topped him in any way since.

Lyle's hot palm wrapped around his shaft. Vivid memories snapped sharply into focus, of things they'd done together and said. 'You could kiss me first,' he gasped.

Lyle chuckled. 'I think I've forgotten how that works.'

A reminder seemed wholly inappropriate given the way that Lyle's tongue stabbed between his parted lips. He held nothing back. Raw passion rolled off him in waves. It infused his breath and his grip, so that they clutched one another, fists closing around cloth and fingertips digging into the exposed flesh beneath, unable to break apart.

The sweetness of kitchen dainties lingered upon Lyle's tongue mingled with the dark residue of after-dinner port. His touch, cradling at first, soon grew bolder and transformed into a sliding caress. Whole languages had surely been invented to describe this very act, but right now Darleston couldn't recall a single word of any of them. All he knew was that he wanted – oh, God, how he'd missed – that touch.

With a few deft twists, he released the placket of Lyle's breeches. There were times when he was all about taking, but this wasn't one of them. He needed to give pleasure too. Following Lyle's movements he curled his thumb over the tip

21

of his cock and rubbed slow circles around the sensitive eye. Not that finesse was really about to play a great part in this.

'Together,' Lyle hissed into his ear, before he pressed their cocks tight to one another and began stroking them as one.

Darleston's hips rolled. He clung to Lyle, fingertips curled into one bicep, the other hand fast upon his hip, while the dual caress upon his cock worked him rapidly towards fever pitch. Strange that Lyle could bring him to this so quickly, when it was his legendary control that had wooed so many matrons in the bedroom.

He guessed the difference was desire. Not only his, but Lyle's too. This wasn't just about satisfying an itch, it was a physical need. The threat of climax loomed. It drew his balls up tight and set him walking a knife's edge. It came as a shock when Lyle got there first, crying into his shoulder as his seed spilled. Darleston's hips still rocked, but he was thrusting his cock against nothing but the cool night air. Bereft, he felt the sting of rejection in his cheeks. Then Lyle dropped to his knees and buried his fair head beneath the hem of Darleston's shirt.

Warm heat surrounded him. Then months of stagnant tension finally ran out of his limbs. His arms fell momentarily limp by his sides. Lyle had always possessed outstanding skills and his ability to suck had only improved in the intervening years. Tricks he played with his tongue left Darleston breathless and grasping at handfuls of blond hair just to steady himself. He'd often wondered what it was about this man that made him so damn special. Well, maybe it was this. He simply had a knack, a certain way, of turning what was usually a pleasurable act into something monumental.

Darleston urged more of his prick into the wet enveloping heat, knowing he was being overly rough but quite unable to stop. Lyle's little grunts of protest only made the moment sweeter. Pain, pushing things to their limitations, had always gotten him off. This was going to be swift or he might have tested those limitations. Lyle's fingers curled claw-like into his buttocks. Damn, his fingernails were sharp. He'd have half-moon-shaped bruises there tomorrow. The heat, the raw intensity of this … He couldn't tolerate much more. He needed relief, not torture.

A week or two would give them plenty of time to draw things out.

Lyle's fingers uncurled. He began to knead the tensed flesh, and then two digits speared into the channel between Darleston's cheeks and headed straight for the sensitive hidden whorl of muscle. Just a tickle there, the very suggestion of a fingertip sliding within undid him completely.

His body gave up its gift in long shuddering rolls of bliss.

Legs, knees, arms – his limbs were jelly. Only Lyle's hold kept him upright.

He heard him swallow.

'Fuck!'

Lyle stood, wiping his lips with the back of his hand.

'Fuck!'

Lyle's kisses tore at his mouth. The taste of his own arousal mingled upon their lips.

'I mean to have you, Robert. I'm not going to let you run away from me. I need a lover, not a wife.'

'Right.' The thought sobered him somewhat. Emma – Lyle's wife, who was sweet and charming and no doubt sitting up waiting for him. Field House wasn't anywhere near large enough to host couples separately when there were this many guests.

'Come on, the Orangery is this way.' Lyle tugged him

23

along in his wake. Darleston followed somewhat unsteadily, still trying to fasten his clothing so that he wasn't walking around exposed. Had it been this chilly before? A shiver rolled through his limbs, and Lyle noticed. 'There's a stove in there. We can keep warm and we don't need to worry about being overheard.'

* * *

Condensation clouded the numerous window panes of the Orangery, obscuring the views of both inside and out. Lyle led the way through the towering foliage to a small stone grotto near the back, which also housed a raised silken divan. Darleston had only a glimpse of its gaudy lamp-lit stripes and then he saw Lyle spread out along it, his dress coat cast aside and his breeches tugged down so that the pale globes of his bottom lay exposed. Though he guessed what Lyle had in mind would involve him being spread out, and while in some ways it would be easy to give in, he'd always enjoyed ruthless self-flagellation.

'This is a bad idea.'

Articulating the thought failed to destroy the rather lovely image. Instead he saw the scenario developing, himself creeping forward and enjoying the firm expanse of muscle laid out for him. Heat rose off Lyle's body as he fitted them together in one slow, delicious push. He heard the hitch in Lyle's breath, the momentary sign of protest. If he said 'stop', would he do it? He didn't know. He wasn't sure he could endure such torment. Things always got complicated when his heart said no and his cock said yes.

He followed Lyle over to the cushioned mattress. Watched him as he kicked off his shoes and perched crossed-legged upon the silk. Lyle wove his fingers together as he settled his elbows upon his knees.

'There's no pressure, Robert. I understand you've had a nasty scare. It's natural that you'd have reservations. Maybe you think we've already stepped too far over the mark.'

They'd certainly taken more of a risk than he cared for. He'd never given up on loving men, but he'd always taken great pains to keep such doings out of sight. It benefited no one to expose that particular part of his persona. What they'd just done constituted lunacy, and this ... this current proposition a spell in the asylum.

'I'm not unaware,' Lyle continued. His eyes remained fixed upon Darleston's face. 'You live in public. I know the company you keep, the clubs you frequent. I've seen the criticism levelled at your family ever since the Earl took it upon himself to marry a whore. As for your recent problems with Lady Darleston –' Lyle raked his hand through the long strands of his fair hair, clearly uncomfortable, finally tugging loose the queue holding it in place. Soft fair curls sprang free and hung just shy of his shoulders. 'I concede that puts you in a precarious position. I trust she can't prove anything.'

The only proof of which Lucy was capable was her own wretchedness, and then only because it was apparent the very moment she opened her mouth. Darleston made an irritated swipe at the leaf of a coconut palm before leaning against the grotto wall. 'I'm not wholly devoid of sense. I never put anything in writing. Also, I trust that any punks that might be rounded up would have the sense to realise their own necks are at stake.'

'Your word would stand against that of a cooper or butcher.'

'Perhaps. Either way it makes sense to lie low.'

Lyle cocked his head. 'This would be why you're attending a prize fight. Because naturally no one at all will spot you or remark upon your presence.'

Darleston conceded a grin. The situation wasn't ideal, but at least he wasn't flaunting his person around town any more. More importantly, he'd stopped playing unwelcome chaperone to Giles and his new bride. He hadn't specifically come to Field House to watch the fight. Supporting Neddy, his twin, in his role as Mr Hill's new trainer had merely provided a reason to be here.

'Neddy's deeply involved,' he said to justify his presence.

Lyle continued to smirk and nod. 'Is that who Hill has brought in as trainer? Ned must have put on some brawn since the last time I saw him.' He unwound the length of his cravat, let it hang in a loose loop between his hands.

Darleston gave a quick shake of his head. 'Not noticeably so, but he's a good weave and a sharp right hook. I'm told his footwork is good.'

'That'd make sense. Getting his legs in a tangle is Jack's main downfall. He has a punch like a ton-weight bull, but the nippier boxers just dance around him.'

'Think he's a chance?'

'Ned or Jack?'

'My brother had better not be going anywhere near the prize ring.'

'So-so. I don't know much about his opponent. He's not local. From Welsh stock, I'm told.'

Lyle cast his cravat aside and undid the ribbon fastening of his shirt. Pale blond hairs pecked provocatively through the opening. The yellow glow of the lamp warmed his skin, giving it a sun-kissed hue. Something about seeing a teasing glimpse of chest hair like that grabbed Darleston straight in the groin. Maybe it was the hint of masculinity or the exposure of all that was wild and was customarily hidden by clothing. They were all beasts when it came down to it. No one remained a gentleman in the heat of passion.

The bottom of Lyle's shirt still hung over the top of his breeches from their earlier sport so it was simply a matter of unbuttoning his waistcoat and peeling the layers off to expose him completely.

'Join me.'

Darleston slipped the top button of his own waistcoat, but paused before unfastening the second. Somehow they'd ventured into territory he was reluctant to retread. There was no question about whether he desired Lyle. He'd always done that. Rather, the problem was Mrs Langley. He saw her pale oval face staring up at him again as the teacup she offered rattled alarmingly upon its saucer. It would destroy her to learn what sort of man her husband truly was – what sort of man *he* was.

'I can't do it, Lyle. I just can't. I'm sorry if I've led you on.' He refastened the button, then bit his lips, wanting to say more, but unable to form the words to make sense of his emotions. It wasn't only Emma he was trying to protect, but all of them. He'd been hurt too recently to stomach any more pain. The ache of losing Giles was too raw. Lucy and her libellous innuendos had provided a perfect excuse to leave London. But they'd never been his main issue. Besides, she'd stopped making them as soon as she'd realised that the chastisement he chose to dole out wasn't to her taste. She'd deserved a hiding, but cutting her allowance had silenced her rather more effectively. No, really he was taking in the country air to mend the ache in his chest. He thought he'd understood loneliness before, but not like this. He'd never felt

27

so bereft of friendship as well as love. All his other cronies, the ones he'd hoped to turn to in order to escape the emptiness inside, seemed to be entangled in bereavements of their own

Of course that was the dilemma of his current situation. Love, of sorts, was exactly what Lyle sat offering. Still, he couldn't sacrifice Emma Langley's happiness for his own. There existed hurt enough in her watery blue eyes.

He hid his face, turning into the shadow. He wasn't going to compete with a woman for a man's affections ever again.

'Long term, it'll never work, and that's what I'm looking for.'

Lyle came up behind him. Strong arms encircled his waist, and Lyle's head rested between his shoulder blades. 'I never once stopped wanting you. You have to understand that Emma and I, we're not exactly compatible. We swore to be friends, not lovers.'

'That doesn't make this right.'

'When were you such a moralist?' Lyle's lips brushed the back of his neck, raising shivers. Darleston leaned into the caress, craving more, yet adamant that he wouldn't capitulate.

'I can feel your pulse, your tension, smell your desire. Why resist, Robert? No one's going to know. Don't think so hard about the future.'

'I can't risk hurting her like that.'

'My wife? Why does she matter to you? Why so concerned about her and not your own?'

He shook Lyle off. 'To hell with Lucy! Because Emma has done nothing to hurt me. She's been a kind and gracious hostess.' And he didn't want to compete with a woman. Not again. Not after he'd lost so spectacularly. Not that he'd ever had a chance with Giles. His friend simply wasn't constructed that way.

'We've never ...' Lyle hesitated. His teeth dug into his lower lip. 'Our marriage, it's never been consummated.' He retreated into the deeper darkness of the grotto, leaving Darleston staring at his back in confusion.

'How is that? Do you mean you've never been to her bed? Lyle, how is that even possible? Aren't you sharing a room in this house? I don't understand.' He'd never wanted Lucy, but he'd visited her bed once a month for the last nine years. Give or take. One had to make the pretence of wanting issue, regardless of his actual wishes. The fact that he'd sometimes paid his twin to go in his stead wasn't something he liked to make public.

'I've no wish to embarrass myself,' Lyle confessed, his voice muted and hesitant. 'Nor have I any wish to engage in such an act. I've no desire in that regard. Women are rather like porcelain dolls. I can admire their crafting, but I have no desire to possess such a thing. There was mutual benefit to be had from the arrangement. I'm hardly the first man to seek the security of marriage as a mask for my proclivities. Society asks fewer questions if you offer them the illusion of normality.'

While Darleston's own preference was for men, he'd spent many evenings equally at home between a woman's thighs. At least there seemed to be some degree of affection in Lyle's marriage, which was more than he could claim in his own. 'And does Hill know about your lack of desire?' Darleston asked.

'He sees that Emma is well settled and contented. That's all that matters to him. Of course he doesn't know of my preferences. He's a good man, not an overly enlightened one.'

'What about Emma? How does she take your lack of

29

affection? I can't imagine she's content to be left virginal, or do you allow her trysts as well?'

Lyle shook his head.

Darleston ground his teeth and found his lips were pursed into a tight moue when he tried to form his next word. 'So you sleep with whom you please but deny her any affection. Lyle, I thought better of you, I truly did.'

The other man turned to face him once more. Eerie shadows swam in the depths of his hazel eyes. 'You don't understand. I haven't denied her anything. She wouldn't let me touch her even if I desired to.' Lyle's sibilant whisper bled into the darkness. 'She's frigid, Robert. Colder than the hoar frost. She doesn't let anyone touch her.'

'So she's nervous. But with coaxing ...' Darleston curled his fingers, imagining pressing them to Emma's prettily flushed cheek. Every woman he'd ever known had warmed to sweet talk and a little charm.

'No. You're not hearing me. She's not skittish. She doesn't let anyone near her. Nobody touches her, not even her maid or her sister. We've been married over two years and the only time I've held her hand was in church as I slid the wedding band upon her finger. Believe me, she trembled enough through that. If she could have avoided it ...'

'That's common enough.' He'd quaked too. Although in his case it may have been down to how much drink he'd consumed.

'This affliction goes way beyond that. Watch her tomorrow, and then you'll understand. It's not coitus she's afraid of, Robert. It's physical contact of any sort.'

Darleston's brows furrowed. 'Have you tried to discern why?' How could a human being survive in such a way?

Lyle half-nodded, half-shook his head. 'She won't discuss it with me. Believe me, I've tried and never made the slightest bit of headway. She just brushes me off. It doesn't help that she knows I like men. So talk of physical affection between us is pointless. It's why she was so keen on the arrangement in the first place. She knew I'd make no demands upon her.'

'How the devil did she know? Did she see you?' Incredulous now, Darleston's mouth hung open. Gentle-born women didn't knowingly marry men whose preferences ran to other men. No one wanted to be wed to that sort of scandal.

Lyle nervously wetted his lips. 'I've never asked and she's never ventured the details. But now you see there's no impediment to us.'

Darleston began to pace in and out of the grotto's mouth, worrying his fingernails as he moved. Did this change anything? Superficially, perhaps. Deep down, he wasn't so sure. Emma might still fight for her husband. She could still be hurt by the scandal.

The humidity was starting to wear him down. Sweat beaded his back and trickled down his spine in much the same way as it ran down the window panes. He still wasn't sure. When had he become so cautious? Not so very long ago he'd made a jape of danger and desecrated a grave to settle a score. Now he was hesitating over fucking a man who was actually prepared to give him more than one night of his life. He couldn't in all honesty use Emma as an excuse for rejecting that. If their marriage was truly as platonic as Lyle described, then he wasn't about to lose Lyle to his wife in the way that he'd lost Giles to Fortuna.

Emma knew the risks. She'd made her choices in full knowledge of what might come.

Lyle smacked him across the arse. The impact jerked him forward and out of his emotional stupor. God help him, but he was going to do this. But on his terms. No more being dictated to by Lyle, and no more pansying around playing go-lightly. If they were going to fuck ... well, they were going to fuck.

'Take off your breeches too.'

Lyle's head twitched, bird-like, in surprise. Then he settled his ruffled feathers and did exactly as he'd been told. Naked he really was a marvel. He had an arse to rival that of a Roman god, though not quite as pale as alabaster. Thighs that were feathered with soft golden hairs, and loins ... there was no denying that's where Darleston was primarily looking. Lyle's prick stood proud. Long and uncut, it reached halfway to his navel. It was striped with pale-blue veins, like some Oriental piece of china. Thankfully, it wasn't quite as fragile as a vase.

'So you've missed me,' Darleston remarked. 'In all these years there's never been anyone else that turned your head in the same way? No one who's fucked you halfway to the moon and back? No one who crept inside your head and steamed up all those naughty fantasies you concoct while you date Miss Nancy and her four sisters?'

'Robert, when I toss myself the only pictures in my head are of you ... and the adorable little vadelect I had in Bangalore.' Lyle's grin stretched wide, growing infectious the further it spread. Darleston smiled along with him. Bangalore? He wanted to ask, but the story could wait for another night. Instead, he perched on the end of the divan and tapped his middle finger against his lips. Slowly he wetted its tip.

'Know where this is going?'

'I know where I hope it's going.' Lyle rolled onto all fours.

'Uh-uh! Face to face. If we're going to do this, let's do it properly. I want to see you come and know that you're mine. And if I so much as think your thoughts are straying towards Emma then it's over. Truly over. I can't go through that again.'

He could see a myriad questions racing through Lyle's mind, but his lover seemed to sense that this wasn't the time. Lyle turned and lay flat upon his back.

'I think you're more likely to think of her than I.'

'Maybe.' Darleston covered him, still fully clothed. He didn't intend to remove a stitch. Instead, he pinned Lyle down and kissed him, revelling in the heat and the clash of their tongues. As their lips made merry, his hands were at work, brushing lightly over Lyle's arms and torso. When they parted, it was only so that he could take a breath and turn his attention to Lyle's flat, penny-shaped nipples instead. He sucked hard, drawing the little teat into a point. He palmed Lyle's cock at the same time, working it up and down until Lyle's contented groans had lapsed into euphoric silence. Only then did he tease the entrance to Lyle's arse with his wetted digit.

Fiercely hot, but eager and willing in his acceptance, Lyle writhed beneath him, lifting up his hips to allow for a deep penetration. One finger soon became two, then three. Finally, Darleston accepted Lyle's hands fumbling at his waistband and feeling their way inside his frontfall. His cock bucked in appreciation of the touch. He let Lyle guide him home. Butted up against him, and slid deep.

It really was that smooth and that quick.

Too perfect, really. He did so like a bit of torment.

He pulled Lyle's hair, raked his teeth along his jaw and began to fuck like he truly meant it. The little yelp of pain Lyle gave in response fired Darleston's senses. So too did his lover's retaliation, right down to adding more bruises to his already marked rear.

'Bite me again,' Lyle hissed into his ear as they were rocking smoothly together with the whole universe collapsed in upon itself and centred on the tip of his cock.

Lyle guided him over towards his throat. Darleston sucked hard. He nipped a little but didn't let his teeth break the flesh. He left a mark though, a deep-purple bruise like a stamp of ownership. He'd known lovers who gave one another love-bites in lieu of wedding rings they couldn't legitimately wear. He didn't want to wed Lyle, he just wanted to sink deeper inside him, until he was no longer sure where their bodies met, or what part of this pleasure was his and what was Lyle's.

He added another mark to Lyle's throat. Let him cover it with his cravat tomorrow. He'd still know it was there.

Darleston's temperature reached fever point just before his body gave in to the little death. Sweat coated every inch of his skin. His clothing stuck to him. Only in the areas where their bodies met skin to skin did he feel true contentment. Next time, maybe he would take his clothes off. Then again the discomfort added something, and he liked that it was only Lyle who was exposed.

He looked down into his lover's eyes as his nerve endings began to sing. His orgasm knocked him about like one of Hill's champion boxers, leaving him punchdrunk and dizzy, full of light and air. He collapsed against Lyle, aftershocks still racing along his shaft, each one provoking a sigh of pleasure.

'That's right, Robert. Give it to me. Let go now.' Lyle's hands kneaded the tension from his shoulders. Darleston floated, acutely aware of the feeling that he'd somehow returned home.

His dexterity was shot to hell and his fingers and thumb refused to make a proper fist around Lyle's cock. He worked it anyway, staying inside his lover's body until he'd wrung every ounce of pleasure out of them both. Only when Lyle's high had mellowed to a contented afterglow, and warm semen coated his fingers, did he finally release him.

Darleston rolled onto his back and sucked Lyle's gift from his fingertips.

'How long are you planning to stay?' Lyle propped himself up on one elbow so that he could make eye contact. The tops of his cheekbones, his temples and the tips of his ears were flushed with a pinkish glow. The hint of colour gave him an almost boyish air, while the glow in his hazel eyes suggested embarrassment over his own eagerness for an answer.

'Not until after the boxing. Though I haven't specified a set length to Hill.'

'So it wouldn't be unreasonable to draw it out into a few weeks.'

'I suppose,' he said, a tad dubious.

Joy replaced hope in Lyle's eyes. Lyle curled against him, wrapping a thigh over his legs and nestling his head in the crook of Darleston's shoulder. 'I'm glad our paths crossed again. I truly meant it, what I said about thinking of you. You've always been in my thoughts.'

'Yes,' Darleston drawled, feeling pleasantly lethargic and sated. 'Me – and the vadelect from Bangalore. I trust he's still in India and not secreted about the house.'

Lyle's laughter rumbled up from deep in his chest. 'Robert, if he were, I'd definitely share him with you.'

CHAPTER THREE

Emma woke obscenely early, just as she had every morning she'd ever spent in Field House. The moment the scullery maid opened her door to lay the fire she snapped out of her repose. She kept as still as she could, faking the even breaths of sleep as she listened to the sounds of intrusion. Sometimes, if she were lucky, she'd slip back into the arms of slumber, but more often she lay awake staring up at the patterns on the bed canopy.

It took a moment to realise that Lyle was not lying safe beside her. At home, he never strayed into her bedchamber, but in her father's house there were appearances to maintain, as well as a shortage of rooms. She'd learned to tolerate Lyle's presence in the bed. A line of pillows down the centre of the mattress formed a clear dividing line. She couldn't have him touch her, no matter how much she cared for him, not even in sleep.

Emma sat up. 'Where is Mr Langley?' she asked the dishevelled maid, who in her shock rubbed soot down the front of her homespun.

'I'm sorry, milady. I don't know.'

'I'm right here, of course.' Lyle sauntered into the room,

still in his dress coat of the night before, carrying his waist-coat. At some point in the intervening hours he'd lost his cravat. The collar of his shirt hung open, revealing slivers of the fair skin beneath. He bore the glazed look of someone who has been awake too long, drunk too much or been kissed too hard. In Lyle's case, she suspected all three. Something the marks around his neck seemed to confirm.

Emma lowered her gaze. Her lips pressed tight together. She hardly needed to ask where he'd been or even who with. It made her stomach churn imagining Lord Darleston kissing Lyle so hard that he'd left such marks. 'Leave us,' she barked at the scullery maid, who gathered her things and fled.

'Do we have something to talk about?' Lyle wandered over to the sideboard and began removing his cufflinks and collar studs.

'Where have you been? Have you slept?'

'You know where I've been. Do we need to discuss it? And yes, thank you for asking, I have slept. Although I still require a good bit more.' His coat and waistcoat followed the cufflinks, forming a jumbled heap upon the floor. Emma watched enraptured as he stepped out of his evening breeches and folded them over a chair back. Lyle was all straight lines. His body fascinated her in much the same way that she sometimes became entranced by a picture. She appreciated the aesthetic quality, but there was really no need to touch.

He strode over to the bed, crushed shirt-tails dangling around his thighs and the neck open to his breastbone, so that the pale-gold hairs upon his chest were clearly visible. Up close the bruises on his neck were a vivid mix of crimson and purple. She half expected to see teeth-marks too. Lyle made no attempt to hide them.

'I know the rules. I promise you, we were discreet.' He

destroyed the wall of pillows, casting all save one cushion onto the floor. The last he plumped instead and settled against.

She couldn't stay with him like this, with nothing between them but air and cold sheet.

'Who was it?' she asked quietly. There were things she instinctively knew about Lyle that only marriage exposed. She knew when he'd taken a lover and she knew when he'd drunk too much, without the need for questions or empirical evidence. Tonight she wanted actual confirmation, even though she knew it would smart to hear it. 'Who?'

Please say it was the footman or Aiken or anyone else. She clung tight to the slender thread of hope.

'I thought we had an agreement that there was no problem with my choices. Why is it so important to know? What do you hope to learn? I wasn't implying anything by removing the pillows. I just find it ridiculous that we have to sleep as though there are three of us in the bed.'

'Don't change the subject.'

Lyle looked at her, his lips slightly parted as if about to speak. Instead, he smoothed a hand over the bedclothes so that he banished the wrinkles in the eiderdown. He frowned. 'Why are we squabbling?

They weren't normally enemies over his infidelities – heavens, rather that than him seeking satisfaction from her – so she supposed it must seem odd to him that she was making an issue of it now.

'Was it … was it Darleston? You know one another of old, don't you? I just thought … I guessed after your greeting –'

Oh, why did it have to be him? The only man she'd ever felt even the faintest connection with. Though hell knows why she felt it. They had nothing in common.

Lyle's eyes narrowed with suspicion.

'Yes, Darleston and I know one another. Why is it important?' The bed groaned as he made a half-hearted attempt to tug the sheet over his shoulders. 'Why the sudden interest in my doings? You've never taken any interest in my lovers before.'

'No reason.' She couldn't confess. What was there, really, to confess to? She wasn't about to act upon the curious tingle she felt inside when gazing at Lord Darleston. 'I just thought it prudent to know. I wouldn't want to intrude upon anything.'

Lyle rolled over and gave her a hard stare. His nostrils flared slightly, causing Emma's heart to thud. What if he suspected her affection? He might treat her differently if he saw she had intentions on another man. He might not be quite so amenable. God forbid, he might actually demand his conjugal rights.

'Isn't he a little notorious? I wouldn't want you to get into trouble.'

'I won't. Not as long as you're with me.' He reached out a hand to her, as if he meant to cup her cheek.

Emma hopped out of bed. 'You know that I'll not make a fuss. Whatever it is that pleases you is quite fine by me as long as you respect my wishes as we discussed.' She glared accusingly at his hand, so that he hid it beneath the sheet.

Lyle's lips formed a tight moue. 'I always do, don't I? I've never demanded …'

She nodded. 'And I appreciate it. Our needs complement one another. I'm eternally grateful for that.'

'Don't you ever long for even a little affection?' Lyle enquired

Emma's nod transformed into a vigorous shake. 'No – leastways, not as you mean it.'

'But do you have any idea what it's like?' He sat up against the pillows with his hands steepled before him. A wistful smile turned up the corners of his mouth.

'No – no, I don't. And I really don't need to.' She shook her head while backing away from him. She really, really didn't need to, because despite still being *virgo intacta* she could well imagine, having witnessed Lyle's exploits before. That's how she'd known she'd find him a suitable husband. She wasn't sure who the man had been; a migrant labourer, perhaps, or a visiting groom. The sort of man she'd never really expected Lyle to associate with. They'd been bent over a mounting block in the stables and she remembered how the cheeks of the man's bottom had flexed and dimpled as he'd driven his prick deep into Lyle's rear. Even now the image still had the power to quake her to her very core. Watching him had been lewder by far than stumbling upon a man and maid. Men were not meant to love one another. She knew what she'd witnessed had been a criminal and ungodly act, yet the men's pleasure had been unmistakable. Worse still, her memory had now metamorphosed, the groom replaced by Lord Darleston, standing in his magnificent baroque coat swiving her husband with depraved abandon.

Fever consumed Emma's body. She pulled on a wrapper and disguised her shivers as cold, fleeing toward the fireplace for emphasis. Her fascination with Lord Darleston hadn't diminished with sleep; if anything it had grown more acute, particularly as she now knew him to be interested in Lyle. Not that she would ever act upon her attraction. Besides, silly ninny that she was, Lord Darleston was clearly inclined like her husband and would have no interest in her.

'Shall I have your breakfast sent up?' she asked. As soon as the chill air in the bedchamber cooled her cheeks she'd dress.

'That would be nice. It was Darleston,' Lyle said with a

sigh. 'I had his cock in my mouth and he tasted absolutely divine.'

Emma snatched an ornament off the mantel. Her fist clenched the slender figurine, as for a moment she was convinced that Lyle had deliberately intended to vex her. She stared at her hand, trying to comprehend the violence of her response. She wasn't normally given to rash actions, but then neither was she invested in any person enough to experience pangs of jealousy over their affections. Emma closed her eyes and breathed slowly until the tension drained from her body and she was able to uncurl her fingers. Thank heavens Darleston would only be part of their lives for a short while. She glanced at Lyle and realised that, in his wistfulness, he was merely thinking aloud. It was hardly the first time he'd shared inappropriate thoughts or descriptions with her. When they were home alone, it even amused her.

* * *

The more thought Emma gave to the prospect of living even a short while with Lord Darleston in the same house, the more terrified she became. What if Lyle recognised her desire? How would it change their relationship?

Her hands shook so hard during breakfast that she gave up trying to crack the shell of her soft-boiled egg and left it and the rest of her food untouched. A walk ought to have made things better, but the heavens opened as she stood upon the entrance steps. Thick grey clouds promised a heavy, lengthy downpour, which left her stuck in the library, flitting ghost-like between the shelves seeking escape, when there was no place to escape to.

Lyle's words echoed between her earholes as if her skull

were devoid of matter. She'd been aware of several of her husband's previous lovers. She'd known their names, their families and backgrounds. Never once had she felt threatened by their existence. Nor had she counted them as anything other than blessings. While Lyle was taking his pleasures elsewhere he wasn't making demands upon her.

Her gaze again strayed through the open door into the billiards room, where the men stood around the table conducting what sounded very much like a plan of war. Her father's voice rose above the others.

'As soon as this infernal rain stops I'll take you down to see him. I want you gentlemen to get a feel for his character before the event.'

'Aye, but what about the Welshman? Will there be a chance to assess him before the fight?'

'Of course. Of course. We'll see what we can do.' Her father guided Mr Bathhouse towards the rear of the room, leaving her with an unobstructed view of Lord Darleston holding a billiards cue. Since he'd been nursing it for a good twenty minutes without taking a shot, it seemed he merely held it to provide comfort.

She oughtn't to have been looking, but her gaze kept straying from the printed words upon the page of her book to the frontfall of his breeches. She saw it not as it was but open, Lyle upon his knees, his mouth wrapped around the thick firm rod that lay beneath. Lyle had touched what she wanted, when she'd never wanted anything before. Not like this. She'd never wanted to press her fingertips to the warm flesh of another living soul. Not since – she shook her head – not since … She needed no reminder.

Darleston would be warm, not cold, the vibrancy of his pulse a flicker of heat running just below the skin. He'd taste of brandy and sin, and of all the wicked things in the world that one ought not to do. He *was* sin. Her sin. One big package of impiety, from the ends of his fiery locks to the sculpted perfection of his coat-tails, and just standing there waiting to be unwrapped. If God could have sent her a gift, then Darleston was surely it.

Emma dropped the book and twisted her fingers in her hands. Pure awareness of his presence needled her so much she had to scratch. The rasp of her nails felt impossibly good, but didn't dissipate any of her irrational need. Some strange part of her that she could barely comprehend longed to stride over to him and comment on the firmness of his bottom. Truthfully, she wanted to say arse, but to hear such a crudity from her would turn her father milk-pale. Not that making a remark about his bottom would be much better.

If she offered to walk with Darleston as Lyle had done, and then fell on her knees in turn, would Darleston allow her to take his prick in the same way?

Was it possible to touch someone and to make them understand that you required no recompense, no like for like? She couldn't bear hands upon her skin. Not even his. Not for a moment. But perhaps she could tolerate the movement of her hands over his body. After all, she'd be in control of that.

Damn, she had to stop looking at him. She jerked her gaze away, only for it to return a second later. She couldn't help it. There was something about him that called to her. Something incomprehensible. Damn, she had to stop damning in her head. It was uncouth – *and damnation* – had Darleston even noticed her existence? Did he recall their conversation last night, or had their *tête à tête* been obliterated by memories of pleasure and her husband's unfaithful mouth?

'Emma – whatever's the matter? You look as if you've been cooked.' Amelia hurried over to her side.

Emma immediately stopped her scratching in order to ward off her sister's approach. Amelia never could resist poking at her. The notion that her overzealous affection might be unwelcome seemed to pass her by. Not that she didn't dearly love her sister, but, heavens, she did wish they wouldn't fuss over her.

'I'm quite fine. Just hives. Horsehair does always set me off.' She scowled at the library furniture. 'I've some lavender cream I can put on. It'll soothe it.'

She left as quickly as she could without seeming to flee, painfully aware of Amelia's gaze upon her back as she hurried towards the stairs. If her sister latched onto her irrational thoughts, it would be worse by far than Lyle finding out. Lyle understood discretion. Amelia understood nothing but her own need for entertainment.

'Mrs Langley.'

Emma squeaked in alarm and clutched the banister. She leapt up the bottom few stairs before turning her head to see who called, although she already knew. His voice sent a dart of energy right through her midriff. Lord Darleston stood in the lobby. Emma remained stock still, fingers locked tight around the wooden rail, while her heart thumped against her ribcage.

'Mrs Langley. The others are heading off to see Mr Johnstone. As I'm not so eager for that pleasure, I wondered if you'd show me the amphitheatre that is to be the stage for the bouts instead. I understand it's located amongst the woodland.'

'The amphitheatre?' she gasped. She sounded choked even to herself.

'Only if it wouldn't cause you any trouble. I imagine I can find it myself if I'm pointed in the right direction. I realise it's an imposition, it still being rather wet.'

Had the rain even properly stopped? More than likely this was a mere break in the clouds.

'No, that's fine. That's not a problem. I'll just fetch a shawl.'

Why should a little rain keep them indoors?

Why was she so excited over the prospect of wading through wet woodland with him?

'Maybe you could see if that vagabond of a husband of yours has risen and would care to join us,' Darleston hollered after her, affection evident in his voice.

'Of course. I expect he's ...' She gave a nod. What was better – to find Lyle still asleep and endure Darleston's closeness all alone, or to find Lyle dressed and eager to accompany them? She didn't wish to stroll along behind or between them in full awareness of what they'd done. Nor did she know any method of extracting such images from her head.

Lyle's valet slipped away the moment she entered the room. She'd never understood Lyle's need to have someone fasten his buttons for him. How she hated the stares, the tugging and pulling sensation of hands upon her skin. Surely he could manage to find the armholes of his own coat.

Ignoring Lyle's inquisitive glance, she hurriedly donned her spencer.

'And where are you off to?'

'Out for a stroll.' She did intend to pass on Darleston's invitation, but something stopped her speaking the words. Why should she invite Lyle? There'd be no fun in watching the two men walk shoulder to shoulder while she waddled along behind like a lost puppy. She couldn't do it. The whole time she'd know what they'd done together the previous night. She'd know she was apart from them, locked out, surplus to requirements. She'd rather have Darleston to herself, even if all they exchanged was a companionable silence. She wanted a friend.

All right, mayhap a bit more than that.

It wouldn't do to have Lyle present if her gaze kept straying as it had done this morning. He read her too well. He'd realise something was afoot, and God forbid that he recognise the true depths of her fascination with Darleston. It would serve them all equally ill if he thought she had real designs on the man. Jealousy was bound to rear her ugly head and, worse still, he might finally insist on his matrimonial rights.

And yet in a purely theoretical sense she did have designs upon Lord Darleston. Practically speaking, it was a hopeless and irrational dream, but then, practicality had rarely served her interests.

Also, deep down she didn't believe Lyle would ever want her as a woman.

'Do you know where my wrap is?'

Lyle crossed the room holding it. He waited for her to turn, so that he might drape it around her shoulders, but Emma stiffened her spine and refused to turn. Recently he'd used such opportunities as a means of getting close to her. Then, all the hairs on the back of her neck stood on end, leaving her feeling doubly wretched.

'What I said earlier, I wasn't trying to needle you, only to be forthright about things. I don't like that we live a constant lie. If there was another way –'

'It's fine,' she cut him off. 'There's no need to go over this. I perfectly understand that you have needs and that Lord Darleston is helping you fulfil them.'

'Yes, however –'

'Don't, Lyle. You've already told me what you've done with him. There's no need to say any more.' She snatched the wrap from his hands, taking care not to make contact with his person. 'Take your pleasure in whatever fashion you please. It makes no difference to me.'

CHAPTER FOUR

While fibbing to Lyle as a defensive measure came incredibly easily to Emma, she couldn't lie in the same way to herself. Hot tears rolled down her cheeks as she fled the bedchamber. It did matter how Lyle took his pleasure. It mattered very much, because in this instance his pleasure was Lord Darleston.

Ninnyhammer! Fool. You've spurred Lyle towards him now, when that was the last thing that you wanted.

Though really, wasn't that for the best? Daydreaming was one matter, but reality quite another. Nothing romantic would ever happen between her and Darleston. They'd never share a touch, while Lyle would find hours of satisfaction in kissing and holding the man. And what she needed was to keep her husband satisfied. That way he wasn't in her bed making demands.

A deep tremble rolled through her body as she imagined being crushed beneath Lyle's weight and of being pressed tight to Lyle's pale skin. No – she corrected – not simply pressed together. He'd be right inside her, so there'd be absolutely no retreat or escape. They'd be completely bound. He'd be under her skin, not just beside it.

The notion froze her in mid-step. Emma clutched the top of the banister and sucked down several steadying breaths. No one else ever seemed to have such a problem with the idea of contact. They were all forever exchanging handshakes, kisses and embraces. The last person to cuddle her had been her nanny, right after she broke the news of Emma's mother's death. The embrace had made her skin crawl as though all the bugs and beetles of the graveyard were clambering over her. She'd avoided such clinches before that point, but that hideous show of false and vile affection had made her determined not to endure further embraces.

She'd grieved by the graveside, alone, invulnerable and aloof.

'Still abed, is he?' Darleston called up to her. He stood awaiting her return in the hall below, his hat already perched upon his head of fiery hair and his cane swinging gaily in his hand.

Since she didn't want to admit that she hadn't extended the invitation to Lyle, Emma remained silent. She mopped her tears, and then continued straight past Darleston out into the fine spray of mist that hung in the air at shoulder level. She fastened her bonnet as she went.

* * *

Darleston strode after Mrs Langley trying not to show his bemusement at her conduct. Although he had no hard evidence for his supposition, he'd lay money on Lyle being dressed and a more than willing companion on their walk. So naturally he had to conclude that Mrs Langley had deliberately excluded her husband from their jaunt. He couldn't help speculating over the reason.

Had Lyle told her of the passion they'd shared the night before? He hadn't hinted at making such intimate confessions to his wife, but Darleston had known couples who reported the details of every extramarital tryst to one another. However, if Emma possessed such knowledge and hated the arrangement, why then had she agreed to accompany him out? Had he set himself up for a scolding? He wasn't sure he could face that. Not after months of rebukes and a night during which recollections of Lyle's welcoming mouth had left him largely deprived of sleep.

The pale sun still seemed a little too bright this morning.

Darleston lowered the brim of his hat. In truth, tired as he was, his body still ached for more robust loving. To hell with what he'd initially said to Lyle, the chance of pleasure, however fleeting, was too rare a thing to casually dismiss.

It was fine to dismiss the need for love, when love surrounded one in abundance and affection could be bought by merely raising one's brow. Things became rather more desperate when you were tarnished goods. Women avoided him, afraid that his homosexual tendencies might be transferred to them and onto their husbands, as if his preferences could be equated with the pox. And men avoided him for fear of – well, because they were preposterously conceited for the most part. He had standards as well as taste.

He thought back over the nights he'd spent alone. The caress of his bed sheets against the hot tip of his cock had been unbearable. Even the satisfaction he'd wrought with his own hand hadn't entirely seen off the seductive ghosts of his imagining. Lyle's presence had relieved much of that tension.

How could Emma Langley possibly survive with no human contact to soothe away the pains?

Learning her secret, if it existed, was paramount. He

wished he could lock himself up that tight, become immune to those around him; no longer need their voices or their nearness to simply propel him through the day.

Of course, he had to touch her, primarily to confirm the validity of Lyle's assertion. Not that he intended to just reach out and grab her, though on one or two past occasions such actions had got him exactly where he intended to get.

Women – he watched the sway of Emma's hips as she walked ahead of him – there was no telling where even the subtlest gesture would get you. One misconstrued tilt of the head and you were shackled for ever.

Emma's purposeful stride came to a halt on the edge of a copse. She peered back at him from beneath the vast rim of her bonnet. Beckoned him forward. Was the bonnet too a guard against affection? Bestowing a kiss upon her would run the risk of serious injury. He eyed the end of her brown ribbons and contemplated tugging upon them so the knot unravelled and he could send the ridge of corduroy flying up into the trees. Its fortress-like confines aside, the colour drained the vitality from her face, giving her a sallow, waxy skin tone. Darleston preferred the deep chestnut of her hair.

'I'm afraid the path is a little windy and overgrown. And I don't suppose Father has recollected to have the briars trimmed. He never thinks of such practicalities, only of his vicious brawlers.' As he approached she strode forth again. 'We'll simply have to make the best of it. I trust you don't mind a few pricks, milord?'

Darleston snorted into his coat cuff, pleased he faced her back once again. If only she were offering something other than a stroll through the brambles then his answer could have been wholeheartedly positive. As it was, it seemed best not to grumble over the nicks in his coat when the excursion had been at his behest.

Not that he had any genuine interest in the venue, only in engaging her as a companion. He still felt uncomfortable about accepting Lyle's affection with only Lyle's assurance that Emma would be unperturbed by it.

'You don't approve of prize-fighting?' he ventured, seeing a lead into conversation.

Emma briefly turned her head to look back at him. 'I confess I find little to admire in such sport. Perhaps you can tell me what the appeal is in watching grown men beat the wits from one another's heads when they possess few enough to start with?' The path widened a fraction and he caught up so that they walked abreast.

'I'm afraid any explanation I offer would fail to enlighten and paint me in very poor light.'

Did he see a twinkle of knowledge in her pretty blue eyes? Did she think just for a minute, as he did, that there were aesthetic reasons for watching shirtless men fight? Although most of the prize-fighters he'd known were sadly spoiled in the looks department. Too many scuffs and broken noses did that. He tended to focus his attention on the parts that were normally left unseen.

'You're not aroused by such a show of strength?'

Emma gave an indelicate tut. 'Intelligence is far more valuable to me than brawn. I think I should rather watch a scholar study than see two hot sweaty men bloody one another's noses and wrestle in the clarts like beasts.'

'Indeed. Yes, I suppose it is faintly ludicrous for grown men to behave in such a way, but then we do love to pit ourselves against one another.'

'We're almost there. We take a right ahead where the

53

path forks.' She gave him a rather hard stare when he stood mere inches from her person. Her normally agreeable mouth formed into a tight pout that made him want to smooth a thumb over it to iron the wrinkles away.

Naturally, he held back from such an intimacy. They weren't friends enough for that sort of action to pass without rebuke, even if she weren't as skittish as a hare over the mere press of a fingertip.

Although, all said, he still had only Lyle's word that that was how she'd react.

'An amphitheatre is an atypical garden attribute,' he observed.

Her expression brightened immediately. 'Yes. My great-grandfather had it built as a fernery, but it fell out of favour once the Orangery was completed. He was prone to momentary passions. He owned three hundred coats when he died. Not a single one had ever been given away. His valet positively despaired.'

'I'm surprised only one valet sufficed.' Darleston swung his cane and knocked aside an arch of thorns. 'Ah, but the ferns remain,' he observed.

They had reached a sheer drop, so that they looked down into a bowl in the earth, with concentric stone-edged tiers cut into the sides. Ferns grew in patches upon the banks, long stems reaching for the sun. It was the most perfect space for all manner of indiscretions, which he suspected was its primary purpose, not the growth of ferns.

Steep steps, worn and lined with cracks, led to the various layers of the amphitheatre and down to the circular base, where sandbags and ropes already marked the extent of the prize-fighters' ring. Darleston jogged down to the base and strolled the perimeter.

Directly opposite the steps, a tree lay fallen across the entrance to a stone tunnel. The huge trunk formed a solid bridge between several of the tiers. 'That's not recently come down?'

Emma shook her head. 'It's been there since before I was born. There are dates carved into the bark.' She wound her way around one tier and traced her hand across what he presumed to be one of the carvings. 'The tunnel leads through to the promenade in the walled garden, but it's rather damp and in ill repair. It'll be hideous if Father traipses all the spectators through that way.'

Lyle ought to have brought him here last night, where they'd truly have been shielded from the house and the chance of discovery, although it would have been a good deal colder than the Orangery. Still, personally he preferred the natural shield formed by the high banks, undergrowth and woodland to walls of transparent glass.

Emma followed him down into the basin. They stood awhile in companionable silence. He liked that quality in a woman. So many of the silly chits in town saw silence as their downfall and chattered on inanely without pause. Of course, she was older than most of the maids out seeking a husband. He guessed her to be a good ten years older than her sister.

'What are your passions?' he asked. When she turned and looked at him he qualified the statement: 'As you're not one for boxing.' He imagined she'd list the normal rote of womanly accomplishments, but instead she simply shrugged. Only after a significant pause did she answer.

'I pickle things.'

'Cabbages, beetroot, that sort of thing?'

She laughed at his seriousness. 'What else? You didn't

think me an amateur naturalist, did you?'

'Well, I confess the thought of pickled mice did cross my mind. You're clearly not a great lover of crowds, so something else must entertain you, and I've come across a few rather eccentric recluses.'

Outrage briefly flared in her eyes. 'I'm hardly that.'

'No. No, of course not. You're far too pretty to be a hermit.'

Emma blushed a little, his ill-chosen words forgotten in the wake of the compliment. She turned away from him still smiling and found herself a perch upon the fallen log. 'Do you have one on your estate?' she asked a moment later. Her fingers worked over whatever names were carved into the tree bark.

'Me? I have neither a hermitage nor an estate. I own very little save a vast array of coats and a plethora of dubious appellations. Everything belongs to my father, including a few of the labels with which I'm blessed.' He was rather glad she didn't enquire into what those labels were as most of them were unrepeatable. 'You don't paint?'

'No. Do you?'

'Sometimes.'

'Any other hobbies?'

He couldn't help it. A wicked grin slid across his lips. 'One or two.' He raised his brow.

'Oh!' Emma gulped, and then retreated into the shadows of her bonnet. She left her perch and went to look at some of the wild flowers nestled amongst the ferns. Still, it wasn't long before he felt her gaze upon his back. He'd been facing away from her, eyeing the tunnel entrance, itching to explore, but wondering if it was too much to ask her if the passage were truly as riddled with dirt as she seemed to suggest.

Darleston turned a little so that he could spy her from the corner of his eye. She was looking – no, staring – at him intently, her expression a curious mix of desire and revolt; hot eyes, sullen lips.

The expression alone raised a purr of interest in his chest. Coupled with his need for affection – well, the possibility of her wanting him set his pulse racing.

Maybe he was mistaking anger for desire. If she knew or suspected what had happened between him and Lyle then it made sense that she'd be riled. Not that their encounters so far suggested that. Additionally, there was something in her gaze that was too curious, too warm to be anger. Plus the stare wasn't focused upon the back of his head as though she intended to deliver a blow, rather it travelled up and down his form, taking in the contours, lingering over his profile and the curve of his arse.

The merry devil was staring at his arse.

Well, that ruled out the possibility of her being Sapphic. It wasn't repulsion over being with a man that was keeping her from Lyle's bed. The notion had briefly entertained him, or at least the possibility of watching her with another maid had done so.

Darleston turned to fully face her. He raised a brow. Emma's chin immediately drooped towards her chest. Four strides brought him to her. He took the obvious course. The same one he'd trodden with many a drooping wallflower. He stretched out a hand and with two fingers lifted her chin, forcing her to meet his gaze.

Shock so deep it bleached every hint of colour from her face transformed her expression. Her eyes opened so wide her blue irises shone like halos. Emma's mouth fell open, and not in a good way. Not in a 'kiss me, I'm yours' way. Instead, he winced, expecting a scream. However, she remained silent. Then, rather than knocking his arm away, she scrambled backwards away from him as though he was Satan and his hellish touch burned.

'Why?' she might have asked. 'Why did you touch me?'

Instead – nothing. Arms wrapped tight about her body, she continued to shiver.

'I didn't mean to startle –'

'Forgive me.' She cut him off. 'I no longer feel so well.'

In truth she didn't look it either.

Darleston watched her flee back up the steps and into the thicket of grass and briars. Considering the shock he'd seen on her face, he didn't envisage her halting before reaching the edge of the copse, perhaps not until she'd locked herself behind her stout bedchamber door.

Naturally any decent man would have followed and seen her home safely, or at least attempted to intercept her flight, but pursuing her would likely cause more harm than good. He'd seen the sheen of tears in her eyes; heard the thickness in her throat. And he and tears never mixed to anyone's satisfaction but his own. His brother Neddy had once observed that what he really needed in his life was a doxy who wept whenever he spoke.

'Satisfied that I'm no liar now?' Lyle emerged from the gloom in the tunnel's entrance and sauntered towards the fallen tree.

Darleston strode upwards to meet him, admiring the buff and cream ensemble in which Lyle had dressed. Pale colours suited him. His breeches had been handsomely cut so they rode over his upper thighs like a second skin, giving rise to all manner of tempting thoughts – and wasn't that likely the intent?

'Followed us out, did you?' he asked.

Lyle offered him a simple shrug. 'It seemed prudent, given your reputation as a licentious rakehell, and, considering what I've just witnessed, it seems I was right to keep watch.'

'And what did you see exactly?'

Lyle cast an awkward glance in the direction of Emma's flight. 'Robert, it seems very much to me that you were attempting to kiss my wife, which is rather unsporting of you, given all the pleasure I advanced you last night.'

'I was merely trying to affirm what you'd told me.'

'Then a handshake would have done.'

Darleston rested against the fallen log in a spot where the bark had completely worn away. This close to the tunnel entrance, he could see that it was indeed damp and riddled with murky puddles.

'I can count on one hand the number of ladies with whom I've shaken hands. A kiss is a far more customary greeting.' Admittedly, he didn't generally aim for the lips, but usually the knuckles. 'And she was looking at me with such obvious desire it seemed rude not to oblige.'

'You've a vivid imagination if you think Emma was assessing anything other than your intellect –'

'She was staring at my arse.'

'– but it's useful to know what it takes to grab your attention.' Lyle counted the pointers on his fingertips. 'A salacious expression, a pout and a prominent "don't touch" label.'

'It was more pleading than salacious.' Salacious rarely stirred his blood any more. In fact, he liked things difficult. In a fit of playfulness, he leaned closer to Lyle. 'I'd like to see you donning a "don't touch" label. I think I know the perfect place to hang it.'

'Would that be where you wish to touch the most?'

'Perhaps,' Darleston remarked cryptically.

'Damn it, Robert! What game are you playing with me?' Lyle brought his palm down hard upon Darleston's knee. The resulting slap echoed around the arena. Birds scattered from the interlacing branches overhead.

Darleston stared at his stinging leg, which he was unable to rub without knocking Lyle's hand away.

'I thought we reached an understanding last night.' Lyle's hand slid upwards a fraction, slipping into the channel between Darleston's thighs. 'So, if you're not set upon becoming a monk, and clearly you're not, given that you were about to kiss my wife –' Lyle turned his head expectantly '– would it kill you to show me a little mercy? You've seen what she's like now. It's never going to be physical between us.'

'Ah, but I do relish a challenge.'

The fingers caressing his thigh turned into claws.

'Ow!'

'Robert!'

A wicked smirk climbed across Darleston's lips. He couldn't help it. A no was always more appealing to him than an easy yes. 'Oh, don't fret. I just have an idea about your little dilemma, that's all. Naturally I'll only pursue it with your permission.'

'Unless it's a plan that involves her becoming jealous because I'm repeatedly swiving your arse, then permission isn't granted.'

'A little jealousy could be part of it.'

With a jerk, Lyle sat up straight. His eyes narrowed, then he leaned forward, lips gently parted, his gaze locked upon Darleston's mouth. His large hand burrowed into the warm space between Darleston's thighs again. The tip of his thumb scored a line over the crotch seam, slid upwards and buffeted the wakeful ridge of Darleston's cock. 'Right here, right now. No running away. Dare you?'

'Permission first.'

Lyle drew in a long breath through his nose. His tongue briefly wetted his lower lip. 'What do you need?'

'Everything.'

'You'll never get close.'

'Then there's no problem.'

Several bated breaths passed between them. Heat flooded Lyle's hazel eyes. He nuzzled Darleston's shoulder, ran a finger around the collar of his shirt, and then quick fingers made light work of loosening the knot of his necktie. 'As you will, Robert. And as I will.' He struck, targeting the soft, exposed skin of Darleston's neck right over the pulse point. 'You know you marked me last night. It seems only right I return the favour.'

'You were begging to be claimed. I on the other hand am hedging my bets.'

'Darleston, if you mention my wife again, I may actually throttle you.' Lyle's fingers stroked the skin his lips had just met. Hot tremors rippled through Darleston's body. Necks were sensitive. He knew that, he'd seduced several past lovers in that way, but he'd never counted on his own neck being quite so riddled with nerve-endings. He barely moved, unable to focus until Lyle's kiss reached his lips and then they sank into one another's arms, sprawled along the length of the fallen elm.

When Emma had first drawn his attention to the inscriptions carved into the bark of the fallen tree, a crude and impossibly tempting vision of Lyle lying bound and prone with a gag in his mouth and his bottom bared had swamped

Darleston's thoughts. Now he saw their positions reversed, Lyle above him, taking charge of things.

Could they do this here? They'd be taking a huge risk. But who else would come out here? All the other guests had gone with Hill to meet Jack Johnstone at one of the outlying cottages. Only Emma remained, and she'd already flown. Having observed the bone-deep fear in her face, he couldn't envisage her returning.

He worked his hands inside Lyle's clothing, and then sucked in a breath when Lyle did the same and found the swell of his cock. 'Fellatio is fun,' Lyle muttered, while working his way down Darleston's body, kissing his chest and the pale skin of his stomach that he exposed en route, 'but what I really need is a nice long fuck. I need to feel you around me, accepting me. I need to make this real between us, not just play acting. I want to know you're committed to this. I can't deal with you blowing hot and cold, whether it's a tease or not.'

Darleston steadied himself a moment. What Lyle was proposing was different to how it had been between them in the past. He'd always been the *indorser*, Lyle the nancy. And yet ... 'Is that what you really want?'

'Robert, you don't need me to answer that. I've lost count of the number of times I've got hard just thinking about it.' Desire made Lyle's voice husky.

'Then do it.' Butterflies filled his stomach at the instruction. Lyle remained tensely poised, as if he couldn't quite credit the reality of the invitation. Darleston gave him a wicked grin. Wits and senses be damned. He hadn't earned a reputation as libertine by acting in a respectable manner, or by waiting around for somebody else to make the definitive move. He curled his fingers into the hair at the back of Lyle's neck and pulled him hard against him.

They fitted together like the two parts of a puzzle, as if they were meant to be together. It made sense. He'd once loved this man. Nay – that love had never died, circumstances had simply torn them apart and then it had been easier to deny his feelings than to live with them. He'd acted in exactly the same way over Giles.

Darleston nipped lightly at Lyle's bottom lip, teased him with the promise of a deep kiss but stayed just out of reach until Lyle's breath became fast and flighty. Only then did he deliver on the promise. As it had been the night before, the kiss left him feverish and uncomfortably hard. Unlike last night, he didn't allow Lyle to take charge. Having tossed aside his hat and stripped the coat from Lyle's back, Darleston jammed their hips together while simultaneously enjoying a good feel of Lyle's bottom. Firm muscle filled his palm. The robust swell of Lyle's cock branded his abdomen, promising … well, promising exactly what he damn well needed.

It didn't matter if this lasted a week, for the summer or the rest of his life. He no longer wanted to deny the pull he felt. Instead, he committed to it. No turning back.

'Swive me,' he purred.

'With pleasure.' Lyle's breath warmed his ear. His lips traced the lobe and descended again to his jawline.

Darleston pushed his hand inside Lyle's breeches and took pleasure in the feel of Lyle's erection filling his hand. This was what they both needed. It was a beginning and an end. They'd never properly said goodbye. This was a welcoming hello.

'Trust me.' Lyle winked as his fingers began to explore beyond the swell of Darleston's shaft. 'I learned a trick or two from that vadelect. All you need do a while is relax and enjoy.' He made swift work of the remaining fastenings and dragged Darleston's breeches down to where his boots prevented any further descent. Then, having first pressed a kiss to each inner thigh, he bestowed a series of ecstasy-inducing licks to the very eye of Darleston's cock.

Darleston lay on his back and stared at the blue sky and swaying bowers. Birdsong filled his ears. Prior to Lyle, the last person to go down on him like this had been Lucy. He might hate his wife, but he'd made a fine job of teaching her how to suck. Yet Lyle breathed fire into his veins in a far more endearing fashion, seeking out tender spots so that the ache in his balls grew almost unbearable. His hips began to roll of their own accord. Fingers gripped him tight. They coaxed his legs further apart, traced circles over his bottom, urged him to lift up and turn over.

As he rolled onto his front, Darleston eyed the long slim wand that was Lyle's cock. It had been too long since he'd allowed himself this pleasure. Butterflies began to riot in his stomach as he positioned himself over the trunk as he'd imagined seeing Lyle. He'd needed, had wanted a good pricking for so long, but circumstances had conspired against him and he hadn't wanted a whore. He'd wanted someone with whom he had a bond.

Lyle's hands settled upon his bottom, the touch so light it raised hairs all over his body. The sensation bordered on ticklish and made him realise just how few really good times he'd had playing the bottom role. No man had ever really touched him like this. Past encounters had been swift and frantic – seedy; something done in the dark, without an exchange of names or meaningful emotions. This was broad daylight, out-of-doors and luxuriously tentative.

Lyle touched him as though he meant to imprint a memory

of himself upon the skin. When his thumb brushed the sensitive whorl of Darleston's anus, he nearly shot up off the bark, it set so many nerves alight.

Dear God – that was only the trace of one finger.

Conflicting messages crowded his pleasure centres. Things became even more muddled, even rapturous, when Lyle bent and set his mouth to work where his fingers had strayed.

Darleston's eyes drooped closed. He'd definitely never been kissed so intimately before. Within moments his blood ran so hot he swore brandy fumes had replaced his blood.

'You really want this, don't you?' A whisper of hot breath assailed his ear. The tip of Lyle's very cheeky tongue wriggled into another sensitive place. 'Tell me how much you want it, Robert. Tell me what you're feeling right now. Having regrets? Any final wishes?'

'Let me feel you.'

'Like this?' Lyle's form moulded itself to the curve of Darleston's back. Loins pressed fast to willing flesh. Why was it that the sensation of a cock poised within the channel of his arse was in some ways more enthralling than the act to which it led? 'Think you're relaxed enough yet? Think I'll slide in without a hint of resistance?'

He wasn't sure about no resistance, but teasingly close wasn't anywhere near close enough.

His senses screamed and his balls ran with an itch so crazy he wanted nothing more than to jerk himself to fulfilment then and there. Instead, he pushed back against Lyle's cock.

The rasp of Lyle's breath whooshed past his ear. 'Easy, Robert.'

'Easy yourself.' He pushed back again. A shot of joy streaked from his anus to his chest as the tip of Lyle's cock eased inside. A groan started deep in his chest and gained vehemence as it left his throat. 'More. Do it and I'll tell you what I have planned for Emma.'

'What makes you think I want to know?' Lyle wriggled his hips a little, but staved off Darleston's attempt to take him all the way inside.

'Because I know you. Give me a chance, Lyle, and I swear we'll have her together. Have you ever had a woman as you're taking me now?'

Lyle grunted – but not in affirmation.

'Imagine it. Then imagine my cock inside her cunt so that you can feel me as though our cocks are caressing one another as we both possess her. All three of us sharing that perfect moment of bliss ...'

A pinnacle he wasn't so very far from now. He arched his back against Lyle again. This time his lover pushed forward at the same time so that their bodies met and Lyle slid deep.

'Oh, God!'

The ache, was it always this good?

Too good.

Incredibly raw.

The border between ecstasy and pain had never been so fine.

'I did warn you to go easy. Relax. Don't tense up.' Lyle pulled out a little, then slid back home. 'There now. Show some bottom. Let's just get you used to it, shall we?'

'Fuck!' Darleston swore. Drawn-out wasn't what he needed right now. 'Harder, Lyle.' His words came out in a rush.

'Like this?' Lyle wrapped his arms tight around Darleston's chest and tugged him into a kneeling position. Chest locked to his back, they swayed together, scaling the path of pleasure.

Lyle's fist closed fast around Darleston's cock and began to jerk him to the rhythm of their hips. 'Almost,' he cried. 'I want you with me. It bothers me when the man I'm fucking can't stay hard. Not that you're having that problem.'

'Keep stroking me like that and you'll know just exactly how into this I am.'

'Are you going to come while my cock's in your arse?'

'If you insist on stroking me like that, I don't think I'm going to have much choice.'

Despite the warning, Lyle persisted in swirling his thumb around the head of Darleston's cock.

'Holy God!'

'That good, eh?'

Darleston fell forward onto his palms. Sweat beaded his skin. His balls drew up tight as he soared towards orgasm. 'Your goddamned wife is watching us.'

CHAPTER FIVE

'Emma, aren't you going to dress?'

Emma glanced up from the sampler that lay upon her lap. The embroidery needle she'd held lay dangling over her knee by a thread. Amelia stood at the drawing-room door, her hands pressed together before her as if in prayer, a pose that was probably intended to mask the ridiculously low and inappropriate neckline of her dress. Only a tiny scrap of lace maintained her modesty. A piece would have to be sewn into it before she was allowed to wear it in public.

'The dinner gong went five minutes ago, yet you're still here,' the minx said, before Emma had a chance to scold. 'Oh, heavens, Emma! Are you so determined to wreck my chances of finding a husband? Isn't that the frock you went out in this morning? There are mud stains all around the hem. You can't wear that to dine.'

Dinner. Hours had passed. Yet she hadn't seen or heard anyone come in. After Darleston had ... after he'd touched her, her heart had raced so fast she thought it would jump right out of her chest. All of her breath had been stolen. She'd had to get away from him as fast as possible, but she hadn't run very far. The mire of brambles made it difficult

69

and her legs wouldn't carry her. Her feet kept slipping. One briar whipped back upon her and left her arm beaded with blood. She cried out but he hadn't heard.

Perhaps it was best that he hadn't heard. He'd been going to kiss her. Hell knows what he'd have done if he'd seen her hurt.

No man had ever kissed her upon the lips. Darleston had looked at her and seen into her soul. He'd read the desire there, had been about to return it. If he hadn't raised his hand first, he might even have captured her. Her heart sped a little at the thought. A knot of tension built in her womb. How wonderful that he recognised her desire, but he had to understand that she wasn't like the society women he knew. She couldn't be with him. She couldn't love him in that way. Any passion would remain unrequited. Regardless of the desire she felt, she would never act upon it.

And yet she'd still about-turned and stumbled back to where she'd left him. There'd been no sense in her head, just as none resided there now. The sound of Lyle's voice had spurred her forward. She'd known why he was there even before she spied the men together. She'd given Lyle permission. She had only herself to blame. But seeing them together like that ... The details of what Lyle practised had never before troubled her thoughts.

Now they were her only thoughts.

'Emma?' Amelia's shrill cry smashed the recollection apart. 'Are you not well? You look ill. See, you've gone crimson and your skin is all blotched.'

Emma turned her head, but she could not see herself.

'Please don't be sick.' Amelia wrung her hands. 'Father won't hear of me being amongst this company without you around as chaperone. He'll send me to Aunt Maude's.'

Shakily, Emma waved away the concern. 'I'm fine. Just a little faint. Too much fresh air and not enough to eat. I'll be right again in a moment.' She staggered past Amelia and into the hallway.

'Should I come up with you and help you dress?' Her sibling shadowed her flight into the hall so closely that her presence added to Emma's nervousness. Amelia craved affection. Like a lapdog she was always underfoot. She saw any sign of weakness as the perfect opportunity to snuggle up close. It wasn't that Emma didn't want to return her sister's love, only that she couldn't bear to expose herself in such a way again.

'No, you go in to eat. I'll be fine once I'm rested. Could you please apologise to Father for me? Tell him I have a headache. And ask if Mrs Dobs would be so kind as to send up a tray.'

'Should I have her send up a tincture of something too?'

'No, quiet will be remedy enough.' She gave her sister a weak smile. 'Don't worry, I'll be fine again tomorrow. I won't let Father send you to Aunt Maude.' Then she hurried up the stairs before Amelia could follow. More than her head, her heart ached. And when she mulled over what she'd experienced her womb clenched tight too, as if her body intended to wring every ounce of feeling from the earlier encounter.

All afternoon she'd sat gazing into space waiting for either Lyle or Darleston to approach her. She hadn't given dinner a thought. How foolish was she? Lord Darleston would be next to her at dinner, with Lyle directly opposite. There'd be no avoiding either of them. Oh, no. She couldn't face them together like that, not in public where everyone would witness her embarrassment.

Hiding in their room wasn't ideal, but at least only Lyle would seek her there.

* * *

Dinner calmed her a little, though she didn't eat a lot. Lyle arrived while she was stirring a spoon around in the mashed-up remains of a lemon tart. He paused in the doorway a moment before sealing them within and striding forward.

'Why are you hiding? Amelia says you have a sore head.' He perched upon the foot of the bed, so that the tray of food formed a barrier between them.

She knew they'd seen her, so there was no supposing he didn't understand her reasons.

'All right, if you won't say, then answer me this. Why did you come back, Emma? After he'd frightened you, why return? Did you change your mind about something?'

'No.'

So he knew Darleston had touched her. She hadn't considered he might be cross with her for that.

'Emma.' Lyle stretched a hand towards her, but stopped short of actual contact. 'Can we speak plainly for once?'

'I thought we always did.' Her words echoed around the room, shrill and defensive.

Lyle shook his head. 'I didn't mean you to see that. We should have been more circumspect. I want to apologise if my behaviour has offended or embarrassed you. I'm sure Darleston would like to say the same. However, I have to know why you watched. Why did you stay when you saw what we were about? You could have left.'

'I – I don't know.' Her cheeks prickled with the heat flooding them. Her reflection in the silver teapot bore the hue of a raspberry. Aghast with embarrassment she curled her knuckles against her mouth. 'I was intrigued, I suppose. I've never seen ... I've never spied on you before. Well, only once.' And that hadn't been anywhere near so enlightening. 'I swear it. And I won't do so again.'

Lyle's fingers curled into the eiderdown. 'I didn't expect you to make it a habit. Not that I should really mind if you did wish to take pleasure in that way, as long as you warned me of your intention beforehand.'

What in God's name was he saying? That he would invite her to watch them fornicate?

'I don't think ... I'm not sure that's absolutely necessary.' The fire in her cheeks spread to her ears and her nose.

'Why is that?' Lyle pressed. He shifted position so that he sat upon his haunches. 'Is it because it's not me you want to watch? It's Robert, isn't it? You're attracted to him.'

Robert she presumed to be Lord Darleston. Robert, she repeated to herself, committing his Christian name to memory. 'I'm most certainly not.' She shook her head desperately.

Lyle crowded her, shuffling up close to the wall of crockery between them. 'You're the most godawful liar I've ever met. Tell the truth, Emma. Do you want to make love to him?'

'Of course not.' She shoved aside the tea tray and leapt out of bed. Her limbs and arms were trembling. It took all her coordination and determination to cross to the fireplace. Lyle followed. He loomed over her. Emma risked a peep to find him dusting sugar from his clothing. The remains of dinner lay strewn across the bed. She reached out to ring the bell for a maid, but Lyle blocked the way.

'I don't think I've ever seen you so roused.'

'I don't want him like that,' she insisted, still seeking a distraction from the conversation. The whole bed would have to be stripped and remade before either of them slept. 'You know my habits. I don't care to be touched by anyone.'

The harshness of her declaration made it sound convincing, but deep down she wasn't so sure of her honesty. Omission still constituted lying and a small white lie lay embedded in her words. She didn't want to be touched, but there was no denying that she wanted to run her palms across Darleston's form.

Lyle frowned at her, his brown eyes riddled with mysteries. 'He claims you were staring at his arse. And I saw you staring at his cock. Do you deny that?'

She blustered a moment, her mouth working but no sense coming out. 'Well – I've never seen one before and I could hardly stare at yours, considering where it was embedded,' she eventually blurted.

Oh, dear heavens, that was quite the most foolish and ridiculous thing to say.

Lyle's jaw dropped. For what felt like eternity, he stared at her, shock engraved in every line of his face. Then, abruptly, he began to laugh. 'Emma!' A deep rolling laugh, which tugged at her lips and made her grin too. He didn't seem so angry either, once their merriment had died down; instead he seemed intrigued.

'Well, I think that's outrageous. That you've never seen one, I mean. We ought to rectify that. Can't have a married woman not knowing what's what. I know you'd probably rather I brought in Robert, but –'

'No, no, don't!' She couldn't have him here making things even more difficult. Darleston didn't understand the rules. And even if he did, she wasn't certain he'd obey them. She supposed being an Earl's son made him rather a law unto himself.

'– but I don't mind obliging you. Really, Emma, you had only to ask if you were curious.' Lyle artfully slipped the buttons of his frontfall, drawing her attention fully to him. 'You can't have seen much detail out in the woods.'

She'd seen detail enough.

'Robert's is very nice, of course. I think you'll find him a little thicker than I. Although I'm longer.'

She had no response to that. None at all. Flabbergasted, Emma watched him step out of his breeches and raise his shirt-tails. Confusion momentarily wrinkled her brow, for what she saw was not at all like what she'd seen earlier. Lyle's prick lay curled against his body as if slumbering, while Darleston's member had stood erect. Yet even as she stood trying to figure it out, change occurred before her eyes. Lyle became stiffer, longer. He woke up and stood proud. The tip peeped out from beneath a hood, rosy and glossy. A slit like a tiny eye was exposed. From it leaked a single shiny tear.

'How much more do you want to see?' he asked.

'I don't know. What is there to see?' She clasped her hands over her mouth.

'I can pleasure myself, as if I were inside him. I can bring myself to climax. Women can too if they touch themselves in much the same way. Not all touch is bad, Emma.'

She'd reserve judgement on that. However she didn't wish to get into a debate at present. Fascination had taken hold. It was nigh impossible not to focus on the slow, steady rhythm of Lyle's hand rubbing back and forth, up and down the length of his shaft. What a delightful picture he made. It made her feel twitchy inside, hot and irritable but in a pleasant sort of way.

Actually, in much the same way Darleston's touch had made her feel.

Well, why should it be such a great thing to admit to desire? She wasn't immune to physical attraction, merely unnerved and quite unused to the sensations of it. She had never claimed not to feel; she only wished not to be poked and prodded.

Lyle caught her gaze. 'Perhaps you'd allow me to get more comfortable.'

Emma gave him a mute nod. She watched him strip naked, desperately relieved that the door was locked.

Two years of life together and prior to this moment she had no clear idea of what he looked like. Her husband was a beautiful man. Naturally she was aware of his shape and how well he fitted into his clothes. But clothes masked plenty of sins, as she knew only too well.

Golden hairs flecked Lyle's chest and the pits of his arms and formed a thick thatch around his loins. His legs were hairy too. She'd never realised that. So too were his forearms. His nipples were two pale-pink pennies, only a shade or two darker than his skin. Smooth muscle gave him a graceful shape. Why, he was even more beautiful naked, especially as he was right now, standing proud.

Lyle left the fireside. Emma followed his movement to the bed, gaze locked upon the firm globes of his rear as he set aside the crockery. He ripped the despoiled eiderdown from the bed. 'Sit here. Come close. I promise I won't touch you.' He beckoned her to a spot just shy of his left hip. Emma sat primly upright, her hands clasped fast together. 'How does it make you feel to watch me do this?'

'I don't know.'

'Good, bad, indifferent?'

'Hot.' Another blush streaked across her face. No similar sign of embarrassment coloured Lyle's cheeks. He seemed supremely relaxed. The only hot and flustered part of him appeared to be his prick. The tip reminded her of the very ripest of cherries, with its dark-red hue and sensual curves. She noted that he swept his thumb over the eye-like slit every time he brought his palm downwards.

'Hot is good,' he mumbled.

'How does it make you feel?'

He laughed. 'It makes me feel fantastic.'

'Are you picturing him, while you do that?'

'Robert?' Lyle shook his head. 'Only in a roundabout way. I was thinking of you watching us and how very much I'd like to see you taking your pleasure. Everyone deserves some, you realise.'

She swallowed slowly, fearing what he might ask, how he might demand that she undress and lie naked beside him, and how he might beg to touch her skin. Enter her.

'I'm not asking you for anything,' he reassured her, perhaps having noticed her shiver. 'Just tell me what would make you happy and I'll give you it. Anything.'

She knew in essence what he meant – that he was offering her the sort of satisfaction other people craved – but she could find no joy in the notion of being caressed. However, watching the steady stroke of his palm back and forth in that rhythmic motion over his cock had taught her something. There was a tingling sort of excitement to be had from seeing someone else touch themselves. Not that she wanted to spend her days watching Lyle alone. No, she'd much rather watch her husband with his lover. The excitement she'd felt watching them fuck was ten times the fluttering, giddy nervousness she felt now.

Would Lyle understand?

What would he think?

Perhaps her greatest fear, far beyond that of being touched, was being thought mad. If she were judged so, every freedom she possessed would be stripped way.

'Say it, whatever it is.'

'I want to watch you with him again.' Shock at her own words engulfed her body like a cold douche. Emma's heartrate sped as she trembled. Afraid of Lyle's reaction, she averted her gaze.

'Go on,' he prompted.

Emma immediately raised her head. Lyle wasn't cross – he remained relaxed, if you could describe the pumping of his fist as such – but he was intrigued.

'What is it you wish to see us doing?'

Emma shook her head, quite speechless. None of this made any sense. The whole conversation ought to have been a dream. Normal couples didn't converse like this. At least she was fairly certain they didn't. But then, typical husbands didn't fornicate with other men, and wives accepted whatever affection their husbands chose to bestow rather than bristling at the mere notion of it.

'You really ought to tell me. I can't bear the suspense. I'm conjuring all sorts of images, most of them lewd.'

Maybe it was his smile and the way it ran into the depths of his warm brown eyes, maybe it was the peculiarity of the situation, but the admission spilled from her lips. 'I want to see you do things the other way around, with him in ...'

Lyle gave another chuckle. 'Emma Langley, I don't think I know you at all. I can't believe you've just said you wish to see me fucked in the arse by another man. What are you thinking?'

'I'm sorry. I should have kept quiet.'

'No. No, you should not have kept quiet. You should speak some more. You ought to tell me why you want to watch things that way. Is it so that you might imagine yourself in my place?'

'No!' she squeaked, alarmed by how her insides seemed to heat at the notion. 'The pair of you looked good together.'

Lyle shook his head, dismissing the answer as the blind it was. 'I don't think that's it at all.' He didn't say what he thought her true reasoning was, for he reached climax at that moment. Emma watched his seed spurt from the tip of his cock. It fell in silvery streaks upon his belly and coated his fingers. For several long moments he held himself still and gulped down uneven breaths. Eventually he opened his eyes and found a handkerchief.

'I believe you are monstrously wicked, Emma Langley, and if I hadn't already married you, I would do so again.' He reached out, but stopped short of embracing her. 'I'll speak to Darleston and arrange a time and a place when we can indulge you. I'm sure he'll oblige. He's quite sweet on you too.'

While she floundered, wondering what in heavens she was supposed to make of that remark, Lyle cleaned himself up and redressed.

'Are you sure he won't think it strange?'

Darleston had not seemed overly perturbed at being watched in the amphitheatre, but that had been accidental. Arranging a situation where she would be their official audience while they did that was different altogether.

'I think he'll see you as a very accommodating hostess. Not everyone is quite so gracious about sharing their husband. And Emma – I don't mind that you desire him, just as long as you don't steal him away. So you needn't feel guilty in that regard. Everyone ought to have someone who makes them feel alive, but I am curious. What is it about him?'

Truthfully, she answered: 'I don't know.'

CHAPTER SIX

When Lyle went upstairs to address Emma, Darleston made his own excuses and left Hill and the rest of his house guests to their port and cigars. He walked out of Field House and set off along the riverbank, using the quiet time to churn over thoughts and possibilities. The sun still lingered on the edge of the horizon and swarms of aphids hovered over the deceptively still water. The river reminded him rather strongly of Emma Langley – or maybe she was simply in his thoughts – placid on the surface but driven by ferocious hidden currents.

Despite the excitement of the day and the prospect of working his way into Emma's heart, he felt calmer now than he had in weeks. He guessed his good mood could be attributed to the sexual release. He'd always pursued his passions, even once they'd become a little jaded and prone to extremes, but for the last few months, between losing Giles and Lucy's hideous rumour-mongering, he'd shied away from any sort of engagement. Maybe that too contributed to why seducing Emma had such a sense of piquancy. Women like Emma, cold on the outside, burned like hot coals once you cracked the surface, but he wasn't sure which element of the challenge he relished most: seeing her passion burn so brightly once she'd surrendered, or planting the initial seeds of temptation required to set her on the path to his bed.

To his and Lyle's bed.

Hell, he shouldn't be so excited by the prospect, but he was.

He'd never had a husband and wife together before. Leastways, not after their vows. It was probably taking an enormous risk, yet there remained something hopelessly alluring about it. It was proving far too easy to fall for Lyle all over again. As for Emma – he liked the heat in her gaze when she looked at him. He loved the glimpses of her spirit he'd seen, like her annoyance at being thought weak and silly purely because she was a woman. And he craved – yes, craved – half her strength. He couldn't survive without others around him to prop him up. The sort of solitude she endured would kill him.

'Robert?'

He turned at the sound of his name to find a small coracle bobbing on the water. It contained two gentlemen, one of whom gave him a frantic wave. Darleston sauntered down to the water's edge and waited for the boat to approach. His twin brother leapt from the vessel and slapped him about the back by way of greeting.

'When did you get here? This afternoon? Hill didn't mention you earlier.'

'My presence must have escaped his mind. Last night. Pennerley wasn't in the mood to be accommodating.'

'I can't imagine why you ever thought he would be. I don't suppose anything has changed there since last November. Is Miss Rushdale still with him?'

Pennerley had split with his long-term lover the previous Hallowe'en and had been brooding in his castle ever since.

'Yes, she's still there.'

'Excellent.' Neddy rubbed his hands together. He turned to the man who remained in the boat, tilting the oars. 'That's twelve guineas you owe me, Quernow.'

The man resignedly bowed his head.

'So, how are you finding the place? Shall we walk?' Urged along by his brother's grip upon his shoulder, Darleston resumed his saunter along the riverbank. The little boat bobbed along beside them, maintaining a respectful distance.

'Why didn't you tell me that Lyle was here?' Darleston asked, though he knew the answer.

Ned released his grip. 'As if you don't know. If I had, you wouldn't have come. I know what you're like when your humours are unbalanced. It's as if the whole world is out to get you. You'd have given me some patter about keeping the scandal at home and not transferring it, when really Lyle's probably the best thing that could happen to you at the moment. You can't mope around after Giles for ever. He's a married man.'

'As is Lyle, in case you hadn't noticed.'

To his vexation, Neddy simply shrugged. 'Not in the same way. He and the wife aren't close like Giles and Fortuna. Oh, Rob, you're not telling me that you've suddenly grown a conscience, are you? Because I don't believe it. I really hate to indulge most of your little peccadilloes but I always liked Lyle. He's good for you. I'd rather see you with him than one of those mollies in town.'

'There's no fear of that.' Not while Lucy still had a tongue to tattle with. He couldn't risk any real scandal, or she'd have him forced into fleeing the country. Not that bedding Lyle wasn't a risk, but less of one. Lyle being married would certainly make things more palatable if word got out. The notion of them wife-sharing was quite a different matter from sodomising one another.

'How is it you didn't come down to see Jack earlier with the others?' Neddy asked

Darleston slowly sucked his lip as he considered his response. Since he'd cut his hair in January, they'd become more alike. He looked at Ned and was disturbed to find such a perfect reflection staring back at him. Since childhood they'd taken pains to be as individual as possible. 'Other things to think on.'

Ned grinned. 'You're not actually cross with me over Lyle at all then. That's good. I would like you to see Jack, though. He's something unique. I think you'll approve.'

'Aye, well, maybe tomorrow.' Having reached a fenced border, Darleston turned back towards the house.

'You say that as if you had another pressing social call to make.'

'You know me. I'm just not that interested in sweaty labourers. I only ever watch you in the ring and then only to ensure you remember to climb out again.'

'You won't say that once you've seen him.' Neddy's jovial exuberance almost convinced him to make it a date, but really he had far more interesting plans for the morrow. He waited as his brother returned to the coracle and watched as they pushed out into the river again. We'll see, he thought. We'll see what tidings Lyle brings.

* * *

She could pleasure herself.

She could pleasure herself.

Emma lay on her back in the freshly made bed in the

room she shared with Lyle, her arms positioned rigidly by her sides. Her nightshift covered her body from her neck to her ankles. The lace around her neck tickled her every time she exhaled. The question really was: did she dare? Also, while Lyle had said it was possible, he'd failed to dictate the exact method of accomplishing such a task.

Who was she trying to fool?

She didn't need a map to know which bits of her body were sensitive and which were not. If she hadn't before today, she certainly did now, following Darleston's attempt to kiss her and Lyle's performance, not to mention having watched the two men fuck.

Oh, dear Lord, had she really started to think in such crude language? Her family would be horrified to hear what went on in her head. She guessed that was another reason to avoid physical contact. People always seemed to read one another better when they were touching.

Darleston remained firmly lodged in her thoughts. The moments leading to the touch and all that followed kept replaying themselves. Even as she'd crept towards them through the bushes with no knowledge of lovemaking as such, on a gut level she'd understood what the sounds were. She'd arrived expecting to find Lyle on the receiving end, and had been doubly surprised and overheated when she'd seen that it was Darleston instead.

He'd had his eyes closed when she approached. His jaw was locked tight too, making her think that there was a measure of strain involved in the pursuit of pleasure. As she'd watched, his expression had slowly changed, a sort of rapture seeming to soften his hard features. Yet her attention had not remained upon his face, rather it had been repeatedly drawn to that point where the two men's bodies were linked.

She had been too far away to really see the details of Lyle's prick penetrating Darleston's pale buttocks, but she'd been close enough to see Darleston's prick standing erect, and to get an illicit thrill from it.

Emma's breasts grew heavy again when she pictured the two men moving together as one. She had never witnessed anything quite so earthy or beautiful. Her nipples tingled and a thread of fire seemed to link the two points to a third, far more sensitive place between her thighs. Lyle would no doubt tell her to explore a little in any of those places. Yet it seemed wrong to do so. Darleston, she suspected, would offer to do it for her, and a not insignificant part of her worried that her response would not be the definite negative it ought to be.

Emma huffed a sigh against the edge of the bed sheet. After his performance Lyle had gone, having expressly told her where to find him. It hurt a little to think of him curled up in Darleston's bed. More specifically it made her shivery and transformed the dark above her into something isolating and oppressive rather than comforting.

She didn't like to have him sleep by her. The soft whisper of his breathing kept her awake all night.

Her only consolation was that Lyle had promised to speak to Darleston about arranging another tryst that she could watch. If she'd imagined such a thing possible even twelve hours ago, she'd have thought herself crazy. In all likelihood she was exactly that.

Emma gnawed her bottom lip. Thinking of how Darleston's long fingers had curled beneath her chin set her pulse racing and restarted the deep-seated ache in her womb. Tentatively, she pinched one taut nipple. Lightning shot down from her breast to the nub between her thighs.

Dear Lord! One might be driven crazy by sensation such as that. Which naturally prompted her to do it again.

Emma rarely luxuriated in the feel of anything against her skin. The clinging cage of her stays and gowns she tolerated. She didn't linger when she bathed, preferring to make it a short-lived exercise in cleanliness rather than an indulgence. She hated anything too cold against her body and always warmed her clothes accordingly.

Lord damn it! She couldn't do this in the bed. There were too many memories associated with lying in this position. Emma hopped out from beneath the sheets and scuttled over to the fireplace, tugging the top cover with her. She lay before the grate on her side, so the flames gently warmed her face, and snuggled the bedspread around her shoulders.

The glow of the fire painted her skin in shades of bronze and orange. Emma slipped a hand between her legs and pressed it tight to the juncture. It'd be better without her cotton shroud in the way. Feeling braver now she was away from the bed, she bunched up her shift around her waist and laid a palm over the fleece of curls covering her mons. Despite her fingers being cold, the touch brought more heat to her flesh. *More*, her body seemed to plead. She gave it, pressing two fingers into the hot slit of her quim.

That press ... damned if it wasn't both shocking and wonderful. Naturally she had to repeat the motion, and repeat it again and again, until the press became more of a slide and her fingers were slippery with fluid.

Pictures of Lord Darleston filled the dark void inside her eyelids. He lay impossibly still upon the library chaise longue. Emma stood by him listening to the soft whisper of his breaths and observing the gentle rise and fall of his chest. For a long while she simply watched him sleep, which seemed invasion enough, but the more she watched, the more she longed to trace the contours of his noble face, slide a fingertip along the bridge of his sharp nose. To begin with, her gaze remained fastened upon his head; it really wasn't right to stare at a gentleman below the waistline– not that it had stopped her doing so earlier that day.

Emma held her palm over his chest. Even at a distance of several inches heat radiated up from his body to warm her skin. With her knuckles she brushed the deep-red pile of his coat. When he made no reaction to the contact, her bravery increased. This was how she always wanted him – passive and still. She slipped open buttons, peeled away his elaborate finery to reveal the skin beneath. She'd be like a ghost to him. Any awareness of her presence would be only on the very periphery of his senses. Yet he would still be responsive to her touch.

Soft murmurs of enjoyment passed his lips as she explored the ridges of his chest and abdomen. She ran rings around his neatly steepled nipples, traced the contours of the curious brand she'd spied on the right side of his stomach. Slowly his sighs became more abrasive as she unfastened his breeches and pulled aside the fabric to expose his loins.

Emma's fingers curled around the imaginary staff of his erection. Supple heat filled her palm. She stroked up and down as she'd seen Lyle do. The noises Darleston made changed from sighs to mewls. Gradually his hips began to roll with the movement of her hand, but he never once opened his eyes.

If she really could make him stay as somnolent as this, then touching him would become simple. Perhaps she would go further than just using her hands. She'd lower her mouth until her lips caressed the fiery tip of his cock, and then take him fully into her mouth as Lyle had professed to have done.

As long as he didn't try and return the touch, everything was fine. Maybe she would go even further. For a moment she pictured it: straddling his lap and tentatively lowering herself over his upright prick.

The nub between her thighs grew as taut as her nipples. Threads of panic jolted through her chest as she imagined the brush of his glans against the lips of her puss. But she couldn't seem to tear her hand away, couldn't stop herself rubbing – couldn't stop impaling herself.

Her whole body froze, every muscle pulled tight – so tight that they ached – then all at once she relaxed.

Emma soared. She floated in her daydream above Darleston's body, joined to him as his prick gave up its seed. Even then his eyes remained closed, maintaining the distance between them. She licked her fingers. Lay basking in the warm languor of the afterglow, soothed and contented. Perhaps not all touch was bad, at least not her own. She'd given herself a lot of pleasure, and only the tiniest part of her regretted that the fantasy wasn't real.

She'd never dare to touch Darleston in such a way.

Nor would the opportunity ever arise. Men like Darleston did not lie passively upon a chaise while married women caressed them until they climaxed.

Although, for all she knew of life in the capital, perhaps they did exactly that.

CHAPTER SEVEN

To Emma's consternation, nothing good occurred the next day. She walked with Amelia, and then rode in the afternoon, hopelessly aware of the saddle rubbing against her sensitive flesh the whole time. Amelia's tattle about the varying qualities of the menfolk didn't help either. Suddenly, the word 'man' only prompted visions of Lyle and Darleston naked.

Lyle she saw at breakfast. Darleston she glimpsed once or twice around the grounds, but he never seemed to be still long enough for her to appreciate the moment. Towards evening she found herself wandering the ground-floor rooms seeking him out. The fact was, she missed his presence, even though the thought of his touch terrified her. However, if she could stay with him in the same room as the other guests, then he wouldn't be able to do anything without raising suspicions and frowns. She eventually tracked him down to the library, where he was taking an early aperitif with Bathhouse, Connelly and Phelps. Phelps had her father's recent litter of spaniels bounding about his feet. He and Bathhouse tossed an apple between them that the dogs kept trying to catch.

They all stood when she entered. 'Good evening, Mrs Langley,' they chorused, making her feel like an elderly governess. Darleston returned to his chair first. Emma walked past him to the window bay. She took a book from a shelf and sat looking out of the mullioned lacework panes at the lawn. Only a minute or two passed before his shadow fell across her lap, although it felt like nine or ten.

'Have you had a pleasant day?' he asked.

'Passable. And you, milord?'

'Darleston, I beg you. I don't think we need to stand on such formality.' She could almost hear the thought echoing through his head: she'd seen him fornicate and what could be more intimate than that? Well, engaging in coitus with him, the very notion of which left her trembling.

'Darleston,' she repeated, noting that he hadn't invited her to call him Robert as Lyle did. 'How did you like the boxers?'

The light from the candelabrum above caught the red of his hair as he shook his head, turning the strands a brilliant copper hue. Shadows masked the glint she expected to see in his dove-grey eyes. 'I haven't been there yet. You'd have to ask one of the others about their merits.'

'Oh – I thought since I hadn't seen you about the house today that you'd accompanied my father.'

Darleston smiled and shook his head. 'Other plans.' The way he grinned dared her to ask him what. He'd been with Lyle, of course. They'd been together. It didn't take any imagination to figure out how they'd been engaged.

Suddenly bereft and bitter, she said the most ridiculous thing imaginable: 'Are you my husband's lover?' As if she genuinely needed him to confirm it, considering what she'd seen.

It was a good thing that the spaniels were yapping so much over chasing apples and kerchiefs, otherwise the question might have raised a lot more than his eyebrows.

'I think you know the answer to that only too well. Are you going to tell me that you object? I shan't believe you, considering the questions I've been asked.'

Emma's nostrils flared as she pursed her lips in vexation. The taste of bile lingered on her tongue. Yes, she knew they were lovers. And no, as a matter of fact, she didn't like it. She didn't like that she was being left out.

'If it's true, then why did you do that yesterday?'

He cocked his head. A frown creased his brow.

'In the amphitheatre,' she explained, still too cross to realise that she wasn't being precise enough in her questions. 'If you're engaged with Lyle, why did you try and kiss me?'

Darleston continued to stare blankly at her a moment, making her think that she'd read it all wrong and that he hadn't meant to kiss her at all. Then his expression transformed and a devilish smile spread across his lips and ran straight into the depths of his eyes. 'Because when a lady studies a man like that, a kiss is generally what's on her mind.'

Emma's breath sat heavy in her chest. It took her a moment to realise she was holding it.

'I'm sorry I so misread you,' he apologised. 'Clearly you were only vexed over my acquaintance with your husband, and you were staring daggers not flames.'

Heat suffused Emma's chest. The prickle of embarrassment ran up her throat and into her cheeks. She knew he didn't believe that, not considering the way his eyes lingered on her mouth, and his lips parted invitingly. Fiend, she wanted to brand him. He had to have been sent by the devil to torment her, as if she hadn't experienced torment enough already.

Darleston angled his body a little closer, so that he stood inclined towards her. Emma curled her fingers into the upholstery of the window seat. Being close to him was dangerous.

He knew she didn't want to be touched. Lyle would have told him how she was. Yet to escape she'd have to brush against him.

He knowingly had her pinned.

'I understand you wish for some entertainment tonight.'

Emma lifted her head. Surely he couldn't mean … Why, yes – yes, he did. He'd been with Lyle all day; it made sense that they'd have discussed the matter. She just couldn't believe he would bring it up in a room full of people. 'Some entertainment would be pleasant, but I don't wish to put you out.'

Darleston cocked his head again, so that a strand of coppery hair fell across his face. His lips parted slowly, but his words were lost as Amelia's voice ran out over the dogs and conversations. 'Entertainment,' she squealed, having hearing as sharp as a hare's. 'What do you propose, Lord Darleston? Do you play the pianoforte, or should we partner up to play whist?' Her oval face lit with glee at the hope of music and games after dinner.

'Sardines,' Aiken called.

Amelia immediately clapped her hands and gazed hopefully at Darleston. Emma's nerves literally sang. She couldn't play such a game and Amelia knew it. Actually, they all knew it. Darleston pursed his lips, while Amelia jigged up and down, impatient for an answer. Thankfully, her father vetoed the proposal with a swift shake of his head.

'Oh, Father …'

While Amelia protested, Emma's heart filled with relief. 'Charades,' someone else suggested and the game was agreed upon.

Emma made to rise, but Darleston refused to move. 'I know you didn't mean us to play charades, Mrs Langley, but shall we humour them for a while? I think there'll still be time to entertain you in the fashion you desire. I always find my passions run hottest after midnight.'

She met his gaze warily, afraid she would find mockery dancing there, but his expression was quietly serious. 'Shall we say: until then?' He lifted his brows again, and then turned away. 'Hill, how goes the training? What day is the fight set for?' He disappeared into the study with her father.

* * *

'We should play charades every night while they are here,' Amelia announced as she and Emma made their way up the stairs to bed, each carrying a candle. The soft light of the flames cast a bronze glow on her sister's face as Emma turned towards her. While she enjoyed seeing Amelia's gaiety, she didn't share her enthusiasm for mime.

'You wouldn't enjoy it so much if that were the case,' Emma responded, exercising some tact. No point in damp-ening Amelia's spirits, even if her own were quite bewildered by what was going on around her. Darleston's parting words to her still echoed inside her head.

'Oh, but I do like charades and how it brings out quite a different side to the gentlemen. Don't you find they're not quite so stuffy? Well, aside from Lord Darleston. Did you notice he didn't join in? He just sat and watched the entire evening.'

'Well, perhaps he doesn't care for the game.'

'I don't know why he's here. Do you, Emma? I mean, he's just not as interested in Father's sport as the rest of the gentlemen. I know he asks questions, but there's no enthu-siasm in his words, and he's not even been down to Field Cottage.'

'Perhaps he's had other things to attend to.' Like making merry with Lyle for one, and keeping her in a state of frenetic excitement for another.

Amelia paused as they reached the upper landing. 'Do let's go with Father tomorrow.'

Despair washed through Emma's chest when she saw her sibling's calculating expression. 'Whatever for? There'd be nothing for us to do, and I take no delight in watching grown men throw punches at one another.'

'Yes, but don't you see it would be a perfect opportunity for me to see what motivates them? Don't you think it important that I know a little about Bathhouse and Aiken?'

'Not especially.'

'Oh, Emma.' Amelia crossly tapped her foot on the creaking boards. 'I shall grow quite vexed with you. You're no fun at all. You know very well that I'm thinking ahead to my future. I know also that you merrily spied upon Lyle before you agreed to wed him. You can hardly blame me for wishing to do the same.'

'Aye, but I was already aware of an arrangement being struck between Lyle and Father. Unless I'm mistaken, Father has had no such talk with either of the gentlemen you've mentioned. It was fine looking in upon them the other night, but you know very well what they are all like now.'

Amelia gave an unladylike snort. 'As I said – no fun at all.' They reached the door to Emma's chamber and Emma turned towards it, but to her dismay Amelia didn't continue along the passageway but lingered by her shoulder.

'What is it? I'm weary now.'

'There's another reason I wish to go. I overheard father talking to Mr Connelly, and apparently there are another two gentlemen staying over at Field Cottage with Jack the Lamp.

I think it would be well-mannered of us to go and see them.'

'You've thought long and hard about that statement, haven't you?' Emma smothered her wrath with a yawn. She didn't believe Amelia cared one jot for who the men were. She knew her sister well enough. No, Amelia's primary motive was to catch a glimpse or three of their guests stripped out of their shirts, proving their manliness. 'Dear heart, I don't think it a wise idea at all. I know what you're trying to do.'

'Find someone to take me away from this dreary place,' Amelia responded brightly. She placed a hand on one hip, which only riled Emma a little more. 'Can't we stay up and talk a little more? You know I have questions about things, and I think it quite uncivilised of you to keep them from me. You don't want me to head down the aisle with a head full of fluff, do you? Oughtn't I to know a little of what goes on in the bedchamber?'

'Amelia Hill, I've no idea what you're talking about, but I know what Aunt Maude would say if you were to go on like this while she were here. Now, it's gone midnight.' The library clock began to chime at that very moment. Its mellow tone echoed loudly up the stairs. 'Please, go to bed and let me do the same. Ask Father at breakfast what he thinks of you accompanying him. I don't think it appropriate and neither would Aunt Maude, but it's not up to me. Don't imagine that I'll go with you, though, for I shan't. I don't like to watch them fighting. I'd much rather see a man finely dressed in his shirt and cravat than scrambling about like a savage.'

More white lies, she scolded herself inwardly. Considering what she'd been envisaging all day, her mind was not so very pure.

With a snort of vexation, Amelia finally stormed away along the corridor. Emma watched her go until all she could discern was the flicker of the candle her sister bore. She wished she could offer Amelia some genuine advice, but what could she say? She had no more experience of men than Amelia, perhaps even less.

Emma turned and grasped the cold doorknob. Light streamed from beneath the door frame, across which a shadow passed. Emma hesitated. She knew it couldn't be Lyle. She'd called goodnight to him in the billiards room just before she and Amelia had climbed the stairs. Possibly it was Lyle's valet, although normally he relied upon the man to dress rather than disrobe him. She didn't believe it to be one of the maids either. They all knew her habits well enough.

A frown creased her brow as Darleston's last words to her echoed through her mind. Had he come to her room? What game was he playing with her? Had he arranged a rendez-vous here with Lyle to which she was to be privy? Or had he come with some other form of entertainment in mind?

To her surprise, when she stepped within, the only light came from the fireplace. No one appeared to be lingering in its glow, but Lyle's bed things were laid out upon the righthand side of the quilt. Her nightshift occupied the left. Emma set her own flame down upon the mantel. Imagination and wishful thinking were getting the better of her again. In the narrow wedge of heat from the blaze, Emma unpinned the bib-front of her dress and began working upon the knot in her sash. Nothing would come of Lyle's promise. It was patently ridiculous to think it would. They couldn't act like that within the house. People would overhear. They would know, and she was worldly enough to realise that what she'd witnessed them doing was a crime. But crime or not, the roll and slap of their bodies still intrigued her.

It was only as she glanced up, having stepped out of

her dress and caught a glimpse of movement in the mirror, that she realised she wasn't alone. Her breath caught. She swirled on the spot, clutching her discarded dress to her chest. Darleston stood in the doorway that led onto the balcony. His gaze swept across her, bringing heat like the brush of a warm sirocco to her skin. She tried to find adequate words for her distress but stumbled over them. Darleston waited patiently, leaning against the inner ornamental curtains of the bay as if he intended to gauge whether she would scream before he made another move.

Emma closed her mouth.

He still wore the clothes she'd seen him in at dinner: a vivid bottle-green coat with a black collar and deep cuffs, all spun from a thick, soft fabric that captured the light as he moved.

'Our assignation was for midnight, was it not?'

'I did not agree to meet you, or invite you here.'

'No,' he agreed, shocking her, for she'd expected an argument. 'We left those aspects unsaid. Shall I add that Lyle invited me here? He seemed to think that there was entertainment to be had in the three of us gathering.'

'He's not here,' she said, stating the obvious, for how could he be without passing her? Unless he had found a way to fly up onto the balcony.

'I'm sure he'll join us in a moment or three.'

Emma didn't appreciate the delay. She needed Lyle here, now, to make this safe and somehow acceptable. She'd be branded a slattern if Darleston were discovered in her room, and Lyle would become a laughing-stock. A cuckolded man rarely retained any respect amongst his peers. No one would understand that that wasn't what Darleston's presence was about.

He emerged out of the shadows, closing the door onto the balcony quietly behind him. Emma stepped back out of reach when he joined her upon the hearthrug. 'I've seen a night-rail or two in my time, you needn't hide over that. Grab a wrapper if you wish, though I must say that the pale colour suits you. There's an overabundance of trimming on that dress you've taken off. You should take the bows off the front, and abandon that hopelessly stuffy fichu-and-lace cap.'

'Are you always so incredibly rude?' She shook her head. 'No, you weren't to me the first evening, but I suppose it was different then. You didn't know who I was.'

'I wouldn't claim to know you now, though in time I hope to.' He reached out to her, but she backed away again.

'Is it my touch that offends you, or just anyone's?'

'I'm sure Lyle's made you aware of my preferences.'

'I think you'd be surprised at what Lyle has said. Or maybe not.' A smile teased the corner of his lips. 'He has orchestrated this all for you.'

'There's pleasure for him in it. He wouldn't have agreed to it otherwise.'

Darleston considered. 'Mayhaps ... there may well be that ... but Lyle isn't here yet, and it's not his role in this that fascinates me. Why do you want to watch us, Emma? What do you hope to get out of it?'

When her mouth fell open again in shock, he dismissed her outrage with a turn of his wrist. 'Let's not mince words over why we're here. I think it'll be simpler for everybody if we dispense with coyness. Why is it you wish to watch me fuck your husband? What incentive has led you to this point?'

'I don't know what you mean.'

'What I mean –' He took another step, closing in on her and trapping her. Emma stared up at him in alarm. He was too close. She sensed the outline of his body as though he were pressing against her. Darleston's smile broadened so that she could see his teeth. 'What I mean is that I don't think you really wish to watch at all. I think you'd like to do, but you can't. Leastways, you don't believe you can.'

'What in heavens do you imagine I want to do?'

'That I'm not altogether certain of. I could hazard a guess or two, but really I'm not sure if it's Lyle or myself you're more interested in. Maybe it's both. If one can't satisfy then two surely can. The idea is not so very uncommon. Is that it, Emma? Would you like to bed down between us?'

'I don't want either of you to touch me. I beg you, don't come any closer.'

'Hm.' He gave a swift nod of the head. 'No contact. I understand perfectly, but you didn't really answer the question.'

Nor was she going to, for the mere mention of such an idea had planted the possibility in her brain, and it burned there like volcanic lava, bubbling, flowing and conjuring up fantastical images of three bodies entwined and filled with rapture.

'I guess we shall just wait for Lyle,' he said in response to her prolonged silence. He turned on his heel and strode over to the bed, where he perched near the footboard with his arms folded over the top of the wood. After a moment he rested his chin, and then his cheek, against the grain.

The knots in Emma's guts gradually unwound. Darleston hadn't done her any harm, even if he had pried into her personal business as if it was a perfectly commonplace thing to do. He also had a point about her dress. It was a frumpy old thing. Amelia chastised her for it, Lyle called it her silly old sack dress, even her father, who had no interest in ladies' haberdashery, had commented on the excess of lace wrapped around her throat. 'Makes you look as if you've lost your bosom,' her cousin, Charles Aubrey, had once remarked. Of course, almost everything he said related to bosoms.

Emma cast the dress over the dressing-table stool and retrieved her wrapper from the armoire. Darleston hadn't moved. She thought she sensed him watching her, but his eyes were shut. Inexplicably, Emma felt herself drawn closer. It wasn't only the dress he'd been right about; almost everything he said was true. She was interested in him – how could she deny it after her fantasy of yestereve, when she'd imagined touching every part of him, had drifted so deeply into the romance of him that she'd fantasised about not only touching but sucking his cock.

And of going further than that too …

She'd grown so aroused that her inhibitions had fled.

Still, all that was inside her head. She never intended it to happen for real. She just wanted to relive the excitement of watching the men. Anything more was quite unnecessary.

As she drew a little closer to the bed, Darleston opened his eyes. He gazed up at her but remained still. Minutes seemed to stretch into infinity. The candle burned low, and she was forced to light another. 'He's not coming, is he? He just sent you here, because he thinks –' She shook her head, not wanting to finish the thought. What in heavens did Lyle think? Had he decided that her avoidance of his touch was purely because of some physical aversion and that it would be simply overcome by setting her up with his lover instead? It would not. The thought of Darleston's hands upon her raised a shiver. Her nipples stiffened as she imagined the slow swirl of his finger drawn in circles around one erect point.

'He thinks he's giving you something you want,' Darleston remarked.

'But he's wrong. I told him that I only wanted to watch.' Panic filled her voice. Emma wrung her hands together and paced. 'I told him. You see that, don't you? How could he even have thought otherwise? Why would he suppose –?'

Darleston flipped onto his feet. 'It's only been a minute or two. Maybe he thought it important to give us some time. This is a little awkward for me too, Emma. It's not my habit to let people watch me make love. An audience is never something I've sought. And my recent experiences with women have not been entirely happy.'

'Your wife?'

'Is not nearly so understanding.' He cast around into the shadowy corners. 'Is there anything to drink in here?'

'I believe Lyle keeps some brandy in the decanter.' Emma waved him towards the side-table, which held a set of three stoppered vessels. Darleston sniffed at them all and then poured a glass. Instead of consuming the contents, he offered it to her.

'Take this. It'll steady your nerves. I want you to be comfortable, because then I will be too.' He gave her one of those elongated smiles of his that was somehow nerve-wracking, debauched and charming all at once. 'Let's sit and talk this through. Set some boundaries, perhaps?' He settled on the hearthrug before the fire, his long legs stretched out and his coat-tails crushed beneath him.

Emma took a tentative sip from the glass, and then swallowed a larger mouthful. The alcohol poured fire into her veins, but did nothing at all for her jitters.

'Come where it's warm,' he said. 'I won't bite.'

If only you would ... 'You bit Lyle.' She immediately covered her mouth.

Darleston nodded. 'Aye, I did, but only because he wished it. He bit me too.' Slowly he unwound his cravat and released the fastening of his shirt so that the neck gaped open, revealing the bruise upon his throat and the pale delight of his chest.

'Why do that to one another? Surely it hurts.' The brown and red speckled mark certainly looked sore.

'I find the line between pleasure and pain is a very fine one. Walking its precipice is a delight that's hard to describe. Yes, it hurt, but in a good way.'

'And when he entered you?'

He briefly troubled his top lip with his teeth. 'The sensations are akin, yes.' He folded his legs beneath him as Emma hunched down on the opposite side of the fire. How could he speak so frankly without a hint of embarrassment? Her cheeks were burning and her sexual peccadilloes were hardly being discussed.

By firelight, he was quite the most lovely creature. The burnished copper of his hair tumbled around his face like threads of fire, while the shadows softened the harder ridges of his jaw and nose. Again she felt drawn, as she had when looking at him through the library window on the night of his arrival. The palms of her hands itched with the need to reach out and make contact.

'Did somebody hurt you, Emma? Is that why you won't let anyone close?'

Aghast, she stared at him. 'No. Good Lord, no! No one hurt me. Why would you think that?'

'Because most women do not tremble if you so much as brush past them.'

'Nobody hurt me,' she repeated, focusing on the knot she'd made with her fists rather than the kindliness in his face. What in heavens did he imagine to have occurred? 'I have my reasons. Not that I feel any need to discuss them. All I need to know is whether you'll respect them.'

'It's hard to respect something you don't understand, but assuming I manage it?'

'Then I shall respect that you and Lyle are intimate together and I shall make no demands or cause any fuss over it. I shall do nothing to endanger you.'

Darleston drew his hand through his hair and looked into the blaze a moment. 'Where do you fit into that equation of longing?' he asked after a moment of quiet consideration. 'I can hear the need in your voice. You don't want to pack us off to do the deed in private. We wouldn't be here now if that were the case. So make some demands. State clearly what you actually want and I'll do my best to oblige.'

Dear Lord, why did he have to be reasonable? Why was he even prepared to indulge her in this? And why did the hum of his voice thread her veins with hunger? Emma looked at him, not seeing him as he was, but as she'd imagined him on the chaise longue – supine, obliging, still and yet aroused by her caress. But she couldn't speak her thoughts. They would only arouse ideas that were simply best not explored.

'I don't want anything. I don't –' Her voice broke off.

Darleston moved so that he was on his knees before her, his expression soft and, dare she admit it, affectionate. 'Well, if you think of anything … you know you've only to ask.'

CHAPTER EIGHT

Darleston rolled backwards off his knees and onto his feet. His hearing was perhaps sharper than Emma's for the bedchamber door opened at that moment to admit Lyle. 'You're late,' Darleston remarked, the softness that had infused his words now replaced by a huskier, more sexual tone.

'One of us has to stay up to see the guests safely to their beds.'

'Did Father retire early again?' Emma asked, rising to her feet despite Lyle waving her back to her former position.

'He did, which was no great surprise. And Aiken and Heath are now securely ensconced too. There should be no disturbances.'

Of course, now that Lyle had arrived matters would progress. She'd only just become accustomed to Darleston's presence and begun to relax. Now her heart thundered again and her jaw locked tight with tension. *I've seen them before. I asked for this. Just relax.* No one would touch her. She'd be like a shadow, clawing at the edges of the room, but apart from their activity.

'I'm afraid Emma has not been entirely forthcoming with

regard to what she desires of us,' Darleston remarked. 'I'm not sure at all how we're to provide satisfaction.'

'I want nothing for myself. I told you that.'

'Well, I'm not sure that's entirely true, but I'll humour you this once.'

Her opinion of Darleston changed in that moment, but only for a moment. How dare he presume to know her? How could he read her so easily? How could he know what she truly desired? Because he did, she sensed it, saw it in the depths of his shiny dark eyes. He recognised that watching two men fornicate was not her true desire, merely a mask for what she really craved – his companionship, his touch.

I can't do it. It'll never be.

Lyle stooped and retrieved Darleston's discarded cravat. ''Tis lucky then that I remember what you asked for, madam wife. I don't think I shall ever forget it. You asked to see me fucked, did you not? You wished to watch while Robert swived my arse.'

Emma sank back onto the rug, the strength gone from her limbs. Why did this have to be so blunt and open? She ought to have said that she wished to spy, to remain hidden while they performed the act.

While heat both internal and external washed colour into her cheeks, she noticed that Darleston was smiling. 'No.'

Her shock was mimicked in Lyle's face. 'No?' he questioned.

'That's a privilege you'll have to earn,' Darleston said to her. 'Tit for tat. You have to give something in order to receive. Are you willing, Emma? Or shall I take myself to my chamber now?'

Her breath caught in her throat. 'What do you want?'

He laughed, his tongue flicking over the points of his

canines. 'I haven't decided yet, but I'm sure that something will occur to me.'

'Then how can I possibly agree?'

'You don't have to agree, because I'm not going to swive him. I'll give you a taste of something else instead and then you can judge if you want to take things further. It's entirely your choice.'

'Emma?' Lyle asked with a hint of desperation in his voice.

'Very well. Show me what you will.'

Kissing – something she'd never understood, but which she now couldn't take her eyes off. In some ways seeing their bodies pressed tight, hands grasping, full of urgency, was more intense than watching them fuck. Her own lips burned with imagined sensations of such a caress – deep, furious, passionate and growing in intensity. The ache of their joining seemed to spill into the air around them and raise the temperature of the room by several degrees. Her heart sped, and then hiccupped when they drew apart. Darleston fell onto his knees so that his head was level with Lyle's groin. Dexterous fingers made quick work of Lyle's waistcoat buttons. He yanked the front of Lyle's shirt from his breeches and unfastened the buttons of his frontfall. Lyle's breeches slithered down his legs with the aid of some tugging. Then Darleston's large palm swept up the inside edge of Lyle's thigh with the fingers splayed.

And she knew what was coming, could see it so clearly. He would do as Lyle had described and take her husband's cock in his mouth.

It was not quite as quick as that. Darleston teased before he delivered. The pink flash of his tongue touched the very tip of Lyle's prick. He paused there, his breath warming the surface. Even then he didn't deliver, but placed numerous light kisses up and down the stem, while with one thumb he gently stroked Lyle's balls.

Lyle's expression told her everything about how it felt to be held thus. Rapture. His eyes fell shut. He sought blindly for some support, initially finding only Darleston's head of fiery locks, in which he entwined his fingers. 'Oh, yes! Suck me, Robert. Please.'

'Like this?' Darleston bestowed a firmer kiss to a point halfway up Lyle's shaft.

'Not quite.'

'Like this then?' Avoiding the cherry-red tip again, Darleston kissed the juncture where the base of Lyle's prick met his cobs.

'A tad higher.'

'Ah, I understand.' But he didn't rise up. He sank lower instead and took not Lyle's cock but one of his bollocks into his mouth.

Emma leaned forward straining to see. It was hard to determine from Lyle's expression whether the touch was entirely pleasing, rather he seemed on the edge of some precipice. 'Ease off.' His fingers curled tight into Darleston's hair, making knots of the coppery strands.

Darleston released him. He sat back on his haunches and directed Lyle to the armchair. Lyle fell gratefully into his bower, his breeches still hanging around his knees. Darleston tugged them off along with Lyle's shoes and stockings. He rose upon on his knees again to kiss Lyle's mouth while stroking his prick before finally taking Lyle's cock in his mouth.

The very act confounded her. Here was a lord upon his knees sucking another man's – her husband's – cock as if it were a joy to do so. Emma shuffled around, needing to know if the act aroused Darleston as much as it did Lyle.

The front of his breeches, what she could make out around his coat-tails and the tangle of their limbs, stood tented. A sort of triangular protrusion strained against the buttons.

It did arouse him. Sucking another man's cock aroused him. She wanted a closer look at the evidence. Longed to see his shaft standing erect and watch his seed spill over his fingertips and belly once more.

Darleston's hips rocked as he fellated Lyle, mimicking the rhythm of coitus, back and forth in a steady figure-of-eight motion.

If she asked, would he expose himself? Would he take his prick in his hand and masturbate as he pleasured her husband and allow her to watch all that? It took every ounce of strength she possessed to open her mouth and ask, 'Can I see?'

She had to move away from the hearth, the heat in her body was now so fierce.

Darleston turned his head towards her. 'His prick?' Lyle's shaft glinted in the firelight, shiny with saliva and precome.

'Yours,' she mouthed, words barely audible.

He heard her though. She watched the delight at the request run into his eyes, filling them with powerful dark magic. His lips were moist and berry-red as if he had smeared rouge on them, and just for a second she imagined leaning in and tasting them and the essence of Lyle's sex left upon them.

'Say that again,' he said. 'Tell me you want to see my prick again.'

Embarrassment tied her tongue in knots. She couldn't look at him as she said it. 'I want to watch you stroking your prick.'

Saying 'prick', that was the truly toe-curling part, followed by the sharp sound of Lyle's indrawn breath and then a terrible moment of silence before Darleston smoothed a hand over his frontfall and cupped the prominent bulge there. He slipped one button, then a second, before teasing the waistband of his breeches away from his skin so that it slid down and clung to his hips.

She couldn't see nearly enough skin. Really, she wanted to strip the clothing from his upper body, so that the lines of his torso were displayed for her amusement, but he could keep his breeches on. Somehow that made the act more sordid and beautiful.

Darleston wrapped his large hand around his cock. He worked his wrist, steadily picking up the pace while he resumed sucking Lyle. The sight of them provoked a fever that made her tremble inside. Later she would lie alone and rub herself to climax, the images of the pair of them playing in her head. Now her fingernails dug into the centres of her palms and she squirmed so that the lips of her puss rubbed together, providing much-needed friction to her nubbin.

Darleston's eyes remained closed while he sucked and stroked, but Lyle watched her writhe, his face full of enchantment.

'Touch yourself,' he mouthed.

Emma shook her head. She couldn't. She simply couldn't while they were watching.

'Please.'

She shook her head again.

'Stroke your breasts.'

Darleston made a *mmpfh* noise in response and tried to turn his head while somehow still sucking Lyle. His eyes blazed as they met hers. The look, wild and ferocious, caused her insides to melt. She stared back at him open mouthed and sopping wet, so desperate for a touch to her clitoris that her hand strayed in that direction without any conscious thought on her part. She pressed herself once, greedily, through her shift. It was as if spring had bloomed all over her body. 'Again,' Lyle urged, while he drew Darleston to himself. She shook her head, but then did exactly as he asked. It was impossible not to. She simply couldn't keep still and remain aloof to what they were doing, not with all those wet clicks filling her ears and the lewd vision of Darleston – fellating Lyle, cock in hand – devouring her control.

'Oh boy!' Lyle's hand returned to Darleston's hair, guiding him, restraining him. His closeness to orgasm glowed in his face. He jerked Darleston impulsively, the motion becoming increasingly arrhythmic.

What happens when you come? She wanted to ask. The answer became suddenly apparent as Lyle raised his hips up off the chair in a final desperate thrust. He gasped, seemed to gargle a host of endearments, unable to articulate any of them properly, as he came into Darleston's mouth.

She watched Darleston swallow and almost cried at the intimacy of the moment. The sheen of Lyle's gift coated Darleston's lips when he turned his head and rested his cheek against Lyle's thigh. He looked right at her as he stroked and rutted against Lyle's leg. A desperate sob escaped his shiny lips. His tongue flicked across them, so that he tasted Lyle's seed as his climax broke.

Emma shared the moment with him, watched the lick of fire in his eyes, knew his heat and pain, his loss and his bliss. Pearlescent fluid coated his hand and made a wet patch upon the rug.

She knew hunger in that moment – deep, desperate, gnawing hunger – like nothing she'd ever experienced before.

He saw it too, and knew her desire, but he didn't act. He

113

remained clamped fast to Lyle's thigh, breath laboured and muscles lax.

They'd both come but she remained unsatisfied. It was the most terrible and traumatic moment of her adult life.

Frustration needled her skin, making the situation even worse, yet she couldn't give in to that need. The same part of her that had kept her free from physical contact for so long now stopped her pursuing the release she so desperately craved. She knelt, frozen in position, afraid to react because who knew where it would lead.

Darleston fell onto all fours and crawled towards her. The dip in his back as he stretched added to the illusion of sleek male beauty. He stopped in front of her and rose to his knees. He and she were mere inches apart, as they'd been in the amphitheatre before he touched her. He reached out now. Emma's breath caught. Tears stung her eyes. She couldn't breathe. She couldn't move. Could only watch in terrified silence as his curled fingers drew level with her face, but he didn't make contact. Instead, he traced the curve of her cheek an inch away from her skin. He didn't speak, but in truth he didn't need to. The message was clear in his eyes. I can give you what you need. All you have to do is grant me permission.

It didn't matter how much she craved release. She could never ask for his touch. Never. 'Please step back.'

'Is that truly what you want?'

She choked upon an affirmative, while tension rippled through the space between them.

'Very well, Emma. Though it pains me to see you left unsatisfied. I would however beg a favour of you before I depart.'

'Wh-what favour?'

'Show me a glimpse of yourself.'

'Now hang on there, Darleston,' Lyle interjected. He pushed himself up from his sleepy repose in the armchair. 'We never agreed to this.'

'Are you protesting?' Darleston raised a brow, while passing Lyle a handkerchief.

Her husband accepted the monogrammed linen and cleaned himself. 'No. Of course not, if Emma's happy with it. You just took me off-guard there. She was only meant to be an observer.'

'I was, yes.' Emma agreed. It had never been her intention to be a part of what they'd shared other than as an observer. Yet they'd both made her part of their lovemaking. Lyle had pretty much ordered her to take part and Darleston continually pushed against her boundaries, urging her to extend them.

'I'll leave what portion you choose to share entirely at your discretion, but know that this is my price. If you wish things to progress beyond this point then give me an image to fuel my dreams. Don't worry, Lyle, you're already there.'

What he asked was fair. She couldn't refuse him. Yet her whole body trembled at the thought of exposing any more skin than she already displayed. All this time she'd been sitting in her underthings with a shawl around her shoulders as if her attire were entirely respectable. Emma cautiously removed the woollen wrap and let it fall onto the rug. She thought he might like to look upon a breast. Men seemed to like such things. She'd seen paintings depicting women with their breasts bared and onlookers' gazes fastened upon them with an almost religious zeal; some even depicted the men reaching to out to squeeze the nipples. But to expose herself thus would require the unlacing of her stays, far too much manipulation for her currently agitated state; and she

115

would have to face him and know what was in his heart as he looked. What if he found her lacking in some regard? She wasn't robustly endowed like some of the ladies in town. Her bosom was rather modest. It would likely only just fill his hand.

Emma turned away from him instead. Tentatively she lifted the hem of her shift, raised it higher and higher, exposing the length of her stockings and the garters clasped around her thighs. Higher still – they were now seeing the bare skin of her upper thigh, lily-pale even by firelight. With one last tug she raised the shift to her waist, exposing the cheeks of her bottom. Why didn't he say something? What was going through his head? What was he imagining? Would the image of her pert, luscious bottom fuel dreams of him swiving her in the fashion she'd asked him to take Lyle tonight?

Emma released the gathered fabric and let it fall to hide her shame. She remained with her back to the men, still aroused and hopelessly frustrated.

'Thank you,' Darleston said. That was all. She heard the click of the latch and turned in time to see the flash of his coat sleeve as the door closed behind him. Lyle had left too. She was alone. The room felt vast and the pit of her stomach empty. And no amount of frantic, solitary masturbation would change that.

CHAPTER NINE

Lyle followed Darleston into his room at the far end of the upstairs corridor. 'You ought not to have pushed her like that. It was too much. Bullying her isn't going to gain you anything. You'll just prompt her to withdraw and then you can call cuckoo on your wretched plan.'

The glow of a single candle lit Darleston's face as he turned. 'She performed, didn't she?' He quirked his brows. 'And I don't think you actually believe it wretched. You want your wife happy, don't you? Believe me. It's preferable to being saddled with a sour old cow.'

Lyle guessed Darleston would know. He'd never met Lucy, Lady Darleston, yet somehow he knew her. Leastways, he knew her type – selfish, insouciant and resentful. It wasn't enough for her that she'd been handed an Earl's son as a husband. She wanted more. Believed she deserved everything. Rumours of her misdeeds and flirtations had passed his ears long before the recent newspaper scandal erupted.

Darleston set aside the candle and sank onto the centre of the tester bed. Lucy, had she been present, would have moaned incessantly about the room, but Darleston seemed remarkably content with it. Owing to his late and rather unanticipated arrival, he had not been given the grandest apartment. That room had gone to Phelps and Heath to share as the highest ranking and most distinguished of the expected guests. The fact that they were also both young and robust helped, as the room was somewhat prone to drafts and damp; even the heartiest fire rarely elevated the temperature to any sort of cosiness. Darleston's current chamber, however, was a good deal more pleasant, having benefited from a warm palette of red and gold and a lower ceiling. It also stuck out on a limb from the main corridor, making it ideal for illicit assignations, which was exactly what Lyle had in mind. Fellatio was all well and good, but it wasn't what they had planned.

Darleston propped himself up on his elbows. 'Be reassured, Lyle, the most traumatic thing I've done tonight is walk away and leave her unfulfilled. No true gentleman would have done so, which shows us both up for the rogues we've become.'

'Speak for yourself.' Lyle poured a stiff drink, which he downed in a single gulp. The most traumatic thing Darleston had done was refusing to swive him. 'You may consider yourself a rogue if you wish, but I was only acting in accordance with my wife's express wishes. I won't push her into something she doesn't desire and, after two years of marriage, I think I know what that is. I agreed only to provide her with a delicious tableau. Nothing was required of her in return. You're the one who insisted upon repayment. Be it on your head.'

'Lyle.' Darleston combed his fingers through his fiery locks. 'If she didn't desire what I'm egging her towards then I wouldn't have been treated to the sight of her very comely behind.' Darleston's lips curved into a smile that accompanied an 'mmm' of appreciation. 'You're a lucky man. Lucy is skinny as a rake and not half so peachlike.'

'You know perfectly well that I have no interest in women's bottoms whether they are legally mine or not.' He took another measure of sherry. In truth he had been more stirred by the glimpse of Emma's flesh than he'd anticipated, perhaps because he'd never seen any part of her except what was strictly decorous to observe. Her skin was impossibly white. Her bottom reminded him more of the lower swell of a teardrop than the chubby flesh of a peach. There had been something stately and elegant about it, but he wasn't sure that his admiration extended to arousal. He didn't long to gaze upon her rear for hours, or cling to it, or dig his finger-nails into its surface leaving brightly coloured marks behind as he wished to do to Darleston's arse. He didn't wish to plant his cock firmly in the furrow between the cheeks and ride them both to satisfaction. No, if he was honest, Emma's frigidity had never truly bothered him. In many ways it had been a relief not to have to worry about whether he could even fulfil his duty.

'You know, you say that, Lyle, but I didn't imagine you giving her orders to frig herself.'

Heat of the moment. It wasn't as if he didn't desire her happiness. They were friends, a partnership of sorts, after all. 'That is altogether different. I can offer her contentment without desiring to couple with her.'

Darleston rolled onto his stomach with a sigh, turning his back on Lyle. 'I swear you're determined to make this twice as difficult as necessary.'

Lyle cautiously perched upon the lip of the mattress. He reached out but kept his hand poised just over the curve of Darleston's thigh. 'I guess things are moving in a slightly different direction from how I'd imagined. You want her. Perhaps more than you want me. Be honest with me, Robert.

119

This isn't merely about fashioning some sort of safety net for the two of us. You genuinely desire her.'

Darleston rolled over again. He pushed up into a sitting position and scrunched a few pillows under his right side. In the dim light of the candle his eyes were like two splinters of onyx. His expression gave nothing away, though, as they looked at one another, something softened around Darleston's jaw. 'I fear my tastes run a little less purely than yours. Your wife fascinates me. How can she stand to live like that? I would die if I had to go more than a week without some manner of touch. I want to know how she does it.'

Lyle worried his lip as he watched him.

'I want her because she won't let anyone close. Good Lord, I wish I had the ability to survive like that.' Darleston shook his head in disbelief. 'And yet, I've also observed the way she looks at me, as though she would strip me naked and ride me until I was completely spent and it's very hard not to respond to such yearning. I know you understand that.'

'Do I not look at you in that way?'

'That's what I just said, isn't it? That you understand. The difference is that you're within easy reach.' Darleston's fist tightened around the open edges of Lyle's shirt. 'I know that you're not going to bolt if I act upon the desire I see.' He further knotted up the linen, pulling Lyle closer, so that he was forced to move, to straddle Darleston's legs and look down into those wide pool-like eyes.

'She is beautiful too, beneath all those dowdy clothes she hides behind.'

Lyle didn't resist, even though he thought he should. Instead he simply let Darleston reel him in until their lips were almost touching and their breaths mingled.

'If I'd acted as we'd planned,' said Darleston, 'there'd be no reason for a next time.'

'I'm not so sure I need there to be a next time,' Lyle said. The thought of Emma in the bed between them gave him jitters that ran through his body and caused his knees to knock against the muscles of Darleston's thighs. 'All I ever wanted was you. That's what I have, right now. I don't want to change that, Robert. I'm perfectly happy keeping my relationship with Emma as one of friendship.'

'We're not changing it. We're safeguarding the future.' Darleston's hands clasped either side of Lyle's face. 'Allow me my fun, Lyle.' He pressed a single kiss to Lyle's forehead, followed by another to the tip of his nose. Then he swept a fingertip over the lower swell of Lyle's lip. 'Do it and I'll make sure you have yours.'

A shudder streamed though Lyle's body like an arc of lightning, sparking arousal so sharp he could taste it on his tongue. Fine. Let Darleston lead Emma in whatever merry dance he wished. He had what he needed right here and, providing that didn't change, Robert was right. There was no problem.

Lyle danced his hips forward a fraction, bringing them down on top of Darleston's, communicating his need by action rather than words. There weren't words for what he wanted. Not really. Yes, there were crudities, but none of them really described the feelings invoked, the pure poetry of their bodies interlocked and moving together as one. Feeling as one.

He tugged at Darleston's breeches, virtually tore them off and dealt quickly with his own. This time it had to be fast.

'Straddle me,' Darleston insisted. He remained supine on the bed, only his shirt left as a covering. His prick stood up proudly. 'I don't think we need to be that quick, do you?'

Lyle sank down slowly until he felt Darleston's cock nudging his entrance. He really meant to take things gradually as Robert suggested, but his body had other ideas. Full penetration occurred a mere moment later, and then he was rising and falling and no longer in control of his movements. Need had taken possession of his body. And he danced the devil's jig until he was entirely spent.

Exhausted, he collapsed into a limp and liquid heap. 'I love you, you know that?' he sighed into Darleston's chest.

Darleston stroked a hand back and forth through his hair.

'I know it. I won't forget. I just want you to love Emma too.'

He already did, just not in the sense that Darleston meant it.

* * *

Emma overslept the next morn. Heaven knows how the scullery maid had managed to creep in without disturbing her, but for the first time ever it had happened. Field House was eerily quiet and not in the pre-dawn fashion she'd grown used to. Rather it felt empty, as though all the other inhabitants had crept away and left her behind. Normally such quiet soothed her, today it left her agitated, especially when she realised that Lyle too had been and gone. He'd left her a short note:

Taking care of Amelia. Last night was fun. Hope you were suitably entertained.
Yours affectionately, Lyle.

Emma hopped out of bed. She dressed rapidly in an old buff and lavender dimity frock. A tray of sweets and stewed tea stood awaiting her by the door. She gagged at the taste of tannin, but swallowed the tepid beverage all the same. Then gorged herself on three macaroons.

If only her taste for Lord Darleston could be diminished in such a fashion, or even explained. It wasn't just his physical form she found attractive, there was something more, as if they'd shared an experience that had glued them together – and not one that had involved sex or Lyle.

Emma gazed around the bedchamber, almost expecting Darleston to emerge from some corner or other. Nothing stirred. She remained alone, just as he and Lyle had left her.

Emma rubbed at the tender circles beneath her eyes. Sleep had quite escaped her until well into the night. Her ears had strained for the sounds of the men together in the Winter Room and her imagination had filled in the rest. Or rather it did and it didn't, because at some point she'd ceased thinking about Darleston and Lyle and started seeing glimpses of herself with Darleston again. Nothing solid, just fragments spliced together in a haphazard sequence – a peep of her bottom, exposed for him, followed by the swell of an uncovered breast and then most frightening of all, her hand stretched out to his, their fingers splayed and almost touching.

She shivered, remembering the acute terror and orgasm it had provoked. For her own wellbeing, she had to cast Lord Darleston from her thoughts. Last night couldn't happen again. Seeing them like that had gained her nothing but a bellyful of despair. Nothing good could come of allowing things to continue. Forget companionship. Nothing so tepid would work with him. Best she maintain the walls that had protected her for so long and avoid further contact with Darleston altogether.

Yet the itch of arousal still remained. Emma resisted the

urge to wet her fingers between her thighs again. Four, five times she'd brought herself to climax last night but her body remained unsatisfied by her efforts. Curse Darleston and Lyle both for awakening her to such need. She'd been content before. Isolated, detached, but quietly contented.

And she was the biggest liar in Christendom for thinking it. She'd wished for someone to come into her life and make it whole where it was lacking. Well, he was surely that person, and the only thing holding her back was her own fear.

Darleston would somehow free her.

Free her – as if she were some kind of slave! What sort of codswallop was she thinking? She didn't believe in fate or coincidence. People made their own paths, some with more help than others. She was just scared of growing old and lonely, and frightened that Lyle would one day find a man he truly loved and run off, or, worse, come to her to beg for his release. She knew she would let him go. She wasn't heartless and never wished to deprive him of the affection he needed. No, she wouldn't damn him to an asexual marriage just to save herself from growing old alone.

'Where is everyone?' she asked Grafton when they crossed paths in the hall.

'Mr Hill and the gentlemen are abroad, ma'am.'

'And my sister?'

Grafton's wrinkled brow smoothed into softer lines as though Amelia were some sort of cherub and the thought of her soothed his soul. 'Miss Amelia departed with Mr Hill.'

Grafton clearly had no idea how much of a ninny Amelia could be.

'She's gone with them to see the fighters?'

'Yes, I believe so.'

Emma gaped at him. She must never allow herself to

oversleep again. Amelia had clearly done as she'd suggested and asked their father's permission to join his band of boxing enthusiasts. Emma had counted on being abroad to advise him against it, but that opportunity had flown while she slept. Now the silly little fool was probably fawning over Bathhouse and making cow eyes at whichever gentlemen were occupying the Cottage. Worse still, pursuing them would only draw attention to Amelia's actions. Really, she supposed, she ought to spend some time with her younger sister discussing realistic prospective matches. Maybe this evening she'd sit her down and go over things properly.

'Could you have a tea tray brought to the Dog Parlour?'

'Of course, ma'am.'

'Thank you.'

'Should I make that for two? Lord Darleston is in there.'

Emma froze to the right of the stairs. She turned to stare back at Grafton.

'His lordship asked that the fire be lit and a toasting fork provided.'

What the devil was the man doing in there? The Dog Parlour was quite the most forgotten room in the house, unloved by anyone save her. It was the one place to which she could retreat and be certain of solitude, more assuredly than in the bedchamber she shared with Lyle. Now Darleston was there, when she needed to mull over the consequences of Amelia's actions and how she ought to handle the situation of Lyle and his lover. Her best course was probably to turn a blind eye to their actions and, what ... forget him? Because that was likely! She couldn't get the man out of her head. She had only to set eyes upon him to be overwhelmed by the tingling need to stroke the stark lines of his face and sift the fiery strands of his hair between her fingers. She needed to know him, to understand what lay in his head and his heart.

Damnation, this would never do. She was going to have to talk to him.

The Dog Parlour stood at the rear of Field House, just below Darleston's bedchamber. It had once been intended as a music room and decorated accordingly, but when both she and Amelia failed to show any promise or dedication in that department it had largely been abandoned.

Contrary to its name, the Dog Parlour never housed her father's pack of dogs. Rather, it held a large portrait of a beagle, which hung over the fireplace, and had done so since the first Hills had settled here in 1655.

When Emma entered, Darleston was reclining upon the old love seat, his long nose buried in a botany book. His coat, of beautiful slate-grey damask, lay draped over the arm of another chair and his shirt sleeves were pushed almost to his elbows so that the soft gold-tinged hairs on his arms caught the glow of the firelight. Emma watched him silently for a moment, afraid to move. If he could have reached into her thoughts, plucked out a single dominant image and made it real, this was it.

Upon her entrance he really ought to have swung his feet back onto the floor and put on his coat. Instead he closed the book upon his fingers and followed her approach with his eyes.

Countless times now she'd imagined him like this, placid and pliant, stretched out for her pleasure.

It didn't feel right him being here.

Her heart was busy hammering its way up her throat. With the fire stoked high, the room was already stifling, and now perspiration tickled as it beaded around her collar-line. 'What are you doing here?'

His gaze swept instantly to the fire, where the toasting fork still lay propped against the grate. 'Can I offer you some refreshment? Perhaps some of this remarkable jam.' A pot of cook's best quince jam stood open on the floor with the knife protruding from it. Dear Beattie would have a fit if she saw it treated like that. Then again, wasn't it what she ought to expect from an Earl's son? The only real surprise was that he knew how to use a toasting prong and didn't require a footman to hold it.

Emma edged around the love seat, avoiding the armchair occupied by his coat, and perched primly on the edge of the rocking chair. Her rigidity prevented its normal swing. 'Why did you stay behind?'

Darleston's brows furrowed at the sharpness of her tone. She had made the question sound like an accusation. 'To see you. I did tell you the fighting holds minimal appeal.'

'This is my room.'

His frown smoothed and the very corners of his lips curved upwards. At the same time the grey of his eyes shimmered like moonstone. 'Is it?' he asked innocently.

The perfect devil of a man knew very well that it was. More than likely his presence here was deliberate. The intrusion made her skin prickle as though he were trying to caress her. There were countless other rooms in the house, all of them more comfortable and better appointed. 'Have Lyle,' she blurted. 'I don't mind.' Her eyes stung but there were no tears. 'You don't have to petition me. You don't have to involve me. It's fine, really. I knew what he was. I know what he is. It's never caused a problem before.'

She couldn't do this. She couldn't play games with this man. It hurt too much. She wanted too much from him, when she didn't want to want anything from anyone.

'And if there's more to it than that?' Darleston's voice was whisper-soft and seemed to curl around her senses as though it were intent on embracing them. 'What if this isn't only about Lyle? You gave me something precious last night. I don't want our friendship to end there.'

Friendship! They were barely acquainted.

'Shall I tell you what I'd like, Emma? Will you hear me out?' He leaned forward and laid his book open upon the floorboards.

'What I'd like ... I don't wish you to just accept Lyle and me. I'd like you to be part of that relationship. You're a beautiful and intelligent woman, and I'd rather you participated in that pleasure than I feel I was stealing from you. Wouldn't you rather join in than stand watching?'

No. No, I wouldn't, she railed silently at him. Emma fisted her hand in the front of her hair. The discomfort soothed her a little, while her arm formed a barrier between them. She was one sorry little liar. Her rebuttal didn't sound convincing even to herself.

Darleston settled back down again. 'Perhaps I'm not explaining very well. What you need to understand is that I'm not entirely like Lyle. His experiences have all been with men. Mine less so. I don't think he truly knows how to please you any more than you do yourself. Oh, I realise that he taught you to –' He raised his index finger and wiggled the tip.

The simulation further heated Emma's already burning cheeks. Why had she donned three petticoats when one would have sufficed? Simple – she'd put them on like armour, as though swaddling herself could somehow protect her from this man and the havoc he caused to her composure.

'– but that's not everything.'

She didn't need him to point that out. She had learned last night just how fruitless solitary pleasure could be.

'I like you, Emma. I'd like us to be closer.'

She wanted to believe that, even as the notion chilled her to the core. None of Lyle's previous lovers had paid her the slightest attention. She didn't exist to them. She might as well have been his housekeeper for all the respect they afforded her. Darleston hadn't exactly apologised or asked her permission to dandy with Lyle, but at least he'd noticed her presence. No, more than that, he was suggesting she become some sort of co-conspirator.

'Don't you want a little pleasure for yourself?'

Troubled, Emma shook her head. She knew what he wanted. More importantly, she realised that hiding, and pretending that he simply wanted her to keep quiet, wasn't going to work. No man had ever been interested in her in that way before. Her marriage to Lyle had been by mutual consent, but desire had never been part of it, and no other gentleman had ever courted her. They all thought her cold and aloof. But Darleston seemed to see her differently.

'Tell me what you want, Emma. Truthfully. I know there's more to this on your part than a simple desire to watch two men fuck.'

She squirmed in response to his language, only to find heat blooming in her cunny. It further raged as she gawped at him, seeing him as he'd been last night, on his knees, with Lyle's cock in his mouth.

'Was there not some part of you that longed to join in and claim some of that pleasure for yourself?

There was, but she could not say that to him. She desired to touch him, but she would not confess it to him. He wouldn't understand. Nobody did.

129

Darleston swung his legs onto the floor and leaned forward. 'Emma, what I'd really like is to be able to kiss you.'

'Stop it!' She screwed her eyes closed to the vision of him. She couldn't kiss him. She couldn't kiss anyone. What's more, he knew it. Lyle had told him, and he'd seen first hand what she was like. 'Just stop it. Oh, God, please. Stop.'

'Emma, look at me.' His words were whisper-soft, yet in her head he was stalking her like a big cat. After a moment, she peeped at him through her fingers and was relieved to find him still sitting upon the love seat. Feeling foolish, she lowered her hands.

'There's no rush,' he said.

She let her heartrate settle before making a reply. 'You're wrong about me. We don't want the same things. You're mistaken.'

'I don't think I am,' he replied, quietly confident. 'You're not the first woman who has ever looked at me with heat in her eyes. Nor the first to refuse me. I'd let it go, but the thing is, none of those other women were quite like you. Come here, Emma. Come to me. I dare you.'

Come to him and do what? He was mad. She wasn't about to sit on his knee and let him take liberties.

'Touch me. It doesn't matter where, a button, my knee, a strand of hair ...'

'I can't.' Even if she'd been like everyone else, she'd have refused to compromise herself like that.

'Ask me what I'll do while you touch me, Emma.'

She didn't need to. He'd already told her what he wanted. He'd touch her too.

Emma shook her head frantically.

'I'll stay exactly as I am now. I won't move a single muscle.'

Her gasp became a wheeze as it pushed past the constriction

in her throat. 'You'll lie still while I touch you?' She ought not to have blurted that, but in her surprise she'd spoken her thoughts aloud.

The look he gave her said he'd do so much more than that, if only she'd give him the chance. 'Perfectly,' he replied.

What am I doing? Emma inched off the chair. *I'm behaving badly.* She ought to sit right back down and behave respectably. Instead, she fell onto her knees at the side of the love seat. Slowly, she uncurled a fist and turned her palm towards him.

Darleston's silver-grey gaze followed her every movement. A tiny encouraging smile played across his narrow lips.

Emma reached out, hardly daring to look at what she was doing. Her arm shook. The very tip of her middle finger made contact first. It slid over the silk of his stocking, bringing the whole of her palm into contact with his shin. Emma bit her lip, then grinned. Triumph. She'd touched him. She could withdraw now, content in the knowledge that she'd fulfilled a hopeless wish.

Only, when she thought of it, she didn't want to live off the memory of that single moment. Why should she, when he remained so accepting and still? Slowly, she turned her hand and stroked upwards, over the ridge of his knee and onto his breeches and the satisfying, solidly muscled wedge of his thigh.

The coals in the fire collapsed causing a sudden crack. Emma pulled her hand back fast and clasped it tight to her thumping heart.

'It's fine. Just the fire,' he said. 'Again.'

Emma uncoiled. Still hesitant, she traced the pearlescent shell of one waistcoat button, then another, following a line up from his stomach to his chest.

'The rest of my waistcoat doesn't bite.'

131

'I like how they feel – slippery.' Perhaps he hadn't guessed she was half-heartedly hoping that one of the buttons would magically slip though the buttonhole and provide a pathway for her to explore the cambric shirt that lay beneath. She realised, when she spread her hand flat, that Darleston had made one leap that she hadn't. The quiet thump of his heart beat against her hand. It stirred her emotions in ways she didn't want to interpret. It was as though she were lost in some thick fog and following that steady drumming was the only way to find her way out. Once, long ago, she'd fallen asleep to the rhythmic comfort of a beating heart.

Emma stroked upwards again and reached his collar bone. The ends of his fiery red hair tickled the back of her palm. She curled one lock around her fingertip. The colour seemed darker against the pallor of her skin. As she slid her hand into his hair proper, she leaned closer. She pressed the tresses to her face, and let his scent wash over her. She had never known a man with hair so vibrant a shade. 'You're family is old,' she observed. 'I mean that you've been a long time in this place. That didn't come out right. I mean …'

'We date back to before the Normans is what you mean. Yes, that's true, at least on my mother's side. All the men of that line have red hair.'

'Have you any siblings?'

'One. A brother. And you have *a* sister?'

And a host of other misty faces she could barely recall well enough to put names to. 'There were others.' She pressed a finger to his lips to silence the questions she saw forming. *Shh! Quiet. Don't ask any more. I don't want to remember.*

His lips parted. The tiniest hint of moisture wet her fingertip. Emma stroked upwards over his top lip too. They were soft, except for one part that seemed to have been bitten. She pressed three fingers across them and Darleston closed his eyes. He leaned into her touch, instantaneously changing everything as she felt the tiny pressure of his kiss.

'No,' she squeaked. Quavering, she backed into the safety of the rocking chair. 'You promised.'

'I'm not sure what I've done.'

Emma knitted her hands together as if in prayer.

'You were pressing quite hard.'

'I'm sorry.'

'Don't be. Come back instead.'

'I ... I can't.' She could see, sitting here, what hadn't been so apparent close up. Darleston was very much aroused. His cock formed a thick diagonal ridge across his abdomen. If she went back to him, she would end up touching him there. Like Lyle, she'd circle her thumb around and around the tip. She'd cup and squeeze the shaft, drive him to a point where he could no longer lie still and remain passive. Yet his grey gaze drew her in.

Only Grafton's arrival saved her. Emma's gaze flew to the door as the butler waddled in bearing the tea tray she'd asked for. He set a low table between her and Darleston, turning the cup handles and teapot towards her before reaching for the violated jam pot.

'Leave it,' Darleston said, staying Grafton's arm. 'I'm not done with it yet.'

'Very well, milord.' Grafton gave a brusque nod. 'Is there anything else?'

'No. Thank you. That will be all.'

He gave a nod and left.

'You've no bread left,' Emma observed. Grafton's intrusion had served only to ratchet up the simmering heat between

133

her and Darleston. A whole sequence of knots was now cramping her stomach.

'I have plans for the preserve later.'

He would glaze her husband's cock in it and lick it clean again. Emma clamped her hands over her mouth, shocked by the image that sprang so fully formed into her head.

Darleston stood. 'I think it might be better if we took a walk instead of tea.' He pulled on his coat and sallied over to the window to take a peep at the world outside. 'I think we'll manage without your pelisse. Don't you agree, Mrs Langley? I find exercise is a wonderful restorative when I'm agitated, and you clearly need some air. I might take a sketchbook.'

CHAPTER TEN

Darleston brought along a satchel containing his charcoal sticks and parchment, though he felt no inclination to draw at present. They walked a fair distance in silence, his tumultuous thoughts having stilled his urge to speak

There was much he wanted to learn about Emma Langley, but he knew it unwise to push her too much at one time. He'd succeeded in getting her to touch him. That would have to be triumph enough for the present. Alas, that knowledge didn't place him in the most comfortable of positions. While his erection had eased as they walked, the urge to seize her and steal the kiss he so desperately wanted only intensified, which perhaps explained his choice of direction. Somehow the notion of being beaten repeatedly around the head no longer repelled him.

'We're headed towards the Cottage,' Emma observed, breaking the silence.

Darleston merely inclined his head. He needed another outlet for his emotions. Drawing simply wouldn't do. He also needed additional company to act as a buffer between them. In the heart of a crowd he was less likely to lapse into folly.

'Why?' She'd been almost as prickly as he since they'd left the house. 'You know I detest it.'

He couldn't explain, not without revealing exactly how much her tentative exploration of his body had cost him in terms of restraint. His nerves were shredded. He wanted her hot little hands roving all over his body again. 'I thought you might like to check up upon your sister.'

'Oh!'

'You are worried about her, aren't you?' he asked, knowing full well that she was. Lyle had made his own concerns plain that morning. Amelia was the only reason Lyle had accompanied the group, as he intended to keep an eye on the silly minx. While Amelia had appeared serious before Mr Hill, Darleston had watched her dance with glee out of sight of the party.

'I'm sure she's only interested for the worst of reasons,' Emma confided.

She peeped up at him with those soft blue eyes and Darleston's reserve slipped a notch. *Pin her up against a tree and make her whimper with need.* He shook off the thought, but couldn't entirely demist his vision. The fact was, he wanted to see her naked. And he intended to pursue this until he did. Furthermore, he wanted to listen to her mewls of delight and pain as she climaxed in his arms.

'Worst reasons?' He raised his brows, indicating that she should elaborate.

'To admire the men,' Emma whispered conspiratorially. How odd that she felt she needed to lower her voice to discuss such a matter, when she'd willingly roved her hands over his body and seen him do much more to Lyle. 'She is being too overt in her admiration. Mr Bathhouse said only last night that he intended to pit himself against Jack today.

136

I know that the boxers are prone to dispense with some of their garments. It's unseemly for Amelia to be watching them.'

Quite unintentionally a laugh burst free of his lips. 'You're worried because she might see a man sans shirt – after what you have done and witnessed.' Of course it was the wrong thing to say, but he couldn't help it. He'd always hated the way women insisted on censoring one another over trifles. He'd never heard of anyone dying from exposure to a bit of bare flesh. And it was hardly the same as performing a sexual act. Not that he'd ever seen any real problem with that either.

'That's different,' Emma protested. Two bright ruby-coloured spots appeared high on her cheekbones. For a moment he felt genuinely sorry to have vexed her, for her pretty face became rather hard when she frowned. On the other hand, the way she pursed her lips simply fuelled his desire to seize a kiss. 'But perhaps you've forgotten that I'm a married woman while my sister is not.'

'I've not forgotten.'

No, he'd definitely not forgotten. He simply wouldn't have paid her the same regard if she'd been unwed. He had nothing to offer an unmarried lady save a great deal of heartache. Mayhap that would also prove true for Emma but he sincerely hoped not.

'Do you genuinely believe it will do her harm to see a few men boxing, or are you merely fearful over other people's opinions? Because if it is the latter than I don't believe you have cause to worry. The other men won't remark upon her presence, not when Hill is sponsoring the match.'

Emma's expression remained doubtful. She worried her lower lip while she considered his response.

'Take heart, there may be unexpected benefits from the situation. Bathhouse is dreadfully hairy, you know. He's a pelt like a goddamned wolf. The sight may actually put her off him. Hell, I've known a maid or two resign themselves to spinsterhood for fear of having to embrace such a man.'

Emma's frown transformed into a pout. 'Now you are simply teasing me.' She turned away from him with a 'hmph'. Darleston stalked after her until he fell into step beside her again.

'It's no tease, Emma, I swear.' He crossed his heart.

'Then ought I to ask you how you know he's so endowed? He's not ... like you and Lyle, is he?'

Startled, Darleston cleared his throat. 'Dear Lord, no! I've seen him around town, that's all.'

'In a state of undress.'

He raised his brows. 'Well, you know, my stepmama does hold some rather wild soirées.'

'Your stepmama.' It was Emma's turn to raise her brows.

'Yes.' Heavens! Did she know nothing at all about him? He'd assumed, because Lyle was *au fait* with his circumstances, that Emma was equally enlightened, but, now he came to think of it, that was rather ridiculous, since the pair were hardly communicative. Lyle couldn't even tell him the reason for Emma's resistance to touch, so why would he share with her the details of his lover's life? 'My father was remarried last year to a woman both my brother and I had formerly bedded. It was a shock all round. She was a courtesan.'

'Then it's no surprise that your wife is scandalised. How can you accept such a thing?'

'Don't be naïve, Emma. I have no control over my father's doings. He's at liberty to marry as he pleases. As for Lucy, let me assure you that the only sourness on her behalf over the marriage was that it usurped her from the role of power at Darleston House. She doesn't care to be second place in any situation. Otherwise she thoroughly enjoys the Countess's affairs.'

Darleston turned away from Emma's scrutiny. There were few if any other people alive by whom he was so repulsed as Lucy. Heaven help him, but if he met her in a cold, dark alley he'd be hard pressed to restrain himself from wringing her sorry little neck.

'Is she aware of what you're doing with my husband? If she were here would Lyle be courting her in the same way you are me?'

Aghast, Darleston stumbled. Once he'd righted his footing he stared at Emma in disbelief. 'Is that what you believe this is about? That I'm simply buying your silence?'

'Is it not? You have what you need from Lyle. You have no need of me as a lover.'

He swallowed carefully, giving himself time to order his thoughts. 'Need and desire are two very different things. As for Lucy, no, she does not know about Lyle.' What's more, he'd do his damnedest to ensure she never found out, because if she did she'd be spreading her nasty tattle to the newspapers again in a trice. Yet that thought was not the one that stuck in his gullet, raising bile. The real trouble would begin if Lucy caught wind of his interest in Emma.

Even though Lucy had never loved him, that fact had never tempered her possessiveness. She'd been jealous of every woman he'd ever set eyes upon. 'What you need to understand,' he explained, 'is that my marriage was not of my choosing. It was a requirement, entirely arranged by my mother as a punishment for loving Lyle.' While there was a little more to it than that, he didn't feel it necessary to revisit every detail.

139

He eyed her thoughtfully. 'Lucy left me, if that's what you are fishing to know. It happened several months back, and for reasons it would take far too long to explain. I've not seen her since and I've no desire to. To the best of my knowledge she is still in London.' Whoring herself to who knows whom. Engaging in Lord only knows what sort of devilment, and generally doing untold damage to his credibility. Still, it was far preferable to her presence by his side.

'I've saddened you now,' Emma observed after they'd walked a little further at a rather swift pace. The breeze ruffled her hair around the edge of her bonnet. 'That wasn't my intention.'

Darleston shook his head. 'You've only reminded me of my woes. That's probably a good thing.' Best he didn't become complacent least he forget how vicious and vengeful his wife could be. 'Emma, let me be direct with you. What Lyle and I have been doing is dangerous. If Lucy, if anyone, were to find out, the consequences could be devastating.'

She cocked her head towards him. Her eyes were thoughtfully narrowed. 'Do you not think I'm perfectly aware of that? You're not the first man I've known him to dally with.'

He'd lay money on him being the first of Lyle's lovers that she'd ever discussed the matter with.

'I accepted the risks when I married him.'

Of course she had. He'd known that already. She'd married Lyle because she trusted his preference for men would keep him from making demands upon her. A role Lyle had performed perfectly until this very week. 'How did you know?'

Her flush spread towards her temples. 'I saw him. Not that I make a habit of spying,' she hastily added, clearly horrified at her own admission. 'It was entirely accidental. I don't even know who the other man was.'

'Quite by accident in the way you witnessed Lyle and me?' he pressed.

'That was accidental. I had no idea Lyle was in the amphitheatre.'

The insistence in her voice stopped Darleston in his tracks. He turned about so that he stood before her, blocking her path to the Cottage, which lay in sight just beyond the hedgerow. Emma lifted her chin, her eyes full of wariness as she lifted her gaze. 'What is wrong?'

'What do you imagine would have happened if I'd still been alone when you'd returned?'

The hiss of her indrawn breath told him she'd considered the matter. 'I didn't … I haven't thought about it.' She bowed her head, presenting him with the pleated brim of her ridiculous bonnet. Still there was no hiding the deceit of her statement.

Darleston continued to stare at her. This impossible woman would be the undoing of him. 'Tell me,' he murmured. 'When you relive the moment, what happens, Emma?'

His nerves grew more frayed the longer they stood there, silence stretching into eternity, Emma staring at her toes, he at the crown of her hat. Yet he remained glued to the spot, unable to propel himself either forward or back, even when the raucous cheers of Hill's fighting fellowship drifted to them on the breeze.

'Tell me.' He only just stopped himself reaching out to her and cupping the curve of her cheek.

Her lip trembled. 'Don't force me. Don't press me over this.' She peeped up at him, and then lowered her gaze again at once. 'I don't want things to be awkward between us. I do like you. I'd like us to be friends.'

'Just not anything more.'

141

He understood. Deep down, he really did. It just hurt to hear it, especially after they'd come so far. She'd touched him. She, who touched no one, had roved her baby-soft hands all over his body. The problem was that he wasn't like her. He didn't possess the same degree of restraint. Right now he wanted to crush her to his chest. He wanted to deliver the kiss he'd meant to bestow back in the amphitheatre. Somehow he knew she would taste of all the things he loved best, tears, fever and sweet, sweet sin.

Darleston forced himself to walk backwards away from her. Forcing the issue wouldn't help.

'I'm sorry,' she whispered, clearly interpreting his retreat as one of anger. Her hand stretched out towards him, and it was all he could do not to take it. 'I can't be what you wish me to be.'

'Go back to the house. I'll check on Amelia,' he said. He needed her to leave before the glitter of moisture in her eyes turned into full-blown tears, because then he wouldn't be able to hold back. He'd embrace her whether she wanted it or not.

'Robert ...' Her voice quavered as she said his Christian name. Frown lines wrinkled her brow. She gave a shiver and then folded her arms around herself. 'I don't want to go separate ways.'

'We're still friends,' he reassured her. 'Nothing's changed. I just need some space. I can't hold myself in check like you. Do you understand?'

He watched her turn back to the house, wondering all the while if he'd done the right thing by holding back. Maybe if he had kissed her, things would have somehow worked out.

Only when she'd become a mere speck on the horizon did he turn towards the old stable block. Within the squat stone structure the temperature dropped enough to make him quiver over the difference. Darleston adjusted his coat. He was in an antechamber that led to a much larger room. Most of the light in the building came from stubby candles glowing inside open-topped glass jars. While the building no longer housed any horses, the scent of saddle soap remained to underscore the whiff of cheap tallow and sweat.

'Hey, there, you've made it,' Harry Quernow hollered through the wedged-open door into the arena beyond. Amelia too put her head around the door. He cast a greeting to her as he stepped through into the second room. This was clearly the space the horse stalls had once occupied. The walls still bore the scars from where the woodwork had been ripped out to make room for the boxing ring, although here and there saddle blocks remained as chairs for the houseguests.

The gnarly figure of Jack the Lamp occupied the nearside of the roped area, squared up against Darleston's twin. He cast his twin only the briefest of glances to make sure he wasn't faring too badly.

Lyle soon sidled over to him. 'Given up?' He'd told Lyle of his intention to spend the day getting to know his wife.

'No, it was just getting a little uncomfortable.' He left Lyle to interpret that in whatever way he chose. 'How has your mission fared?'

Lyle cast a glance in the direction of his sister-in-law. 'It's been tiresome. She's been all eyes for the fighters and not said a word to any of the men besides a few things regarding tactics. I'm not sure what Emma's worried about. That, and, in all honesty, what is there to fret over? It would do her well to marry. It may as well be to someone she likes.'

'Aye, I agree with you on that. However, Emma seemed more concerned with the possibility of Amelia compromising herself and thus being unable to wed.'

143

A brisk shake of his head set Lyle's long hair falling forward over his face. 'With whom exactly? For God's sake, Robert, they're hardly notorious delinquents. Three of them are married and I trust have more sense. Aiken's besotted with the Walsh girl and Johnny there –' he nodded at Bathhouse '– he's not going to do anything. He turns into a stammering buffoon if she so much as looks at him. Let's be honest, the only real concern here is over your brother. Quernow's not going to risk his position.'

Darleston cast his gaze over the assembled men, focusing last on Hill's secretary. A year ago, Quernow had been only weeks away from the debtors' prison. 'Are you saying I should have a word with Ned?'

'Would it do any good?'

'It's never influenced him before, leastways not for the better. It might just draw attention to her. He seems suitably focused elsewhere at present.'

'Aye, he's taking his role as trainer seriously, I'll give him that. Do you want to stop and talk to him, or shall we head back?'

Darleston shrugged. He had nothing important to share with his brother, but he understood code for 'I want to know what you've been doing with my wife' well enough.

'Well, if you're sure Amelia's safe?'

'I think Hill's perfectly capable of watching her. He's not as doddering as he likes to make out, and I think he knows her well enough.'

CHAPTER ELEVEN

'So, there are to be five other guests arriving for the fight on Thursday.'

Five more reasons to fret. Emma remained focused upon her reflection in the mirror. Turning her head towards Amelia would only encourage her sister's interest in their new guests when the ones they had were concern enough. Not that any of the gentlemen had behaved at all disreputably; rather Amelia's desire for attention grew increasingly blatant.

'I overheard father talking to Beattie. You should have heard her complaining. Apparently Lord Darleston made off with a whole pot of one of her best preserves and there are simply not enough stocks to accommodate so many new guests for so long. Of course she's lying; she's been bottling every blackberry, mushroom and cat's whisker she can lay her hands on since before I was born.'

Emma slapped down the perfume bottle she held. 'Don't speak ill of her.' Beattie had put food on the table for them when they might otherwise have starved. She understood how rapidly fortunes turned and might do so again. Her housekeeping wisdom was not to be mocked; in fact, Amelia would do well to learn from it. Rather than lecture, she turned her vexation to the topic they'd been avoiding ever since Amelia returned. 'You ought not to have gone with the menfolk today,' Emma snapped.

Amelia slunk over the threshold with a grin upon her face. She came to stand beside the dressing table, where her fingertips left imprints in the loose layer of powder that coated that end of the glass surface. 'What would you rather have had me do, sister dear?' A deep-woven thread of laughter belied the contrition on her face. 'You were abed. Surely it would have been even worse if I'd remained here – alone with Lord Darleston. Heaven knows what sort of naughtiness I might have got up to.' Her po-face fractured into a smile.

Emma scowled, unable to dispute the reasoning. She could not even claim Darleston would have maintained a decorous distance, because look what he'd enticed her into – running her hands all over his body, as though he were simply a pet or a luxurious shawl, or she some cheap harlot. What's more, Amelia would not have been nearly so timid. God help them, she needed to ensure such an opportunity didn't arise. Not that she believed Darleston's interest extended to her sister, but how could one really tell? She knew enough of him now to know that licentious, perverse and many of the other adjectives he'd collected were perfectly accurate. The other gentlemen could no doubt boast epithets just as disquieting.

'You must have thoroughly bored him, for he joined us at the Cottage soon enough,' Amelia pressed.

Amelia had changed. Over the last few days she'd grown sharper and more direct, not that she hadn't always been tactless. There was a difference in the way she held herself too, more upright, which somehow added to her grace.

'Oh, Emma! 'Tis no wonder Lyle chooses other company when you scowl so.'

Emma turned sharply to look up at her sister. What did she know? Did she indeed know anything? It would do her no good to press or even address the matter. 'You need to wear a fichu with that,' Emma snapped instead. And she needed to keep a closer eye upon Amelia's dressmaker the next time she visited. The swooping neckline descended far too low. The dress was one of the collection Amelia had had made in anticipation of the London season: an ivory affair with bronze and russet detailing. Additionally, her maid had arranged her hair so that it fell in tumbling curls on either side of her face and the ends lay enticingly upon the upper curve of her breasts, which bore evidence of powder and rouge.

Amelia continued to smile. 'Don't be such a stick-in-the-mud. I don't wish to have a frilly oversized kerchief around my neck, scratching my skin and leaving me all blotchy. I'm not showing off anything God didn't intend me to display.'

'I can almost see your nipples.'

'Don't be absurd, Emma. There's plenty of whalebone in place between me and disgrace, and it's not as if I'm about to start picking pins up off the floor, so nothing is likely to fall out.'

Emma stood. 'You … you …' Somehow, while always being wilful and stubborn, Amelia had still shown a degree of respect for her elders. That had gone now, lost behind a facetious grin. 'Go and get changed.'

Amelia clamped one hand to her hip. 'I shan't,' she said with an uncharacteristic swagger. 'You are not my mother to tell me what I should and shouldn't do. You're not even Aunt Maude, who at least shows some affection whilst ordering me about.'

'You will do as you are bid.'

'Oh, is that so?' Amelia stepped back away from her. 'Exactly how are you going to make me do your bidding? Will you drag me to my room and strip me down to my shift, dear sister?' She waited, body tensed, ready to fly if Emma took the bait.

They both knew she wouldn't. Never once had they embraced or held hands or shared any physical contact as sisters ought to have done.

Amelia sucked in a deep breath. 'I don't want to be like you,' she blurted. 'All stuffy and countrified and aloof. We're not alike, Emma. We've never been alike. I want their attention. I like to be touched.' A sly gleam lit her eyes as she hissed the last part. 'I won't sit idly by while you and Aunt Maude find some horrid old miser to wed me to. I want to live. Do you hear me? I want to live, and I want to know affection and pleasure.' She turned her back on Emma and strode purposefully out of the room. 'And I will.'

'Wait,' Emma demanded. 'Come back.' She followed her sister onto the landing. Amelia had already reached the head of the stairs. She cast Emma a stony glance, and then swept down to the lower level as proud as a duchess.

For several moments, Emma remained frozen, one hand closed fast around the banister. Her hair lay free around her shoulders. There were no shoes upon her feet. She couldn't be seen downstairs like this. And what would she do even if she gave chase? They could not shout at one another like fishwives while their guests looked on. Furthermore, in any row their father could be relied upon to take Amelia's side. He never saw any wrong in his youngest child. Emma had done her best with her sister, but she'd never wanted to play mother. The supposed rewards never seemed to outweigh the heartbreak. Fifteen children, and only she and Amelia survived.

'I'm just trying to protect you,' she whispered. If only Amelia would see that. When the right man came along, then she would do anything and everything to help.

'Problem?'

Emma snapped to attention. Her hands fell to her sides. Darleston stood only a few feet away. He had dressed in the exquisite baroque coat that had so enchanted her on the night of his arrival. It seemed even more magnificent now, the candlelight catching the pattern woven into the fabric. Emma stared at him. 'No ... I mean ... no, there's no problem.' She crossed back into her chamber, only to find Darleston at her heels when she turned to close the door. 'What is it?'

'Let me help you.' He pushed his way inside, and then pressed the door to behind them. 'Problems with Amelia?'

'It's nothing. She's at an awkward age. And bitter because we are here rather than in town where she could participate in the season.'

'She's unlikely to find such attentive company in town.'

'Amelia doesn't see it that way. She believes we are depriving her. She thinks that I'm cruel because I seek to curtail her involvement with the gentlemen. I only mean to keep her safe.'

'Let her be, Emma. Allow her to make her own mistakes. We all must.'

Emma stubbornly shook her head. 'I can't do that to my only sister. I do want her to be happy.'

'You can't make people happy. That's something they have to discover for themselves. And how do you expect to make her happy when you're not yourself?'

'I'm ... My God, Darleston, you can't be in here.' How

had she grown so used to his company that she'd barely noticed his invasion of her room?

He gave a nonchalant shrug. 'I was in here last night for long enough.'

'I'm dressing.'

'And then you were undressing.' He raised his hand as if to touch her. Emma scuttled away, returning to her former position before the mirror. 'We need to talk, you and I.'

'What about?' Emma reached out to take her hairbrush, only for Darleston's hand to close around the shaft first.

'Allow me.'

No one had combed her hair since Beatrice died, nigh on twenty years ago. The memory of Bea's squeals of laughter and the sensation of her chubby little hands tugging at the knots lent additional steel to her already straight back. She couldn't do this. She couldn't sit still and allow him to brush.

Emma remained frozen in the chair watching him warily. Darleston stood so close she could hear his breathing. If she moved, she would have to squeeze against him in order to escape. She'd gathered all her strength in order to touch him this morning, but couldn't find the same resolve to push him away now.

'Relax, Emma. Push your hair back over your shoulders.'

For some inexplicable reason she complied. Why could he make her do these things? Why was she simply prepared to listen and obey?

She closed her eyes in anticipation of the first stroke of the brush, only to snap them open again equally fast. The darkness amplified the unknown and awakened more memories. Better she stay in the here and now than descend into the darkness of her past.

Darleston lifted the first lock of her hair. Slowly, with

excruciating care, he pulled the bristles over the length of one entire brown wave. The process was repeated, again and again, with Emma steeling herself against the initial contact each time. Though she had to accept that he kept his word. If his fingers tangled in her hair, it was only momentarily. While she was all too aware of his body, he didn't crowd her.

'I'm sorry that I pushed you away earlier,' he said, voice buttery soft and full of contrition. 'I didn't want to do anything that I'd later regret. You have to understand, I haven't your control, and nothing would please me more right now than to be able to hold you properly.'

Emma gently shook her head. 'You don't mean that. I'm sure Lyle's a much better prospect, even given the unholy complications of the situation. He loves you. He can give you all the affection you want.'

'Unholy!' He grinned. 'Yes, I think the church would agree with you on that. But you are wrong about the rest. Lyle can't give me everything I want. Although, heaven help him, he's trying his damnedest.'

Warily, she bowed her head, refusing to meet his mirrored gaze. She wasn't even sure whether to believe in his interest. 'I can't give you anything.'

He bent low so that his mouth drew close to her ear. 'You've already given unimaginable pleasure. Even now ...' Darleston closed his eyes. His smile stretched across his face. 'I have a fertile imagination, Emma. I can make much of little.'

The simplicity of his words raised extra shivers. Emma hugged herself tight. They were walking a dangerous line together. One she knew she couldn't cross. He just didn't understand. She hadn't chosen to be this way. Life had simply conspired.

She lifted her chin when Darleston resumed brushing again.

151

Despite the soothing, rhythmic rise and fall of his hand she couldn't entirely shift the tension from her shoulders. Heavens knows what truly lay in Darleston's heart – he certainly had the reputation of a devil – but what she saw in his reflection was fearful enough.

Darleston was not the sort of man to be denied. Yet he would eventually have to accept that she couldn't be the woman he wanted.

'You must know this will never work. This ... whatever it is between us.'

'You say that with such conviction, and yet you're sitting here allowing me to brush your hair. Has Lyle ever brushed your hair?'

She shook her head, disquieted by the thought. She'd allowed Lyle to touch her only once, when he slipped her wedding band onto her finger. That wasn't something she could escape. However, she'd turned away when he'd tried to kiss her.

'Yet,' Darleston continued, 'we've known each other only a few days now and you've allowed me a privilege you deny your husband.'

She had. Somehow Darleston seemed to sneak past all her defences, or perhaps he was simply more belligerent than Lyle. More likely still was the possibility that he was genuinely interested in her.

'You forced the issue,' she murmured.

'Hardly.' A small chuckle escaped his throat. For some reason the sound seemed to warm her. 'Forceful is something else entirely. I don't think you'd care for that, though your husband certainly does.' Darleston came to her side and knelt. He set the brush upon the table top. Emma stared at his fingertips curled around the lip of the table. 'What is

152

it you fear so much, Emma? What is it that makes you so resistant to another person's touch? Something made you this way, did it not?'

He looked up at her with his smoky-grey eyes and she seemed to fall into his gaze.

Bodies. That's where the fear, the desire for numbness came from.

Bodies pressed close, squirming against her, holding her captive. Frozen limbs locked tight, forever curled around her flesh. Hair plastered to her clammy body. Short fine blond strands and thick, long darker ones, hair that wasn't hers, but nevertheless covered her, strangled her.

Emma bolted out of her chair, knocking the hairbrush from the dressing table so that it skittered across the carpet and landed with a clang against the coal bucket. She saw Darleston move – just a rising grey blur in the mirror – and turned to face him. He had his arms outstretched, ready to hold her, to offer comfort. 'Please don't.' Emma raised her palms to ward him off, and her fingertips made glancing contact with his chest. The effect was like a scald. She pulled back, whimpering in pain, colliding with the vanity, which she then tried to clutch, but her palms slid over the powder-covered glass and prevented her gaining a purchase.

Darleston slowly backed off, two steps then a few more, until he reached the bed and sat down. His head drooped a little, but he continued to watch her.

'We weren't always wealthy,' Emma gasped. She had to give him some sort of explanation for her behaviour.

Life had become easier the older she'd become, but the memories remained of going to bed with her stomach cramped from hunger, and of sleeping squashed together in one bed with her siblings because that was their only source of heat.

153

'Jack Johnstone and the others changed that.' She couldn't recall the name of the first fighter her father had trained; only that he smiled a lot and all his front teeth were missing. It had taken her years to equate that gentle, smiling man with the fiend he became in the boxing ring. His was the first fight she'd watched, huddled on the sidelines of that seething, blaspheming crowd, between her brothers Thomas and George, holding tight onto little Beatrice's hand – Bea, who was too young to be there but nevertheless refused to be parted from her and held on tight right to the bitter end. Bea, whom she'd cosseted and loved in ways she'd never loved Amelia.

The crowd that day had been particularly fierce. Ale and gin ran freely. The sun had baked the ground into clay and everything stank of stale sweat and pigswill. When her father's man went down, the baying for blood reached fever pitch. He only just escaped with his life, battered and torn, his nose forever misshapen.

Even now, it still didn't seem right that such a handsome life should be built on the back of such raw brutality, but that's how it was. Slowly the family's fortunes had turned around, little by little, season by season, until now they were wealthy enough to host an Earl's son, and her father's prize-fighters were good enough to attract the attention of the *ton*.

'Are you suggesting your father's business practices are responsible?' Darleston asked. His brows furrowed.

'No.' Emma sauntered towards the window. She let herself out onto the balcony. A chill wind had risen since the sun began to set, which whistled around the side of the house and tugged at the hair that spilled over her shoulders.

Her father's enterprise had come too late. Oh, the deaths had slowed once the prize-fighting money began to roll into the household coffers, though there were few of the family left for the reaper to claim. Her mother had fallen to puerperal fever ten days after the birth of her fifteenth child. The boy – she did not do well with boys – was stillborn, and entombed with her in a single coffin. Emma had raged against it, but her grieving father had dismissed her concerns as childish. They'd needed the money too much to go to the expense of two coffins. But then he didn't understand the true horror of being pressed together like that, while Emma could never forget the sensation of waking to find another curled against her like a frozen crab.

Darleston caught her. She hadn't heard him move, but neither had she been aware of the floor rushing up to greet her until his arms encircled her body and shocked her out of the faint to which she'd succumbed. 'I'm fine,' she barked, trying to push him away. Lord, the heat of him was intense; it burned through the layers of their clothing to sear her skin. It made her pulse fire so fast and so hard that her head ached from the pressure.

She'd forgotten … she'd forgotten how it felt to be encompassed by so much warmth.

'You're not. You just collapsed.' As she frantically wriggled in his grip, Darleston carried her all the way to the bed, where he laid her upon the quilt. 'Emma, I'm sorry I touched you, but I couldn't let you fall.' He crouched by the bedside. 'You were damn close to the edge.' She saw the horror in his face then, the fear that penetrated right to his eyes. His pulse had been racing too; the thud of it had beaten against her arm as he'd carried her. If she'd swayed forward and toppled that way instead of back into his arms then the low balustrade might not have saved her.

She turned her head away from him, tears welling in her

eyes, frightened as much by his concern as by the aftershock of his touch.

'Mayhap it would be best if you skipped dinner.'

'No.' Emma pushed herself upright. If she hid here then Amelia would be completely unmanageable. The silly twit would believe she'd triumphed with her little show of autonomy. She needed reining in before she did something ridiculous and disgraced them all. Nor could she lie here and fret over what had just occurred and what might yet be. The normalcy of dinner would serve her better. 'I'm all right. I'm all right.' She rubbed at each of the points where he had touched her, as if the action would somehow wipe away the contact. Instead, it made her skin tingle all the more.

Emma rose and hurriedly bound her hair. The call to dinner came while she was still pushing pins into place. It was only as she scuttled toward the door that she realised Darleston still sat upon the bed. His expression remained thoughtful. 'Are you coming?' she asked.

He slowly bowed his head. 'Go ahead. I'll follow you down.'

She hesitated a moment. 'What is it? Is something wrong?'

He tentatively shook his head. 'No. Not at all. As I said, I'll follow.'

* * *

The situation at dinner only exacerbated Emma's unease. Their father turned a blind eye while Amelia acted the jade. And she ... she could do nothing for the memory of Darleston's touch spinning around in her head, as though at any moment she might leap upright and be forced to blurt that he had held her and that she had touched him too.

Only Lyle's watchfulness curbed such rashness. His attention repeatedly returned to her throughout dinner, as though he were checking to ensure that she remained where she ought to be and he hadn't somehow mislaid her. His soft brown eyes were somewhat mournful this evening. He reminded her of an old family pet, beloved and yet left behind while they went out for a walk. Perhaps he worried over the potential for tragedy they were brewing between the three of them. While Emma felt no desire for Lyle – she had never wanted passion from him or been inclined to offer pleasure to him – she did not harbour any wish to maim him. He had held Darleston dear first. She knew the men had known one another long before Darleston's arrival at Field House. Darleston: it was he who made everything different and difficult. If she had been another woman, matters would surely have culminated before now. Only her fears and pantheon of old ghosts held her back, else she might well have given herself up to his love.

Emma dipped her head when Lyle's gaze lingered a little too long. Perhaps he realised the discomfort he caused, for he turned away too, only to look upon Darleston with much the same expression of woeful longing. Lyle had said to her that he did not mind her lusting after his lover, if only she promised not to steal him away. *I've not deliberately coaxed him in any way.* She was sure she'd tried to thwart Darleston's efforts to persuade her into his bed, yet things kept occurring between them that she could not explain as normal interactions between one man and another's wife.

'Miss Amelia, have you some entertainment for us this evening?' Mr Aiken asked, raising his head from the political meanderings of Mr Tipton.

The only entertainment of which her sister seemed capable at present was raising her skirts to flash him her garters.

She'd never owned any musical talents, nor was she overly proficient at cards or any other game. The silly girl needed a London season under the wary eye of a chaperone just to set her straight about gentlemen's expectations of a bride. Only the bounders and rakehells sought the company of a coquette. That said, all the gentlemen were now focused upon her.

'Well, Mr Aiken, I had thought it might be pleasant to stroll a way, but that was before the wind got up. I fear we may have to content ourselves with poetry readings and a hand or two of piquet.'

Did Amelia even know how to play piquet?

'It will be a delight to hear your choice, Miss, and perhaps if the wind drops again as rapidly as it rose we might take that stroll together too.' Aiken turned to Hill. 'Ain't all this gusting a little unseasonal, sir?'

It was Phelps who looked up from his lamb chop to reply. 'For London, perhaps, laddie, but not for these parts. The wind she does blow as she pleases.' He licked a greasy smear from his lips, before burying his gravy-stained fingers in the household's best napkins.

'I suppose we'd better be hoping that this gale blows itself out before this bout of yours, Hill. That old stable's as drafty as hell and it won't hold a handful of the folks that'll come to see Jack. We need the punters in if we're to make a bean.'

Hill chewed thoughtfully on a limp cabbage leaf. 'The fight's to take place in the copse, not over by the Cottage. The trees muffle the noise better and stops folks hereabout at the other big houses getting too curious. One or two of them lack vital humours. The commoners, they know where to go, and if they don't, Dan Furrows at the Arms knows where to point them. You've arranged that with him, haven't you, Harry?'

Harry Quernow confirmed that he had.

'Are we to host any more guests, Father?' Emma enquired, remembering Amelia's assertion.

'Just the two, lass. Oxbury and Littleton should be with us around noon tomorrow.'

Two, not the five Amelia expected. 'No ladies.' Some additional female company might set Amelia back to rights.

'Not that I'm aware of. Though I dare say we could accommodate one or two should the need arise.'

Should the need arise … Why did Darleston stiffen at those words? Why had his jaw tightened at the mention of Oxbury and Littleton? She would have to ask. Only he never presented her with the opportunity, for both he and Lyle slipped away the moment dinner ended.

'Aren't you joining us?' Amelia flounced past Emma as she stood in the entrance hall trying to determine which way to go. The proper thing to do would be to help entertain their guests, while her chief desire was to run after Darleston and Lyle. It wasn't so much that she wished to spy upon their loving, but rather that she wished to know what lay in their hearts. She felt sure that Lyle would be bemoaning their current situation, even though it was he that had initially brought them all together. She simply couldn't accept that he'd wish to see her in a different way. She'd been his wife two long years, but never, ever his lover. Intercourse was something he indulged in with other men. And Emma had never been interested in those men before Darleston arrived.

'I expect my poetry choices would be too dour. Besides I have a sore head.'

Her sister paused on the threshold of the drawing room. She turned her head to look back at Emma. 'You're not about to order me to bed too, are you? I don't have a headache, and I don't see why my pleasure should be dependent on your whims.'

'I'm sure you'll be perfectly fine with Father. After all, you managed one another all day.'

Amelia's eyes narrowed but, despite her stubborn pout, she didn't retaliate. Instead, she swanned into the centre of the company and accepted a glass of heaven only knows what from Harry Quernow. Still, Darleston was right. It was time she let Amelia manage herself. Then it was her responsibility if she stuck her head out so far that she lost it. 'Take care, dear heart,' Emma muttered under her breath as she chose the pathway that led upstairs. She had worried over her sibling since the moment of her birth. Now it was time she turned that care to her own afflictions.

She braced herself before pushing open the door to her bedchamber, expecting to find the two men within. Instead, darkness met her. There was no evidence to suggest that either Lyle or Darleston had set foot in here since before dinner.

They'd sought to deliberately exclude her.

They'd gone to Darleston's room.

A chasm opened in her chest as she coaxed a flame from the coals stacked in the grate. She lit a candle and took it over towards the bed. She could still see Darleston kneeling beside her, his concern almost palpable. The warmth of his embrace still chafed against the painful cuddles of her past, leaving her struggling to make sense of her warring emotions. 'I can't do this,' she said to the empty room. There was safety in isolation, an ease of existence, and yet … She slumped heavily onto the bed with a sigh.

Something crinkled beneath her weight. Emma turned her head to find a writing-case lying beside her on the counter-pane, from which poked several sheets of parchment. She gathered them up without giving them much thought, only considering the oddness of their appearance as she stretched to place them on top of a nearby trunk. Lyle was normally fastidious over the storage of documents. It seemed unlikely that he'd leave them upon the bed.

Emma turned over the leather case. She was not sure Lyle owned anything so pretty in which to store his papers. Emblazoned upon the front of the oxblood leather was the Darleston coat of arms. So the case was his, not Lyle's. Curiosity immediately got the better of her. She didn't precisely mean to snoop, but it *had* been left upon her pillow. Perhaps he'd even intended her to find it.

She flipped open the case, only to drop it immediately. Charcoal-drawn images scattered across the bed. From each of them her image stared. Or rather there were drawings of her, but it wasn't her. She'd never posed in such a fashion. She'd never been touched in such a fashion.

Her sensuality leapt off the paper, her expression an intense mixture of torment and bliss. Only a sweat-dampened shift covered her womanly curves. *Me. This is how he sees me.* Yet such sensuality was beyond her. However, it was not her rapture or grace that captured her attention, but the cause of it. Her hand was cupped over her mons, the middle finger extended to brush against her nubbin. In other drawings she was caressing her own breasts. One depicted Darleston's head between her thighs, doing something unspeakable with his tongue. She'd seen him suck her husband's cock, so it was no great leap to imagine a man might pleasure a woman in a similar fashion, but seeing it depicted in such a way gave her such palpitations that she'd have reached for the smelling salts if she'd owned any. Her constitution was normally robust enough to ward off any such missishness.

161

Still her heart bounced into her throat, almost choking her, at the sight of actual coitus. Thereafter, each picture seemed more lewd than the last – and more enticing.

As she sifted through the drawings, it became clear that they were not all of her. Here lay one of Lyle erect, while another showed him spent. The final one depicted the three of them together. Not just posed beside one another, but together. The notion left her so shocked she simply stared at the image until the drawing was burned into her mind, ready to haunt her in both the waking world and her dreams.

They could never touch her like that. She could never lie between them naked, could never … Good Lord, the situation was impossible. How could Darleston think for a moment she would consent to such an act? Yet the heat in her cheeks was not caused by revulsion. Rather her pulse fired over the possibility of such a situation happening. How would it feel to be held in such a way, to be touched thus by two men at once? Heaven help her, she was not even accustomed to being held by one man. She had been unable to tolerate even the briefest brush of Darleston's lips against her fingertips.

Only something had changed inside her, an ache in her belly, curiosity about what might be. Yet how could anything come to pass in the short time they had left together? Jack the Lamp would fight in two days' time, and then there would be no reason for them to remain here at Field House. Lyle would find yet another lover, and as for Darleston, he would move on to wherever it was he made his home.

CHAPTER TWELVE

Emma didn't intend to burst in on the men. After all, they had presumably retired to the Winter Room because they didn't wish her to be present, but the thought didn't stop her hasty steps, nor did it prevent her opening the door when there was no reply to her knock.

She couldn't let this one chance she had at love slip away from her. Bravery would henceforth be her motto, although deep down she did not feel remotely brave. The butterflies in her stomach had been replaced by something with a far greater wingspan, which fluttered all the harder at the cosy warmth of the room.

Two thick beeswax candles stood either side of the hearth, their scent heavy in the air. Beside them, only the crackling blaze gave any light. Emma's head turned towards the bed, only to find it empty, the drapes drawn back to the posts.

'Close the door,' Darleston said.

Emma turned back to the fireplace. A wingback armchair stood positioned before it, over the top of which she could just make out the bright coppery waves of Darleston's hair.

After a quick glance back down the corridor to make sure she was unobserved, Emma closed the door and turned the key for good measure. There was no sense in inviting observers – observers other than herself.

'Now come here.'

The brevity of his welcome kicked her pulse into a gallop. Come here, do this, do that. Then again, what did she expect, considering she was intruding upon a tryst?

Lyle knelt in exactly the position she imagined she'd find him, his head buried in the shadows of Darleston's lap. The only difference from her mental picture was that he was naked as a newborn and, if the wet sounds she heard were any indication, suckling just as contentedly.

'Closer.' This time, Darleston turned his head in order to beckon her. Fires blazed like warning beacons in his eyes. Challenging her, warning her to take heed and think before she drew any closer. Was this truly the path she sought? Deep down she knew it was. She wasn't here to watch. She was here because she couldn't bear not to be, because she was afraid of missing out, and watching them love one another was the best she could hope for. At least this way she could live vicariously through their pleasure.

'I said, closer. If you're going to watch, then at least stand where you can see what's what.'

They formed a perfect copy of one of the drawings Darleston had left upon her pillow. They were responsible for this desperate sense of longing that filled her and for quickening her pulse so that it raced and beat a heavy tattoo between her thighs. Looking at them, all long elegant lines and hard angles, linked as if it were the most natural thing in the world, she had to wonder if it wouldn't be better for them all if she simply turned around and fled. The men were meant to be together, that was clear from the affection that infused every interaction, while she was different, apart from them, unable to share those delicate busses and signs of endearment that everyone else took for granted.

She couldn't get out of her head the picture of Darleston on his knees, being simultaneously, kissed, masturbated and swived by Lyle. In her dreams she'd revisited that moment countless times, in each instant becoming a little braver. She wanted to knock Lyle's hand aside and bend down and claim Darleston's cock for herself. He wouldn't be touching her, only she him.

'Get out of the darkness, Emma. Lyle, tell her to come here, where we can see her.'

Lyle mumbled something that might have been a command or a mew of content, or even 'Tell her yourself.' His blond head never ceased bobbing.

Still remaining in the shadows, she did shuffle a fraction nearer, so that she caught a glimpse of Darleston's cock each time Lyle drew back. How much ruder it seemed seeing that part of him poking out from beneath his underthings, lewd and appealing.

'Emma!' Darleston snapped, startling her so much that she jumped forward. 'You don't get to barge in uninvited and then hover on the sidelines. If you wish to stay then get over here where I can look at you. And give me something to look at.'

Look at! Well, she couldn't see why he'd want to, considering that Lyle was a far more captivating sight at present. Her husband had always turned heads, particularly, in her experience, other men's heads, but he frequently attracted female glances too. Then again, the majority of the sketches Darleston had drawn had not been of Lyle but of her. She wasn't sure how to interpret that. Maybe there were others of Lyle that Darleston had chosen not to share. Maybe

Darleston appreciated curves as much as muscle. She was not at all sure.

'Emma,' Darleston growled again. The sound of his gruff voice brought a smile to her face. He was not really cross with her; she knew that, because she could detect the humour, the warmth in that rumbling purr. Nevertheless, she inched into his field of vision. If he wished to gaze at her, well, she supposed there was no harm in that. She had never longed to blend into the wainscoting like some of the wallflowers she'd met. No, she had always required to be seen and have her opinion counted, regardless of how little most menfolk of her acquaintance listened. Darleston was different on that score at least.

'There you are.' Darleston's lips quirked at the corners, adding another layer of pleasure to what was already evident, but then she suspected there were few men who could still manage to frown while being loved in such a fashion. Her quim was awash with slippery heat merely from observing it.

'It's not cold in here. Do take off that ridiculous shawl.'

'Stifling,' Lyle muttered. The skin of his buttocks, which were pointed towards the fire, glowed a pleasant shade of pink, though, judging by the localised pattern, she wasn't entirely sure if the heat was the cause.

'What was it you wanted?' Darleston asked. 'I assume you did want something.'

For a moment her focus remained upon her husband's rear. Then she shook her head. What precisely had she come here for, other than to bear witness to this? If deep down she longed for something else, she was not about to confess it.

Darleston made a small dismissive 'hmm' and turned his attention back to Lyle, until she drew the shawl from her shoulders. Then he looked at her again.

The décolletage of her dress was far wider than usual, scraping the edge of her shoulders and scooped low at the front to reveal a good deal of creamy flesh. Without the layer of cashmere hiding her bounties she seemed lewdly exposed in a manner she'd crossly denounced Amelia for only a few hours ago; but Darleston evidently appreciated it.

'Very nice,' he drawled. 'Your sister ought to be grateful you didn't appear thus for dinner, else she'd have lacked for any attention. Now bend forward a little. That's right. Show me.'

Lyle made to turn his head, but Darleston's fingers wove tight into his curls and held him in position. 'Not you. You don't need to look. You've had years to appreciate her assets, and God damn it, you're a fool for not doing so.' He tugged at Lyle's hair until his knuckles whitened and Lyle jerked away. Her husband knelt before her, naked, his erection curving upwards like a white sabre, looking, if not happy to see her, then untroubled by her presence. That was well; she didn't want to be at odds with him.

'Why are you here, Emma? What is it you wish to see … or do?' Darleston asked.

They both knew the answer. It was what had been initially promised to her. She needed to see them fuck. But couldn't put words to the desire. It sounded so crude, so aggressive. Instead, she floundered, opening her mouth and closing it again without making a sound, while praying they would help her out. Neither man did.

Instead, Lyle mumbled something into the root of Darleston's cock, and began fellating him again.

Darleston chuckled in response. 'Yes, you're right. You're absolutely right. I would dearly like to lick her quim, especially while you're doing that, but a kiss is a more typical first move, and I don't think Emma's ready to allow me even that.'

She couldn't allow it.

Her heart sped. All the devils that haunted her yelled for her to flee. Yet her muscles locked tight, keeping her on the spot. Would pressing her lips to his really be any different from troubling them with her fingertips as she had done that morning? If he promised not to react, not to press back, might she not dare to try it?

Only he wouldn't remain passive. He wouldn't be able to help himself. He'd warned as much earlier. Affection, physicality came naturally to him. How difficult had it truly been for him to lie still upon the chaise and not react?

Darleston ran a fingertip back and forth along his lower lip. 'Unlace your bodice, Emma. Pretty as your dress is, it's obscuring the real view.'

'She's not a landscape.'

'That's exactly what she is, Lyle, a panorama of swooping hillsides and valleys, of pretty chasms and charming hidden arbours.'

'You read too much bloody poetry.'

'Are your nipples brown or dusky pink?' Darleston asked.

'I ...' In all honesty, she wasn't sure herself, having never paid them much attention. How they tingled now though, almost as if they were excited by the prospect of exposure. Almost as if they were begging for a touch.

'She has a brain,' Lyle protested.

Darleston concurred with a nod. 'A very fine one, but I'm not really looking for a discussion on politics or natural history right now.'

Lyle rested his cheek against Darleston's thigh. He shot her a quick glance, his expression unfathomable. 'I'm not sure I like the attention you're giving my wife. Observer, remember. It's rather unsporting of you to be thinking of giving her a pearl necklace while I do the hard work.'

Darleston pressed a kiss to Lyle's forehead. 'You know, I hadn't actually considered that. It is a little crude to be thinking of doing that to another man's wife.'

Lyle rose to his feet. 'Everything about this is crude.' He shrugged in response to Darleston's frown. 'No matter, I like crude. Matter of fact, let's be really goddamn crude.' He took Darleston's hand and pulled him upright, then led him towards the bed.

Emma floated ghost-like behind them, hooked on the spicy scent of their arousal. She remained at the foot of the bed when they hopped onto the mattress. They fell upon one another, kissing and rolling over and over, fighting for dominance. Only when Darleston was securely straddled across Lyle's waist did he look up at her.

'Emma – floating on the perimeter again? Won't you undress and join us?' He cast aside his own waistcoat and shirt at that point.

'I can't.'

'Truly?' Lyle raised a brow. 'When was the last time you required a maid to unpin you?'

'No, no, I didn't mean it like that.' Of course she could disrobe herself, but in privacy, not to stand before two horn-mad men.

'Undress or leave,' Darleston said.

Truly, did he mean that?

'You have to give something in return. We established that last time.'

'We did.' Lyle added. Both men were looking at her now, one naked, one partially undressed, both potently erect, the hunger in their eyes doing nothing to quash her fears. Tit for tat – she'd shown her bottom. This time they wanted her to stand in the altogether.

'What will you do? You know I can't participate.' The edge of fear crept into her voice, so that her words came out shrill.

It was Darleston that edged towards her, while Lyle turned to plumping the pillows. 'I know what you can give. I know exactly what you can give and what you can't. Are you forgetting this morning, Emma? Perhaps I dreamed you running your hands all over my body.'

Her palms burned as she relived the moment. So too did her cheeks.

'Is that true, Emma?' A flicker of hurt shone in Lyle's eyes. Oh, God, now he thought her unfaithful, when the caresses had been largely chaste.

'I did nothing wrong, Lyle, truthfully. Besides, that was different.' She stared pointedly at Darleston. 'You were still. And fully clothed. It wasn't sexual.'

'The hell it wasn't. You left me with an acute attack of priapism.'

Her gaze immediately sought his cock. He stood proudly to attention now too, the head ruddy and taut, shaped just like a perfectly ripe plum. No wonder Lyle enjoyed licking it so, although at present her husband's teeth were pressed hard into his lower lip. His eyes were narrowed, and his gaze darted between her and Darleston, hurt seeping into the fine lines of his face.

Emma quailed. 'I think maybe it'd be best if I left.' It had been a mistake to assume she could intrude upon their happiness. She reached to pick up her shawl, only for Darleston's hand to close tight around her wrist. She'd never even heard him leave the bed.

Lyle crossed the room too and claimed the latch key. 'I really think you should stay.'

Stay. She couldn't move. Emma stared numbly at the circle of fingers around her wrist. No one had held her thus since she'd left the schoolroom. No one had truly touched her for years. Darleston's hold bit hard into her flesh.

Let go. She ought to have shouted it. The cry ran loud enough in her head. She knew he sensed her distress too, but still he held on. Then somehow he managed to turn her palm so that it fastened tight to his, interlocking their fingers so that heat surrounded the whole of her hand, as if she'd slipped on a mitten that had been warmed by the fire.

'Come and watch.' He gently tugged her towards the bed. 'Hold my hand and watch me fuck your lover.'

Her lover! His lover, more like. She and Lyle had only ever shared the most polite sort of affections. They had never loved one another in the sense he meant.

'Rest here.' Darleston kept a tight hold of her hand as he urged her onto the bed. 'Settle yourself and then just hold my hand. I won't ask any more than that.' Not even to unlace her bodice? Maybe she'd have been wiser to comply with his first desire. Lyle sat on his haunches and watched her smooth her skirts around her legs.

'That's all that you want?' Emma questioned. If he truly only wanted to hold her hand, then perhaps she could do this. The sensation was not unpleasant: his touch was nice, his hand much larger than hers, so that it enfolded hers in a cocoon of warmth. It was not at all like the hand-holding she remembered, when Bea's pudgy fist had filled the centre of her palm. 'What are you going to do?' she whispered, already aware of the answer. They'd do exactly what their disrobed state suggested, exactly as she'd bid them do for her entertainment. They would swive one another as they had done in the woodland. 'Won't you need two hands free?'

'That wholly depends on who is doing the doing.' Darleston mounted the bed behind her, causing the mattress to dip and shake. He had removed the rest of his clothing, so that he crawled towards her completely nude. Emma stared at him. She had not seen him entirely naked before. He was long and lean, broader than Lyle across the shoulders and slimmer at the waist. The raised brand she'd earlier spied on his stomach drew her attention. Darleston spread his hand across it to cover it from view. 'What is it?' she longed to ask. Instead, her gaze became transfixed upon his cock. She had seen it before, of course, but this was different. He had not been pursuing her in quite such a predatory fashion before. He settled beside her, the lengths of their bodies a mere two inches apart, which was far closer than she'd ever lain with Lyle. That knowledge was clear in Lyle's expression, but he did not seem overly angered by it.

'For example, if I were to lie upon my back –' Darleston reclined so that his head lay upon a pillow '– then you can hold my hand without impinging on anything. Matter of fact, we might lie here and leave Lyle in sole command of our pleasure.'

'Sole command, eh?' Her husband gave a jocular little laugh. By candlelight, he really was most handsome, his sweeping widow's peak giving way to a halo of golden curls, even if his expression remained more lecherous than beatific. 'When do you ever relinquish control? Lie down, Emma. You're making me nervous and nerves play havoc with *amore*.'

She did. She lay down with her head on the pillow beside

Darleston's and looked into his eyes while holding his hand, and her husband grinned at them both in that endearing way of his that lit his eyes with dark magic. When he dipped his head and pressed first one kiss and then another upon Darleston's bare torso, she jumped a little, sensing those fleeting caresses as though he were pressing them to her belly and not his lover's.

Darleston's pulse raced, growing faster as Lyle's attention strayed upwards to one of his pale nipples. Emma's own nipples steepled in response, poking against the boning of her stays, making them feel over-tight, so that her breaths became laboured just as Darleston's were rasping. The heaviness that filled her breasts soon spread to her abdomen. An ache started between her thighs. Her gaze shifted from the faces of the two men to their pricks, which bumped gently against one another. Lyle encompassed both members with one hand and proceeded to stroke them as one. The buzz of energy continued to fill her. It uprooted all her long-held virtues and threw them out of the window. She longed to be as wild and free as the men, to know the heights to which they sailed. 'How does it feel?' she asked, not really expecting either of them to reply.

'Incredible,' Lyle sighed.

'There's no easy way of describing it.' Darleston stared straight into her eyes as he spoke. He was not quite on the same plane of existence, she realised, but lifted to some rapturous state that she'd formerly imagined was only reached by religious devotees. 'Say the word and I'll kiss you there, and then you'll know for yourself.'

He meant to press his lips to her breast. She shivered, imagining the sweeping touch of his tongue to her nipple. Her back arched in anticipation, but she shook her head.

She wasn't ready yet. 'I'll just watch.' Best her skittishness didn't destroy the bond between them

'As you wish,' he said and turned back to Lyle.

* * *

Darleston held onto Emma's hand, slowly increasing the intimacy between them. Anything faster and he knew she'd take flight. He didn't want to wrestle her to keep her in the room, nor risk chasing her out of his life. She'd given him such pleasure earlier – unintentionally, of course – but he wanted the chance to return it nonetheless. Her earlier engagement had lit the whole of her face, turning her frequently worried frowns into joy. Still, like the virgin she undoubtedly was, she trembled at the thought of his touch, held herself so rigidly, wrist and arm – indeed, her whole body – so stiff and unyielding that any attempt at penetration would leave bruises on both of them. It was a blessing, then, that it was her husband he intended to tup and not her. Not on this occasion anyway. Though he'd be a liar if he denied that his pulse raced at the thought of sliding deep inside her.

Maybe he really had become jaded, if only the very antithesis of eagerness could raise his pulse.

Lyle's lips traced the edge of his jaw, drawing him back into the present. The man had learned a thousand tricks in the years they'd spent apart. He knew exactly how to give pleasure and take it away with the simplest of touches. Worse still, over the last few days he'd been learning all Darleston's ticks, like the tickle of warm breath against his ear. The touch of a tongue to that delicate organ captivated him every time. On this occasion, though, Lyle was merely teasing, his hovering lips refusing actual contact.

'Where are we going with this?' Lyle hissed. 'Can I expect any sort of satisfaction from you, or is this all fluff? Can't we say, "Enough with the performance" and cut to the final act? I want you now. I'm sick of drawing things out. It's obvious what she wants. She wants to see you spend. She's only ever been interested in seeing you.'

'In both of us,' Darleston hissed back.

Lyle solemnly shook his head. 'In you. She's lapping up your every murmur as if she can imbibe your pleasure right out of the air.'

'This is for all of us. It won't work if you back out.'

'Then you might want to reconsider lying there quite so passively.'

Silly boy didn't understand at all. 'Lying still is exactly what I'm going to do. You get to be on top.'

'What the devil are you trying to prove? You're a fool if you think you're really going to convince her you're some passive little lamb. You're a fox, Robert. You always have been and, no matter what you think, you're not going to be happy unless you find yourself a vixen. Emma's never going to be that.'

He was wrong. Just because Lyle was blind to her charms and the torrent that raged inside her, that didn't mean it wasn't there. He'd seen the way she looked at him. He knew it was only a matter of time. I can be patient, he reassured himself. It'll work out somehow.

'Work with me, Lyle,' he growled into his lover's mouth. 'Let's show her how it's done.' He squeezed one cheek of Lyle's arse. To hell with Lyle's doubts, just because he couldn't see or at least didn't appreciate his wife's sexual self.

Darleston glanced downwards between their bodies to where their erections branded their stomachs and the tip of Lyle's cock leaked beads of shiny pre-come. Darleston wrapped his hand around the thick shaft. 'Come up here. Let me give you an incentive.'

Lyle's grin stretched from ear to ear. 'Now you're talking.' He clambered up the bed until he sat with his knees either side of Darleston's head, his fingers curled tight around the headboard.

Playfully, Darleston trailed his tongue up Lyle's inner thigh. He avoided contact with Lyle's cock, and directed kisses towards his cobs instead, licking, sucking, and drubbing their sensitive surface until Lyle's hips jerked involuntarily.

'Yes,' his lover gasped. 'Yes. Suck me like that. Oh! Gently … gently.' Darleston tenderly formed his lips around one of Lyle's bollocks and sucked. Few men he knew liked this. For most it was too sensitive, or they lacked trust enough to relax and enjoy it, but Lyle found immeasurable joy in the act, something he'd realised the first time he'd stroked him there and caused him to prematurely ejaculate. Lyle had learned a little more control since then, and Darleston knew when to wind things down a notch. On another occasion he might have drawn things out, but it was more important now that Emma witnessed the intense pleasure wrought by their coupling rather than lingering overmuch on the foreplay.

Lyle gave a low wail when Darleston transferred his attention to the smooth stretch of skin behind his cobs. From there it was only a step or two more to his tender opening. He traced the wrinkled whorl, coaxed it over and over with the tip of his thumb. Hell, he knew how sensitive just a persistent caress there could be. However, if a finger was good, then a tongue dabbed against those hundreds of nerve-endings was definitely better.

Emma let out a scandalised gasp. She tried to free her wrist, but Darleston held on tight. No escape. He refused to let her run, or rather he wanted her to witness this. She had to know the truth of him. He was done with hiding. Maybe what he was doing was shocking, but really, was it any more lewd kissing Lyle's arse than putting his cock there? The latter was what he wholly intended to do once he'd relaxed Lyle enough to make the slide in effortless. This couldn't be rough and ready. Pain was not what he wanted Emma to behold. The sort of congress that left one tousled and sore would have to be reserved for an occasion when he and Lyle were alone.

Sometimes it felt good to ache and have bruises the morning after.

Right now, though, Lyle was begging him for more with mute little rolls of his hips. *Deeper, delve your tongue a little inside.* He didn't need to hear the words to know they were Lyle's desire. *Yes, just there. Now a little ... oh, my!* Lyle wrapped a hand around his own cock and began to rapidly masturbate.

Darleston pushed him away and closed a hand over the top of Lyle's. 'Easy now. This is for Emma, remember.' Emma, who lay beside them, her pupils as wide as saucers and with a healthy blush colouring both cheeks and breasts. 'Are you sure you want to see this?' he asked.

She croaked, and then cleared her throat. 'You know that I do.'

'Even though you know us to be dirty, devilish and obscene?'

To his surprise she laughed. 'Is that not meant to be the appeal? It would not be half so intriguing if it were acceptable.'

Sometimes the clarity of her self-awareness surprised even him.

'Is this how men are with one another – you obsess over one another's pricks and kiss in unspeakable places? It is not how love between husband and wife was described to me. This is altogether more raw.'

'Who the devil described lovemaking to you?' Lyle asked. His hot hands pressed tight against Darleston's torso as he shimmied backwards so that he straddled Darleston's waist again.

Emma sniffed. She coyly dipped her gaze. 'Aunt Maude. It was just before we were wed. She sought to prepare me, as I hadn't a mother to instruct me in those facets of a relationship.'

Lyle groaned. 'No instruction at all would have been better than advice from that grimalkin. I'll warrant she told you to lie stiff as a board.'

'She said that I should put out the lights, close my eyes and that it would probably be best if I lay on my stomach so as not to encourage kissing. Also that such a position would enable you to perform your duties without being distracted by other sins.'

Lyle's brows shot up his forehead. 'Other sins?'

Still smiling, Emma shook her head. 'She didn't elaborate, only intimated that you might be swayed from what God intended if my breasts were in any way presented.'

'The woman's a genius.' Darleston chuckled into the pillow. 'Don't you agree, Lyle? Emma's breasts are very distracting. I'm distracted by them right now.' He let his gaze wander over Emma's bosom. Sometime soon he was going to enjoy becoming lost in their voluptuous curves. 'Of course –' he switched his attention back to Lyle '– clearly she doesn't

178

know you very well or she'd never have suggested Emma present you with her arse.'

Lyle's back stiffened.

Beside him, Emma pushed herself up on one arm. 'You mean that he might have ... Why – why would a man do that to a woman? I understand that it's the only way for you two, but it's entirely unnecessary in a marriage, surely. Isn't it?' She cast her gaze back and forth between them.

'Nothing that gives pleasure is ever unnecessary. You might find it unexpectedly good,' Darleston said.

'I wouldn't have,' Lyle murmured. 'I won't. Women's bottoms hold no interest for me.'

Darleston groaned and poked him in the stomach. 'I swear you don't have a single natural urge.'

'Which is just as well for you, or this arrangement wouldn't work, and I wouldn't be about to do this.' Lyle chose that moment to pinch Darleston's nipples so hard, he actually squealed in surprise. However, the rush of blood running back into his abused nipples brought with it a fresh wave of arousal. Lyle's hand splayed over his chest. The globes of Lyle's bottom rubbed up against Darleston's bucking cock. Yet Lyle's gaze was not on him but on his wife. 'Why don't you help me, Emma? Really, what's the difference between holding his hand and his cock? It's all touch, isn't it? You know that thing you don't do?'

'Lyle!' Darleston hissed. This was not the time to begin a squabble, or start exhibiting jealousy. 'Emma.' He spoke soothingly, or at least as softly as he was able while grasping the thought of her hot little hand wrapped around his cock, guiding him into Lyle's hole.

'I can't. You know it. Don't ask it of me.'

The same objection she'd made before and would no doubt

179

make again. Well, he didn't accept it. Her pulse was racing and her limbs trembling, and he didn't believe it was due to fright. Emma was excited. Emma wanted to touch. Her only real fear was about how he'd react.

'Do it,' Darleston urged. 'Guide me home.'

'Yes, do,' Lyle added. 'Be honest. I know what's in your heart, Emma. I can see it every time you look upon him. So acknowledge it. Accept it. Do it.' He fell forward, grabbed Darleston's wrists and tore him away from Emma. Hands pinned either side of Darleston's head, Lyle looked down at him with a feral grin upon his face. 'I'll hold him still, so it's all down to you, Emma. Rob's not going anywhere, and we're not going to fuck unless you help. Either way, I hereby absolutely revoke any permission I may have given him to touch you.'

Darleston bared his teeth. *Why the dirty little ...*

Emma's fist closed uncertainly around his cock.

He wasn't sure what he'd been expecting, only that it wasn't that. Blood surged. Physical need roared in his ears. Her grip was feather-light, the span of her fingers not wide enough to encompass his girth.

'What now?' she asked. 'I don't know what to do.'

'Guide him to me,' Lyle instructed. A fine line of perspiration hung above his top lip. He closed his eyes as Emma joined them.

The first moments were always some of the most intense. Lyle sank down onto him slowly, squeezing him, encompassing him, while shredding what remained of Darleston's nerves. He wanted fast, not this excruciating slowness. But then he understood. Emma's hand still remained around the base of his cock. It was as if, now that she'd gained her nerve, she couldn't let go again; but he could not achieve full penetration with her holding him. Instead, he was locked into a rhythm of shallow thrusts, good but not quite good enough. 'Emma, you need to let go now.'

She withdrew as though she'd been scalded and sat looking at her hand, rubbing her fingertips.

'Forget her a moment, will you?' Lyle hissed into his ear. 'Fuck me.'

Yes. Fucking, swiving this gorgeous man was exactly what he needed. He did so, picking up the pace until they were both lathered in sweat.

Sweet mercy! He'd succeeded in getting Emma to touch him. Correction – they'd both played their parts. What's more, Lyle understood. He realised now that they could make this work for the three of them. They all had unique roles, and if Lyle and Emma didn't desire one another in quite the same way as he desired them both, it didn't matter. It didn't matter at all.

Nothing mattered, because he was going to come.

It hurt. But in such a good way.

Lyle locked them together in a kiss as Darleston bucked into him, coming into the tight confines of Lyle's impossibly lovely arse.

CHAPTER THIRTEEN

For all her bravery, Emma still woke alone the next morning. Admittedly, in a room and a bed that were not hers, and surrounded by rumpled sheets, but that only served to make the situation more terrifying. They'd left her, slipped away while she slept. The abandonment hit her more acutely as she dressed. She'd reached out to them last night. Fought against every demon she possessed, in order to try and win a place in their hearts – only for this: to wake as she did every morning.

Isolated.

Alone.

God damn them. Couldn't they see that she wanted sustenance beyond the thud of her own heartbeat? Touching Darleston and feeling his incredible heat melt into her bones had changed things in infinitesimal ways. Maybe not for them, but for her. Definitely.

She'd changed.

She wanted their love. Well, Darleston's love ... and maybe Lyle's blessing. She thought he'd given her that last night when he'd deliberately held Darleston down and invited her to coax his lover. Though perhaps she ought to address the question directly.

Lyle had always taken lovers, but she'd never had cause to. Until now. Would he really share Darleston with her?

Emma left the Winter Room, closing the door quietly behind her. As she walked, her mind fluttered back to how the men had been last night. She'd watched them cuddle after they'd made love, sticky with sweat and with their brows pressed together, excluding everything else. She had no doubt that they loved one another. The way they communicated without the need to speak told her that. No, the real question was whether there was room in that bond for her. Perhaps the only way for her to really find out would be to do something genuinely daring for a change.

She would kiss Darleston.

If that didn't win his attention, then nothing in old England would.

'What are you smirking for?' Amelia emerged from her room. Given the flouncing she'd done the night before, she'd dressed rather conservatively this morning in a becoming pink gown that buttoned to her neck and bore a delicate lace yoke. Sprigs of apple-green embroidery covered the skirt.

'You look nice today,' Emma said.

Her compliment met with a shrug. 'This old thing? You've seen it a dozen times. Um, would you like help with your hair?'

Emma shook her head. 'You know I don't care to be fussed over.'

'I know it, only you seemed to have fashioned a bird's nest rather than a chignon.'

In fact she had not brushed her hair at all. It was as it had been when she'd awakened.

Amelia squinted at her. 'Why are you still dressed for dinner? You wore that gown last night. It's hopelessly rum ...

pled.' Enlightenment seemed to dawn, whereupon her frown gave way to astonishment. 'You didn't!' Amelia glanced down the corridor in the direction from which Emma had come. 'You did, didn't you? With him! And you say that I'm a strumpet. Does Lyle know what you're about?' Tears trickled down her sister's face. 'Good Lord, Emma, you don't care for me at all. How could you think of ruining my chances like this? How many of them have you enticed to your bed this week? Just because you and Lyle are unhappy doesn't mean you have to steal suitors from me.'

Emma's jaw dropped, her mouth falling open in outrage. 'How dare you suggest –? We're not unhappy. You've no idea what you're talking about. Whatever it is you think you know, I swear that you're perfectly mistaken.'

'And you believe me a fool. I ought to tell Father.'

Tell Mr Hill what precisely? That Amelia suspected Emma of being a hopeless bawd? She had no evidence beyond a crumpled gown and unpinned hair. There were thousands of reasons why Emma might have been coming down the corridor from that direction. Well, a few at least.

'What purpose could there be in saying anything to Father? It would do you more harm than good. He would simply send you to Aunt Maude's.' Emma wasn't sure where the strength was coming from. Only that it pleased her that she felt able to protect her two men. 'Go ahead, snitch if it pleases you,' she snarled. 'See what it gains you. And you are wrong on all counts, by the way.' Darleston had not ravished her, though he'd touched her more than most.

Emma strode past Amelia and continued to her room. Safe inside, she locked the door and shed the offending dress. Dear heavens, she had handled that badly. Now Amelia was sure to believe she'd spent the night in Darleston's arms, and knowing Amelia she wouldn't be able to keep it to herself for very long at all.

Emma sucked her lip while starring at the locked door. If she went back to Amelia, further denials would only make things worse and she couldn't apprise her of the real facts. Doing so would place them all in danger. Men and women were hanged for lesser crimes every day. Not that she believed what Lyle and Darleston – what they had all – done actually constituted a sin. How could something as beautiful as love be wrong? But she was not a judge. Heaven help her, but it would be better all round if an affair between her and Darleston were seen to be the truth. Assuming anyone would believe it. They all knew she despised being touched.

* * *

Lyle sat at the breakfast table when Amelia flopped into a chair beside him. She was turned out impeccably this morning, looking exactly like a piece of apple-blossom. It was simply a shame her expression didn't live up to such delicacy. She scowled at him when he wished her good morning, before grasping her spoon as though it were a dagger aimed for his heart.

'Do you know where Emma is?' she barked.

Was that the reason for her choice of seat? Amelia didn't often grace him with her presence, particularly when other more engaging company was to be had from Mr Phelps and Mr Bathhouse, both of whom were seated at the far end of the long table.

'I don't.' The last he'd seen of Emma, she'd still been tucked beneath the sheets of Darleston's bed, sleeping contentedly.

Leastways the most contentedly he'd ever seen her. Normally she was taut as a hamstring even in repose.

Amelia made a sour clucking noise. 'Well, oughtn't you to keep a better check upon her?'

Someone had clearly got out of the wrong side of the bed that morning. Lyle laid his cutlery aside. 'Whatever do you mean to imply by that?'

'Only that no one seems to be able to locate her of late. No one keeps track of her comings and goings, or whom she's engaged with.'

Lyle pushed aside his plate and reached for his teacup. Amelia would genuinely benefit from some time abroad in society. She seemed to see every convention as a means of spiting her alone. 'My wife's pastimes are her own to choose. She does not require a chaperone.' He placed extra emphasis on the word 'wife' to try and drive home the difference between Emma and her sister, only to be rewarded with another scowl from Amelia.

'I know that. I don't know why everyone assumes I don't. I'm perfectly aware of our difference in status. Heavens, I can't even stroll about the grounds alone. That wasn't what I was saying.' She took a spirited swipe at the top of her boiled egg, neatly decapitating it in one stroke. 'I only meant to say that perhaps it might be wise to ask her what she'd been engaged with these past few days. What company she's kept, that sort of thing, since she's not been with me – hence the need for you to accompany me on the excursion with the other gentlemen.'

His chair shrieked as Lyle scraped it backwards. He stood and turned towards Amelia with his back to the other guests. *What the devil was the little minx getting at?* 'If you're trying to tell me something, then I suggest you say it outright.

187

Subterfuge is not an appealing quality in a woman.'

Amelia relinquished her spoon and folded her hands upon her lap. 'I don't mean to imply anything. I'm merely pointing out that she has spent a deal of time alone with one particular gentleman. I thought you should know that.'

'You mean Darleston, I suppose.' He raised his brows. 'Well, what of it? We're old friends. Of course my wife is doing her best to entertain him.'

'Yes, but ...' The little virago continued indelicately, 'She retired very early last night and –'

'As did I.' Lyle cut her off, and treated her to a particularly hard stare. 'As did I. Now wash whatever presumption you've made from your head. Emma slept soundly beside me all night, exactly where I'd expect my wife to be.' The fact that they had both been in Darleston's bed was none of Amelia's concern. Nosy little minx. He heartily wished one of the men would make an offer for her, just so that he could wash his hands of her. If she started digging into his affairs, matters would rapidly escalate into unpleasantness. He stalked indignantly from the room. He would have to warn both Emma and Darleston what was going on, because the likelihood of Amelia dropping the subject was precisely none.

* * *

Lyle stumbled across Darleston first. His lover sat in one of the window seats in the library, his legs folded and a book balanced upon his knee. 'There's trouble brewing,' Lyle warned as he pulled over a chair so that he could perch by Darleston's side.

'Are Oxbury and Littleton already here?' Darleston asked. He cast his book aside and inclined his head towards the mullioned glass. 'I've been keeping half an eye upon the approach.'

Lyle's brows crumpled. Was there trouble beside Amelia he didn't know of? 'You're worried about them. Why so?'

Darleston gave him a weary smile. 'I'm wary of anyone whose path I've crossed in recent months. Inevitably certain issues come up, and I've no wish to endure another round of accusations and slights upon my name. Besides, they are not really the sort I'd expect Hill to invite, not with Amelia present.'

'Fortune hunters?'

Bright strands of coppery hair fell forward over Darleston's face as he shook his head. 'Far worse. Money isn't an issue for either of them. Rather they're a pair of rabid muff-mongers.'

Lyle tapped Darleston's knee, then gave it a squeeze, as much for his own comfort as Darleston's. 'If I had any idea what you were talking about I'd be worried. However, it's about Amelia I wanted to speak. She suspects you of conducting an affair with Emma.'

Darleston carefully lowered his feet to the floor. 'She told you that?'

'At breakfast. Caught me perfectly unaware.' He never thought anyone would pay the slightest regard to the shenanigans between the three of them. His whereabouts and affairs generally passed unremarked upon, and Emma in her dowdy outfits blended into the wainscoting. Lyle hid his head in his palms, only looking up at Robert again after several seconds. 'What do we do?'

'Nothing.' To his surprise, Darleston showed no sign of alarm. He slipped from the window seat and strode across the room to a bookcase, where he squeezed the book he'd been reading into a narrow gap. 'I assume you told her it was nonsense.'

'I did, but … but what if she finds out about –'

'She won't. You're forgetting the initial purpose in having Emma involved. An affair – an affair conducted at a house party – is perfectly commonplace. Providing you stick by her there's nothing to fear. Amelia's a fool for drawing your attention to it. I can't think what she hoped to achieve.'

Darleston might not, but he did. 'Spite,' Lyle enlightened him. The relationship between the two sisters had never been entirely comfortable. Yes, Emma called Amelia 'dear heart', but that fondness had never satisfied Amelia's hunger for affection. The girl believed herself entitled to Emma's affections as though her elder sister were her mother, not her sibling. 'I expect she's paying Emma back for allegedly thwarting her chances of gaining a husband.'

'Hmm. Sibling rivalry, a joyous thing. Do you think she's actually seen anything?'

Lyle tugged at his cuffs. He didn't think there was anything Amelia could have observed. He and Darleston had been as discreet as circumstances allowed, and, as for Emma, she didn't allow anyone to get near her, so what was there to observe? 'I'm not sure anyone will believe it of Emma. They'll know she's hiding, covering something. I mean, how can she be conducting an affair? Anyone who knows her will realise how ridiculous the notion is. She abhors physical contact.'

'She's had her hand around my cock, or did you forget that bit?'

Darleston's interjection failed to soothe away Lyle's apprehension. He stared pensively at the other man, expecting … he wasn't sure what. Either way, Darleston didn't offer any more answers.

'I didn't forget it,' Lyle said quietly. He wondered which of them, he, Darleston or Emma, had been the most shocked when Emma had complied with his instructions the previous night. It had certainly added unanticipated zest to the moment. However, none of that mattered right now. 'That's not something I'm about to announce. All I'm saying here is that if we're going to mask our affair with one between you and Emma, then the possibility ought to be convincing. People need to observe that there's a physical closeness between you and Emma that isn't there between her and anyone else.'

Darleston thoughtfully tapped his fingertips to his lips. 'I take your point. It is a dilemma.' But it was one he didn't seem remotely troubled by, particularly when his introspection gave way to a grin. 'Are you granting me permission to touch her again? For you did revoke that right last night.'

'You may do whatever you wish, and would no doubt have done so regardless of permissions.'

'Hm.' Darleston's fingers curled around the chair wing. 'Possibly, but that doesn't change the fact that I want to hear you say it. Lay things out straight for me.'

'You're a devil,' Lyle muttered under his breath. Then he looked Darleston straight in the eye and added, 'You have permission to tup my wife. Happy now?'

'Delirious.' The grin that Darleston already bore stretched wide across his narrow face.

Lyle nodded, but even as he did so Darleston's gaze strayed back to the driveway of the house, diminishing Lyle's faith in the plan.

* * *

Emma skipped breakfast. Her stomach churned at the mere notion of food. She had warned off Amelia, but knew her sister well enough to realise that the matter wasn't done.

191

Amelia for all her naivety could also be as wily as a cat. She loathed the fact that Emma possessed freedoms she didn't, hated the fact that Emma remembered their mother's embrace, while she had only Aunt Maude's sparing affections to thrive upon.

Emma needed to act and quickly. Better that Amelia genuinely believed she and Darleston had formed some sort of attachment than the silly goose discovered the truth. Amelia wouldn't consider the consequences of revealing the gentlemen's love for one another. She'd think only of the attention and sympathy it would bring her way. Without question, Amelia simply couldn't be allowed to delve into the truth of her relationship with either man.

To that end, Emma endeavoured to find Darleston at once. She would explain things discreetly and then act. It was only what she'd planned to do anyway to determine if her place in his affections were genuine or not. She didn't want to linger on the fringes any more, observing him and Lyle. Rather she dreamed that every one of Darleston's lewd etchings was made a reality. All she had to do was find some bottom, as the men would say. Only then would she know how Darleston truly felt.

Emma made a slow, laborious circuit of the house, hoping to happen upon Lord Darleston alone. Yet every step she took while failing to find him drove her a little closer to panic. She couldn't do this, and she could. She had to, for all of them. Amelia mustn't learn the truth. She mustn't sacrifice herself and gain nothing. From the first moment she'd set eyes upon Darleston she'd known there was something different about him. No other person, living or dead, had ever made her want to reach out so ardently. It didn't matter that she'd already touched him more intimately than any woman ought to touch a man to whom she wasn't married. Kissing him would be different altogether. He'd react. He'd press back. The contact would no longer be one-directional. When she thought of how he'd look at her breasts, hold them, press his lips to them, then her resolve almost faltered. Yet while she shuffled from one foot to the other, afraid to press forward and unwilling to turn back, there remained a tingle of heat in her puss.

Deep down, Emma knew it wasn't just kisses she wanted or needed from him. Darleston would make her whole, if only she'd let him.

By the time she turned the corner into the west frontage by her father's study and found Darleston alone, her teeth were aching so much it proved impossible to gasp anything other than his name.

He'd dressed more simply today, in a russet coat and buff breeches, devoid of the frogging and lavish embellishments she usually associated with his clothes. Emma rushed to his side. She had to act immediately, before she had a chance to overthink things or find an excuse to prevent her actions. 'I ... was looking for ...' She pressed a kiss to his dry lips.

He must have been shocked, for he didn't fold his arms around her, nor kiss her back. Rather, he remained stiffly aloof. His palm closed around her elbow and he eased her gently away from his person.

Emma's nose tingled with the threat of coming tears. She'd read everything wrong. Darleston's pale-grey eyes shone with a glassy light. Nothing in his expression hinted at the slightest pleasure over her action. He pushed her backwards against the wall, holding her away from his body as his gaze raked her face.

One tear escaped, followed by another. They rolled down her cheeks and onto the front of her gown.

'Hey.' He wiped away the glistening beads and slowly his lips tweaked upwards at the corners. 'That was an unexpected pleasure. Are you sure it was meant for me?'

What sort of nonsense question was that? Of course she'd intended it for … Dear God! His voice … his voice, it wasn't at all the same. Emma stared at the man before her, marking other differences too, such as shorter hair, the extra ring of lilac fire around his irises and a nose that was not quite so straight or pointed as Darleston's, but looked as though it might have been broken some years before. Most importantly of all, there was no recognition of her as somebody he knew, certainly not as a woman he'd lain still for and shared intimacies with.

'Who are you, by the way?' He leaned forward, cocking his head so that she thought he intended to return the kiss.

Emma squealed, causing him to step back and straighten up immediately. At that moment two other figures came hurtling around the corner.

'Ned?'

'Did somebody just scream?' Mr Hill asked. 'Is there a problem?' He scratched at his mop of grey-white hair.

Darleston … her father! Emma shook free of Ned Darleston's hold and fled away from all three men as fast as she could. She ran through the study and left the house by the French doors.

CHAPTER FOURTEEN

Tears blinded her flight, but she didn't stop running until she'd crossed the lawn and forced her way into the abandoned dovecote. There, in the inky shadows, away from the harsh sun and the censure of the men, she stopped and pressed her brow to the cold bricks.

What an absolute ninny she was. How ridiculous to put herself through all that mither only to kiss the wrong man. She even recalled Darleston telling her that he had a brother. Although he hadn't stated that his brother was also his identical twin.

The dovecote door creaked open behind her. A slash of daylight penetrated the gloom, but only for a moment, before Darleston ducked low and entered. 'You're not the first to make that mistake. I probably ought to have warned you, only I hadn't anticipated you kissing him.'

'Your twin.' She cast a swift glance at him over her shoulder before returning her gaze to the wall. Of all the imbecile things she could have done. She gave her lips a surreptitious rub with the back of her hand. 'He told you, I suppose. So Father knows.' Amelia's interference wouldn't make any difference now.

Darleston stole a little closer. 'Neddy didn't give you away. That was purely my guess based on your reaction. I'm only sorry that my brother gained what I desired.'

'You desire it.' She turned and gawped at him with her back pressed tight to the wall. Her fingernails scraped at the spongy moss growing in the cracks between the stones.

'Emma, you know I do. I wonder if, perhaps, you'll find the nerve to do it again. What do you think are my chances – good, even ... poor?' The last word was delivered with a worried frown.

Why was it that the sensation of his lips pressing against her inner wrist and forearm permeated every word he spoke, even when he stood several feet away?

Emma hiccoughed. 'I'm not sure. I've made a mess of everything. First Amelia saw me and made all manner of assumptions and now I've kissed your brother and Father is probably wondering what the devil is happening.'

'Don't worry. Neddy's explaining. He told Hill that he'd come up behind you too quietly and startled you. I volunteered to check you were all right.' He'd inched towards her as he spoke so that he stood as close to her now as he had in the amphitheatre. Only, unlike on that occasion, when he reached out to her Emma didn't flee. She swallowed the lump in her throat and braced herself for the contact.

The pad of his thumb brushed her cheek, then spread the salty wetness of her tears over her lips, leaving them tingling. He kept looking at her mouth, looking and looking and looking until she tilted her head and her gaze began to follow a pattern of sliding back and forth between his grey eyes and his lips. Any moment he would lean forward and claim her. The mere notion threaded her veins with fire. This might be what she wanted but it didn't in any way make it easy. 'Kiss me,' she said, straining upwards so that she was balanced on tiptoes. 'Do it quickly.' She closed her eyes to await that magical event.

'Don't you want to savour the moment a little longer?'

Emma's eyes snapped open, only for him to lean forward and claim her in that instant. This was not at all like the impromptu kiss she'd given his brother. That had been rushed and – she realised it now – too forceful. This was softer, lighter. Each brush sent tremors of pleasure racing down her throat and through her breasts. It was something to savour and cry for. If there had not been a wall at her back she would have fallen. Her knees buckled when he drew back a fraction, but Darleston held her steady.

His clothing was soft beneath her fingertips, his warmth compelling. She didn't want this moment to end. When he drew back, she boldly rekindled their kiss.

This second kiss was different from the first. He held back less, was more exploring, less tentative. Ever since that first time when she'd glimpsed him through the library window she'd wanted to rub up against him. The way he cradled her in his arms meant she could do just that, curling her hands around his lapels, while his tongue darted against hers. Back and forth, give and take, with more of his body pressing up against her as each moment passed, until she was completely trapped, sandwiched between the brickwork and his chest, with the hard ridge of his cock branding her hip.

'Will you allow me to touch you again? As I did in the Dog Parlour?'

Darleston sucked in a hasty breath. 'I was rather hoping for a more mutually satisfying arrangement.' She leaned into his chest and her lips fluttered over the topmost button of his waistcoat. 'Very well,' he agreed, 'but a little differently,

I think.' Then, slowly, he backed away from her, shrugging off his exquisite coat as he moved. He stopped when his back hit the opposite side of the circular dovecote, whereupon he dropped his coat and started upon the row of mother-of-pearl buttons on his waistcoat. Once that had come off, it was a simple matter to release his frontfall, unwind his cravat and pull his shirt over his head.

Of course she'd seen him naked before, but this was different. This time he'd undressed for her in broad daylight, although one might imagine it otherwise in the gloom of the tiny chamber. She would not have dared expose herself in such a way. Nakedness seemed trebly obscene at this early hour, with no bed anywhere about.

Emma gawped at him with her mouth hanging open. In many ways his body mimicked Lyle's. They were both possessed of a lean, wiry frame, but Darleston was longer. Freckles covered much of his arms. He also possessed that curious raised mark upon the right side of his abdomen, stretching from just below his navel to a point just above his hip. In the excitement of last night it had passed unnoticed; now that imperfection seemed to call to her.

Slowly, she padded towards him, her arms partially outstretched. Closer to, she was not sure if the mark was a scar or a brand. Almost without thought she traced a finger over its silvery surface. 'What happened?'

He shook his head and moved her hand from the mark to his chest. 'I don't want to discuss it.'

So he had his secrets too.

He might not wish it, but Emma couldn't quite shake off her curiosity. It seemed there was almost a pattern to it, as though he'd been stamped. Darleston curled a finger and lifted her chin. 'You claimed you wanted to touch me. Well, now I'm all yours. Anywhere you like, as hard or soft as you like. Use your mouth, your fingers, the tip of the feather you have in your hair ...' He hesitated a moment while he plucked a grey feather from her cascading locks, then blew it away. 'On second thoughts, I'm rather ticklish.'

Ticklish. For a moment she pictured him writhing, laughing as he fought off her hands just as Bea ... no, not Bea, but Eliza – who had died before Bea had even arrived in the world – had done.

Emma stiffened, then immediately forced her shoulders to relax. She refused to sink into the past. She wouldn't let the ghosts isolate her any more. Darleston was her chance to live, and she was damn well going to take it.

She leaned into him once more, her nose pressed to his skin and her lips closed around the furled peak of one of his nipples. She sucked upon it while she let her hands rove across his body. He was not as smooth as he first appeared, for in several places grew patches of soft springy golden hair, the most prominent, she knew from past experience, being the one around the base of his cock. The moment she thought of it, she knew she wanted to touch him there. Her gaze wandered downwards, but she paused. Darleston nudged her in that direction. 'Let's not pretend you're unfamiliar with it.'

Emma curled her fingers around the shaft. She had held him while he slid back and forth into her husband's arse– how could she feign shyness now? She stroked upwards, cupped her palm over the vibrant tip and listened in delight as his sighs became mews and then moans.

All too soon his cock began to weep. Then she knew what she wanted. Without looking down, Emma sank to her knees. Darleston's cock curved upright before her, pressing tight against his stomach. He groaned when she opened her mouth. 'Holy saints, Emma.' Groaned again as she did what she'd previously watched Lyle do.

He tasted of salt and musk. Smelled of it too.

As she sucked harder, his hands groped at the brickwork behind him, seeking further purchase, but she knew right away that she did not want him to spill in her mouth. Rather she wanted him as she'd originally envisaged, lying flat as he had been in the Dog Parlour. That way she could straddle him and rub her puss up against his rampant cock, finally obtain some of that pleasure that was constantly being dangled before her.

If only they had a blanket, but all they had to cover the scuffed and pitted floor was Darleston's coat, an item too beautiful to contemplate crushing and messing with dirt.

Frustrated, she drew back and tore at her arms, lacerating the skin with rows of parallel scratches.

'Emma!' Darleston caught her. He clasped her hands tight in his curled fists. 'What is it? Talk to me. Why?' He stared at the marks upon her skin in deep concern.

'I wanted you,' she blurted. 'Properly, as a man might take a woman. But I can't. I can't do it. I don't know if I can –' Her words broke off as he cupped the swell of one of her breasts so that her nipple lay taut against the centre of his palm. 'Oh!'

His irises were no longer quite so pale in hue, but had darkened to the colour of wet slate. Grey, shot with lilac, so enticing, so compelling. It was hard to stand still as he touched her. Hard to let his fingers walk upwards and pluck out the pins holding the front of her dress in place.

'I have to see,' he said, head dipped forward to compensate for the dismal light. 'You know a dovecote is hardly an ideal location.' His humour went a little way to relieve her tension.

'The other thing you have to understand is that I'm not an ornament. I can't stand idle and let you polish me. The true pleasure in sex comes from sharing it with somebody.'

Emma's pulse beat a rapid tattoo against her temple as he worked open the front fastenings of her stays. She didn't spill from the confinement, though she certainly felt the air rush into her lungs, allowing her to take deeper breaths. His hand worked inside her stays. He cupped the swell of her breast again, only this time the contact was like a scald, too hot, too intense. She wriggled, trying to escape its intensity, even as he captured a nipple and caused desire to blossom deep within her womb.

'Steady now. You're not going to bolt, are you?' She did glance towards the door, but then shook her head as her hands found anchorage amongst the moss-covered stones at her back. 'Good. Then let's make things a little easier.' He unfastened more of her clothing, so that her dress hung open around her waist and her stays were opened almost to her navel. Her breasts filled both his palms. Darleston crushed them together and his breath whispered across their surface before he buried his nose in the crevice between them. Next came the press of his lips, trailing kisses that culminated in his taking one nipple into his mouth.

He was only doing to her what she had done to him.

The sweet sensation came as a shock. Her own explorations had made her realise that she was sensitive there. Pleasure was to be had by repetitive circling of the tip, squeezing a little, tugging upon it. None of that had quite prepared her for what Darleston was doing with his tongue.

'Good?' he asked when he paused briefly to take a deeper breath. Between breathlessness and the fluttering of her heart, Emma couldn't voice a reply.

'Let me show you more.' He trailed kisses up the side of her neck, lingering for a long time over her pulse point.

The heat in Emma's womb grew more insistent, so that she rocked her hips, and angled herself so that she bumped against his loins. She forgot her fears, and forgot the past.

Darleston's feet crushed his coat. He paid it no regard. His attention remained entirely upon her. To Emma's dismay, he did not return immediately to her breasts but stood looking at her for several long moments. Finally, he tucked behind her ear a stray lock of hair that had escaped her chignon. Then he clasped one of her hands and tore it away from the security of the wall.

'Touch me again. Give and take, remember?' He turned her palm, positioned it over the swell of his cock. His eyes closed briefly at the contact and the tip of his tongue brushed his upper lip. He didn't make a sound, but she could sense his pleasure. It was a bone-deep ache, a mixture of longing and frustration, like an itch that had to be scratched.

His hand strayed down to her thigh. Slowly, he began to hitch her skirts, exposing first her ankles and calves, then her knees and her garters and stocking-tops. He released her skirt at that point, let the fabric fold over his arm, while his hand made contact with the bare skin of her thigh.

The urge to bolt reared again, but she suppressed it.

Unhurriedly, maintaining eye-contact with her all the time, Darleston moved higher. Then one finger stroked upwards along the split of her quim, feather-light but sweet enough to have her rearing onto her toes.

He leaned in and possessed her mouth again, while wet, slick evidence of her arousal coated his questing fingers. He found her nub and the intensity of that first touch struck her so sharply that for a moment she feared for her sanity. He seemed to know how to drive every sensible thought from her head, leaving behind only the desire to couple with him.

Yes. That was it. That was what she wanted. She stroked him, so that the head of his cock drove repeatedly through the ring of her fingers, hoping, praying that somehow he would understand what it was she needed from him, but to her surprise he did not lift her or slide her onto his shaft. Instead, he fell to his knees and set his tongue to work, flicking back and forth over her ripe little nubbin.

First fingers and now his tongue spurred her towards some bright pinnacle. Her hands laced in his hair. She held him close, guiding him and mewling over each touch. The expression 'silver-tongued' rolled around her mind. She knew no other way of describing him. Perhaps there was a proper word, but if there wasn't there ought to be, for what he was about was a skill surely worth perfecting. He was pushing her further and further into the light.

She was going to come.

Emma stretched so that her head tilted back against the wall. She let out a groan that seemed to come from her toes. Nay, her peak was already upon her. She came, bucking against him, while his tongue flicked feather-light across her bud.

Darleston blew softly upon her overheated flesh, but even that blessed breeze evoked another tremble. Every part of her seemed jittery and boneless. He enfolded her within his arms and she drooped against him like a wilted flower, no longer concerned about the close contact of their bodies.

Minutes passed. It seemed as if eternity slipped by before her wits returned. She might be sated but the persistent rock of his hips informed her that her lover's needs remained unsatisfied. Emma stared at him. She would not be accused of leaving him hanging twice. 'Are you? I mean, do you want to ...' It didn't matter how she tried to phrase it, the words simply wouldn't come out.

'Do I want to?' He stroked all the escaped hairs back from her face. 'You have no idea, but I confess that a dovecote is not the best place for a first time.'

'I want it. I want you to.'

He raised one elegant brow. 'Aye, maybe you do. The barn would have been perfect, by the way.'

Emma chuckled along with him, a broad smile stretching her lips. 'I'll remember that the next time I've cause to flee.'

'But only if you've a tupping in mind. Don't go rushing in there seeking sanctuary.'

Although his humour relieved the awkwardness of their position, there remained obvious hunger in his movements. His breath came in rough bursts and the rock of his loins grew more insistent, despite his hint that penetration was not on the agenda.

'Surely there's something ...' Heavens, she wanted to give him something in return. 'Will it hurt?' she asked, changing tack suddenly. She didn't want to delay the moment; it might never arise again. She wanted to know, now, before her nerve faltered.

'Coitus? It might a little.'

'I want to feel you.'

He hesitated before shifting his stance so that his cock butted up against her belly. 'Like this?'

'Closer.' Tears prickled the corners of her eyes.

Darleston angled himself downwards and the thick shaft speared between her thighs, where it rubbed up against the still sensitive lips of her puss.

Immediately her slickness coated him, making his glide so

impossibly smooth that they both let out sighs. Still, he held back, nudging close but not entering. Emma wriggled, trying to get more of his prick in contact with her clit. 'Please, I want you to.'

'You're crying,' he observed.

Emma wiped away the tears with the back of her hand. She gave him a smile, even though her vision remained blurry. 'Please.' Another tear trickled over her cheek. Darleston caught it with his tongue. 'I'm a bad man,' he confessed. 'And you're undoing me. Oh, hell, Emma.' He lapped at her tears, while the tip of his cock pressed home.

Oh, Lord! Was that truly only the head of him? The pressure – the intensity would surely split her in twain. But the moment he drew back and the pressure ceased, she craved it all over again.

Darleston lifted her leg and hooked it around his waist while he pressed himself into place again. He held her there, just the very tip of him inside her, poised, waiting while her muscles fluttered with both urgency and trepidation.

'You're sure? Because once it's done, there's no going back.'

'I know it.' Yes, she knew it. She'd thought of this moment often over the last few days. Wanting it. Being alarmingly afraid of it. Curiously, despite her racing heart, she felt quite calm.

'Good,' Darleston sighed. 'Because I want this too.' Then he kissed her hard enough to bruise. At the same time he surged forward, trapping her betwixt the wall and his body, so that he drove into her. A sharp splinter of pain fractured the moment of elation, then – oh, my – he was inside her, touching her where no one had touched her before and in a way she'd never thought to experience.

After barely a moment he drew back again, allowing her

to breathe and bury her head against his shoulder, before he began to stroke in and out. Her body welcomed him. She was slick and wet from her earlier orgasm. She briefly entertained the thought that he'd planned everything this way, but how could he truly have known she'd surrender?

Within a few moments, he lifted her full off the floor. Legs entwined around his waist, hands clasped tight to his shoulders, her back braced against the wall, Emma rode his prick and no longer feared him touching her. For a few peaceful minutes the old ghosts were locked away, or maybe she simply couldn't hear them over the pounding of her heartbeat. His touch was so very different from their icy grasp that she could not compare them, but then this too was a very different sort of love. It was not built upon blood and filial affection. Rather their two separate souls had somehow found one another and sought a way to entwine.

She wondered if this was what all lovers felt. Was it what Lyle experienced when he and Darleston made love? Could one person truly split their affections between two people? Would one of them end up being hurt?

Did it matter?

If the whole world fell apart tomorrow, then everything was still worth it for this single magical moment.

Dear God, he was going to bring her to another peak.

He held her a long time after she'd come and let her cry into his shoulder. 'It's all right, Emma,' he soothed and she actually believed him. Leastways, she believed in his solidity. 'No one is going to hurt you.'

CHAPTER FIFTEEN

Most of the hot colour had faded from Emma's face by the time they'd left the dovecote, except at the tip of her ears. Darleston helped her to relace her stays and pin her dress, which had been a feat of restraint in several senses. Her bosom protested at the binding, and he – he protested at hiding those luscious curves from view. He might always have liked men but, when his interest was roused by a woman, it wasn't because she was built like a boy. No, indeed, he'd always preferred his maidens curvy.

'Will you tell Lyle?' she asked as they rounded the hollyhock that shadowed the door through which Emma had originally fled. The winds of the previous night had left small branches scattered across the grass and had overturned several potted plants. She righted some containers of spilled begonias as they passed, reinstating them amongst the borders of pinks and vibrant, rather phallic, red hot pokers. Darleston watched her dust the earth from her fingertips. It stung him a little that she did seek his support as another woman might. Sex had not fundamentally changed her. She still stiffened whenever her skirts brushed his legs. Someday soon he'd get to the bottom of why that was. It had, he supposed, been arrogant to think that, whatever ill she'd suffered, he could cure it with one good fuck. No one had ever cured any of his ills in such a way, though there'd certainly been a few who'd tried. Then there'd been others like his mother whose methods had been far less pleasant.

'Are you asking me to break the news to him?' He wasn't certain if that had been her meaning or if she desired him to hold his tongue so that she could tell Lyle. 'I don't wish to keep secrets from him, Emma. He won't be shocked. I think he recognised the inevitability of things, considering what we all shared.'

'Inevitable ...' She gave an awkward high-pitched laugh, and then tumbled the word over her tongue several times as though she needed to convince herself of that fact. Perhaps she'd believed otherwise. He'd known the first time she'd looked at him with fire in her gaze that they'd share some sort of sexual denouement. The very fact that her desire was so apparent, yet to be avoided at all costs, immediately caught his attention. Likely that made him the appalling roué some society mamas had cursed him as. He didn't care. He hadn't bedded Emma for some stupid sense of satisfaction. He'd done it to give her pleasure, and because, along with Lyle, he wanted to share his life with her. He'd been searching for someone to love like that for a long time, with so little hope of ever finding them.

'Still, what if he thinks that I'm trying to come between you?' She raised her clenched fist to her mouth as she spoke as if to ward off the possibility of such an event. Troubling worry lines etched her fears upon her brow. It fascinated him that she and Lyle had come to care for one another so devotedly, having built a marriage upon little more than passing friendship. They cared for one another, bore mutual respect, even if neither understood the other terribly well. They didn't judge or make great shows of one another's faults. Would that he could have had such a relationship with Lucy. Life might have been different then. But Lucy was just like his mother had been, selfish, full of pride and cruel.

'Listen, just because Lyle's not interested in bedding you, that doesn't mean he doesn't see sense in the three of us being together. He wants you to be happy, Emma.' He genuinely believed that and he prayed that belief came through in his words. The years had changed Lyle: where once his lover had been possessive, he now seemed more adaptable. Certainly he better understood the constraints society placed upon them as men whose urges ran outside the norm. Mayhap, too, Lyle understood that their tastes were not identical. They were not cast entirely from the same mould. He would always seek the company of both sexes, while Lyle would never find or even seek contentment with a woman. No other man of his acquaintance had put off matrimonial duty for so long. Emma's frigidity had played nicely into Lyle's hand.

Emma continued to walk alongside him, her hands clasped before her, which lent an air of uneasiness to her gait.

'And you?' she asked, stopping momentarily to face him. 'What is it that you want? Do you wish us to all be together?'

'Oh, God!' he cried. The approach to the house was visible over the top of her head. Always, always the tide of fortune turned so fast. Oxbury's landau stood before the main entrance and the man himself was upon the steps, with Edward Littleton at his flank. But neither of those foxes was the reason for his outburst. The problem came in the shape of his wife, framed perfectly by the carriage doorway, her hand pensively extended towards the waiting footman. She'd dressed in a gown of ivory taffeta, overlaid with yards of burgundy Chantilly lace. A feathered cap perched jauntily atop an abundance of corkscrew ringlets. It'd had been months since he'd set eyes upon her. The last time, she'd been bound to the foot of their marital bed with silken cords, dressed in stockings, shoes and nothing else. He couldn't even claim she'd been posed there for him. He'd caught her with another man, one whose fetish complemented hers. Lucy did so like to have her backside reddened. Maybe if she'd enjoyed it a little less he'd have had less trouble controlling her.

'What is it?' Emma tugged upon his sleeve.

He faced her, surprised by the contact. His own horror was duplicated in her expression. Her eyes were open wide, the sheen of tears glazing their surface, while her lips were drawn into a tight grimace.

'You have to get indoors. We can't be seen.'

He wanted to explain, but it was more important to ensure that Lucy didn't spot them. It was imperative that his wife had no opportunity to make a connection between them. He'd have to find a way to silence Hill's chit. Her babbling could prove particularly damning now. What a vile mess. In trying to protect himself, he'd played into Lucy's hands. Her jealousy knew no bounds. The merest hint that he held Emma in any regard and Lucy would use a full-on broadside to destroy her. He had to protect Emma from that, regardless of what it cost him. He would not make her the subject of Lucy's vile tattle.

'Go into the house.' He opened the French door into the study.

'Aren't you coming?' Emma asked when he made to fasten the casement behind her.

'I can't. We mustn't be seen together. Do whatever it

takes, but silence your sister. Find Lyle, too. Tell him that my wife is here.'

She seemed determined to speak, so he pulled the door to. Whatever questions she had would have to wait until Lucy had been dealt with.

* * *

Darleston hung back. He allowed the new arrivals to settle in the parlour before he sauntered in behind Mr Hill. Littleton, sporting newly grown side-whiskers, sprawled across the love seat in his customary corduroy tail coat. Meanwhile, Oxbury, clean-shaven and bewigged, stood by the fireside with Lucy next to him. She had her back to the door, for she was stooping to warm her hands. Why in heaven's name could he not be rid of her? What was it that she found so marvellous about their marriage that made her cling to the remnants of it? They had never been compatible. Surely she realised that the differences the last few months had wrought were irrevocable.

She lifted her head and met his gaze in the huge gilt mirror that sat above the mantel. Malicious delight scored deeper creases into the lines of paint she used to disguise her complexion. Beneath the layers of porcelain white and her rouge blush her skin had always been rather sallow. The patches she wore covered pockmarks left behind from her childhood. She turned an exquisite pirouette to face him, and then stepped forward in greeting with her arms extended.

'Husband.'

If she thought to trick him into an embrace, she'd seriously miscalculated. The possibility of causing embarrassment or offending some other party no longer swayed him at all.

From the mild animosity they'd borne from the moment of marriage they had moved to outright loathing.

'Why are you here?' he asked, folding his arms across his chest.

Lucy stilled immediately and pressed one gloved hand to her mouth as if in shock. 'Such a delightful greeting. How foolish of me to presume you'd pay me at least passing respect. You always did have the most appalling manners.'

'Your behaviour doesn't warrant my respect. Look to correcting that before you find fault with my manners.'

She maintained a look of hurt, despite a calculating glint in her eyes. 'How curious. I was under the impression that it was you, not I, who fled London under a cloud of scandal. You're the one who has blackened the family honour and caused us such disgrace.'

Sometimes the audacity of the woman astonished him. He knew plain and simple that she had been responsible for all the enlightening newspaper epithets. Having made her speech she turned her head, glancing sideways at the others present. Interestingly, neither Littleton nor Oxbury offered any support or defence, while Mr Hill merely eyed her sceptically, as if he were not entirely sure what to do with her, and thought it might be best if he simply washed his hands of the problem. In fact he did just that, ringing for a servant and suggesting that the gentlemen might adjourn to the library for refreshments, leaving Darleston behind to speak with his lady.

The moment the parlour door closed, leaving them the sole occupants, Lucy flounced over to the love seat and settled in the spot Littleton had so recently warmed.

'Why have you come here?' Darleston demanded.

Lucy peeled off her gloves and tapped the seat with them.

'Come sit. Honestly, Robert, don't be such a bore. If you will insist on gallivanting about the countryside without leaving a forwarding address, how else do you expect me to contact you?'

He ignored the instruction to sit. 'You have no cause to contact me. We're done. A fact you're perfectly aware of.'

'We've had a few misunderstandings, that's all. Now sit down. Be a good little lord. We've matters to discuss.'

Darleston instead wandered over to the window. It pained him to turn his back upon her – she was certainly capable of making a fatal attack – but he refused to bow to her wishes. Why couldn't she have stayed away, contented herself with her flock of admirers and debauchers and left him to the wonder of sharing Lyle and Emma's love?

After a few moments of letting her stew, he turned to face her once more. 'I say again, what do you want, Lucy? I've no interest in any sort of reconciliation. Your actions are neither forgiven nor forgotten.'

Now that they were alone, her smile drooped. She clasped her hands tight upon her lap, opened her mouth but for several seconds failed to speak. Darleston waited. Surely she hadn't really imagined that all would suddenly be right between them, simply because they'd spent a few months apart.

'I thought you ought to know that I'm pregnant.'

For several unsteady moments he stared at her tightly corseted form in bewildered silence. There was no obvious thickening of her waist yet, but he knew enough to be aware that not all women showed so early. Besides, elegance mattered far more to Lucy than the welfare of any babe she carried. He doubted she'd abandon her tight lacing no matter how swollen she became around the middle.

213

'Well?' she prompted.

'No,' he said. Not refuting her claim, only the claim upon his person. 'You can't honestly expect me to believe it is mine.'

'I need money to set up a household.'

That was confirmation enough to quell any lingering doubts. She couldn't even be bothered to argue the point. 'Then you had best go and petition the father for funds.'

'I'm your wife.'

He nodded. 'Only through dire misfortune. That in itself changes nothing. I won't acknowledge your bastard as mine. I won't see a child of yours inherit.' Clearly the fact that he'd tolerated her indiscretions with his brother had given her the impression that he'd accept whatever base-born child she cared to give him. 'My resolve is quite unshakable in that regard. I suggest you take yourself abroad to the Continent for a while if you wish to avoid scandal.'

'If I wish to avoid it. What do you think they will say about you, if you refuse to acknowledge the child as your own?'

Quite startlingly he found his humour. 'To be honest, I don't actually care. It won't be anything that hasn't already been said about me and plenty of others before. Now, see if you can find it within yourself to vacate the premises and stop embarrassing the good people who live here.'

'What if I told you that the father is Ned?'

'Then I would know you were lying. He's seen no more of you than I and is equally disgusted by your actions. Who is the father?' He stood before her so that his shadow loomed across her seated form. 'Do you actually have any inkling?'

Lucy's lips became tightly pursed. She stood abruptly, so that they were breast to breast, a mere inch apart. 'Of course I do.' She jabbed him hard in the stomach. 'It's you.' He knew then that she'd never say otherwise, whatever the truth.

* * *

Find her sister. Find Lyle. Emma couldn't find anyone while she remained stuck in her father's study. Grafton and an army of servants occupied the hall and front steps, busy organising the delivery of luggage to relevant quarters. She didn't want to intrude or become embroiled in a discussion of where the new arrivals ought to be housed. Additionally, after Darleston's warning to avoid his person, she dared not take that particular route, for fear that her father might spy her and call upon her to greet the new guests.

Could she bob Lady Darleston a curtsy and then look her in the eyes and not give away the fact that she had been intimate with her husband? How had she come to dismiss his wife so easily in the first place? Darleston had seemed so apart from her, she supposed, as if there was no connection between them. She'd only worried over what Lyle would think of her stealing his lover, not about this shadowy spectre that rumour suggested was responsible for the scandalous slights to Darleston's reputation.

The fact that she had seen him disporting with Lyle did not prove that he'd engaged in such practices in London. Well, it was nice to turn a blind eye to such thoughts, even though he'd spelled out to her that he'd never been a saint. Still ruminating the problem, Emma returned to the window casement and stepped back out onto the lawn. She turned away from the front of the house and strode around the protruding east wing to the kitchen yard.

Waddling geese and a few ducks frolicked on the edge of a vast puddle that covered two thirds of the cobblestone yard. A line of rags hung over it, steadily being bleached by the sun.

Now, where would she find Lyle at this hour? Presumably

he'd led the party of guests out somewhere so that her father was free to greet the new arrivals. That meant she'd most likely find both Lyle and Amelia over at the training grounds. A weary sigh wound its way free of her throat. Everything had seemed so wonderful a few moments ago; now her nerves were in shreds and she would have to brave the old barn and the possibility of Lyle's wrath.

'What is it? What's happened?' Lyle rushed straight to her the moment she set foot inside the old barn. He knew how much she hated coming here, if not the intimate details of why. Emma deliberately kept her head turned away from the sounds of fighting, but somehow that made things worse. She'd turned away in the past too, and turned Bea's head as well in order to hide the worst of life from her. That dirty flea-ridden pit where her father had held the first fight had been no place for his offspring, and, although this current training room was rather more salubrious, she still balked at seeing Amelia squeezed in alongside the gentlemen.

'The new guests have arrived,' she said tersely, aware that those gentlemen were all looking at her. Lyle waved their attention back to the fight and guided her through to the little antechamber that had once housed tack and saddles. Even ten years on, the cobblestone room still retained a lingering smell of saddle soap. He huddled close to her without touching.

'What –?' Lyle asked, not bothering to complete the question.

'Darleston's wife is here. He said I should tell you, and that we're to keep our distance. He begged that we keep Amelia from making insinuations too.'

Lyle's nostrils flared a little. At once his shoulders rose. He paced, one fist pressed to his lips. 'What does she want? Do you know?'

Emma shook her head. 'I haven't even seen her.' She wished Darleston had allowed her that much, but he'd pushed her inside before she'd glimpsed more than the back end of the landau. Would Lady Darleston live up to her husband's exquisite taste and flair for fashion? She couldn't imagine her to be a sorry little dower mouse.

Lyle uncurled his fingers and began gnawing his thumbnail. 'We'd better do as he says and stay here. We don't want to provide that storm crow with any more ammunition against him.'

'What about Amelia?'

Lyle gave a snort followed by a woeful shake of his head. 'I suppose Darleston told you what she said.'

What she'd said? She'd already mentioned something beyond the exchange they'd had in the upstairs corridor.

'No. I only know that she made certain assumptions after she spied me coming from Darleston's room this morning. She threatened to say something to Father, but I'm not sure she will. She knows it would backfire and result in her removal to Aunt Maude's house, which is the last thing she wants.'

'Ah!' Lyle's response failed to inspire confidence. 'Then perhaps we might quell her with a few leniencies.'

Emma shrugged. 'It's possible, I suppose, but I'd still be wary of trusting her. She's been ghastly the last few days. I'm not sure the gentlemen are paying her as much regard as she'd like.'

A brief smile quickened upon Lyle's lips. 'Actually, I think one gentleman in particular isn't paying her as much regard as she'd like.'

When Emma opened her mouth to enquire who, Lyle merely brushed the issue aside. 'I'm not even sure that saying any more to her than I already have will do any good. Matter of fact, it might simply draw further attention to the subject. Mayhap we should just let things play out.'

'Who is it, Lyle? You know Father won't allow her to marry Bathhouse.'

'Not him. She's simply teasing him. I think her genuine affection lies elsewhere and has been brewing for rather longer.'

'Who?'

Lyle shot a glance over his shoulder.

'Harry?' Emma hissed in surprise. 'Goodness. I'm not sure that's any better.'

'Your father trusts him.'

'As his secretary.'

'It could work. I don't want to inherit this – do you?'

No. No, she didn't want Field House or her father's stable of prize-fighters. She'd gladly never expose herself to either again. 'So he's why she's been coming here?'

Lyle gave her a discreet nod. 'I don't think you need to fret over it. Harry's not given to risk-taking. He's learned his lesson on that score. I've promised him that I'll sound your father out over the idea of a match once the fight's done with. That might win us a little favour with Amelia. We just have to survive another twenty-four hours or so.'

'You're buying her silence.'

'Not just that, Emma. I genuinely believe she and Harry will make one another happy.'

Emma wasn't as convinced, but they left it at that. She spent the remainder of the day idling in the amphitheatre. She couldn't linger within the barn and listen to the sounds of the men belting nine shades of hell out of one another, especially as the ghostly voices of her siblings seemed to rise with those of the gentlemen. Nor could she avoid casting concerned glances at Amelia and Harry Quernow. Were they in love? Could it work? Would her father approve?

The questions troubled her even in the tranquillity of the amphitheatre, but at least she was free to entertain her concerns without being spied on.

Come evening, when the aphids droned in swarms beneath the trees and the scent of mulchy earth permeated the still air, Emma finally returned to the house. Grafton stood in the hallway when she entered. 'I'm so pleased you're returned, Mrs Langley. I wondered if you could peruse the seating arrangement for dinner? Since there are additional guests I've had to switch things around a little from how you've been sitting.'

Emma gave the butler an appreciative smile. He always took extra care of such matters as sitting precedence. 'I'm sure whatever you've decided will be perfect, Grafton.' The man had more experience of society dinners than she did. Lyle had offered for her before she'd ever begun a season.

Emma realised her mistake after she took her place at the dining table and found she'd been placed between Darleston and Mr Phelps, with Lady Darleston diagonally opposite. That lady was a rather intriguing antithesis of what she'd presumed her to be. She'd expected aloofness, dissatisfaction, rather than the winsome, smiling and complimentary woman whose gaze often locked with hers. Try as she might, she couldn't discern the harpy Darleston made her out to be. Then again, perhaps that was because he was entirely absent. His chair beside her remained empty throughout the entirety of the meal. She exchanged significant looks with Lyle across the table, but there was no opportunity to enquire about Darleston's absence. Her father, who sat closer, offered no enlightenment on the subject either, and she did not wish to interrupt his conversation with Mr Oxbury to draw attention to the matter.

'Good gracious, what are those?' Mr Littleton prodded a fork into a carefully arranged pyramid of peas slathered with butter. 'Are they some manner of pickle?'

'Peas,' Amelia supplied brightly. 'We grow them in the garden.'

Horror transformed his rather rubbery features into a mass of folds and turned his complexion an unflattering shade of puce. 'You mean they come out of the ground, all covered in dirt?'

'No,' Amelia replied, clearly uncertain if she was being made the foil for some sort of joke. 'They grow in pods that dangle down from the plant. Aren't they fashionable in London?' Trust Amelia to think along those lines. Suddenly the ins and outs of the *demi monde* were of utmost importance and to the devil with common sense.

'Oh, I never eat anything that's come out of the ground save the occasional onion soup,' Littleton enlightened her. 'Really, you're much safer sticking to a good diet of meat, with a little fish for variety, and I do like to steer clear of too much piecrust.'

'Really?' Amelia sought the opinion of the rest of the diners, but no one was forthcoming. Codswallop, Emma longed to bark, but good manners prevented it. Naturally, Amelia declined the peas and the small mountain of glazed cauliflower that was normally her favourite, in favour of griddled kidneys and a rather large portion of fish.

For her own part, salmon, pheasant and potted endives had never taken so long to consume. By the time Mrs Beattie's desserts were added to the table Emma was ready to solemnly swear that nothing but bread and ale should pass her lips again. Lady Darleston, she noted, barely touched a morsel, despite the eloquent praise she heaped upon dear Beattie.

The small talk of current affairs and Jack's chances of victory on the morrow droned on around her, until it became no more than a background irritation. Why hadn't anyone commented upon Darleston's absence? Had he gone? Her stomach cramped at the possibility, almost relieving her of the food she'd swallowed. What if that were true? Would she ever see him again? Would she ever know pleasure again? She stared at the cushioned seat of his empty chair, tears welling in her eyes and distorting her vision, and felt acutely sick.

Darleston made everything different. She didn't want to touch anyone else. The thought of any of the fools seated around the table reaching out to stroke so much as the back of her arm sent shivers coursing through her body, until she scratched at her skin, leaving marks like tiger stripes behind.

He wouldn't leave without saying goodbye. She refused to believe that of him.

'Are you well?' enquired Lady Darleston.

Emma stared at her bloodied forearms and flushed with embarrassment. 'I went walking earlier. I'm afraid I've been rather badly nettled. If you'll all excuse me, I think I'd better find some ointment to put on them.'

Nettled – she'd have to have rolled in the things for the stings to be so bad. What a fool they must all think her. Emma sat at her dressing table and slathered cold cream onto the scratches. It wasn't very long before Lyle found her there.

'What the devil are you doing still up here? You have to come down again. Heavens knows what Amelia has already said in your absence.'

She'd quite overlooked the fact that she'd be forced to entertain Lady Darleston while the gentlemen were at their

221

port and cigars. 'I can't, Lyle. How can I exchange pleasantries with the woman when I've intimate knowledge of her husband? I'm not that good a liar.'

'Why is it different from any other time? You've poured tea for countless of my lovers' wives, sometimes for their daughters too.'

Emma glowered at him. 'Do you think I enjoyed being made complicit in your infidelities? I hated it. I hated that you were always sneaking away. I kept waiting for the time when someone would expose you.'

'I'm not asking you to become bosom friends with the woman, just to act normally.'

'I can't, Lyle. This time it's different. It's not just about your actions. I've wronged her. God help me, I didn't mean to. I didn't think of her at all.'

Lyle crouched by the side of her stool. She suspected that had she been any one else he would have shaken her. 'What – what do you think you've done? For heaven's sake, so what if you've observed us fuck? It's not as if you could have done anything to prevent it. Emma, do you want give your sister free rein to share her sordid assumptions? You must go down.'

In her guts she suspected it was already too late. 'They're not assumptions.' She hid her head in her hands, and only peeped through her fingers when he didn't reply. He'd left her side and wandered over to the window. She watched him tweak the curtains and look out onto the grounds. Maybe he sought a sign of Darleston's whereabouts.

'Lyle?' She rose and pattered towards him.

'What do you want me to say, Emma? Am I supposed to give you my blessing? You shy if I so much as reach out to you.' He did just that, forcing her into a retreat. 'Yet you

222

happily slip into my lover's arms. I know I've had a hand in arranging it, but it still smarts to hear it.'

'I didn't mean it to happen.' That wasn't entirely true. She'd longed for Darleston's embrace, even if she hadn't anticipated ever consenting to it. 'I only meant to kiss him. I wanted to know how it would feel. Please don't be vexed with me. He's the only one … the only man, the only person even, that I've ever wanted to reach out for. I told myself I would never let myself care in that way for anyone again. I'm sorry I don't feel that way about you.'

'I'm not.'

Mouth agape, she stared at him.

'What I mean is that it would have been frightfully awkward. I can't satisfy you. What I'm saying is that I'm not interested in you like that. I know Robert is. It's probably a good thing. It'll keep us safe. At least it would if it wasn't for his wife. I don't think he expected to see her here. There's nothing but bitterness and resentment left between them.'

'You'll let me share him?'

Lyle shoved his hand into his hair, making a mess of his queue. 'I'll try.'

Emma knew that the pact would have been cemented better with a cuddle, but she still couldn't bring herself to engage with Lyle in that way.

'Why is she here? Is he certain that she's responsible for all those nasty letters to the newspapers? She seems pleasant enough.'

'Appearances are often deceptive.'

Yes, they were. Hadn't she learned that, only that morning, when she'd unwittingly thrown herself at the wrong man?

Lyle's brow rumpled. 'What is it that's so amusing? I can't see anything to laugh about.'

'Only that I kissed the wrong man this morning. I meant to kiss Darleston, but I didn't. I kissed his brother instead.'

'Love really is making you blind if you mistook one for the other.'

'They're identical,' she protested, contemplating Neddy's features with her mind's eye. 'And I was harried.'

'Looks are all they have in common. It's miraculous that you didn't receive far more than you bargained for. Darleston may be known for his perversity, but it's Neddy that the society mamas warn their daughters about. He's purportedly seduced half of London.'

'More rumours. Hearsay. Besides, he didn't do anything ungentlemanly.' Unlike Darleston, who had been delightfully crude and wicked. If she closed her eyes tight and squeezed her thighs together, she could almost recapture the feel of him swiving her. 'Where do you suppose he is?'

Lyle shook his head. 'If you ever let me escape this room then I'll consider going looking for him. My absence will hardly be commented on since it's so routine.'

'You've an inkling?'

'Not really. I thought to wander over to the cottage to see if he's with Ned.'

'You don't think he's left, do you?'

Lyle shook his head, although the action lacked decisiveness. The way he then wrung his hands as he waited for her to return to their guests ahead of him also magnified her twitchiness. Emma didn't presume to know her husband, not really. The last few days had taught her how little they had ever discussed. She knew virtually nothing about his childhood. Had no idea why the love between the two men had petered out in the past, only to be rekindled so brightly on reacquaintance. None of it made sense. 'Where do you know him from?' she asked, lingering at the top of the stairs. She didn't really want to go down to sit between Lady Darleston and Amelia.

'We lived within a half-hour walk of one another as children. I often spent time with both Robert and Neddy.'

'So you were just boys when you knew him before?'

'Men,' Lyle corrected. 'Don't make the mistake of thinking we didn't know what we were doing. It wasn't some childish game we shared. We were old enough to be considered adults. Nor did we drift apart, Emma. Our families intervened.'

The sharp hurt that filled his eyes made her spontaneously reach out. There were scars rent across her husband's soul, perhaps as wide as those across her own. She'd just never known it.

'I never stopped loving him, though there were plenty of nights stuck in that hellhole that was India when I truly believed he'd abandoned me for ever.'

'He's not gone. He hasn't abandoned us,' she said, unsure if she believed the words herself.

Lyle gave one slow blink and then straightened his shoulders. 'Of course not. Lady Darleston wouldn't still be here if he'd fled. Whatever she wants, she must want it badly to have pursued him thus far. I don't think she'd sit down to dine and calmly let him slip away. He's with Neddy, I'm sure of it. They always pull together in times of crisis.'

CHAPTER SIXTEEN

The crumbled remains of pork pies and apple cores lay between them on the upturned base of an old beer barrel. Darleston hung his arms over one of the low supporting beams that crisscrossed the interior of the barn. Only in the very centre, where the boxing ring was marked out with hay bales, was there any real space. They had three lanterns lit, barely enough to eliminate the shadows from a four-foot circle. The wax from the cheap candles lent a sour note to air already perfumed with straw and body odour.

Neddy worked diligently, stuffing straw into hessian sacks that he'd then hang from the rafters as punching bags. A row of similar fake torsos already swayed upon meat-hooks.

'What do I do?' Darleston asked his brother. They'd already been over the point a half-dozen times. 'I'm not even sure whether to believe she's increasing.'

Neddy looked up from his work. Bits of straw clung to his red hair and dust coated the front of his waistcoat. 'I don't think it's something she'd make up. Besides, a lie would be obvious enough within a few months. You may as well accept it as fact. What you need to prove is that you're not the father.'

'Prove it!' Darleston slammed a fist into one of the hanging bags, which left his knuckles stinging.

'That one is grain. That's why it smarts. It toughens the knuckles. Further along is gravel.' Neddy took hold of Darleston's hand and inspected the scuffed and reddened skin for damage. It was a minor bruise, nothing that wouldn't fade in a minute or two.

'Ned, we've had no contact since February. What's there to prove? She's clearly not four months gone.'

'I hear you.' Neddy released his hand and resumed his packing. 'So find out who she has entertained. We both know there are a few obvious candidates. One of the pair she arrived with would be my first bet.'

Darleston continued to massage his knuckles, which just seemed to aggravate the throb. 'Mine too, but there's no way to prove it, not when she's prepared to swear otherwise until she's blue in the face.'

'Now you're being ridiculous.' Neddy cast the three-quarters-filled sack to one side and came to lean upon the barrel. He glumly prodded at one of the browning apple cores. 'I know this has taken you by surprise and you're worried that she'll learn about your current indiscretions, but you're not so naïve that you can't handle a matter such as this. We all know servants talk. Especially –' he widened his eyes for emphasis '– when you wave blunt in their faces. Speak to her maid. Find out where Lucy's been staying and who's courted her. Provide incentive enough and she'll give you the precise date of her mistress's last menses and who was in her bed a fortnight after.'

Ever practical, that was his brother. Always ready with a plan of action, even if he did normally go off at half-cock. 'Ah, you're right. I do know it. I know her maid too, if it's still the same one. It's just ...' He shook his head. There were spectres he didn't want to raise. Any sort of conflict with Lucy would rapidly turn into a full-on war. He knew what she was capable of. He'd been on the receiving end these last few months. 'I'm just wary of her dragging Lyle and Emma into this.' Lucy would delight in destroying them.

'Rob, you embroiled them in this the moment you started dallying with them. I have to say, though, I'm impressed.' He jabbed his knuckles into Darleston's shoulder in a friendly punch. 'Husband and wife – that has to be a first even for you, especially given Emma's reputation. You'll have to tell me how you did it.'

'Don't be perverse, and keep your voice down, Ned. I don't mean it to be some passing fling, and someone might overhear you.' No, he'd been building plans for the future, far-fetched, idealistic dreams, but wonderful nonetheless. Why shouldn't they all settle down together and be happy? Really only Lucy stood in the way of that. Yes, Emma was still taciturn and nervous, but he knew that given time and plenty of gentle coaxing she'd truly open up to him, perhaps even to Lyle too. He wanted that, wanted it so badly that it caused an ache in his guts that threatened to bend him double. After Giles had tied the knot, giving him to know that there was no chance for them – he'd been kidding himself for years that there ever had been – he hadn't thought he'd feel so strongly about anyone again. He'd wanted love, but he'd feared it in equal measure. He and Emma were alike in that regard.

He'd taken a chance on Lyle, because he owed him. Plus, the sparks that burned brightly in their youth still remained. Now rekindled, they burned brighter still. As for Emma – she'd intrigued him from the outset. He didn't understand how she'd come to be the way she was. Rather he knew that he loved and admired her as herself. Whether her touch was tentative or bold, he wanted her. If he had to spend the rest of his days tied to a bed, spread out for her in a way that ensured he didn't return her touch, then he'd do it. Even if, by God, he'd prefer that their lovemaking be more robust.

'Rob, you do realise that Lucy won't care one whit about your relationship with Lyle? She's never been bothered in that regard. It's mere ammunition for her cause. Emma will be another matter altogether. If she garners so much as a whiff of evidence against her, she'll make the woman's life living hell. We both know how she's acted in the past. How many of your past lovers has she scarred?'

The reminder did nothing to ease his stomach cramps. If anything the pain simply spread up toward his head. Lucy was irrational and frighteningly possessive, even of his friends and their relationships with other women. She insisted on being the centre of attention. She'd never been concerned about his meddling with other men, but if she so much as caught him eyeing up a pretty girl, then she'd see the woman ruined.

'I know it, but I can't seal the mouths of everyone around me. Lord knows, we've been discreet. At least I thought we had, until her sister started bleating.'

'Amelia suspects?' Neddy's surprise doubled his doubts over the care they'd taken to avoid discovery. Then again, he hadn't precisely hidden his interest in Emma. That had been part of the initial plan of courting her after all, to draw attention away from him and Lyle. This all made it sound horribly premeditated, which in no way reflected his actual feelings for her. The fact was he'd fallen hard and fast, and he didn't want to give her up, not for a single minute. However, he couldn't allow Lucy to hurt her.

'How so?' Neddy asked. 'She's been here the last few

days, crowing over the fighters and generally getting in the way, when she wasn't busy playing Bathhouse and Quernow off against one another. I'm surprised she's had time to pay you any regard.'

'I don't think she has paid me any regard, but she seems to feel slighted by her sister and is evidently looking to retaliate.'

'Then you'd best prepare yourself for the worst.'

'Hm!' Darleston turned his back to the barrel and crossed his arms across his chest. He'd relished life the last few days more than he'd done for years. He supposed it was too much to hope that such merry times would last.

Neddy circled around to face him. In the dim light, with his normal easy-going smile replaced by a frown, it truly felt like looking into a mirror. Even the pain he saw reflected in the black of his pupils was the same. The only difference lay in the source of that pain. He knew his own. He'd never enquired too deeply into his brother's.

Neddy reached out and squeezed his shoulder. 'At least you're not entertaining thoughts of running.'

'What would be the point?' He shrugged off the hold. 'Credit me with a little more bottom than to leave them to face her mercy alone.'

'I wasn't suggesting you would.' Clearly hurt by the rebuke, Neddy stuffed his hands into his coat pockets. 'I only wish you'd shown such fortitude in the past, so that a life of heartache might have been avoided. You really ought to have refused her hand.'

The topic had come up so often he saw little point in retreading it. Yet he still found himself defending himself. 'I don't recall being given a choice.'

'Oh, come on. What was dear mama going to do to you? She wasn't about to let her eldest son starve to death by cutting you off. It would have been an idle threat anyway. The title will be yours. The estates and all the coin are entailed down to the last bloody farthing. She wasn't going to expose you and risk forfeiting that to the crown.'

Grumbling annoyance at the accusation brought pain to Darleston's chest that he tried to relieve by coughing. It didn't work, just making him sound consumptive. At least he wasn't bringing up blood. 'Perhaps not, but I had no real concept of what I was getting myself into. I'd met Lucy twice and had barely spoken to her. There was nothing to indicate she'd be such a venomous harpy.'

Neddy gave a nod. He turned away and began lifting the filled sacks onto empty hooks. 'Speak to the maid. Don't let her ruin you. You know my opinion on your preferences, but if you can make this arrangement of yours work, then all well and good.' He frowned. 'Well, mostly well and good. You realise this way you're saddling me with the burden of continuing the legitimate line.'

'Only if I ensure that Lucy doesn't get her way. I suppose I ought to get to it.'

'And I ought to rest. I've a fight to oversee tomorrow. I best check Harry's seen Jack off to bed too.'

Darleston lingered outside the barn after he and Neddy said goodnight. Bright stars filled the heaven. Across the fields, lights gleamed in the windows of Field House. He'd go up to the maid's room once everyone had settled for the night. That wouldn't be for another hour or two. Meanwhile, he was torn between seeking out Lyle and Emma to reassure them, and wariness over drawing any attention whatsoever. He lit a cigar and watched the smoke curl away. A baby – God pity the poor mite in having Lucy for a mother. He'd never met a more self-centred woman. He prayed one didn't exist.

Ten minutes later he spied a figure heading towards him. Darleston stubbed out his cigar and strode to meet his lover. Even from two field-lengths away he recognised Lyle's striding gait. Closer to, his coat and blond curls provided further identification. They met where the stile crossed the bramble-entwined hedgerow. A tiny brook babbled over a rocky bed nearby, filling the twilight with a gentle music.

'Rob?' Lyle's shadow extended halfway across the field. 'You are still here. I feared ...' He heaved a sigh of relief. 'I ... We weren't certain what you'd do.'

The way Lyle's broad shoulders were hitched with tension spoke volumes about how precarious their relationship was. He thought they'd built a relationship upon trust, but now he wasn't so sure that trust was mutual. Lyle might have forgiven him for what had happened years ago, but he remained wary over the present.

'Did you really believe I'd go, without a word?'

'Of course not.' The tick in Lyle's jaw said otherwise. 'Emma's worried. That's why I came out to look for you. She's fretting.'

Naturally, what woman wouldn't? Somehow they all expected the worst of men, particularly one with whom they'd been intimate. He rubbed his brow, irritated to think that she'd even considered him so despicable as to run away now that he'd worn down her defences enough to indulge in pleasure. *Damn!* He wasn't so jaded that he had to resort to such measures to whet his palate. He hadn't gone to her offering reassurances because he was trying to protect her – Lyle too, for that matter.

'Lucy remains?' he asked.

Lyle gave a meagre nod. 'She's frightfully charming.'

Dear God, his wife was anything but that, but she certainly knew how to act.

'What happened this morning, Rob? I don't mean with your wife. I mean with mine. Emma said ...' Lyle choked back the rest of the phrase as if he couldn't bear to utter it. Doubts swam in the depths of his dark eyes, and he appeared momentarily gaunt. 'I mean, how far did it go?'

Darleston held his tongue. He ought to have anticipated this moment. Not Lucy's arrival and the trouble she caused, but Lyle's reaction to the growing intimacy between him and Emma.

Jealousy, doubt – they were always difficult emotions to weather.

He reached out and curled his fingers around Lyle's shoulder. 'How detailed would you like me to be?'

Lyle placed his hand over the top of Darleston's and removed it from his shoulder. He held on to it, though, turned their palms and laced their fingers together. 'I don't need to know any details. I just wanted to be certain of what has passed. Emma wasn't particularly explicit, and she's not exactly experienced.'

'She's no longer a virgin,' Darleston offered as clarification.

Damn, this ought to have been a pleasant moment, not a cause of this tension between them. Lyle ought to have been there when in happened. Instead, he seemed entranced by something on the grass and refused to hold Darleston's gaze.

Darleston squeezed his hand. 'It doesn't change anything between us.'

'Are you sure about that?'

'Yes – I'm sure. Lord damn it, Lyle!' He shook off Lyle's hold and grasped him around the waist instead. Fist tightened around the fabric of Lyle's coat, he tugged him forward, meaning to embrace him, show him what he felt through the fever of his kiss. But, instead of sailing into his arms, Lyle stumbled. His shoulder hit Darleston square in the chest, winding him. His knees buckled under the unexpected weight and they both dropped like stones.

In dazed silence, Darleston stared at the dim stars. Cold seeped out of the earth beneath him. It penetrated his clothing, setting a chill in his bones. Overhead the purple haze of twilight had now melted into the black of night.

Lyle's shadowy form reared over him, blocking out the light of the waning crescent moon. 'I don't know how I feel about it, Rob. It makes me uncomfortable. She's my wife. I don't desire her in that sense, but it feels damned wrong condoning what she's doing with you.'

'Doesn't she deserve the same freedoms as you?'

The wag of Lyle's head was wholly indecisive. 'I want her to be happy, but –' he caught the edge of his lip between his teeth '– I just wish it wasn't you she'd fixated upon.'

'It's what we wanted, Lyle. It's what we planned.'

'It's what *you* planned. I know I agreed, but agreeing to it and experiencing it are two very different things. I'm torn. I'm –'

'– frightened,' Darleston supplied. It was easy to forget that Lyle's experience of relationships amounted to a platonic, touch-free arrangement with his wife and spur-of-the-moment encounters with men who sought swift satisfaction and nothing else. This was his one experience of anything deeper; hardly surprising he was terrified of losing it.

'You're worried that I'll love her more than you. That you'll get left out. It won't happen, Lyle.' He wanted them both equally. More than that, he needed them. 'Lyle …'

They stared at one another, locked in wordless conversation.

Somehow that made it easier than actually spitting out all the things that needed to be said.

Lyle touched Darleston's face, brushing aside the red strands of his hair. Darleston's lips tingled as Lyle's caress became a slow sweep of his thumbs around his open lips. Lyle dipped down and kissed him. The moment their mouths met, heat ripped through him, relaxing everything apart from his cock, which woke with the appetite of a hungry wolf.

Only one thing was going to appease it and, thank God, Lyle seemed set upon delivering it.

Darleston squirmed, the tight front of his breeches making for an unwelcome pressure on his erection. He needed freedom to breathe and a firm five-fingered grip around him. Only suddenly Lyle didn't seem to be in any hurry to oblige. His touch was tender, exploring rather than demanding. The same remained true of his kiss. Their tongues danced, but in slow tremulous circles rather than a lively gavotte. Yet Lyle had to be aware of the reaction he'd triggered. Their hips were stacked one above the other so that their loins were pressed tight together.

Friction. He needed friction. Only one thing was going to satisfy him. He lifted his hips. Lyle met him, roll for roll.

'Will you do to me what you did to Emma?' Lyle breathed the husky whisper straight into his ear. It was far more than a request, rather a plea dredged up out of Lyle's gullet and spoken through clenched teeth. The notion that he'd somehow missed out and been replaced dangled like a lodestone around his neck. His kiss took on a note of aggression, became far more insistent. 'How did you do it? No one ever cracks her core.'

Darleston tasted his kisses and matched his fervour. 'It's not about what I've done. I've simply made it easy for her to take what she already wanted.' He clasped his hands over Lyle's arse and pulled him closer so that their loins were squashed together with no space between. 'You know as well as I that attraction isn't something you can predict or pretend to understand. For some reason she sees something in me that makes her want to break down the barriers she's created. I don't know what that is or why. I'm just grateful for it. Regardless –' he looked Lyle straight in the eyes '– none of that changes how I feel about you.'

Lyle reared up onto his knees and went straight for Darleston's frontfall. 'She can give you things that I can't,' he said, but the statement lacked the power of his earlier assertions.

Darleston knocked Lyle's hands aside and dealt with his own fastenings. 'The reverse is also true.' His thoughts ran to all manner of crudities as he spoke the reassurance. Things he would never ask Emma to do, even if they were physically possible. Some things were best left between men. Some aspects of his psyche he never wanted exposed to a woman. Leastways, not one he actually liked.

Having finally freed his erection, Darleston stared up at Lyle expectantly. His cock jerked, leaving sticky dots behind on his stomach as the night wind blew its cool caresses over its surface. Yet despite the hunger that turned up the edges of Lyle's mouth, Lyle didn't reach out to stroke him.

'What does your wife want?' Lyle asked instead.

'The same things she always wants – money, social clout, dominion over me.' Darleston covered his shaft with his own palm, took up the stroking Lyle had failed to provide. He needed relief. The day had been one long trauma. Tomorrow might well be worse. 'Lyle,' he gave a tormented plea, while his fist took up a faster pace of slip and slide.

Lyle dipped forward a little, but still made only passing contact. He tilted his head to one side. 'If I just sit here are you going to stroke yourself to eruption?'

'Shit!' What in God's name was this torment about?

Lyle released his own breeches, which fell open around his hips. The blunt head of his cock reared beneath his shirt, tenting the cambric. 'What if I just stay here and rub until I spend too? Are we simply being sordid or are we actually together?'

'Deliberately vexatious is what it'd make you.' He didn't trouble himself with thoughts of what it made him. Desperate, most likely.

'Did Emma stroke you? Is the taste of her still on your cock?'

Why the hell did it matter? 'Why don't you lick it and find out?'

Lyle stuck his tongue out, but nevertheless he bent and troubled the slitted eye with the very tip of his tongue. He followed that up by gently sucking the head, which rapidly had Darleston trying to count stars in the heavens just to hold onto some focus. No denying that Lyle had learnt a trick or two since their youth. Darleston's hips bucked involuntarily, driving his cock deeper into the warmth of Lyle's heavenly mouth. Hell! Lyle just swallowed it down too, as if it was effortless. That's why it came as so much of a shock when Lyle abruptly released him. He got right up close to Darleston's face. 'I've got something for you. Think you can lie still and take it?'

'Lying still ain't a great favourite.'

'Yeah – I've heard you're rather good at it.'

'Lyle.' Darleston lifted his arm to push his hand into his lover's thick golden curls, only for Lyle to brush him off. 'A-aah! You don't get to touch.'

'What, you expect me to lie in the open with my cock hanging out and accept whatever it is you've got planned? Why are you doing this?' Couldn't the silly fool see that different was good? He didn't want the same thing from Lyle as he did from Emma. Hell, all the restraint he had to employ when dealing with Emma would likely give him a hernia if it carried on much longer. Yes, they'd done the dreaded deed – and didn't that notion make him smile – but he was under no illusions about that being anything other than the first hurdle in a long, long steeplechase. That, more than anything, was why he didn't need to be duplicating the experience with Lyle.

'I'm doing it,' Lyle laughed, 'because it excites me. Now keep still, Robert. Be good, or else I'll have to tie you up.'

* * *

Tie him up. Tie him up. Lord damn it, if he had some rope he'd have done it. As it was, he just had to make do with ordering Darleston to lie still. If he could manage it for Emma, he could damn well attempt it for him. Although Lyle conceded that he intended to be far more taxing with him than Emma would ever be. Unlike his wife, he had no time for tentative caresses, but then he wasn't expecting to be bitten at any moment, or rather the prospect of being bitten didn't frighten him. Rather, he was excited by the possibility of pushing Robert past his boundaries so that he threw Lyle down and reversed their positions. If he were fastened securely enough, blindfolded perhaps – he wondered if even Emma's touch might be enough to bring him off.

No – he wasn't going to think of her right now. Lyle banished her to the recesses of his brain. He intended this

239

moment to be entirely about the here and now. Situations were changing. There were no certainties about tomorrow, about their future with Emma or the outcome of whatever trouble Lady Darleston intended to cause, but for this moment Darleston belonged entirely to him. He wanted to remember that and he intended to make it a memory worth remembering.

After arranging Robert's hands on either side of his head, and squeezing his wrists tight enough that the sensation of restraints surely lingered, Lyle sat back on his haunches. 'Remember, you're not to move.'

Darleston eyed him cagily, but did as instructed. That is, all of him apart from his cock, which nodded enthusiastically.

Lyle palmed the eager length and started rhythmically stroking. He played particular attention to the underside of the rose-hued helm, which he knew Darleston found particularly sensitive.

As his lover's breathing quickened, his features scrunched into an ever more impressive frown. Judging by the stiffness of his cock, it wasn't from lack of pleasure, rather the war presumably raging in Darleston's head. His stomach muscles rippled and clenched with the strain of holding himself still. His hips dipped, ready to roll with the motion of Lyle's fist, only to abruptly lock still.

'Fuck!' Darleston's explosive gasp punctuated the balmy night air like a thunderclap. 'How long do you expect me to keep this up? I've a wife back at the house intent upon my torture. You don't have to best her in order to win my affections.'

'Your wife's presence never crossed my mind. I know exactly what you think of her. And you'll keep this up until I say otherwise.' Lyle palmed his own cock and worked the pair of them in tandem. He had this all planned out in his head. It's all he'd thought of since Emma's absentminded confession. He knew what came next, and exactly how damn good it would feel.

Lord, he didn't want to share Robert with Emma, but he'd do it. It was for the best of reasons, although knowing that did little to ease his apprehensions.

It'd been easy while Emma's no-touch policy had remained in place, but now that things had progressed way beyond that … Oh, hell, he didn't know. He only knew that he had to prove something to himself with this, but what that was …

He concentrated his focus back upon Darleston's body. Beads of his dew hung like silvery pearls from the tip of his cock. Lyle caught them upon his thumb and swirled them around Darleston's glans. He pushed both their pricks together and worked them as one, until finally, when he knew Darleston was almost ready to throw off his invisible bonds, Lyle turned around so that he perched over Darleston's cock, facing his toes.

Somehow he envisaged this as how Emma had imagined taking his lover, squatting over him and slowly lowering herself down onto his upright prick, probably while he was restrained or, more likely, sleeping. Although he defied any man to sleep through someone toying with his cock. And he didn't mean to think of Emma.

Lyle slowly lowered himself over Darleston's cock. He guided the helm into place against his arse, and then slowly sank down. Slowly – yes! Because Emma would take things slowly until her maidenhead was torn asunder and she was able to take her lover properly to the root.

Slowly, slowly, he took more of Darleston's prick. It whitened his knuckles to keep the pace so slow, but … 'Ah, yes!'

Finally, he hilted. Beneath him, Darleston gave an appreciative jerk, accompanied by a blissful sigh, but he otherwise kept still. He didn't roll his hips. He didn't clasp Lyle's waist and hammer him back home when he lifted.

Slip and slide. Up and down, Darleston's cock filled him.

It stung so much to find he'd tupped Emma.

He'd known all along it would happen, but he'd really expected to be part of it. The anticipation, what the three of them had shared, had led him to expect it to happen while he was present. He'd sit back and watch Darleston swive his wife, after he'd helped to arouse him. He'd look Emma in the eyes as she took his lover into her body, accepting him in a way she'd never accept him or any other man.

'Damn it, Lyle! I can't take much more. Turn around, will you?'

Momentarily ignoring Darleston's plea, Lyle continued to take his pleasure at his own pace. Only when he felt the tremors running through Darleston's tensed limbs did he turn around to face him.

'Come here.' Darleston's silver eyes shone like the moon-light. 'Kiss me. Take whatever it is you need.'

He wasn't really sure what he needed, or what he was trying to achieve, but he could no longer resist the satisfaction to be had from Darleston's kiss. Their lips only just brushed at first, butterfly-light and full of promise. He couldn't bear it to remain like this, so sweet it bordered on chaste. His need was already ramped up too high. Darleston's prick filled his bottom to distraction. He needed more, but was reluctant to relinquish the control he'd usurped.

'Let me move, Lyle. Give me the word and I'll give you what you need. You know I can.'

Maybe.

Darleston's lips were soft and smooth. Heat radiated from his body, taunted him with the promise of further warmth if only he'd give in. He held off though, maintained a ribbon of resistance, until his whole body throbbed from the strain. With a sigh of surrender he parted his lips to accept the press of Darleston's tongue, which only proved how little the light mussing of their lips they'd previously shared resembled a true kiss. This explosive show of passion was a far bolder demonstration of their love. Kissing Darleston, he was lost in the tangling of tongues and the ache of his need, which in turn drove the rise and fall of his hips.

Eventually he had to break away in order to catch his breath. Darleston's mouth remained open, slack from their shared kisses. Lyle pushed his curled fingers into it, then changed his mind and fed him his thumb to suck instead. The quick pulls against his flesh felt like a direct assault on his cock.

He couldn't do this any longer. He needed more. 'Move,' he ordered Darleston.

'Thank God!' Darleston's husky tones rumbled up his throat from deep in his chest. Lyle felt the vibration right through his body. It fired up his nerves and set his cock tingling with delight.

Yes! Oh, yes! That was better. Sod the slow, one-sided burn he'd been intent upon. This was infinitely better. 'Hell, Rob! Give it to me.'

Darleston let out a brusque laugh. 'Give it to you. I'll give it to you all right.' He flipped them over, so that Lyle found himself abruptly looking skywards, the cold earth against his back. Only for a moment though, then Darleston loomed over and filled him. Why he'd held off from doing this, he didn't know. The throb of Rob's cock in his arse filled him in a way that caressed him inside and out and drove him wild. Fever gripped him tight. He sobbed against Darleston's shoulder, meeting his thrusts and welcoming the demanding pace. There were no thoughts to distract him, only the buzz of sensation in his brain. All that mattered was togetherness and his trajectory towards the stars.

Darleston hooked Lyle's legs up over his shoulders and changed the angle of his thrusts so that the blunt head of his cock hit a patch of raw nerves inside Lyle's body, which in turn set him panting with shock. That pressure, that touch, was both too intense and impossible to resist.

Inarticulate moans escaped his throat. He basked in the moment. The sensation tore through his body leaving him buzzing all over, while a blazing pulse throbbed inside his bottom. Darleston's cock pierced him like a shaft of light that pushed right though his body and seemed to fill him right to the tip of his own erection.

He was going to come, or have an apoplexy, or quite possibly both.

A burst of light stole his vision, and then darkness surrounded him like a shroud. His seed jetted over his chest, soiling his clothing. Lyle didn't care. Every cell in his body was screaming in ecstasy.

'Rob!' he gasped as the darkness peeled back. It was suddenly all too raw. He couldn't take any more motion, though remnants of his seed continued to ooze from his tip.

Thank the Lord, Darleston seemed to understand. He withdrew and used his own hand to finish off. His climax added to the mess upon Lyle's clothes. Heaven knows what his valet would make of the stains.

Darleston rolled onto his back on the grass beside Lyle. They remained in companionable silence for several minutes, just watching wispy grey clouds drift across the heavens.

'It'll work.' Darleston's soft murmur broke the silence.

'Maybe. I guess we'll find out.' Maybe the gamble would pay off and existing as a threesome would make them stronger, maybe it'd descend into an unholy mess; either way, he knew he was in it for the distance. 'Why is Lucy here? You never really said.'

Darleston sat up, got to his feet and straightened his clothing. 'She's claims she's with child.'

CHAPTER SEVENTEEN

As he climbed the stairs to the servants' quarters, Darleston thought how fortunate it was that the Hills housed their guests' servants apart from their employers, in attic quarters that were also separate from the household servants'. Finding an opportunity to accost Lucy's maid would have been infinitely harder if she'd been sharing her mistress's room, not least because he had no intention of setting foot anywhere near his wife's boudoir. As it was, he had to navigate the winding, slant-ceilinged attic passages with a single paltry candle to light the route.

Despite Lyle's instructions, he found the layout disorientating. In the servants' domain there were no pictures or pieces of furniture to use as landmarks. What was underfoot yielded no help either, since it was all pitted, badly laid floorboards, which groaned so much at each footfall that it seemed pointless to attempt stealth. Right, right, left and then fourth door along on the left, just past a narrow window that looked out over the woodland, or at least it apparently did if you could boost yourself high enough off the floor to see outside. He didn't bother to check. Dear God, he was glad he hadn't been born a servant.

Outside the appropriate door, Darleston took a moment to compose himself. At first, his gentle knock prompted no response. A more solid rap resulted in hurried scurrying about within, and then finally, the door cracked open an inch.

'Milord!' Panic filled Sally's blue eyes and she dropped a hasty curtsy, although she took care to keep the door between them. He doubted it was out of modesty. He'd seen Sally Scott in her nightrail on countless occasions and once or twice naked in his wife's bed.

'I require a word.'

Fear smudged darker streaks through the cornflower-blue of her irises. 'Yes, milord. Of course.' She dug her teeth into her blood-flushed lips, but made no move to allow him within.

'You may send your lover out before I come in.' Darleston folded his arms across his chest. 'I've no mind to be overheard.'

Immediately she stepped back from the door, bobbing up and down in acquiescence. Darleston followed her in. The room, which was under the eaves, had a pitched ceiling that required him to bend uncomfortably in order to avoid knocking his head. It possessed plain whitewashed walls, a simple straw-stuffed mattress on a short iron frame, and a squat cupboard that held a washing bowl and jug. Sally's clothes hung from a hook upon the back of the door. Spartan and unappealing, it was exactly what he expected of a maid's room, except the pair of man's trews poking out from beneath the coverlet.

'Leave,' he repeated.

Sally turned to the bed. 'You heard him. Time to go.'

Darleston averted his gaze as a squat, sturdy male emerged from beneath the bed frame with the tails of his shirt tucked around his privates as if to disguise their obviously aroused state. 'I won't keep her long,' Darleston remarked as the man hastily pulled on his breeches. 'Not that you should be in here. What's your name?' He waited for the man to provide it, which, having been indoctrinated through years of household service, he naturally did.

'Cobbs, milord.'

'Aye, well, Cobbs, you won't remark upon my presence and I won't speak of yours. You're Mr Aiken's man, correct?'

'I am, milord. You won't hear a peep out of me. Ain't none of my business what the quality do of a night.'

'Very true. You may leave.'

Cobbs gave a sharp nod and scuttled out of the door. Darleston toed it shut behind him. The moment he turned back to Sally, she flicked open the ribbon fastening of her nightrail and swooned onto the lumpy bed in a pose of virginal surrender. Darleston paused a moment, holding back a burst of laughter. Sally was bonny in a simple earthy way, wide-hipped and big-thighed, softer by far than the bed on which she lay. He had no doubt she could provide a soul with endless pleasure, but he had no more desire to sample her voluptuous curves than he did to fuck his wife. 'That's not what I'm here for.'

She sat up and crossed her arms, clearly disappointed. 'What do you want then, if not pleasure? You cut off mine so that all me bush's a-tingle and you've seen off the means to satisfy it.'

'I said I wouldn't keep you long.'

She grinned, showing off a curiously symmetrical smile. 'Few gentlemen ever do. A quick poke is all they're ever about. They don't think of anybody's pleasure but their own.'

He'd always suspected that she topped up the pittance of a wage she earned primping his wife by bedding the gentlemen of Lucy's acquaintance. 'I want to know what your mistress has been about these last five months.'

In an echo of the flounce Lucy had made earlier when he'd addressed her in the parlour, Sally rose before him, her full lower lip extended into a pout, and tapped two fingers to his chest. 'Why should I tell you? You offer nothing in return. You won't satisfy my whims – assuming you know how to offer a woman carnal pleasure, and one has to speculate not, given my mistress's complaints – and I've no cause to betray my mistress's trust.'

He turned two shiny guineas out of a pocket. 'And think that Mr Cobbs' reputation is on the line along with your own.'

She shook her head. 'He knew the risks when he offered to tickle my fancy. You'll have to offer more than that.' A calculating gleam lit her blue eyes.

'More than two guineas.' He dashed a hand through his hair. 'Very well, name your price.'

'Twelve guineas.' Darleston stared at her, incredulous. 'Or four and a good poke.'

Lord damn it, no amount of information was worth that much. The woman was downright insane. She sidled closer to him, dipping her palm to cover his loins. 'Just 'cause one woman ain't to your taste, don't mean another can't satisfy.'

He'd never had any problem with women, only with Lucy, and his predilection for men had nothing to do with that. It wasn't something the love of a good woman – or a bad one, in this case – was going to solve. He simply enjoyed the pleasure of both sexes.

'Fine.' He knocked her hand away. 'Twelve guineas. This had better be worth it.'

Vexation etched lines of rage across her pretty face. They vanished equally quickly. She gave a tut and twirled away from him to compose herself, and then sat primly upon the bed. 'I suppose you want to know who she's entertained, all that sort of flummery?'

He gave a nod. 'And when she last bled.'

Sally shook her head. 'There ain't been anyone that she's entertained in that way.' As if possessed of sudden energy, she rose and paced right past him to the rear of the little chamber. Being much shorter she did not have to duck her head.

'I pray you don't expect me to believe that. Lucy can't go above four days without some manner of shafting, before she starts rutting with the furniture and whatever else is to hand.'

Sally remained with her back to him, clutching the edge of the washstand. When she finally turned, her teeth were scraping ruts into her lower lip. 'There's been frolicking, of course there has, and some bottom-warming, but I swear none of the gentlemen have taken her like that. I know, for I've had to satisfy her with the jade wand.' Her words petered off.

'Sally, for God's sake. Do you expect me to believe that she's let Oxbury and that fox Littleton do nothing beyond suckle her tits and redden her arse since February? Or am I supposed to believe they've swived her arse but haven't indulged in the taking of her cunt?'

'It's true.'

'The devil it is! And how many others have there been alongside those two?'

'A few,' she huffed, 'but the arrangement's been the same throughout. They're allowed to use her tits and her arse, but no man's to dip his wick in her honeypot.'

'Fine,' he snapped, not accepting her word for a second. 'A few' in Lucy's case would likely amount to half of the aristocracy in London. 'Then be so good as to explain how she's come to be with child, because it's not divine. She's not giving birth to Jesus Christ and I'm damned sure it's not mine.'

Sally dug her teeth into her lips so hard it drew blood. A thread of scarlet clung to the edge of her front teeth. 'She's … she's increasing?'

It this were an act, it was an improbably impressive one. How could her maid not know?

'Aren't you supposed to know that sort of thing? You're in charge of her rags.'

'I am, but … I'm not sure of the count.' Suddenly on the defensive, Sally stuttered over her words. 'She's … we've moved around a lot, and she prefers to conduct her intimate toilette alone.'

Darleston ticked the tip of his nose with his steepled fingers. 'How long since she's bled?'

Sally swore under her breath, and then began totting dates up upon her fingers. ''Twere before Bath. Prior to leaving London, I think. Yes, it was the night of the Pemberton ball, I remember, because she had such appalling cramps that we had to send word at last minute that she couldn't attend.'

'And that was?' Lord, he had no patience left for this extraction. All he wanted was a name, something he could throw in Lucy's face come morning as proof of her infidelity and lies.

'April,' Sally announced. ''Twere April. Middle of the month.'

'And it's now June.' Thus making Lucy a mere two months gone. Hardly surprising that she wasn't showing yet. Still, it was confirmation enough for what he needed. Prior to Lucy's arrival at Field House, they'd not seen one another since mid-February, a fact that entirely ruled out the possibility of him being the father. It would have to do, since he didn't believe for a moment that he'd extract a name from Sally. 'I'll have your payment sent to you.' He paused on the threshold of her room, and glanced back at her worry-etched countenance, so different from that of the saucy, flirtatious woman he'd initially faced. 'You said you were in Bath. What for?'

Sally slowly tilted her head, so that she looked up at him from beneath her brows. 'So Lady Darleston could take the waters.'

'She's been ill?' he asked, his mind suddenly whirring with possibilities. The waters wouldn't see off the clap or the pox, but that didn't mean folks didn't soak themselves in some misguided hope. Given Lucy's love of sexual excess, a dose of either couldn't be ruled out. Of course, most bathed there for gout, but he didn't suppose that to be her problem. She tippled, but not generally to excess. Lucy preferred to keep her wits about her and her senses sharp. Alcohol dulled the sort of pain she craved. 'Has she seen a physician?'

The fright that bleached Sally's skin told him he was finally asking the right questions. It was not a babe he had to worry about, or who his lady wife had lain with, but whatever malady had sent her to a quack.

'Just some stomach cramps. Seems plain enough what they are now.' Sally's eyes suddenly came alive and glittered. 'You're sure I can't persuade you to partake?' she crooned, giving her hips a saucy wiggle.

The girl was terrified, afraid that before long she'd be without a position, but not because of anything he might say or do. Rather, she knew that whatever was afflicting his wife, it wasn't likely to be pregnancy.

'No,' he said quietly. 'I'll away and leave you to your rest.'

* * *

253

'Darleston.'

He stirred slowly, waking from the dark dream with cobwebs of woe still clinging to his skin like a dusty raiment. He'd slipped back into his past, falling through layers of memory to the days before his marriage. He hated ... *hated* anything that forced his hand. He could no longer look at his mother and see her as the same woman who had nurtured him, brought him into this world. She'd severed the link between them, accused him of unnaturalness and satanic practices, when all he'd wanted was to love and have that love returned.

The parchment upon which the words he had to speak sat crumpled within his fist. His brother's hand curled tight around his shoulder. 'It won't be that bad.' Neddy offered in reassurance. 'One night, that's all you need offer her and then you can ignore her if you wish.'

If he wished ... All anyone cared about was that he should produce an heir, a squalling babe to carry on the family line. What he wanted, what he craved, wasn't of interest or relevance. There was no way he'd be allowed to ignore his wife's bedchamber.

'Darleston ... Robert.'

Someone shook him and he rolled over, trying to ignore the tug back to reality.

The delicate rose scent of Emma's perfume delivered him fully from the dream. He lifted his head off the pillow just as she settled her derriere level with his waist. 'What are you doing here?' His words came out slurred. Darleston pushed himself up a little and gave his head a shake for good measure.

'I had to make sure. Lyle said you were back, but I had to know it for myself.' Her shoulders hunched up towards her ears as she spoke. She'd come to him wearing nothing but a simple linen nightdress that even in this dim light – he'd left the curtains open – left nothing to the imagination.

Mouth suddenly dry, Darleston stared at the long plait of hair that dangled over her narrow shoulder and longed to tug upon it and pull her to him. He'd known that she would fret from the moment he'd pushed her into her father's study and shut the glass door between them. Lyle had confirmed it, as did her presence, but he'd still been right to stay away.

'You shouldn't have come here.' It made him ill to see the pain in her eyes at his words. 'It's too risky,' he tried to explain. Couldn't she trust him over this? 'I won't abandon you. There's nothing to fear on that front, but while Lucy's here, 'tis better that we remain apart.'

Emma folded her hands neatly in her lap. Every muscle in her body had to be pulled taut. If the strain increased, he feared she'd snap.

'I know it. I understand. I do.'

Yet she was here in his bedchamber and his cobs felt achy because of it. Through the thin weave of her shift he could make out the puckered tips of her nipples. The memory of tasting them, of being inside her, flooded his senses with feverish warmth. It didn't matter to his heart that his brain told him there was too much risk associated with her being here. Like any warm-blooded man, he wanted what lay before him. 'Does Lyle know you've come?' he asked, trying rather unsuccessfully to get a grip on his rampaging libido. He wanted to soothe away the tension from her limbs and replace them with a very different sort of ache. The memory of sliding into her and having her sheath grip his cock and being allowed near enough to hold her close clamoured at his senses.

'He's asleep,' she said. 'But I couldn't. I didn't mean to

come, or cause you alarm. I just needed to … I made sure that nobody saw me.'

Of course she did, and why should anyone see her slipping down the corridor like a woeful spectre at this hour of the night? It was impossible to make out the mantel-clock, and he didn't care to reach for his timepiece, but he'd swear to it being nigh on three, maybe even four o'clock.

'Emma.' Her shoulders quivered as he reached out, but, rather than touch her, he tugged back the covers, exposing a space in his bed for her to climb into, so they might sit side by side.

At first she made no move to join him. 'Do you love her?' she asked instead.

Who? Lucy? 'Good Lord, no! Never. The marriage wasn't my choice.' However, it had been his choice to accept it. He could not lay the fault of his marriage entirely upon others. After all, he had stood there and spoken his vows. No one had pressed a gun to his head, or a sword to his heart. For a time he'd even done his best to honour the promises he'd made in the cold, dismal church. 'All that exists between me and Lucy is wretched. She's here only to make worse what is already rotten.'

'I feel that I've slighted her.'

Darleston's mouth fell open as he stared at her. 'You've not. How could you have?'

'I've lain with you, her husband.'

Heaven help him, but the only wrong he could see in that statement was that she'd only lain with him once, when he'd like to make it a good score of times.

'By the same token I've slighted you, by lying with Lyle without ever seeking your consent. Lucy has wronged me hundreds of times over.'

'Two wrongs don't make a right.' Nor did two hundred.

'No, they don't, but I won't have you carrying the guilt for something that was already broken. Don't grieve for her. She doesn't deserve your pity or sympathy. If she learns of this, she'll destroy you, not because she cares for our marriage but out of pure malice. She's made other lives hell for doing much less than lying with me.'

'I have upset Lyle too.' Raw pain twisted her pretty face into a mask of anguish. He didn't believe she'd willingly hurt anybody. Rather she'd choose to absorb all discord into herself and keep everyone harmonious and safe.

Darleston patted the vacant space beside him again. 'You have not.' That was a little white lie, but Lyle would get over it. 'He's just adapting to the changes in our relationship. Emma, please. You're cold.'

Finally, she consented. The moment she settled into the space he'd made, Darleston tugged the covers all around them. 'Lie down and talk.' Not that there were any words to make things right. Ignoring the fact that she stiffened, he cuddled up close so that she might feel the warmth of his body. Only the thin cloth of her shift stood as a barrier between them. Couldn't she see that love had nothing to do with marriage vows and puritanical moral codes? Cupid's arrows struck where they pleased. He'd been pierced the first moment he saw her. Moreover the wound hadn't healed; it'd deepened, so that his whole body throbbed from needing her.

'Emma.' He propped himself up on one elbow so that he could see her more clearly. With any other woman things would be so simple. An embrace, a simple kiss could lead to so many places, but she still flinched whenever he reached out to her. 'I want you to know that I stayed away from you tonight because I deemed it safer, but that doesn't mean I didn't desire things to be different. Part of me wishes that you, Lyle and I could simply walk out of the house tonight and flee, never to be seen again. We could live somewhere remote where we'd be free of censure.' Not that he believed such a place existed. 'However, I've been running for the whole of my adult life. It's time I stood firm. I'm no longer prepared to have my life dictated to me by that venomous harpy.' His mother was dead. His father had chosen to make a whore his second countess, and Lucy had done everything in her power to destroy him. He wasn't going to be henpecked any more.

Despite her intake of breath, Darleston splayed a hand over the flat of Emma's stomach. The contact made her jolt, but she didn't move out of reach. Instead her eyes filled with woeful longing. 'Will you stay?' he asked.

'I shouldn't.'

By which she meant she wanted to, but didn't know if she'd cope with what she believed he intended.

'That's not what I asked.' He swept his hand upwards until he captured a nipple in the centre of his palm. The tip immediately crinkled. Emma gave a low gasp.

Lord, it hurt to see the anxiety wrinkle her brow. 'We could just cuddle,' he suggested. The frantic coupling they'd made in the dovecote would never have been his choice for a first time. He didn't want to think it always had to be that way. He opened his arms to her so that she might rest her head against his chest.

'I don't know.'

He thought she would leave, but then she slid into his arms and her cheek pressed lightly against his chest.

'I wish you'd tell me what you are so afraid of. What happened to you that makes you fear this closeness so much?'

He felt her shake her head. 'I just never wanted the

hollowness to swallow me up entirely. Sometimes it's easier not to feel.'

He guessed he understood that. From the outset, her ability to cut herself off had been what intrigued him most about her. He'd never been able to sever his emotions like that, no matter what his many acquaintances believed.

Closer. He wanted her even closer now.

Darleston tugged off his nightshirt. 'Let me lie naked beside you.' He wasn't thinking of sex, only of skin-on-skin contact. Emma tentatively tugged open the ribbon fastening of her nightrail. She wore a white linen affair, decorated with swirls of embroidery all the way up to her throat. She lifted the hem and drew the whole thing off in the same way he'd removed his nightshirt.

Lord, she was beautiful. He hadn't had the chance to really appreciate that before. Emma clung tight to the sheet, but he refused to let her hide. This woman had enchanted him when countless lascivious whores couldn't even raise his pulse with their jiggling and their pouts. Darleston pushed back the covers so that the moonlight fell on her skin and turned it silvery. Soft, creamy flesh the colour of buttermilk greeted him. She seemed so sharp in her clothing that part of him had expected her to be all angular; rather she was rounded and curvy as a woman ought to be. Her breasts were plentiful but not heavy, and her thighs slightly plump. 'You're beautiful.' He rose over her, wedging himself between her knees. 'May I kiss you?'

She gazed at him as if uncertain, then tentatively nodded. Her lips parted ever so slightly in invitation. A grin curving his lips, Darleston dipped his head, not to meet her lips. He bestowed a kiss on her belly instead. His tongue flicked lightly into the hollow of her navel. Emma reacted as though she'd been singed, bucking up off the bed and shaking. Her heart thumped so strongly he could hear it. He had no intention of letting it slow back to a normal rate.

So maybe he wasn't playing fair; nor was she, by coming here in the dead of night. Even the illusion he upheld of being a gentleman faded after midnight.

Slowly he shimmied backwards until his head was positioned over her springy curls. 'May I kiss you again?'

This time she had a better idea of what to expect. It showed in her voice as she squeaked, 'Yes,' and in the way she gazed at him in petrified adulation.

The scent of her quim filled his nostrils. Darleston bent and tasted her cunny with one slow lingering sweep of his tongue – salty and so utterly feminine, so completely different from Lyle, but just as heavenly.

Her thighs quivered as his lips worked their magic. 'Easy now.' He used his hands to push her legs a little wider, forcing her muscles to relax. He had the taste of her on his tongue now, and she lay completely open to him. She was all his.

If that weren't intoxication enough, her gasps transformed into groans that she tried to muffle by pressing her mouth against the back of her hand. Another flick of his tongue and she exchanged that hand for the silencing effects of the pillow.

He could see the point – they didn't want their loving overheard – though he longed to throw it across the room. Hearing her muffled cries called to him, so that his blood sang in his veins. Arousal tingled through his shaft, but for now he was content to listen to her sighs and let the fever of anticipation burn. 'That's right, tell me,' he crooned. Damn, he knew how to satisfy a woman, but he'd never wanted to offer contentment in quite the way he did now.

He took things slowly, savouring her taste and avoiding

her little swollen nubbin until he was certain that to do so any longer would simply be cruel. Then he turned his kiss upon the pearl peeking shyly out from beneath its hood. That was enough. Her shoulders rose off the pillow and her thighs clamped tight around his head. 'God! Oh!' She came, the pitter-patter pulse of her climax beating softly against his tongue.

Rather than waiting for her to calm, Darleston slid his cock into the heat of her channel. She stared up at him, wild-eyed, blissful yet still afraid.

He'd do anything to remove that fear and have her know true ecstasy.

'I ... I ... I can't.' She battered at his hands in panic. Still, her hips lifted to meet him and her sheath hugged his shaft.

'Shh!' he soothed, stroking inside her. 'I want you to feel good.' Then he remembered Lyle's words about how he imagined Emma would want sex to be. Control played an essential part in her ability to cope with the invasion of her personal space. He'd taken that from her. Time he handed it back. 'Roll over.'

Bodies sandwiched tightly together, Darleston rolled them so that he lay on his back with Emma astride his hips. 'At your own pace,' he instructed as she rose above him. Her breasts bounced. The nipples were coral-pink.

Darleston locked his hands around the bedposts. It killed him to do it. All he wanted was to smooth his hands over her creamy skin and give her every last bit of pleasure he could, but he'd pushed things too far, gone a little too fast. Time he accepted his punishment. Though, considering the rush he felt as she danced delicately on his chest, it was hardly a penalty at all.

Emma's panic settled immediately now that she was above

him. The fear washed out of her eyes. She moved too slowly at first to satisfy the intensity of his need. His knuckles ached from gripping the bedposts. He wanted to grab her and buck into her hard and fast. However, the more she relaxed and the more he fought his urges, the more her movements fell into line with his desires. Soon they were rising and falling in perfect harmony, their shallow breaths perfectly synchronised. He was so close, so very, very close to coming that her frustration didn't register at first. Then it hit him. The way she moved, the way her teeth were ground together, all spoke to him of something out of reach.

'I can't. It's not working properly.'

Was she talking about them? The hell it wasn't working properly. It was divine.

'I can't … I want to …'

He understood. 'It's all right, Emma. Stop chasing it so hard. Relax.' No way on God's earth was he leaving her frustrated. Darleston adjusted his grip upon the bedposts. 'Pet yourself. Let me watch you.' His gaze fell to the juncture of their two bodies. Obliging her would be his pleasure. He just wanted to make sure it was hers too. 'Go ahead, touch yourself. You know how to do that, right?'

Emma tentatively lifted one hand from where it rested upon the bed. She extended her index finger and curled the rest.

Darleston's breath quickened as she slowly drew her hand up her leg to the juncture of her thighs. She looked down at how they were joined, her mouth open, tongue flicking back and forth over her small white teeth. Then gently, she tapped her finger to her nub.

Wow! He watched pleasure lick colour through her irises. Her mouth opened, but no sound emerged. Hell, he was desperate to feel her come around his cock, but this was about taking things at Emma's pace, even though every strategy he knew for slowing things down was failing him utterly.

Restraint? After the week he'd spent, his reserves were spent.

'It feels wrong to touch myself like this.' A rosy blush spread across her cheeks.

'Why should it be wrong?'

'It's lewd.'

'Emma, you've no idea. This is nothing compared to what I'd like to do.'

She grinned. 'I've seen what you've done with Lyle.'

Darleston bucked upwards sharply, toppling her forward over his supine form. She only just caught herself before she landed flat upon his chest. 'There's nothing wrong with a little lewdness, nor a little lust. And I get a whole lot lewder than what you've seen me do to Lyle. I've done things that'd make your hair curl.'

'That would save me the effort of applying rags.'

Her snappy comeback shocked a laugh from him. 'Oh, my God! I can't believe you said that.' He kissed her tenderly upon the lips, only for Emma to open up to him. More than that, she darted her tongue inside his mouth, which damn near undid him completely. When she relaxed, she was incredible – every inch the woman he'd always expected she could be. Somehow she had forgotten whatever evil lurked in her past that had led her to isolate herself. If only he knew the key to releasing her permanently, then truly things would work out between her, Lyle and him. He wanted that. Wanted it so desperately. Lucy be damned. Come morning, he'd do whatever it took to get rid of her. Divorce her even, if necessary.

'Emma.' He wedged a hand between their bodies and found her clit, and then kept on rubbing it as they writhed together.

He'd come to the country determined to hide away and disassociate himself from the pleasures of the flesh. Rejected, and disillusioned, he'd believed himself unworthy of love. Instead, he'd stumbled upon the two people in the world who could make him feel whole.

'Emma, I can't hold this much longer. I'm going to ...' The pulse of his orgasm already beat at the base of his cock. Pressure flowed upward through his balls and into his shaft. He pushed her away as best he could. 'I really probably ought not to come inside you.'

'Why?' Her words were a dry, husky caress against her cheek, her eyes two blue pools inches above him, so open and unafraid that he instantly regretted his words. To hell with consequences, he wanted a life with her.

Only then the realisation hit her. He saw it first in her eyes. Vapours of pain clouded their bright surfaces. She froze. But he was already there, spilling his seed deep inside her.

CHAPTER EIGHTEEN

In the nauseous silence that followed, Darleston lay on his back, body glowing, but his heart rent in two. Never had he felt so vile, so villainous. He'd meant only to give her pleasure. Instead he'd delivered a blow from which she might never recover. He ought to have taken better care of her. Considering his extensive experience of matters of the flesh, he ought to have spared a little more thought to the repercussions of indulging his desires.

Emma lay curled on her side on the farthest edge of the mattress. Each sob that wormed up out of her throat carved another slice out of his soul. She flinched when he rolled over and extended a touch toward her. The mere brush of his fingertips against her shoulder made her curl up tight like a hedgehog being scrutinised by its prey.

'Emma, I'm so sorry, I let things get out of hand. I just ...' He just what? Telling her he loved her would sound incredibly hollow at this juncture, as if he was dismissing the issue of a pregnancy because love conquered all, when in truth that was utter bollocks. In his experience, love rarely triumphed over anything, and a baby was evidently the last thing Emma needed in her life. Hell, it wasn't something he relished as part of his. Who the devil wanted a lovelorn punk as a father? At least now he half understood some of Emma's behaviour. He'd mentioned offspring the very first evening at Field House and watched her expression cloud. Then he'd simply put it down to shame. So many wives blamed themselves when children didn't promptly arrive after a marriage. After two and a half years with Lyle and nary a patter of tiny feet, she must have felt pressure. But that hadn't been the reason for Emma's frown. 'What happened?' he asked.

'I can't have children.'

Instinctively, he knew she didn't mean in a physical sense. Fertility wasn't an issue, else she wouldn't have leaped away from him so fast after he'd spilled his seed. No, she meant that she couldn't tolerate the notion of growing or supporting a babe. Only he didn't understand why. He knew several women who balked at the idea of offspring, but they were all self-centred, harridans to the core, with no love for anything beyond self-indulgence. Emma no more fitted that bill than he did that of a saintly verger.

'What happened?' This time he risked a rebuke and curled his fingers around the top of her arm. Emma didn't shrug him off, though she did bite her fingers. Even in the half-light, he could see the shimmer of tears trickling over her cheeks.

'Emma, did you have a child?' All manner of possibilities warred in his thoughts, most of them too dark to contemplate.

'No,' she croaked, and shook her head. 'I just lost so many.'

Miscarriage? No – that made no sense. He'd swear he was the first man with whom she'd lain. No point in pretending he understood what she was trying to say. He didn't.

Instead, he hunched over her, unable to offer the comfort she so obviously needed. 'Tell me again, I don't understand.'

He sought her gaze. Tears had turned her eyes pink. Still their brightness shone, impressing upon him how much he'd come to care for her in such a short time. 'Please, Emma. I want to understand.'

After a while, she pushed herself upright and got out of the bed. She didn't try to speak, just cast about the floor for her shift.

'God, Emma! Don't go. Not like this.' Horror at the thought of her departing set him rolling across the eiderdown to reach her.

'Not going. Come with me,' she croaked as she pushed her feet into delicate satin pumps. 'Can't explain properly. Put on some breeches. I'll show you.'

Darleston lumbered rather ungracefully off the bed on the side nearer to Emma. Wherever she intended them to go he'd follow, if it helped make sense of what afflicted her. He pulled on his breeches and tucked into them the shirt he'd worn to bed. Given her apparent need for haste – she was rocking agitatedly from one foot to the other – he eschewed the rest of his attire.

She took his hand as they crept along the upstairs corridor. If anyone happened upon them, no amount of explaining would convince anyone that they were not lovers. But, damn it, they needed that fact to remain secret at least until he'd seen Lucy off. The floorboards creaked considerably less once they descended the stairs. Emma, her pert little bottom distractingly tempting as it jiggled beneath the thin weave of her shift, headed for the front door. While she worked the locks, Darleston pushed his feet into the hessians he'd left in the bootroom and shouldered his greatcoat. He ended up sprinting down the steps after her, carrying a pelisse.

A chill breeze blew in from the east, making the pre-dawn air biting, though not a single cloud tarnished the blue-black sky. They'd have fine weather for the boxing later.

'It's Amelia's,' Emma said when he offered her the coat. He ought to have realised. The fussy decoration didn't reflect Emma's tastes. Still, it was warmth that she needed. The cold had whitened her limbs, and she had goosebumps. She shivered too, with each fresh gust, though he didn't think she noticed it.

'Please.' He held open the coat for her to slip on, and then fastened the buttons all the way to the hem. 'Where are we going?'

'The church.' Her tears had dried upon her cheeks. They left her skin oddly streaked. Although she'd accepted his hand earlier, she shook him off now. They headed in the same direction they had ambled that first morning when she'd taken him to visit the amphitheatre. On that occasion she'd worn a ridiculous wide-brimmed bonnet. Now her hair danced about her shoulders, torn from its bedtime confinement by his hands and tangled by the wind.

The first traces of dawn were peeking over the horizon, glimmers of orange and bronze that pierced the thick foliage as they skirted the edge of the woodland. On towards civilisation they trotted, Emma leading, him following like a faithful lapdog, down into the dell that led towards the hamlet on the other side of the river.

Understanding came to him when they reached the graveyard. At the back, in a gated preserve, Emma led him along a row of moss-covered headstones. So many names and dates. The eldest a mere sixteen when he died. So very many of them. All of them Hills.

Dear God, she was one of fifteen!

When she said she'd lost so many children, she'd meant her siblings.

Glittering blue eyes met his. 'Amelia and I are all that remain.' The tears that had choked her earlier were gone now, replaced by a cold, reserved aloofness, as though she had to step back from the raw emotion of her loss and view it from a distance.

The youngest child had died within hours of her mother. Five had been lost within a few bitter weeks.

'What took them?' he asked.

Emma gently chewed her lip. 'Sickness. A fever.' She knew more, he could see it in the gauntness of her expression, but it was obviously distressing her just to revisit it. 'They died one by one beside me in the bed.'

'Emma, I'm so sorry.' His mother was the only person he'd truly lost, and by that point there'd been little love between them. All his other tragedies had been on a lesser scale, like Lyle the first time around, and giving up Dovecote to Fortuna. His love line had been cut, but those involved remained. They still lived and breathed. Death was rather more final – and to have it strike so close at such a tender age!

Emma paused before a simple rose cross, over which an iron ring had been looped. 'Bea.' She crumpled, crushing her shift on the dewy earth beneath her knees. 'I fell asleep, when I knew I ought not to.'

'You can't blame yourself. How old were you? Were you sick too?'

'Nine. I was nine.' She shook her head. 'I'm never sick. I'm never sick.'

Darleston soberly covered his mouth with his clenched knuckles. Nothing he said would make any of this right. Still, she'd brought him here. He doubted she'd ever told a soul how deep her pain ran. 'Tell me about the others.'

Her pink tongue flicked once across her cracked lips. 'I was twelve when mama passed. Amelia was only ten months, Abigail two, and Elizabeth three.' Emma's gaze swept solemnly over the moss-strewn cross at the end that stood a foot higher than the row of children's graves. 'Aunt Maude oversaw most things, and a string of nannies and governesses. William went away to school. I wanted to go too, to get away from the house and the bed and the constant stench of decay, but I was expected to oversee things.'

She'd known no escape until Lyle had come. It may have been a marriage of convenience but it had hardly freed her.

'I kept myself apart from the little ones, because I knew they'd only be taken. William died in a carriage accident. Elizabeth contracted bronchitis. Abigail drowned when she was five. I'm not sure how Amelia survived.'

'Maybe she's built of the same stern stuff as yourself.'

Emma conceded that with a grudging nod, perhaps recognising that both she and Amelia were stubborn and staunch in their own ways.

'I know it's impolite, but where do you fit into the family tree?' He'd already guessed her to be ten years Amelia's senior, and the string of dates before him seemed to attest to that.

'I'm the third eldest. Thomas and Thomas came before me.'

Thomas and Thomas. One of them was among the five who'd been taken by the fever. A tiny misshapen rectangle in the turf denoted the other's exceedingly short life. Emma watched him uncover the headstone by stripping away a thick layer of moss.

'Mama was forever plump and round. One babe seemed to arrive and then another was immediately expected.'

Darleston reached out and pulled Emma tight to his chest.

Ramrod-straight, she merely tolerated his hold.

'I can't abide children. They flout rules. I can't have them climbing on my lap.' Tears twinkled in the corners of her eyes again, but they refused to spill. 'You're the only person I've wanted to touch since Beatrice died and the only person I've allowed to touch me. I wanted to run away from you when we met, but I couldn't. You were like a magnet that drew me. The more I tried to deny what I felt, the stronger the need to be next to you became.'

'I know.' He pushed his hand into her unbound hair.

'I thought maybe time enough had passed that I could force myself to be strong.'

'Emma, you have been.' He pressed a fleeting kiss to her brow. Relief washed through him when she allowed him that without pulling away. 'I'm so sorry about earlier. I should have planned better. There are things that can be done, ways of preventing a pregnancy.'

''Twas I who invited myself to your room. You couldn't plan for that. And I did it knowing you meant me to stay away. Why did she come? Why does she have to be here?' Emma did turn away from him then. 'Lord, she makes me feel so sordid and grubby, as if my skin is tainted with this unholy deceit that I can't wash off. She's your wife and I know what she's done to you, and that there's no love left between you, but still …'

'Forget Lucy,' he said, taking her in his arms once more. 'Forget Lucy and forget the past. Think of the future we can have together instead. You and Lyle are all that I want.'

Emma pressed her lips tight together. Then she rested her cheek against the soft wool that covered his chest. Her arms wound tight around him and squeezed so hard that it pinched. No matter, he didn't try to release himself. It was contentment itself to be cradled thus by her. 'You turn me into a giddy fool,' she whispered. 'I want us to be together too.'

'We will be.' Somehow he'd make it happen.

'We were poor,' she said into his coat, and he understood that she trying to find a reason for the deaths. 'That's why it happened. They were never given the opportunity to thrive. The fight money came too late.'

* * *

By the time Emma and Darleston returned from the church-yard, thick golden rays were striping the roof of Field House. Everyone would be up, all buzzing with excitement over Jack Johnstone's fight. Emma had no wish to attend, though as hostess for her father it was her duty to do so. At least this time she might find a spot in which to stand behind Lyle and Darleston, so that she could block out the grisly smacks of fists meeting flesh. The hollers and stench of the crowd were oppressive enough, without having to watch as well. Lyle always tried to shield her, but two men would make a far more robust barrier, and at least her smiles would not have to be entirely faked, for what better view could a woman ask than her lover's pert and lovely rear? She would imagine Darleston surreptitiously touching Lyle. Images of their lovemaking would sustain her through the fight. No one would push her forward. They all knew she couldn't tolerate the press of the crowd.

Emma squeezed a practice smile onto her lips. Explaining, sharing her grief with Darleston, had diminished the weight upon her chest, but the initial cause of her distress remained. After keeping herself apart and safe for so long, how could she have acted so irresponsibly? She knew well enough the facts of life. One could not live in the countryside and not know them, even if, until Darleston's arrival, she hadn't comprehended the true depth of the act. Yet, thinking back to that point where she'd been astride him, riding his cock, her thoughts had been concentrated on seeing him climax, feeling the pulse of his cock inside her, and knowing that it was her actions that were bringing him such bliss. No other thought had entered her silly head, and, even if it had, she did not think it would have entirely changed things. Lord help her, she deserved to be on edge until her flow resumed.

Robert Darleston affected her in ways she could hardly comprehend. He squeezed her hand, reminding her of his presence. Emma looked up at his sharp profile and knew beyond doubt that she not only trusted him, she loved him. It had come to that. The notion of being parted from him was simply unbearable. She had no idea how things would work out, but somehow they must.

She and Darleston had walked back from the graveyard as any man and woman might do, her hand resting lightly upon his arm. Now, within sight of the windows, Emma relinquished her grip. Folks would be about, likely at break-fast, but Darleston had impressed upon her the continued need for discretion, at least until her ladyship departed the house. Emma did not see how she could possibly keep their relationship closeted for ever. People would see the closeness between them. They'd recognise the fact that she didn't flinch in the same way when he reached out to her. It'd start as whispered observations, but the gossips would put two and two together. Perhaps that was better than them realising the truth about her husband and his lover. The possibility of Lyle's preferences being discovered had always worried her. Now she had double reason to fret.

'We ought to try and slip in unnoticed,' Darleston said.

Emma nodded her agreement. 'You go in the front. They'll think you've been for an early morning stroll.' In his enveloping, caped greatcoat, Darleston at least passed for respectable, save for the oversight of a hat. His lack of proper attire beneath could easily be concealed until he'd reached his bedchamber. Not so her. Grass stains marred the front of her shift, beneath which her legs were bare and chilled. Additionally, without her stays, Amelia's pelisse constituted an extremely ill fit.

'Where will you go?' he asked. The sun glinted off his burnished copper hair.

'I'll walk around and come in through the back.' She regularly left the latch open on the window in the Dog Parlour. The room stuck out from the back of the house so that it wasn't overlooked, and with any luck she'd be able to shimmy through the gap without attracting attention. From there she could slip up the back stairs to her room without anyone making assumptions as to what she'd been about. The worst she might expect was a few questions from Lyle.

'Very well.' Darleston briefly enveloped her in his embrace. She breathed deeply, basking in the musky scent of his body, as she committed his strength and heat to memory until they could be together again. His lips buffed her brow. 'Go now. We'll speak later.'

Emma relinquished her hold and scuttled away, staying out of sight of the frontage by hugging the line of conifers until she had rounded the left-hand side of the building. Rather than head upstairs, she lingered in the stuffy warmth of the Dog Parlour, where she dressed her hair to the best of her ability without a hairbrush. Although unlikely to meet anyone on the way to her room, if she could pass muster from a distance it would mask her attempted deceit should she be unlucky enough to happen upon one of the servants or guests. She had not forgotten Amelia's assumptions of the previous day, when their paths had crossed and she'd seen Emma's hair unpinned.

Thankfully, the route remained clear. Lyle had already dressed and left by the time she reached their bedchamber. Emma performed a quick toilet and chose a conservative gown in cream, with a high-waisted, thigh-length caraco jacket of nightshade blue. The colour reduced the sallowness around her eyes due to lack of sleep, although it did emphasise the pink tinge of their whites. She could only pray that with all eyes on Jack's performance her pallor would pass unnoticed.

Halfway down the stairs, Lady Darleston rudely stepped in front of her, blocking the way. Emma immediately recoiled from the fierce white wraith to cower against the banister. 'Good morning,' she muttered, not really wishing to speak, but determined not to appear rude.

'Hmph!' Lady Darleston snorted. She had dressed in white satin, from the tip of her head, where a feathered sailboat perched atop a white tricorn hat, to the floor, where the train of her heavy skirt dusted the boards. Such starkness might have drained the colour from some faces, but not hers. Lady Darleston's cheeks glowed crimson. 'For some perhaps, but I do not perceive it so.'

'Oh. Does something ail you?' Emma enquired. Social manners were ingrained in her makeup, though she felt like kicking herself for asking. 'I expected everyone to be in good cheer this morning over Jack's fight. Was your room not to your satisfaction?'

Her agreeableness met with a chilling glare from Lucy.

'How dare you?' the Lady hissed. 'My room was tolerable, unlike the reception afforded me by my hostess.'

Lucy's words might as well have been slaps, for they brought blood rushing to Emma's cheeks as readily as any blow would have done. ''Tis bad enough my varmint of a husband treats me so abominably without having his doxy flaunting her good spirits in my face. Don't think I don't know of your actions. I know my husband, Mrs Langley, and his pitiful attempts at subterfuge are just that. You should hang your head in shame.'

More taken aback still, Emma clutched the banister for support. In truth, she could not deny Lady Darleston's accusation, but she had not been prepared for such a direct or immediate assault. How had the woman come to know? Had her sister betrayed her? Amelia had certainly been peevish over the last few days, but surely she wasn't that spiteful. Her embarrassment swelled further when she realised there were other guests milling about the hall below and that Lady Darleston's words had almost certainly been overheard.

'Can't even utter an apology?' Lucy remarked of Emma's gaping response. 'Well, know this, you little fool. I don't tolerate anyone meddling with my husband. He is mine and, if you are wise, you will desist in your liaison at once. There's many who'll pay a handsome price for tattle, even about a country bumpkin.'

Would this have been worse if Lady Darleston had come upon them abed and torn Darleston from her side? In her mortification, Emma didn't think so. She had no way of lulling the woman's fury, nor could she feign contrition and beg forgiveness. Artful deception was not a trait she'd ever acquired.

'Leave her be, Lucy.' Darleston's voice preceded him as he

strode over to meet them. 'She's done you no ill, and you have no right to label any woman a whore without first labelling yourself as the biggest one of all.'

Lucy turned towards her husband and met him eye to eye, he at the bottom of the stairs and she three steps up. Darleston remained dressed as he had been when Emma had left him, in his greatcoat and boots and with his fiery hair curling gently upon his shoulders.

'Are you denying she's your tart?'

'Of course I am. What trouble are you hoping to stir by even suggesting it? Mrs Langley is happily married and not the sort to dally behind her husband's back –'

'Dull, you mean.'

'– so you may keep her out of your attempts to destroy my good name.'

'Your good name! What name?' Lucy jabbed Darleston square in the chest with two of her heavily jewelled fingers. 'Your perversities are bandied about town as synonyms for unnaturalness. What have I to do with that?'

Darleston maintained a curiously stoic air of resilience throughout his wife's response, leading Emma to wonder if they had played out this particular scene before. Despite Darleston's coolness, Lucy hammered on at him as if greatly maligned. 'What have I done?' she howled, while she fanned herself furiously. She had become quite red about the face, and seemed likely to be overcome by a fit of the vapours. Emma wondered if she ought to call for some smelling salts before the woman expired.

'How have I displeased you in such a way that you'd leave me bereft while you gallivant about the countryside pursuing such vices, and when I am quickening with your child?' Lucy smiled rather maliciously as she spoke the last words, and cast Emma a particularly hateful glance.

For just a moment Darleston's urbane façade slipped, which transformed his coldness into the most dreadful fury. If she hadn't known him to be most gentle and tender, Emma would certainly have quailed at such intense wrath.

'It is not my child,' he growled and brushed Lucy's hand aside a lot less gently then he might. She staggered as though he had struck her, though he had not, and began to shed piteous tears. Darleston took a further step back from her and clenched his fists by his sides. He spoke rather more calmly when he addressed her again. 'As for your accusations of abandonment, as I recall it, madam, you left me. You climbed out of a window and ran into the night after I caught you being swived by another. Not content with that, you launched a campaign of terror upon me and my friends, spreading scandalous rumours for which there is no sound evidence at all. I find it incomprehensible that you should come to me seeking reconciliation only to immediately launch into yet more rumour-mongering.'

''Tis untrue,' Lucy wailed, but the protest lacked sincerity.

'Is there some problem?' Mr Bathhouse strolled over to them. He'd shown some adeptness at dissolving minor quarrels over the course of his stay, which made Emma grateful for his involvement. Her relief didn't extend to Mr Aiken and Mr Littleton, who appeared in the doorway of the dining room, their faces full of morbid curiosity.

'Only one that perpetually ails me,' Darleston replied. He did not to turn to address Bathhouse, choosing instead to deliver his response with an artful turn of his wrist.

'My husband is an unconscionable cad,' bemoaned her ladyship. 'I am quite the most unfortunate of wives. Why must you deny your future heir?' She jabbed at her husband

again, at the same time as seeking Bathhouse's hand to
clutch in support.

'It is not my child,' Darleston repeated in a more conversa-
tional tone, though the purr of his former anger still rumbled
deep in his throat.

'Who else's do you suppose it to be?'

'That is a very good question, and one for which I shall
endeavour to find an answer. What I do know is that you
are not above two months gone and until your unwelcome
arrival yesterday I had not set eyes upon you for four. So
explain to me how the babe could possibly be my son?'
Darleston turned and looked questioningly at the assembled
guests, who raised their eyebrows in unison.

'I repeat my comments of yesterday when you first
presented me with this nonsense, that you should make your
doe eyes at the child's real father. Petition him for money, for
I will not support you. Your bastard will never lay claim to
the earldom. I will not acknowledge the child.'

'Perhaps this dispute might be better resolved in private,'
Mr Bathhouse interjected. He seemed most uncomfortable,
having come to smooth things out and instead found himself
forced into the thankless role of Lady Darleston's protector.
She would not release his hand, no matter how many times
he sought to withdraw it. 'Milord, the library might afford
you such.'

Darleston waved aside the suggestion. 'There's nothing
more to discuss. The facts are entirely straightforward.'

'Still ... well ...' Bathhouse muttered, trying to extract his
hand from Lady Darleston's death grip.

Ignoring Bathhouse's straits, Darleston addressed his wife
once more. 'Leave,' he said simply, then turned his back on
her.

Lucy blanched in response to such a direct cut. 'Oh!' she cried dramatically and fell into a faint, so that Mr Bathhouse was obliged to catch her and lower her gently to the steps. 'You foul beast. You monster.' From betwixt her bosoms she produced a handkerchief, which she applied liberally to her eyes, though there was no evidence of tears. 'I cannot believe you accuse me so when I have always been such a good and faithful wife.' Perhaps that was stretching credibility a little too far, for there were several rather disrespectful murmurings from the assembled gentlemen. Her ladyship ignored them. 'All you care to do is free yourself to indulge in further wickedness. Do you imagine you are so discreet that your nocturnal habits pass unobserved? I have been here but a day and they have already reached my ears.'

Still with his back to her, Darleston paused. 'I think you mistake me for someone else, unless I've taken to sleepwalking, for I have spent every night here in my own bed.'

'Sleepwalking,' her ladyship scoffed. 'Is that the newly fashionable term for it? Do you deny that you approached my maid last night? You went to her quarters.'

Darleston did not respond. However, as if on cue, Lady Darleston's maid appeared at that very moment with vile-smelling salts to waft under her employer's nose. 'Tell them.' Lucy gestured to the assembled onlookers. 'Go ahead, girl, as you told me. Isn't it so that milord made certain demands of you last night?'

'It is,' the girl responded. She was a plump lass with wide hips and an ample bosom. However, her mock-serious expression couldn't entirely hide her all-too-knowing worldliness. She was no innocent, and likely a very saucy piece instead. 'He came to me after midnight, he did. I was quite at my wits' end as to what to do.'

'You poor soul.' Lady Darleston petted the maid in a soothing fashion, her own affliction clearly forgotten.

Darleston groaned and rolled his eyes, but refrained from offering an explanation, a fact that perhaps worked to his advantage, for no one seemed at all concerned about his supposed visit to the servants' quarters. Even Emma felt certain it'd been for a legitimate reason, rather than the one Lady Darleston implied.

''Tis no new thing for you either, Robert.' Lucy clambered once more to her feet in order to tick her fingers back and forth before his face. 'What devilment is it that provokes you to accost innocents in this way? Oh, if I'd only known the extent of your depravity when I agreed to marry you, I should have saved myself such misery.'

'That is the first truth you have spoken all day,' Darleston said.

'Well, let me speak another. I know you have a lover and I know who it is.' She turned her steely gaze once more upon Emma. 'You need not stand there so primly. I'm not fooled. Even your own sister is appalled by your behaviour. She was positively distraught when she confided last night.'

Amelia – Amelia had betrayed her, though whether out of malice or simple foolishness it was hard to say.

'What is the meaning of this?' Mr Hill shuffled in from the direction of the study, followed by a trickle of other guests. 'I shall have the townsfolk and the constable here if this shouting keeps up, enquiring if we are to have the boxing in my hall.' He eyed Darleston and Mr Bathhouse standing at the base of the stairs and asked, 'Is there some quarrel between you gentlemen?'

Bathhouse's eyes widened in alarm. 'Good Lord, no.' He gave his host to know that the discord was between husband

and wife, a fact that turned Hill's poker face compellingly stern. He offered a hand to Lady Darleston – thus freeing Bathhouse, who made a speedy retreat into the dining room. Her ladyship dipped immediately into an exquisite curtsy. When she bobbed up once more, a triumphant and unflattering – for you could see the badness of her teeth – smirk stretched across her cheeks.

''Tis rather unseemly to air one's grievances in public,' Mr Hill reprimanded her, immediately extinguishing her smile. 'Whatever complaint you have against his lordship, my hall is not the place to declare it.'

Lucy's eyes narrowed at the remark, but she offered her host no apology, whereas Darleston did so with unfaltering politeness, to which he received a nod in return. It seemed as though the drama was done

The tension in Emma's chest eased enough for her to take an unsteady breath. She and Lyle and Darleston needed to speak with one another most urgently. While she still trusted Darleston, the issue of Lady Darleston being with child thoroughly complicated matters.

However, as Mr Hill turned to return to his other guests, Lucy stopped him with a woeful moan. 'Please, sir, I'm sorry to raise such matters at this time, but I cannot let this go. For all his nice words my husband has cruelly abused your hospitality while here. He has made your daughter his mistress.'

'Good God!' Hill released Lady Darleston's arm. Surprisingly, he did not round upon Darleston, but instead turned forthwith to Amelia, who had followed him from the study. 'What devilment have you been about, young lady? I knew I ought to have sent you to your Aunt Maude's.'

'Not I,' she squeaked, though the way her lip trembled

suggested a degree of deceit in her answer. Foolishly, her gaze swept at once to Harry Quernow, who at least was less obvious in giving a tremulous shake of the head. So Lyle was right. That was where Amelia's affections lay. Thankfully her father seemed not to notice. If such an obvious hint at a liaison had occurred in the past, Emma would have taken Amelia aside for a sound lecture, but considering her own promiscuity and its imminent revelation she no longer felt in a position to sermonise.

'Um, no, you misunderstand,' Lucy helpfully clarified. 'I meant your other daughter, sir. Mrs Langley.'

Much to everyone's surprise, Hill burst into peals of helpless laughter. When he caught Emma's gaze, his mirth vanished equally fast. He might occasionally be insensitive and treat her like a dolt, but he was not an unkind father, and generally endeavoured not to cause her distress. His attention returned abruptly to Lady Darleston. 'You are trouble, madam. I knew you would be the moment you stepped down from the landau yesterday. While I'm delighted to know my instincts are as sharp as ever, I'm sorry that I've had to listen to you besmirch my daughter's reputation. I know you to be a liar.' Mr Hill drew himself up to his full and rather considerable height, showing himself to be a stout and hearty man still, despite his thinning grey hair. 'You will not make such idle accusations again. Whatever quarrel you have with my lord Darleston, I find it intolerably rude of you to try and embroil my family. Please collect your things. I can no longer welcome you as a guest in my home.'

'It's the truth. Ask her,' Lucy protested. She had turned a rather ghostly shade, so that the white of her outfit thoroughly overwhelmed her. 'Ask Amelia.'

'I have no intention of asking anyone, let alone the opinion

of an impressionable girl barely out of the schoolroom. Please
have your maid assemble your trunk.'

'Come, milady.' The maid gently tapped her mistress's arm.
Lucy threw her a scathing look. 'Take off your coat, Robert.
Show them what lies beneath. 'Tis no ramble you've been
upon this morn, but rather face-making with your harlot.'

Darleston remained buttoned to the throat. He observed
Lucy calmly. 'Making up tales in order to embarrass me will
not better your situation. How do you suppose me able to
conduct an affair with Mrs Langley when she doesn't permit
even her family to touch her?' He sniffed. 'Then again,
perhaps you have not noticed that fact since you've been
such a short time in this house.'

It seemed from Lady Darleston's silence that she had not
been aware of that particular fact, nor did it please her to
know it. With a terrific flounce, she stormed past Emma up
the stairs, presumably to collect her accoutrements, only to
stumble near the top and topple forwards onto the landing.
Harry Quernow took the stairs at once, closely followed by
Mr Phelps and Mr Connelly.

'Are you well, milady?' Harry asked. Emma didn't hear the
response, only saw her father's mouth set into a grim line.
He nodded at Harry. 'She can rest while the maid packs. I'm
not so heartless as to send anyone away injured.' Between the
three gentlemen, they carried Lady Darleston to her room.
Once they were out of sight along the upstairs corridor,
Darleston caught Emma's eye. 'Forgive me,' he mouthed, his
expression one of grim softness.

Forgive him! Why she could barely comprehend what had
just occurred.

'Emma, dearest, are you all right? You look quite faint.
Has she shocked you very much?' She realised it was her

father speaking, but could not meet his tender expression. Instead, she worried her lip and fought hard to hold her fast-brewing tears in check. 'Oh, my poor child,' continued Mr Hill, 'it's been quite horrid, I'm sure. You look nearly overcome. Perhaps it would be best if you retired for a spell. I'm sure Amelia will take charge of the guests.' The knowing look that passed across his face at the mention of his younger daughter made Emma suspect that he hadn't missed that little exchange between Amelia and Harry Quernow after all. Keeping Amelia busy with the other guests would also keep her away from Harry, who had duties of his own to attend to.

'Yes,' Emma agreed. 'I think I should like to lie down. Excuse me.'

CHAPTER NINETEEN

Child! A child! Emma felt only the cold reality of the linseed-polished wood beneath her hand as she made her way back up the grand staircase to her chamber. Why had Darleston not told her? Paternity doubts aside, he must acknowledge that it had bearing upon the situation. She knew Darleston did not love his wife and, if all he said were true, she did not deserve his affections, but surely he was not knave enough to leave his wife – the woman, however wrongly, he had sworn before God to cherish and protect – to fend for herself while pregnant?

Worse too was the fact that her own frigidity had been bandied before everyone. They had all thought her odd enough before; now she'd be discussed like a prize heifer, and Lyle's virility was bound to be called into question. They would all be at risk.

Nauseous to the depths of her stomach, Emma swayed, suddenly overcome by light-headedness. She longed for a steady arm to hold onto in that moment, but no one came to her assistance. They had not even followed her up the stairs to see that she was well. They were all so used to her rebuffs – even Lyle knew better than to attempt any sort of affectionate contact – yet that was the very thing she craved: someone, be it the lowliest servant, to put their arms around her and tell her that all would be right, though that was a lie no one had cared to offer her since her mother's funeral. Yet what she wouldn't give to hear it said. Sometimes one had to believe in little deceits in order to stomach reality.

Head still swimming, Emma entered her room, fell onto the bed and closed her eyes.

She awoke some time later in response to a persistent knock upon the door. 'Emma, please open up.' After thirty or so *rat-a-tat-tats* achieved him naught, Darleston lifted the latch and let himself in. Groggily, Emma lifted her head from the pillow, only for her hair, which had come loose from its pins, to tumble over her face. 'The others are at the fight,' he explained, while she brushed the strands aside. 'I came back as soon as I was able. Oh, Emma, I'm sorry you had to hear that from her. I ought to have told you what she'd come here for, but in the wake of everything else it clean slipped my mind.'

Even if she had not already trusted him, the sincerity with which he spoke would have assuaged any doubts. Still – 'You can't send her away penniless to rot,' she said. 'Not when there's a child involved.' She hunched herself up so that she sat cradling her knees. She'd experienced first-hand what poverty did to children, even those who were loved. Lady Darleston didn't seem the type to make an affectionate or even interested mother. The best the child could hope for was a doting nursemaid or to be claimed by an adoring father, but the latter would be impossible so long as Lady Darleston insisted upon the child's legitimacy.

'I confess I'm not even sure she's quickening. I did go to see her maid last night, but not for any sordid reason. I meant to discover the name of the actual father.'

Darleston perched on the foot of the bed, barely finding purchase on the rumpled coverlet, his full coat-tails fanning out behind him. He had dressed in some of his most magnificent finery, a charcoal-grey silk suit overlaid with a cobwebbed pattern of embroidery and diamonds. His waist-coat alone, a fiery shade of taffeta that matched his hair, sported more rubies than the lacework necklace Lyle had given her as a betrothal gift. The ensemble gave him an air of grandeur that would elevate him far above the rank and file of the fight crowd. It might single him out as a target for the pickpockets, but it would also buy him a great deal of respect among those with pretensions of grandeur. Emma wondered if he was expecting further trouble. He always dressed beautifully, but this excess seemed to her to be a kind of mask.

'Do go on.'

He shook his head. 'Sally was far from forthcoming, but she did let slip a few details that make me think it all a ruse to extract money for some other purpose. I'm not altogether sure what, but something is afoot.'

So he had armoured himself by making his status absolutely plain.

'What do you suspect?' She tilted her head, taking the pressure off her chin and resting her cheek upon her knee instead.

Uncertainty turned his eyes a watery grey. 'It could simply be creditors exerting pressure, but I do wonder ... I'm not sure ... I think perhaps she's ailing in some way and not quickening at all. The maid said that she'd been to take the waters at Bath, something Lucy's been fervently dismissive of in the past. Sally had no notion of her being with child.'

Emma straightened. Upper servants were privy to all manner of delicate information. 'How is that possible?'

'I've asked myself the very same. I may write a letter or two later. There are one or two physicians whose opinions I respect and who might be able to shed some light upon the matter.'

'No baby.' Emma rubbed at the tension building in her temples again. 'Do you think it a tumour or some other malignancy growing inside her?'

'Oh, that, definitely,' he agreed heartlessly, only to apologise a moment later. 'I'm sorry. Lucy does bring out the absolute worst in me. I don't want to offer her anything. I can't help suspecting that giving her money will only open myself to future demands.'

'Blackmail?'

'Nothing is beyond her.'

Emma nodded. 'I still feel it's wrong to leave her with nothing, no matter how heartless or cruel she is. Would it hurt you dreadfully to offer her some modest amount?'

Darleston gave her an inscrutable look, one that turned his grey eyes almost the same hue as his coat. She doubted many would notice it, but she knew a war raged inside him over her request. Externally, only the faint wrinkling around his eyes gave any hint of his thoughts. After an awkward pause, he said, 'I fear you are a far better person than I, for I should dearly like to wring her neck. I've certainly no desire to look after her, but I suppose I have not really told you the half of what she's done. Nor have I any wish to recount it,' he hastily added. 'However, if it pleases you to be kind, then I will see she's given a stipend, enough to live comfortably if modestly upon. I'll have my lawyer oversee it. I hope not to meet her again outside of hell.'

'You're a good man. No one who sees into your soul would ever send you there.'

Darleston gave a dubious snort. 'I think you are forgetting some of my preferences, my love.'

Not for a moment would she ever forget that he'd been her husband's lover before he'd become hers, or that he remained so still. They might all stay for a day or two more, once today's fight was over, but she sensed that life was moving on. Some sort of decision and arrangement had to be agreed upon by the three of them before the tide of departures from Field House sent them off in different directions.

'Emma, may I move up this bed?' Darleston asked. He seemed to sense her depression. 'Leaving here needn't be an end to anything. I should like you to think it a beginning.'

Emma held her hands out towards him. He didn't take them. Instead, he enfolded her in his embrace, so that her head moulded to the crook of his shoulder and his familiar musky scent evoked a warm glow inside her, though it didn't entirely quell her fears.

'How will it work?' she asked. How could it work? She and he might feel the same way about each other, but she and Lyle were more like brother and sister than husband and wife.

'It'll work because we'll take measures to ensure it does.' He gripped her a little tighter as he spoke, but the extra closeness didn't eliminate her doubts. 'Lyle's prepared to be adaptable. Can you be?'

She clove to the silky smoothness of his coat. 'I'll try.' That truly was the very best she could offer, not knowing if she would ever be able to tolerate any touch but Darleston's. Desire had driven her to open up to him, but that was something she simply didn't feel for Lyle. Maybe it would come in time. They did love one another in their own curious way.

'Shall I tell you how I imagine us to be?' His breath stirred the disarranged curls that hung each side of her face. Emma kept quiet, knowing he would take that as a cue to continue. 'Don't think that I don't know your preferences. I do, which is why I see myself in the centre.'

'In the centre of what?' she enquired.

He hesitated and, as his chest pressed against her back, she felt too the tremulous leaping of his heart. He had reservations about sharing this. She wondered if this was something he'd shared before, perhaps with Lucy, and had had thrown back in his face. 'There are certain things I've always imagined myself part of. Having both you and Lyle is already more than I ever hoped to gain.'

'You want us together, though.'

'Yes – like we've been, but more so. Do you think you could do that, Emma? Could you let me make love to you while Lyle was present? He wouldn't have to touch you, but it's likely he'd be touching me.'

Likely! She had a sudden, startlingly clear image of what Darleston was tentatively hinting at. She'd seen the men together often enough now to know how things worked between them, and if Darleston were in the middle then, yes, it would be possible for them all to be joined at once; but did he really believe that they could manage it without her and Lyle touching one another? The strange thing was that, in the situation he envisaged, the thought of accepting Lyle's touch when lost in a sensual haze didn't disturb her nearly as much as the idea of tolerating even an everyday embrace from Amelia.

'I can try,' she said. 'Will I be able to feel him through you?'

Darleston turned her head so that he could look at her.

His grey eyes shone with wonder. Maybe he hadn't expected her to understand so completely, or to accept it with such grace. He seemed pleased that she had. She supposed most women didn't want to hear about their lover's past deeds, or their love of other people, but somehow she didn't feel threatened by his desire for Lyle, only intrigued.

'I don't know. Some of his movements, perhaps. I've never really been in that situation to know.'

'But you have performed … made love in such a way?'

He stroked her hair, and then pressed his lips against hers. 'No. Not exactly in that way. You have to understand that the two halves of my life have never really crossed. I've loved two men at the same time, and I've bedded women in the company of another man, or two, but the woman in question was always centre stage. That's not how it's going to be between us.'

'So many lovers, and yet you find time to be intrigued by me and my coldness.'

'You're not cold at all.'

She accepted his words with a nod, while not entirely believing them. 'Has Lyle asked you to stay with us?'

His expression grew dark. 'I think he intended to talk to you first.'

'Ah.' They sat in silence a moment, until Darleston bent and gave her another gentle kiss.

'He knows how I feel,' she said. 'I can't see why he'd delay making the offer, unless he feels threatened or uncomfortable in some way.'

Darleston cocked his head to one side as if considering. 'Perhaps he simply wants to talk it over thoroughly in case there are terms to negotiate. It's a big step, inviting me into your lives like that.'

'He wouldn't have thought twice about it if I weren't involved. We've entertained his lovers before.'

'This is meant to be rather more permanent.'

Emma mulled that over for a moment, but she couldn't see that permanency was the issue. Lyle lived too much in the moment for that. He didn't think in the long term, only of the now: how things affected him now, not how they would be in three days' time, let alone longer. 'He's not going to present me with some ridiculous plan whereby we get you for three days a week each and only share you on Sundays, is he? I hope he knows that's not going to work. That would be tiresome and awful.'

'Then how do you propose we arrange it?' Darleston steepled his fingers before him and tapped his fingertips to his mouth.

Emma frowned at him, incredulous. 'That we go about our daily lives and see what comes of it. I'm sure we'll all desire privacy at some point, but we can address that as adults, can't we?'

'He's already jealous of the time I spend with you.'

'Oh, is he?' She was already aware of that. 'Well, I don't suppose he's thought about the amount of time the two of you spend together gallivanting about the estate and how that excludes me. In fact, you're able to see a whole lot more of one another than I can ever hope of doing with either of you. I might be seen as peculiar, but I'm still obliged to entertain the ladies of the district. They'll be constantly calling, once it's known you're staying with us – an actual viscount.'

Darleston's fingers stilled and he lowered his hands from his lips. 'It's only a courtesy title, and I've a reputation that's foul enough to scare off most.'

'You're the son of an earl. You could dance about naked

painted all over with yellow spots and they'd still come to simper and titter before you.'

Vexed now, she pushed him away a little, a move that instantly brought a frown to his face. 'I think we're all a little nervous of how things will be. I know I don't desire to start a war. You've said yourself that Lyle's never been forceful or discourteous to you. He wishes you the very best.'

'But only if it's not with his lover, and don't try to pretend otherwise. I know my husband well enough to read his moods. He was far from pleased when I told him what had happened between us.'

'I won't deny it,' Darleston said. He rubbed the side of his rather long nose. 'He has expressed some doubts but, like you, he's nervous, he's frightened. None of us truly knows how this will work out. What's important is that we're all committed to trying it. For my part, I want you both in my bed, and I just pray that I can persuade each of you to go along with that.'

As a first act of persuasion, he pressed a lingering kiss to the juncture between her neck and her collarbone, a touch that left her boneless and trembling in his arms. Darleston eased her down against the pillow, where he fanned her brown hair around her head. Two long strands framed her face. He curled one around the tip of his index finger.

Emma lifted a hand to touch his face, but he laced their fingers together instead, before placing a kiss upon the back of her hand and then another on her wrist. 'Come closer,' she whispered. The mattress creaked as he changed positions so that he lay stretched over her, braced upon his knees and elbows. She smiled up at him, knowing this was the position he planned for them to take when the three of them lay together. 'Have you secreted Lyle close by?'

A crease appeared between his brows. 'No. I left him supervising the fight with your father.' She hadn't realised that the boxing match was already under way, but nap-taking did tend to skew one's sense of time.

'There'll be talk over your leaving.'

'I doubt anyone has noticed. They were far too engrossed in the brawl. Only Quernow saw me leave and he was more concerned with the book Littleton and Oxbury were running. Regardless, it was far more important to come and see that you were well than to avoid comment. I had to apologise.'

'Have you apologised?

He dipped his head again. 'I believe I was just about to.' He kissed her in a slow, meandering way, one that roused her senses slowly and made them burn all the brighter for it. Emma clung to him. After all that had passed that day, she couldn't bear to let go. The flick of his tongue against hers coaxed her into relaxing, as did the reassuring weight of his body above her. How strange that she should consider it so, when if it were anyone else she'd be half out of her wits with fright, desperate to scrub even the memory of their touch from her skin with a scouring brush.

Not content with a simple kiss, Darleston hitched her cream petticoat and sought the bare skin that lay above her garters. 'Let me,' he whispered, when she modestly pressed her thighs together. 'I can give you pleasure like this without raising unnecessary complications, just as Lyle once showed you, I believe.' Lyle had never demonstrated that. He'd shown her what it was like for a man, and described how she might apply such knowledge to her own fulfilment. Still, it remained a lesson for which she was grateful. Lyle did care for her in his own quiet way, and she for him. Perhaps they might grow to appreciate one another in more intimate ways, given proximity and time. If anyone could bring that about it was Robert Darleston.

Emma gazed at his narrow face with its frame of red hair around it. His mouth took on a sultry expression, turning up ever so slightly at the corners. It wasn't so much that the expression invited her kiss, more that it promised wickedness. 'Are you plotting something?'

'Only this.' His hand moved from where it lay warm against her thigh and came to rest over her mons, while his thumb traced the seam of her labia.

'Oh!'

'Oh?' he repeated, while his thumb stroked back and forth, wakening her body, so that the head of her little nub peeked out. 'Did you ever put into practice Lyle's lesson? I think I would have enjoyed observing that *tête à tête*.' The pad of his thumb brushed her nubbin, making her jerk at the sheer intensity of the spark that dashed through her innards.

Emma's cheeks blazed.

'Don't be shy about it. I think a woman ought to know her own body. I refuse to be hypocritical about it. I've indulged myself often enough. More than a few times while thinking of you.' He kept his stroke light, so that his thumb, followed by his fingertips, danced over her skin. 'I half thought that I'd go mad from the possibility of not having you. I might well have done, if it weren't for Lyle, and even then it was hard to dispel the thoughts of you. You've haunted me, Emma.' His lips joined in the delicate dance and he drew circles over her throat and décolletage. 'And after you showed me that teasing glimpse of your derriere ... well, I certainly gave it and several other parts of you considerable thought. I stroked myself, in the way you've watched your husband give himself pleasure, and all the while I pictured the soft swell of your breasts and skipping my palms over them, and the roundness of your belly. I thought of how it would feel to have you hold me. But most of all I imagined doing this.' He fell back on his haunches and with an elegant flick lifted her rucked-up petticoats fully out of the way. He paused, leaned over her, breathing in her musk, then brought the intense pleasure of his kiss to her peeping nub.

He had done this thrice now. Each time its power seemed magnified. Emma clutched at the sheets, then at his back, then his hair. She wove her fingers into the bright strands, blindly guiding him, while he worked magic with his tongue. After a while, she realised that he was speaking, not just kissing her, but whispering endearments and secrets to her cunny. His tongue probed her entrance, filling her, but not nearly as well as his cock.

Despite the nightmares of dawn, her need for him began to build. His tongue, beautiful and talented as it was, didn't satisfy her as his prick could. He'd claimed there were ways of managing things to avoid her conceiving. 'Robert.' She tried to lift him to her. 'Robert.' Rather than responding to her pleas immediately, he applied himself more precisely to the task, sucking and licking and drubbing the very tip of his tongue at lightning pace against her nub. He'd surely bring her to climax before he even thought of sliding into her. Maybe that was the way. If her little death didn't happen while he was inside her, the spark that brought a child into the world wouldn't occur. Maybe he'd have to withdraw too, before he reached a peak.

'Robert ... please ... I need more than this.' She opened her eyes to beseech him the more, only for an astonished gasp to burst from her throat. A second later she inhaled enough to scream.

CHAPTER TWENTY

Lady Darleston stood at the side of the bed. She had softened the stark white costume she had donned earlier by adding a mid-blue fur-trimmed pelisse. A hat composed of the same materials, with tassels to one side, perched upon her abundance of ringlets.

Darleston started to lift his head. 'No, don't get up, Robert. Stay right there.' Lady Darleston pressed the barrel of a flintlock to his temple. 'I see my assumptions weren't so very far off. Mrs Langley seems to tolerate your touch perfectly well, or is it that she just doesn't mind licking, without the press of a hand?' With her own free hand Lucy tugged at the front of Emma's dress. The pins gave way, exposing the layers of linen beneath and the swell of Emma's breasts. 'I can see why you're charmed by her. You always did like nice tits.' She grabbed one of Emma's breasts and cruelly squeezed the nipple.

'What do you want, Lucy? Let her be.'

'"Let her be." Oh, I don't think so, for I can see how very much she hates this. Am I making your skin crawl, dear Mrs Langley?' She pinched again, hard enough to bruise, and then squealed in delight when Emma flinched. Emma turned her head away, determined not to show her tears. This woman would not see her pain, or how much it cost her to tolerate this rough handling.

'As for what I want, husband mine, you already know that. You'll accept the child as your heir, or I'll pull the trigger and rid us both of the problem. I'm sure with a small degree of manipulation I can get both you and Mrs Langley off together.' Amusement bubbled from her in the form of another laugh. 'Isn't that what lovers are always questing for, to die the little death together? Only in your case it won't be so little and it'll be a tad more permanent.'

Considering the pistol barrel pressed to his head, Darleston maintained his impassive expression. He might have been greeting a neighbour at a ball, not facing a deranged woman with a gun. 'If you pull that trigger you will splatter yourself from head to foot in gore and bring every servant in the house rushing here. It's unlikely you'd go unpunished, no matter how fine you think your acting skills.'

'I'd get what I wanted. The line would continue in your name.'

'You're not remotely concerned about the title, only the status it gives you. I don't think you're prepared to sacrifice yourself for a child. Though, having said that, isn't it time we ended this ruse? What is it you want, Lucy? Money? I'm not going to argue paternity with you any longer, because we both know there is no child.'

Surprise flickered in the heart of Lucy's pupils, to be quickly consumed by rage. 'Of course there's a child. I have all the symptoms. I have fainted and been sick and I have had no flow of blood.' She clutched her hand to her stomach as though a sharp pain ran through that part of her body. 'What else makes a woman ill in that way?'

'I'm sure I don't know.'

'Nothing. It's a child, you fool.'

'Of course,' Darleston agreed in a soothing tone, but in a way that suggested that he knew her to be hiding from the truth. 'Very well, so you require money. I'll provide money. Let Emma go and we'll talk. She's irrelevant to this.'

Lucy's grip on the pistol relaxed a fraction, but then she gently squeezed the trigger. A maniacal grin stretched across her milk-white face. 'Do you think so, Robert? I've never found your mistresses to be irrelevant. How sad to find you think so little of them, but then you have always been a selfish rip. Seven years we have been together and not once have you planted your seed in my belly. What is the point of marriage if not to produce an heir? Dear God, you even set your brother to the task of performing for you. I thought it could not be me, that it was merely a function of your unnaturalness, only here I find you with a mistress. There have been tens of them, have there not? It is just me you've spurned. You even made love to your best friend's wife.'

Emma tried to quell her shock, but she had not known the extent of his past debauchery. She would let him explain himself before making any judgements.

'You will accept this damned child as your heir, Robert. You will.' Lucy's voice became a shriek.

'As you wish.' He said it so quietly that at first Lucy did not seem to have heard him over her escalating screams. When it did sink in, she stared at him coldly. After a moment of silence, she began worrying her lip.

'You agree. You give your word as a gentleman and won't go back on it?'

'I agree.'

'I want to set up my own household. Not as I have had

301

to endure these last few months, but a proper establishment such as my rank entitles me to.'

'Of course.'

She laughed. 'How delightful to find you so amenable. I should have put a gun to your head years ago.'

'I would prefer if you could remove it now.'

'Would you? Then I don't think I shall. I'm finding this all rather enjoyable.' She clutched her hand to her stomach again. If there had been a chair nearby, Emma suspected she would have sunk into it. 'Besides, I do so wish to get to know Mrs Langley better. Mayhap we can cosy up and become intimate.' Her face lit up then as though she had been struck by the most wonderful idea. 'Why don't you introduce us properly, Robert? Is your cock still at a stand?'

'What?'

From where Emma lay beneath him, peering up into his face, it was plain that he regretted the outburst, but Lucy had taken him by surprise. The corners of his eyes wrinkled with rage, but somehow he forced his voice to remain urbane and unworried.

'No. I'm afraid I don't find any eroticism in the situation.'

'Do you hear that, dear?' Lucy sighed. 'He finds nothing inspiring about your muff, even with his nose pressed to it. Tut, tut. We shall have to pray he is lying.' She grabbed hold of the hair upon the back of Darleston's head. 'Rouse yourself. I want to watch you poke her.'

Darleston paled to the core. If they ever got out of this bed and this room, Emma was certain he would murder his wife. A coldness she had not seen before swept over him like an icy wind. His face became a sneer, full of haughty aristocratic abhorrence. 'You'll have to shoot me. I find myself disinclined to put on a show.'

Lucy's mad grin transformed into a scowl. There was a sort of glazed sheen in her eyes that made Emma wonder if she hadn't taken laudanum or some other potion to temper the aches that were so obviously afflicting her.

'Oh, Robert, you are no fun. And just when we were getting along so well.'

The chamber door swung open at that moment, whoever it was not bothering to knock. 'Emma?' the intruder enquired. Lucy turned sharply, gun in hand. As she moved, Darleston rolled towards her. Catlike, he landed on his feet and sprang up between Lucy and the bed. He made a grab for the pistol, which went off with a deafening roar. For one horrid moment, as smoke billowed around the matchlock, Emma feared for Darleston's life, but when Lucy staggered backwards from the recoil Darleston followed her. He wrenched the pistol from her grip and cast it across the room. It skittered over the polished boards and came to rest in the window bay.

Lyle stood in the doorway. He caught Emma's gaze for just a second before he dropped like a felled tree.

'Lyle!' Emma leapt from the bed. Her husband lay on his back, eyes and mouth open. A spreading puddle of blood was forming under his right arm. 'Oh, God!' she cried. 'What do we do? He's hit.' She knelt down beside him.

'I didn't,' Lucy protested. Her face took on an even wilder expression, slack-jawed and trembling. 'You pushed me.' She clawed at Darleston accusingly. 'You shoved me so that I'd hit her husband and you could claim her for yourself.'

'Shut up!' Darleston shook her hard. 'If I hadn't knocked you, you'd have shot him dead.' He tried to hold onto Lucy and drag her over to a chair, but she scratched at his face like a wildcat, forcing him to maintain his hold on her rather than go to Lyle's aid. 'Is he badly hurt, Emma?'

'I don't know. Yes.' She'd never dressed a wound larger than a scrape. 'He's been hit in the upper arm. I think the ball has gone straight through.' The misshapen remains of the projectile lay in the middle of the hallway runner, looking like an innocently misplaced marble.

'You need to fetch the surgeon. Head over to the fight. Hill has a man on hand to see to Jack after the match.'

She knew him. Jimmy Bolden, the village butcher. The man had a good grasp of medicinal herbs but he was also over-eager with his knives and prone to lopping things off with little hesitation. She couldn't let him sever Lyle's arm.

'Emma.' Lyle, who, despite his injuries, clearly had the same thoughts about Bolden, grabbed her wrist with his unhurt hand as she made to rise. 'Stay here.' He gripped her so tightly that even her instantaneous urge to recoil from his touch didn't free her. 'Stay with me.'

'You're hurt,' she said soothingly, reaching out tentatively to stroke back the golden curls from his damp brow. 'I have to fetch help.'

Lyle shook his head. 'Not Bolden. I've seen his work. He'll only spill more of my blood on the floor. Get Drummond, if anyone.'

His valet? What could he possibly do? He might remake Lyle's coat sleeve, but now wasn't the time to think of clothes.

'You need to examine the wound. See that it's clean. Then sew it closed and bind it tight,' Lyle continued.

Emma watched his blood continue to pool. A wave of nausea slowly rose in her throat. 'Lyle, I can't do that.'

'I trust you. I've seen you embroider. Please. If you love me at all, if we've a chance at anything good together.'

She tried to pull away from him again, but only so that she could run for help. She did want him to live, but she could not dress his wound. Yet if the bleeding wasn't stopped his life would drain away. There were servants downstairs. They would know what to do and whom to fetch.

'Emma,' Lyle croaked with some effort. 'I've been a soldier. I've seen such wounds and helped treat them. Please, do as I instruct.' A glaze was slowly coming over his eyes, leaving the intense dark pools softly shadowed. 'Please.' The rigid tension in his jaw faded into relaxation. 'Please. Find Drummond to help you.'

A maid and two of the upper servants, one of whom turned out to be Drummond, appeared in the doorway at that moment. 'We heard the bang,' Drummond said, before kneeling at his master's side. 'Have you a sewing box? We need scissors to remove his coat sleeve.'

'In the drawing room, downstairs.' Perhaps he'd hoped it lay closer.

'Betsy.' He addressed the maid, while the other footman went to aid Lord Darleston in his struggle with his wife. 'Go and get Mrs Langley's scissors, and fetch whatever strong liquor you can find. Gin if it's there, otherwise brandy or rum. Be quick.'

'Do you know what you are doing?' Emma enquired. Lyle's tight grip upon her wrist was gradually slackening, which only added to her distress. 'Shouldn't we call for help?'

'I was with him in India. He'll be fine, as long as we get him sewn up and keep the wound clean. The house is almost empty, ma'am. There's only cook and the scullery girl downstairs. Everyone else has permission to watch the boxing.'

'Pillowslips,' Lyle mumbled. His eyelids fluttered, and then closed.

'Lyle?' Emma shook him, but he didn't rouse.

'It's probably for the best, ma'am,' Drummond said. 'He

won't feel it so much.' He fetched several of the pillows from the bed. One he placed beneath Lyle's head, the other he stripped of its case, which he tore into long strips.

Betsy arrived back from her trip to the drawing room clutching a decanter and Emma's best embroidery scissors. Her mousy hair had escaped its cap in her flight and stuck out in frizzy curls, an offence that in any other circumstances would have earned her a reprimand. She'd also brought a needle and a reel of bright-blue thread. Drummond set to removing Lyle's sleeve, cutting through both the soft wool and the cambric shirt beneath.

Lyle had worn one of his better coats today, one he normally reserved for special occasions, finely worked around the buttonholes and less coarse and squire-like than some of the garments he wore for overseeing matters of the estate. He'd curse the loss of it, for he loved to look well. Emma had often suspected that, if they'd spent more time amongst the city set, her husband would have become something of a peacock. Maybe that was one of the things he found so appealing about Darleston.

The blood flow, which had become sluggish, quickened again once the sleeve was stripped away. Drummond made her press two pieces of wadding made from the pillowslips against the wounds, one on either side of Lyle's arm.

'Give me that thread,' Drummond ordered.

Betsy wet the end of the yarn between her lips and set to threading the needle. She had a good eye and nimble fingers and handed it over at once. Drummond started on the upper wound first, pulling the skin together with a chain of bright blue stitches that turned purple as blood seeped into the cotton. He bade Emma hold Lyle's arm upright by the wrist as he worked on the back of his master's arm. Once the flesh had been drawn together on both sides of the arm, Drummond poured neat brandy over both of the wounds. Then he bound Lyle's arm with the remainder of the strips torn from the pillowslip and lifted him onto the bed, a notable feat, for he was a good deal shorter than her husband.

'If there are any signs of infection tomorrow we can use blowfly maggots to clean out the necrosis. They'll eat up whatever's rotten and keep the gangrene at bay.'

At that, Emma voided the contents of her stomach. The image of wriggling, crawling things gnawing on putrid flesh was too close to one that routinely disturbed her sleep. She didn't stumble, though she did feel faint. She reached out and grasped the bedpost. She would not lose Lyle to a fever as she had lost so many of her siblings. He would live, even if that meant trusting in Drummond's horrific methods.

'Maybe you should lie down too, ma'am,' Betsy suggested. She fussed around Emma, taking care not to touch her.

Emma accepted the kerchief she offered, but shook her head at the notion of retiring. She had thankfully only made a mess of the floor and not herself. Since she had missed breakfast there had been little in her stomach anyway. Nor was she tired, and a room would have to be made up for her, since Lyle was occupying their bed. 'I'll stay here, and sit with him.'

'Very well, ma'am.' Betsy ran at once to fetch another chair and settled Emma in it.

'Should I run over to Mr Hill?' asked Drummond. 'Will the constable need to be called?' He glanced uncertainly at Emma and Lord Darleston, as if not sure whom he should best consult. Darleston, with the aid of the footman, had finally secured Lady Darleston in an armchair. She had her hands bound before her in her lap, tied with what looked suspiciously like one of Lyle's galluses. She had succumbed to a fit of weeping, but her tears were now and then punctuated by a hysterical laugh.

She would have to be removed to another part of the house.

Darleston came over to where Lyle rested deathly pale upon the bed. 'Dear God! This should not have happened.' He took Lyle's good hand in his and bowed over him as if in prayer. When he straightened up, he kissed Lyle gently upon the brow.

'Bring Hill,' he instructed Drummond. 'Tell him what's afoot, and that I'd prefer it if we could avoid the involvement of the constable. I should like to speak with him first and see if we can't settle the matter amongst ourselves. I'm sure neither of us wishes to court a scandal.'

'She mustn't get away with it,' Emma exclaimed.

'She won't.' Darleston regarded her calmly. He cast an inscrutable glance at his wife before returning his attention to Drummond. 'Send for a physician too, and a midwife. There's a matter I need to clear up before I speak to Hill.'

CHAPTER TWENTY-ONE

'Rob! Robert ... where are you, damn it?' Neddy's voice echoed inside the glass walls of the Orangery like a series of cannon blasts. Darleston didn't reply. He remained at the back of the grotto, watching a steady stream of water trickle past his feet, numb to the noise but little else. Life had become so twisted and tormented over the last few hours that he wished he could lock himself away from it all. Staring at the water seemed to be the closest he could get to that.

'Rob. Thank the Lord!' His twin hunkered down beside him. Neddy still wore the tweed outfit he'd donned for the fight, which was now creased and rather grubby. 'I've been looking for you for ages. What are you doing out here? You're needed inside.'

Was he? What could he do? He couldn't offer comfort; Emma had retreated into herself. He couldn't bear to look upon his wife, and Lyle's fate was way beyond his skill. The only option left to him was prayer, and, since he had no faith in God, that seemed altogether pointless.

He raised a hand to wipe away the sweat that lathered his brow. 'Will he live?' It was the only question that mattered now. He knew that Neddy didn't have the answer. It was too soon to say. The ball had passed straight through Lyle's arm, damaging muscle and sinews. Bolden thought it might have splintered some of the bone and wanted to dig around in the wound. Drummond had held him off, backed up by the physician that Hill had called in, Waddington, Waddingbeck or whatever his name was. At least they'd all agreed that further bloodletting wasn't the answer. The maids had mopped bucketfuls off the floor already.

'Rob, I don't know. He might mend. He could lose his arm. The main worry is keeping him free of fever. If they manage that, he might make it.'

Fever – like those five tiny bodies Emma had shown him in the graveyard. He couldn't allow her to suffer another loss like that. He'd promised her that everything would work out. She'd trusted him, opened up to him, and all it had achieved was the pain she'd striven so hard to avoid.

'God, I'm so sorry.' His brother bowed his head as though this were all somehow his fault. Ned had guided him here, but he hadn't pushed him into Lyle's bed, and had hardly encouraged him into Emma's. It was no more Ned's fault than it was anyone else's – except his.

'Here.' Neddy passed him a silver flask. 'Take a swig. You need it. And for heaven's sake talk. Spit out all that nonsense I know you're thinking.'

The brandy burned as it hit his gullet, leaving him coughing and fighting back the tears he'd been restraining for hours. 'I thought … I thought maybe it would work out, and we'd manage to be happy together.' He ought to have known better. Lucy was never going to agree to free him. If she hadn't spoilt it now, she'd have found a means to do it later. It'd been foolish to think she'd walk away quietly from being publicly humiliated. She'd intended to appear the stricken party in her little performance on the stairs, and instead she'd shown herself up. He ought to have known she'd retaliate.

The only good thing was that she hadn't realised the depth of his feelings for Lyle. If she had, then likely the shot would have been fatal from the outset. Instead, she'd meant only to strike fear into Emma and make him bow to her wishes. Lucy hadn't understood that this time he'd found something he had no intention of giving up.

'Emma?' he enquired.

'She's by Lyle's side.' Neddy reclaimed his flask. He drained it dry before returning it to his inside pocket. 'Let's go in. Waddingthorpe wants to talk to you about Lucy's condition.'

'Is she pregnant?' He knew in his heart that she wasn't, but he needed an unbiased opinion to confirm that. Trusting to his guts alone seemed too treacherous these days.

'I think that's what he wants to talk to you about.' Neddy tugged upon his arm, encouraging him to stand.

Did he really want to know? What difference would it actually make? He ought to have her arrested and tried, but he was not about to send for the constable, who would no doubt find reason to poke his nose into his privacy, regardless of its tenuous bearing on the case. Hill had no desire to invite such attention either. It had been the first thing he'd said after he'd been told that Lucy had shot his son-in-law.

'Stay with me when we go in, Ned.'

His brother promised with a solemn nod. He rose and offered Darleston a hand to get up, squeezing a fraction too hard as he tried to communicate some measure of reassurance. 'It'll work out, Rob. Somehow it always does.'

For Neddy perhaps. He couldn't honestly say that anything in his life had worked out quite as he'd wished it.

* * *

Dr Waddingthorpe's robust figure occupied the whole of the drawing-room sofa. He sat alone in the large chamber beside a rapidly collapsing heap of coals. For a country doctor he dressed rather finely, his waistcoat clearly grosgrain silk, even if his curled periwig showed signs of age. He started out of his repose the moment Darleston entered, and his jowls quivered as he shifted his enormous bulk upright.

'Milord.' He dipped his head in a gesture towards a bow, then waited, sweat bubbling above his lip, for his lordship to sit.

Darleston chose to stand. He'd always found bad news easier to stomach that way. He waited until he was sure that Neddy was present too before addressing the doctor. 'I understand you've examined my wife.'

Waddingthorpe swayed uneasily. He looked at his hands as if expecting that something to eat would suddenly materialise there. 'I have, milord, though with some trouble, I may add. She was not entirely co-operative.' He rubbed at something on his finger that Darleston suspected might be a bite mark. 'Though she is resting peacefully enough now that I've administered a small sedative.'

Darleston wondered idly how many of Hill's servants it'd taken to pin her down in order to administer the dose. 'And?' He had no time for niceties at the present. He wanted straight answers without any dither. There'd be plenty of time to wallow in misapprehensions during the dark of the night. He straightened his shoulders, bracing himself for a blunt, hard shock.

'There is a growth in her belly, part way down on the right side.'

Darleston sagged a little, releasing a sigh. The news was far better than he'd hoped for, though obviously not good. 'Not a child?'

'No.' Waddingthorpe hesitated long enough to wipe his kerchief over his mouth. The action didn't seem to suggest uncertainty about his answer, but rather about the response he'd received. 'I don't believe so, milord, though it's hard to say for certain. There are cases where the embryo grows external to its proper abode, but such a body is unlikely to come to fruition, and hence ought not to be considered a child but rather an imp. However, in Lady Darleston's case it is more likely the lump is a cancerous growth. I was able to palpate it quite thoroughly through the abdominal wall. The tumour is quite large for one so petite.'

'How large?'

The doctor made an imprecise gesture with his hands, and then turned about, looking for something of a representative size. He seized a fruit bowl and emptied the oranges out of it into Neddy's hands before holding the vessel aloft for them to see. The whole of her abdomen had to be riddled with it, if Waddingthorpe were not exaggerating. 'It likely extends into her liver and spleen and some other organs. Most likely it started within her lady parts and spread.'

Part of him wanted to laugh at Waddingthorpe's attempt at delicacy. Could the man not manage slang, or even anatomical terms, for such organs? Then again, he suspected Waddingthorpe had rather enjoyed his exploration of Lucy's abdomen.

'Curable?' he asked, though he already guessed the answer. He concentrated on the doctor, rather than on his brother's ashen face, while Waddingthorpe put aside the fruit bowl. Neddy was taking all this harder than him. For himself, he wanted nothing more than to see Lyle and know he was well. To the devil with Lucy.

Waddingthorpe gave his head another solemn shake. 'If it were earlier in the process I'd normally recommend extraction. It'd make her barren, but there'd be a chance of recovery. In this case, that would necessitate too much cutting. However, there are some tinctures and medicines I can prescribe to ease the burden and which may help reduce the load. If she'd seen me sooner ... Well, there's a penetrative ointment too that might work. I've had some success with it in the past. It's rubbed into the skin over the afflicted area four times a day. I'm sorry I can't give you better news than that.'

'No, I thank you for your honesty.' At least the good man hadn't tried to string him along with some assurance of recovery. He could read it in the man's posture, in his subdued, stoic sense of calm. He wouldn't be Lucy's physician long enough for the endeavour to be profitable, so he was saving himself the burden of having to lie.

'Rob?' Ned asked, reducing his multitude of questions to that one word. Darleston waved both his brother and the doctor away. He left the drawing room and went straight to find Hill.

That gentleman sat behind his desk in his study. He looked particularly gaunt this evening, his eye sockets hollowed by the grey smudges around them. His irises were a watered-down shade of Emma's blue. 'What can I do for you, Darleston?' He looked up, flicking away powdery snuff stains from his waistcoat.

Darleston ignored the impolite address. In the circumstances, it was hard to find offence. 'I've spoken with Waddingthorpe regarding my wife.'

Hill took another pinch of snuff before putting aside his little silver box and giving Darleston his full attention. He sneezed violently, but remained in a defensive pose, his arms crossed and resting on the blotter before him. 'He concludes that her ladyship is ill, and not of sound mind, is that right?'

No mention had been made of Lucy's mental functioning, only of her physical symptoms. Regardless, Darleston nodded in affirmation.

'I trust you understand that I cannot allow you to remain here with her. I'm willing to keep this matter quiet between us. I've no wish to involve the justice service in my affairs. I think we can agree that it was an accident amidst the crowd at the prize-fight that resulted in Lyle's injuries.'

'Absolutely,' Darleston agreed. Given the recent scandals that had hounded his person, discretion was in everyone's best interests.

'I'm sure you understand that I cannot extend you any further hospitality. You may depart this evening or with my other houseguests on the morrow, but you must remove yourself and your lady wife from my property.'

'Yes, of course.' He had no wish to deal with Lucy, but couldn't shirk his responsibility in that regard. He'd married her, for better or worse. That made it his job to deal with her. Ned had already sent word ahead that they'd be arriving at the family estate in Shropshire imminently. Once there, they'd have Lucy confined to her rooms. The situation wasn't ideal, but would hopefully prevent the worst of the tattlemongers' speculations.

Of course, it would mean leaving Lyle and Emma behind at the very time he wanted to be with them the most. 'I'll arrange for us to depart right away. I would like to see Mr

Langley before I depart, if that's possible. I feel I owe him a grave apology.'

Hill scraped back his chair and rose at once, shaking his head of thinning grey hair. 'I'll pass on your sentiments when and if he wakes.' He poked out his chin and his words emerged in a flat tone, squeezed through his gritted teeth. 'Lyle's condition is much too grave for visitors. Lady Darleston's actions may yet deprive him of his life and my daughter of her husband. I think you'll agree, given those facts, that your presence will only aggravate an already volatile situation.'

Did he imagine Emma would run at him and beat her fists against his chest, or that Lyle would wake and bellow at him in outrage? He might deserve both, even if he expected neither. 'I needn't disturb him.' He only wanted to say goodbye and explain his departure. 'Lyle needn't be roused. If I could just speak with Emma, so she could pass my words on.'

Hill gave a more vigorous shake of his head. 'I will pass them on. What did you wish to say?'

Darleston stammered for a moment. He was not about to whisper 'I love you' to Hill to pass on. 'Just that I am sorry, and that I hope he mends, and that I hope this will not sever our friendship.'

Somehow he doubted Hill would even pass on that much. His whole demeanour had changed. Darleston almost said as much. He bowed instead and backed away. Regardless of what Hill wished, he'd pay his respects to both Emma and Lyle before he left.

'I'm not blind to what goes on around me, sir.' Hill's voice snaked its way across the carpet towards him. 'I know what part you played in this. Don't think to go against my wishes and aggravate the trouble you've already caused.'

Had his intentions been so plainly written on his face? Darleston tried to readopt the mask he wore in town, but found he could not smile, even thinly. 'Sir.'

'Milord. Both my daughters have made suspect decisions of late. I cannot find those choices acceptable. Do I make myself clear? Don't increase the trouble you've already caused. In fact, I'd henceforth advise you to sever all contact with the Langleys.'

Darleston steadied himself against the back of a chair that stood by the doorway. The soft leather moulded to the shape of his grip. 'Are you accusing me of something?'

'No, Lord Darleston. I am not. Provided you do as I suggest I have no cause for complaint.'

Which meant that the man suspected certain things but had no evidence to back them up. Darleston met Hill's eyes and saw the truth staring back at him – coldness and hatred, and not because of any damage Lucy had done, but because Hill knew that he and Lyle's relationship had encompassed more than friendship. Heaven knows when he'd begun to suspect. Hell knows what he thought of his daughter's involvement. Maybe he still questioned it. Certainly he'd dismissed the notion of Emma engaging in any sort of physical contact when Lucy had hinted at the affair that morning.

'The servants have their instructions. Leave, milord. I don't want to make things uncomfortable for you.'

Darleston turned on his heels and left without bidding his host goodnight.

* * *

Emma woke to daylight with cramp slicing into the side of her neck. Lyle still lay in the bed, swaddled within a thick layer of blankets. Someone had stoked up the fire so that the room was stifling and grey wisps of smoke belched from the sooty chimney.

Emma eased herself out of the chair in which she'd slept, stiff muscles protesting at the effort, and leaned over Lyle's prone form. Having satisfied herself that he was still breathing, albeit with an uneven rhythm, she hobbled over to the window and cast open the door onto the balcony. The fresh breeze rushed in to greet her, lifting her skirts and freeing her skin from the clammy grip of her clothes. The sky stretched out before her, bright blue, with not even a wisp of cloud. The day would be glorious, perfect for idling away picking blackberries or splashing her feet in the stream. They might have taken a picnic hamper packed with Beattie's pickles and freshly cooked pies. The three of them could have sat together, learning who they were. Darleston knew so much more about her than she'd ever told Lyle, but he knew more about Lyle too. The two men shared a past she wanted to unravel. She wanted to listen to their stories and laugh with them over ancient misdeeds. Instead – Emma glanced back at the bed and a sense of foreboding made her hug her arms to her chest – she didn't know if Lyle would make it through the day.

Perspiration peppered his brow and the bridge of his nose when she returned from the window to perform a more thorough inspection. His blond hair hung in damp curls that stuck to his skin. Emma combed one away from his cheek. It sprang back into place like an unwound coil.

He'd always been well dressed. Lyle turned heads, but he'd never turned hers. She'd never appreciated him in that way until this last week, when Darleston had made her see Lyle differently.

Darleston loved him.

He loved her too, at least she thought so. She shook a little as she reached out to trace a fingertip over Lyle's cracked lips. They were bleached almost to the tone of his skin. Why hadn't Darleston come to see them? She understood that he had Lucy to deal with but, once she was securely locked away, she'd expected Darleston to sit beside her and wait for Lyle to wake.

Her husband lay so still that Emma thought nothing of extending her touch across the rest of his face, then down his neck into the collar of his nightshirt. The wound in his arm had been bound with strip upon strip of clean white linen. Drummond had removed the sleeve from one of Lyle's nightshirts to accommodate the injury.

Emma touched the bandages lightly, counting the lines down from his shoulder to his elbow. The linen was wet.

Alarmed, she drew back. Drummond had closed the wound. She'd held Lyle's arm and watched the seams of the hole being drawn together by the thread. The bandages ought not to be wet.

She looked at Lyle anew, and saw the sweat beaded on his skin and his deathly pallor. Fever. 'No, Lyle,' she told him. 'I cannot lose you.'

Emma rang the bell for assistance, but didn't wait for it to arrive. Instead she poured tepid water from the jug on the nightstand into the basin and bore that over to the bed. Lyle groaned a little as she pressed a damp cloth to his skin. She cleaned his face and upper torso, delving into the open collar of his shirt. His eyelids fluttered once or twice but never fully opened. Instead, his stillness mocked her. This is how she'd asked Darleston to be – still, almost lifeless. She no longer wanted that. She wished Lyle to be as he had always

319

been. They had a future together, an uncertain one, yes, but a more positive and fulfilling one now that Darleston had come into their lives. She didn't fool herself into thinking they'd ever be intimate in a conventional sense, but they'd forged a bond over the last week more meaningful than their hollow wedding vows.

'Wake up, Lyle. Please.'

Amelia arrived in answer to the bell, instead of a maid. She'd brought up a plate of sandwiches and a bowl of broth. 'You're touching him,' she observed, before sinking into the chair Emma had recently vacated. She looked almost as wan as Lyle, with her bright-blue eyes red-ringed.

Emma nodded. 'It's hard to bathe someone without doing so. Where's the maid?'

'Must I be ill for you to touch me?'

A rebuke sat on Emma's lips, but something in Amelia's expression stopped her. 'I'm sorry,' she apologised instead. 'I'm sorry I've been such a dreadful sister to you. I never looked after you as I should have. You deserved my affection and I never gave it.'

'I understand why,' Amelia replied. 'At least I do now that certain things have been made plain. Aunt Maude tried to explain it once, but I didn't understand how you could hold all those dead things dear and not me. You never comforted me, not even when I scuffed my knees.'

It seemed strange to talk of such things with Lyle lying between them, yet somehow appropriate. 'I couldn't. It wasn't you. It wasn't your fault. You survived, Amelia, like me. We survived and none of the others did. I never expected that to happen. I always believed I'd have to give you up too. So I was determined not to love you too much.'

Amelia held out her hand. Emma hesitated, but then took

it. Her sister's hands were slender and cool, utterly unlike the pudgy sibling fists she'd held before.

'How is Lyle?'

Emma shook her head. 'Not good. I think Drummond ought to look at him again.'

'Not Dr Waddingthorpe?'

'I trust Drummond over him.'

Amelia nodded. 'Father's sent him away. He's dismissed Harry too, and sent all the guests home.'

It took a moment for the full extent of Amelia's news to sink in. 'All of them? Whatever for? Harry had nothing to do with this, and Drummond saved Lyle.' Their father's actions made no sense at all. 'All of the guests?' Her stomach seemed to drop into her feet, which suddenly seemed so heavy she could hardly move them enough to guide herself into the chair on the opposite side of the bed to Amelia.

'Darleston went first. He and his brother drove away with Lady Darleston last night.' Her horror must have shown, for Amelia scuttled around the bed to her. She knelt by Emma's side. 'I don't think he wanted to go. He tried to get in here, but Father set the footmen on guard.'

'I never heard anything.' Emma jumped up, too agitated to remain still. Darleston simply couldn't be gone. She needed him. He was her backbone. Without him, she was not nearly so brave.

'Father had something put into your tea. He made me, Emma. He said you needed your rest. I swear I didn't know what he was going to do. He had Grafton put something into mine too. I slept like a log for twelve hours.'

If it was not lack of sleep that had ringed her sister's eyes, then what was it?

'He dismissed Harry. He's dreadfully angry, Emma.'

Why did she keep twittering on about Harry Quernow? 'Did the fight go badly, then?' Emma asked.

Tears tracked down her sister's face. Amelia rubbed at her eyes, making their redness all the more lurid. 'No. Jack won. It was an overwhelming victory. He sent Harry away because he knew I loved him. Harry made a bet upon the fight. He hoped it would give him enough independent means to support me. Father never even gave him the chance to ask for my hand. He just packed him off with all the other guests.'

Emma braced herself with her hands on the footboard. There was so little clarity at the moment, or maybe she simply refused to see the truth. 'I still don't understand why he'd dismiss Lyle's valet. They've been with each other for years. He had no authority to do that.'

Amelia clambered to her feet once more, her conservative dress now thoroughly rumpled. 'I don't believe Father thinks he'll survive.'

Emma shot a quick glance at her husband. Lyle's condition was by no means good, but to have already dismissed him as if he were gone – that stung. She had never believed her father a callous man, and he had always got on so well with Lyle.

'Emma, in his head I think he's already buried him.'

All she could do was pace and shake her head. How could he think that? Nay, even if he thought it, to precipitately send the healers away was madness. 'I need to speak to him.'

'Emma.' Amelia backed towards the door, successfully blocking her exit. 'He knows what you've done. What you and Lyle have both done. He said some frightful things before I came up here. I can't believe that they are true. Tell me they're not true. I know I said some things, but I only meant to vex you. I never truly believed them.' She swallowed hard, and then burst into a fresh bout of tears. 'I can't see a season or anything else to look forward to now. Father means to punish us. He says we're both a disgrace.'

Emma idly patted her sister's shoulder while her thoughts reeled. She knew the bond that Lyle and Darleston shared was not one accepted or even tolerated by society. She'd always known that if Lyle's proclivities were revealed she'd have to forfeit her life with him, but she'd never expected her father to act so cruelly as to wish her husband dead. 'What did Father say?'

'That Darleston incited you both to lewd practices. He made me read from the Old Testament, but I can't believe any of you did such wicked things.'

They had, though she wasn't about to confess to it. Besides, letting a man die without fighting to save him was a far worse sin than loving one, or even two. 'I've done nothing of which I'm ashamed,' she said. She grasped Amelia's hands tight. 'My husband is not dead. Help me, Amelia. Help me save Lyle and my life. I'm not allowing him to die because Father thinks it's just punishment for some imaginary sin. Love isn't wrong. It will distress me far more to lose him than whatever ills father believes we have done will harm him.' She handed Amelia a handkerchief to dry her face. 'Drummond said we should use maggots if the wound became infected. I think it might be. The bandages are wet when they should be dry.'

Amelia gazed at her, her face alight with wonder behind her uncertain frown. 'You've changed. Knowing Darleston has changed you.'

'He opened my eyes.' She refrained from giving any more details. Amelia didn't need to know the complexities of the triangular relationship she, Lyle and Darleston and formed.

All she needed to understand was that it was something worth fighting for.

'You don't deny that you made love to him?'

'We can ask Beattie to help, and her daughter. They both know about poultices and compresses. So it was Harry all along that you were making eyes at?'

'I liked him from the very first day that Father employed him, but I didn't know for sure that it was more than that until the other gentlemen arrived and I had something to compare him to. It's no good now, though. Father won't hear of it. And don't lie to me that he will.'

For the first time in her life Emma embraced her youngest sister. 'I won't, but that doesn't mean it has to end badly. If Harry's still true to you, you can elope.' Amelia's eyes lit with hunger. She dried away the last of her sniffles. 'But not yet. Not until Lyle is healed. Help me, and I promise I'll help you.'

CHAPTER TWENTY-TWO

Nine weeks later: late August 1801

Few turned out to witness the interment, only the diehard barnacles and those unfortunate and desperate enough to have no other social engagements. A funeral simply didn't hold the same appeal as a coming-out ball, several of which had already been announced for the coming season, and while the rumours about Darleston's preferences had quieted over the summer, the scandal surrounding him hadn't been entirely forgotten.

He stood by the graveside nodding his acknowledgements to the other attendees. His father, the Earl of Onnerley, had come, as had Neddy, bearing condolences from Giles Dovecote and some others of their set. Most surprisingly, Oxbury had dragged himself out of the woodwork to pay his respects, but then, considering how often he'd shared Lucy's affections, perhaps he felt he owed her that much. Littleton, on the other hand, remained notable by his absence.

Only one buffoon was foolish enough to suggest he start hunting for a new wife. Darleston immediately cut him. One marriage was plenty for any lifetime. Let his brother produce an heir for the title, or let it fall to some distant cousin. He didn't care either way. No woman would ever shackle him as Lucy had done. He'd watched her suffer these last nine weeks and regularly wondered if he ought to have taken up the pistol she'd used to maim Lyle and turned it upon her. It certainly would have been a swifter, more satisfying sort of justice. Instead, he'd watched her become stick-thin apart from that swollen, tender belly. She'd maintained it was his child even with her dying breath.

Neddy fell into step with him as they walked from the graveyard back to the waiting carriage. In their muted black ensembles, they were perfect duplicates, their red hair luridly bright against the dark velvet. Only their stocks and shirts were white. Yet they remained steadfastly different. Few saw it, but little things separated him from Ned, small but fundamental things.

'How badly has she left you off?' Neddy asked as the crested landau pulled away from the cemetery gates. 'I know her creditors have been circling like vultures.'

Rumours of Lucy's illness had spread surprisingly fast, considering they'd kept themselves confined to the Onnerley estate. All manner of folks had washed up at his door demanding their dues. 'Nothing too colossal, and only her mantua-maker made any fuss. The poor woman hadn't been paid since Lucy and I married, but she was too worried about losing custom to risk making a fuss prior to her death.' She'd been the first to arrive with a bundle of logbooks and receipts in hand to substantiate her claim. He'd paid her extra just to be rid of her and out of fear over who would turn up next. If news of Lucy's illness had spread, rumours of her involvement in Lyle's injury would surely follow. But they never did.

'Still no word?' Neddy asked, accurately interpreting the direction of his thoughts.

'Nothing substantial, only what Drummond's managed to glean from the locals.' Lyle's valet had come to him in despair after Hill dismissed him without warning or references and for no discernable reason. The man had done his best for Lyle, which made his treatment all the more abominable. The best Darleston could do was offer him a position – one that predominantly involved keeping tabs on the goings-on at Field House. Things had been overly quiet there for far too long, although the residents had been stirred up somewhat over the last sennight.

Damn Lucy to the eternal pits of hell, she'd given him naught but anguish and taken from him the only good thing of recent years. No matter how much he longed for it, he wasn't sure he'd ever see Lyle or Emma again. His only consolation was that there'd been no similar entry to Lucy's in the newspapers, announcing Lyle's interment also.

'You could have gone back and insisted upon seeing them.'

Darleston turned his head to the window and watched the green field rolling past. If only it were as simple as Neddy made it all sound. He'd known when his carriage left Field House that there'd be no returning; to insist upon it even now would only provoke a scandal. Lucy might be dead, but he doubted whether Hill's outrage over the unlawful conduct in which he and Lyle had engaged themselves had calmed in the least.

'What are you going to do, Rob?'

'Wait. I don't see that there's anything else that I can do. I don't even know how they feel about me after what happened.'

It was Neddy's turn to peer out of the window. Although accepting of his foibles, Darleston knew his brother still found the topic uncomfortable. Ned thought nothing of hopping into bed with another man providing they had a maid to share, but exchanging affections with another man beyond some playful ribbing was a step beyond his comprehension.

Regardless, Darleston pursued the topic. He needed to vent, and Neddy was the only one prepared to listen. 'They're everything I want, Neddy. Lyle always was. I just never dared think about what might have been after he'd been packed off to India. There seemed no sense in making an issue out of something that I'd already lost.'

Neddy's gaze remained steadfastly set upon the sheep outside. 'I know how much it hurt. I heard you sobbing through the night. It's why I brought you together. I didn't know if you'd still feel the same way but, when I saw Lyle again, he was carrying that same sort of lonely shroud I've seen you wear. I never anticipated you making Emma part of it. I'd heard the rumours about her iciness.'

Darleston stared hard at the back of his twin's head until Neddy turned to face him.

'I don't have any answers, Rob, other than for you to walk away and start afresh somewhere else now that you're free of Lucy.'

'You don't mean me to do that.'

Neddy bowed his head. 'No, but someone had to state it as an option. You've wasted years of your life already, waiting for something that was never going to happen. I don't want to see you stagnate like that again.'

'It won't happen.'

The flicker of irritation that briefly furrowed the space between Neddy's brows betrayed his doubts over that, but Darleston chose to let it go. He had no intention of allowing things to carry on like this indefinitely. At some point either Emma or Lyle or both would appear in public, and then he'd be there. Hill could warn him off, but he couldn't prevent them meeting outside his territory. His main fear, however, was not Hill, but that it had been Lyle and Emma's decision to shun him. They hadn't spoken after the shooting. He had no way of knowing how much that one incident had influenced their thoughts. Perhaps they saw him now as a passing summer folly, something best forgotten and never spoken about. It would kill him to hear that, but one way or another he had to find out.

* * *

Two weeks later

'We're leaving, Father. It doesn't matter how much you object to it. Lyle is recovered now and we have our own property to tend.' That was explanation enough for their departure, without bringing up the myriad other reasons why they were so keen to hurry away. He'd kept them here as virtual prisoners for nearly three months. For much of that time she'd had no choice but to weather his scrutiny and disdain. He'd only softened his censure a little when he saw how much effort she'd put into saving her husband's life. He'd been genuinely pleased to see Lyle recover, so she guessed he'd shuffled all his low opinions onto Darleston's shoulders. It was easy to blame someone who wasn't present and already had a reputation as a fiend. She hadn't heard a good word spoken about the entire Darleston clan since the day they'd left Field House.

'Your sister is missing. How can you even think of going home?' Mr Hill blocked her path across the hallway, though there was still room to flit past him.

Emma looked up at her father's wrinkled brow and saw

his fears and loneliness. 'Amelia is not missing, father. She's eloped. I'm sure we'll hear from her in a week or so.' Her sister wanted nothing more than to be able to return home a wedded woman and show off her new husband.

'And this elopement doesn't bother you?'

'No. I'm afraid it doesn't. It was her choice, her mistake to make, if that's what it turns out to be, though I don't believe it shall.' She had initially wondered, just like her father, if Amelia's interest would wane through lack of contact, but her love for Harry had remained remarkably steadfast. 'She loves Mr Quernow. It's who she wants to spend her life with, and you like him father, for all your grumbling.'

'He was a fine secretary is all I said.' Mr Hill placed particular emphasis on Harry's former role.

'Well, perhaps he will be a particularly fine son-in-law too. He's more interested in your business of prize-fighting than Lyle will ever be.' And more able too, after what had happened, she might have added but didn't.

'Hmph,' her father snorted. 'And I suppose you think I should just welcome them back without a quibble?'

'Exactly.' Emma walked around him. She did not want an argument to be the last words they spoke to one another before parting. For all his faults, he had tried to do his best for her. He'd been a good parent to her for most of her life. He'd done his best to provide for them, but at the moment he seemed so blinded by the horrors of his own past that he refused to imagine anything but the worst outcome for everybody.

Mr Hill tapped his walking stick hard on the floor, signalling her to stop. Emma turned back to him reluctantly. 'And who do you love? That's what I should like to know,' he asked.

Her nose prickled at the question. Memories she fought daily almost overwhelmed her. Emma stiffened her spine and pushed her shoulders back. 'I should have thought that was perfectly apparent, given that I've spent so many weeks nursing him.' She did love her husband, just not as her father meant.

Luckily, Lyle emerged from the bootroom at that very moment, upon his lips a thank-you to Grafton for his aid. He smiled when he saw her, which warmed her from inside and at least seemed to calm some of her father's suspicions. She smiled back.

'Yuletide,' Mr Hill announced. 'I'll expect to see you both then. No excuses, unless it's for a confinement.'

Maybe they'd come back, maybe they wouldn't. Too much depended on what happened next. She was fair certain that a baby wouldn't be it.

Lyle had grown thinner during the summer, so that his clothes fitted a little less well, and Drummond was no longer around to adjust them. His hair was cropped short. It had made it easier to tend while he lay bedridden, although it was just now starting to show a tendency to curl again.

Four times she had nearly lost Lyle during the night; three times she'd prayed that her life be forfeit in place of his; the last she time she'd sold her soul to the devil instead. She'd climbed onto the bed and lain beside Lyle, their bodies stretched out like two matchsticks, and she'd whispered to him about all the reasons he had to live. She'd recounted the paired vision of loveliness he and Darleston had made when their bodies were entwined. She'd told him how it felt to take Darleston's cock inside her, and speculated how it would be between them if they all made love to one another at once. She'd touched him to show him how brave she'd become and how it would work.

Miraculously, the next morning Lyle woke. She wouldn't pretend he'd been immediately hale and hearty. It'd been a long fight to get him back on his feet. Now, though his arm was whole and appeared to be healed, apart from a small ruddy gouge at the top, he was still handicapped. He could no longer hold things or form a tight grip. Sensation there was unreliable too. He didn't always know when she was touching him.

Lyle held his arm stiffly as Grafton fastened up the buttons of his greatcoat. He still wore his injured arm out of the sleeve, though he no longer kept it bound in a sling.

'Mr Hill, we really, really must be off. Your hospitality has been incomparable, but I can no longer abstain from seeing to my affairs. Things have to be dealt with, and I can no longer use this –' Lyle lifted his injured arm '– as an excuse. Good day, sir.' He gave a very formal bow, which Emma copied in the form of a curtsy.

'Father. We'll see one another soon. I'll write to you, if I hear anything from Amelia.' She thought he might cry as they made their way outside to the waiting carriage. She prayed he had Amelia back with him soon. Maybe she and Harry would give him the houseful of offspring he wanted. Mr Hill had always forgiven his youngest daughter in the past, and she knew he had a soft spot for Harry Quernow. As for Harry, he knew he'd made mistakes in his past, and he'd worked ridiculously hard to fix them. He now seemed to be doing very well for himself.

'Free.' Lyle pushed down the window and stuck his head outside to breathe in a lungful of air the moment they left Field House and turned into the lane. 'I didn't think he'd ever allow us to go. Now, have you managed to locate Darleston's address?'

Emma delved into her pocket for the note she'd made of it. She'd written several letters of her own over the last few months, only to find their burnt remains in the library fire. Whatever offences her father had decided she'd made, he'd been determined to ensure she didn't repeat them. This address was new, though, acquired in the last week through a network of servants. 'Here it is. It's a small cottage he's taken in Derbyshire. Drummond is working for him.'

'Excellent. Tap on the roof and have the driver take us straight there.'

Emma hesitated in carrying out the instruction. 'I thought you meant to write first.'

Lyle took the card from her and transferred it to his injured hand before he pulled her firmly to his side. 'I've written to Darleston before. He's abysmally bad at sending any sort of reply. No, I think the best thing would be to face him and ask him straight out what he wants. That way, at least we'll know.'

'Yes,' she said meekly. Lyle was right, of course, but, God help them, what if Darleston said no?

* * *

Tangled thickets of wildflowers bordered Grindley Grange, the riverside cottage Darleston had hired. A climbing rose straddled an archway that led onto the driveway, from which one gained one's first real sight of the house as the road sloped down towards the river. It was not as grand as Field House, though it dated from a similar era. Nor was it a property one expected to find inhabited by a lord.

'Why is he here?' Emma asked, as they waited for the carriage steps to be folded down.

The bulk of the building was formed of thick slabs of grey stone, to which a more recent red-brick façade had been added. The grounds too were modest, bordered all around by steep slopes and farmland. There were no near neighbours save the occasional stray sheep.

'Why do you think?' Lyle replied. He descended ahead of her, and then used his good arm to help her down. 'To hide, of course.' Whether he meant as a result of the ever circulating rumours or from society mammas eager to introduce him to their daughters, he didn't explain. Either, she supposed, might induce a man to hide.

She let go of Lyle's hand once her feet were safely on the track. How quickly she'd come to depend on these little shows of affection between them. Not that she accepted them from everyone, only from Lyle and sometimes Amelia. Occasionally, she wondered how she'd managed to get through life before their comfort. 'Do you think he's mourning his wife?'

'No.' Lyle loosed a little laugh, which did nothing to ease the tension wrought by their arrival and magnified by the isolation of the property. 'Emma, he hated her. She did nothing kind the entire length of their marriage. She branded him as her property and cared not at all how he felt about that.'

'Do we knock?'

There was no need, for Drummond emerged from the cottage. He immediately hurried over to greet them, and to instruct their driver and footman about the disposition of their luggage. 'You look well, sir,' he said to Lyle, having ushered them both into Grindley's modest hallway. He took her pelisse, and then helped Lyle shed his greatcoat. Drummond's gaze lingered over the fact that Lyle still wore his frockcoat with one arm outside the sleeve. He gave a tut of displeasure, but made no further remark. 'Milord isn't expecting you, is he?'

'Isn't he?' Lyle asked.

Drummond sucked in his cheeks and gave a swift shake of his head. 'No, I don't think so, sir.'

'Then perhaps you'd better announce us.'

'Very good. If you'll just wait a moment, Mr Langley. Mrs Langley, there's a chair behind you if you need to rest.'

Emma accepted the chair by the bootrack, which seemed to house as many walking sticks as items of footwear. She had wished so ardently for this moment over the summer months, but now trepidation made her stomach clench. Why had they not addressed him in a letter first? It was so much easier to speak one's mind on paper, although she understood it was not always wise to do so. Letters could go astray. Folk other than the recipient could read them and make light of the contents. Still, she had to question if they'd done the right thing in coming here without giving him due warning.

He might not want them here. Perhaps he was hiding from them.

The house smelled of linseed oil and dried flowers that had been set there to mask the mustiness of long disuse. The windows in the entrance hall were small and let in hardly any light. They were still mired with cobwebs and grime around the edges. She didn't think Darleston had been in residence all that long. It wouldn't surprise her to find several of the rooms still masked with drapes.

Drummond returned within seconds to show them the way. He threw open a door onto a lovely sunny parlour that overlooked the river. Here at least the furnishings were clean. The walls were painted an appealing yellow, giving everything a homely glow. The room reminded her strongly of the Dog Parlour that she'd made her own at Field House, though there was a stag's head set above the fire instead of a pompous portrait.

Emma's hands flew to cover her mouth as she set eyes upon Darleston. It had been midsummer when they'd last seen one another. He'd dipped his head and kissed Lyle upon the cheek before her father arrived and the doctors set about probing the hole in Lyle's arm. He had not said goodbye to her in any way. Nor did he greet her familiarly now.

In appearance, he hadn't changed from how she remembered him. Red hair, the same burnished shade as the copper kettle that sat upon her kitchen stove, still framed his narrow face. The strands had grown a fraction longer, so that the ends bobbed just short of his shoulders. His clothes, too, still enticed her to reach out and touch.

Darleston's gaze strayed first to Lyle and then to her. 'Will you take a seat?'

How different this was from the way he and her husband had greeted one another at the start of the summer. She'd looked on them then as they damn near winded one another, and cursed the closeness that excluded her. Now she longed for such a display of devotion, so that it could unravel all the knots that held their affection in check.

Lyle prodded her into a seat beside him on the sofa facing the unlit fire.

'How is your –' Darleston began.

'We heard about the funeral.'

'– arm?'

Both men settled back, neither giving a response to the questions asked. Lyle crossed his legs before him, an action Darleston soon duplicated. They gazed at one another, but without truly seeing each other, almost as if their images were warped like a reflection in a pond beset with ripples.

'There's a little stiffness.' Lyle hitched his right shoulder to rub at the wound. 'The feeling's returning slowly.' He bent and stretched his fingers, but Emma knew he didn't have the same degree of sensation in them that he'd possessed before.

Darleston's jaw relaxed a fraction. 'I'm glad you're healing.'

'Are you?'

Lyle's response brought back all the tension that had just been released.

'Of course,' Darleston insisted. His grey eyes opened wide, and he leaped out of his chair.

Lyle stood too. 'No, you misunderstand me. I meant, how are you? Not to imply that you weren't glad. Have you let go of her memory yet, Robert?'

The look in his eyes – lightning meshed with thunder – suggested ire at the question. 'I don't think of her. Other matters have occupied my thoughts.'

Us, Emma hoped, but he in no way implied that.

'You'll stay for dinner?' Darleston insisted. 'It's no trouble. And the night too, considering the hour. There are no inns locally that could accommodate you.' He rang the servants' bell and passed messages to Drummond for his housekeeper and cook. 'I insist on it.'

* * *

Darleston splashed his face with water. He prayed he knew why they had come here, but dared not believe in it. He'd waited months without hearing a word, and now they were here without announcement or warning.

He dressed formally for dinner, in a claret-coloured coat and cream breeches. His waistcoat had enough embroidery to be considered a tapestry. Still, it was to good effect. Presenting himself at his best helped him hide his tumultuous feelings. It was impossible not to hope, when they had turned up upon his doorstep, yet he hardly dared to let his thoughts stray in such a fanciful direction.

Emma was in the dining room when he went back downstairs. She'd changed into a lilac satin dress that he'd never seen before. The waistline rode high and tightened just beneath her breasts, which for once were not completely covered by a glorified handkerchief. Instead, their curve was provocatively framed by a spray of lace. Sadly, the sides of her gown were crumpled, as though she'd been twisting the satin. Indeed, when she saw him, her hands flew to those very spots.

She looked well. Delightfully so. Her chestnut hair held a glossy sheen and hadn't been so severely tied as she'd previously been inclined to wear it, but her expression was one of measured anguish.

'Are you well?' he asked.

'Very.'

'Why did you come?'

Her fists made further creases in the satin. 'Don't you know? Can't you work it out?'

He knew what he hoped, but didn't dare speak it.

Emma was braver. 'We needed to know how things stood. Whether there was space for us still in your heart. We've heard nothing from you. You left without a goodbye.'

Darleston squeezed his fists tight to stop himself grabbing hold of her. He longed to shake her and tell her it wasn't his fault. If only he could show her the depth of his feeling, and how much it had cost him not to make an unholy fuss. He'd kept away out of loyalty to his family, who couldn't stomach any more disgrace, and because he didn't want to draw scandal to Lyle and Emma's doorstep.

'Not out of choice. Your father –' he barked.

'I know what he did.' Emma cut him off. 'This isn't about that, it's about us, and what we want now. It doesn't matter what my father thinks.'

He took a step forward, eager to touch her, but restrained himself, thinking that perhaps he had forfeited that right. 'What do you want, Emma?'

Her eyebrows lifted slightly, and her delicate, kissable lips parted. He watched her tongue flick over her lower lip, leaving a thread of moisture. 'You. Is that not obvious? I want what we had before.' Her eyes blazed with inner warmth.

Darleston bowed his head. 'Things changed when Lucy pulled the trigger.' *Many, many things.*

'Yes,' she agreed, nodding, yet with a note of enquiry in her voice.

'Changed so that you no longer want us?' The question came not from Emma but from Lyle. His soft voice reached them from the adjoining room. Both Darleston and Emma turned in time to see him approach. At first he lingered in the gloom at the end of the sideboard, so that shadows masked his expression. 'Mayhap you don't care to associate with a man maimed by your wife.'

Darleston immediately swept towards him. 'Good God, is that what you think? You're not maimed, and even if you were –' He broke off, took a deep breath. 'I've wanted you both every minute of the last three months. It's been agony maintaining my distance. Hill made it absolutely plain what the outcome would be if I came even as close as the village.'

Lyle remained silent, though he emerged from the shadows. He had not dressed as if for dinner but in a swathe of multicoloured silk that made joyous curves of his figure. It emphasised both his physique and his height, which damn near stole Darleston's breath. He looked his former lover up and down with his mouth slightly agape and his heart thumping fast.

Lyle wore curled-toed slippers upon otherwise bare feet. Darleston recalled the shape of each of his toes, long and quite slender, the nails always perfectly clipped and buffed. But he couldn't keep staring at the man's feet to avoid what lay in their hearts.

Meeting Lyle's gaze didn't help. All he could think was how goddamn good Lyle looked.

'Is that true, Robert? That you wanted us?' Lyle stepped a fraction closer.

'It's always been true,' he muttered, letting the words seep up out of his heart as he gazed into Lyle's eyes. 'It killed me to leave you when you were so badly hurt, but I had no choice. I've hung on every scrap of news that Drummond has brought.' He reached out to Lyle, who accepted the touch with his head bowed.

'We were parted once before, remember, Robert? Fate intervened eventually. I couldn't leave things to chance a second time. I didn't want to spend years yearning for the time when our paths would cross. What made it worse was that I sometimes thought you didn't enquire after my health because it was really only Emma that you wanted. Your past reputation would have supported that. Or maybe the whole thing had been no more than a bit of summer fun for you, a bit of a challenge.'

Hurt, Darleston rushed to his own defence. 'I wanted you both and could do naught about it. What we had, what we were building, it was never a game for me.'

Lyle gave a quick nod. 'Then I beg you'll forgive my darkest thoughts. You see, I had too much time to think while stuck in bed, and fever causes strange dreams. You never ran to me when I fell.' He shushed away Darleston's attempt to explain. 'I know that you were holding Lucy, trying to keep us safe from further attack, but I damn near lost my arm, and you never comforted me. It made me wonder if you'd deliberately goaded Lucy into making the attack, so that you could remove me and have Emma to yourself.'

Darleston leapt upon the notion at once, determined to stamp it firmly into the ground. 'Dear God, how could you think that of me? I told you from the start how it was. I never hid anything. I wanted to be with you, but there was never the opportunity to allow that.' He turned away from Lyle, shaking his head.

'He did offer you some comfort,' Emma said. 'It was just before the doctor came, after Drummond had sewn you up. I envied that you had that, while I had no goodbye at all.'

As if in response to his name being called, Drummond appeared at the door, but on seeing them deep in conversation he turned away again and closed the door behind him. They heard him shooing the maid back to the kitchen in a loud whisper.

Once it was quiet, Darleston took up the thread again. 'I know you were hurt, but how could you make the accusation you just did?'

Lyle shook his head. 'You're not hearing me properly. I haven't accused you of anything, just shared my dark thoughts. All I'm asking now is that you speak truthfully about what you want – not just now, but in the long term.'

Hellfire! Had he not already said it? Ire caused him to clench his fists. Darleston turned and looked at their expectant faces and realised that he'd have to say it all over again, stating it plainly and simply. 'I love you.' He turned his head to make sure he meant them both. 'Time isn't going to change that. Come here, you obtuse bugger.' He grabbed hold of Lyle and pulled him into a tight embrace. Initially stiff, Lyle soon relaxed into his shoulder until there was no room between them.

He hadn't dared hope to feel or be held like this again. 'Emma too.' They opened their arms and she hurried to them, so that they stood in a triangular embrace, grinning like fools.

'I want you both, for as long as you'll put up with me.' Emma was as much a part of his dreams as Lyle.

'Then all's fine and we should eat,' Lyle said, raising a chuckle. He took a step backwards, rubbing his injured arm.

Darleston looked from Emma to the table and then back to Lyle's face, and knew what he wanted. 'Cobs to food! Are you naked beneath this?' He slipped one of the fastenings on the front of Lyle's patterned robe and pushed his hand within. As he'd anticipated, bare skin greeted him. A grin creased his face. 'What on earth possessed you to wear such an unsuitable outfit to dinner?'

Lyle ran his fingers over the front seam. 'I thought it might make things easier once it was time to retire. You've stolen my valet, and it's damned hard to get in and out of a coat one-handed.'

For all the laughter that erupted, Darleston recognised the seriousness hidden within the remark. 'You can have Drummond back right away,' he insisted. He'd only taken the man on because he'd been dismissed so unfairly. It damn near broke his heart to know that Lyle wasn't fully healed. His alarm eased a little as Lyle leaned into him so that their lips met. Shivers raced down his throat and into his groin. Darleston tore at the remaining fastenings on Lyle's robe until the silken knots gave way. Lyle wore only a pair of underbreeches beneath. The cotton clung to his hips.

Lyle's years of hard toil in India had fashioned him into a sleek white tiger. He'd lost a little tone because of his illness but his skin remained smooth and unblemished save for a golden patch of hair that grew in a diamond between his nipples, and the tear in his shoulder. His brown eyes burned with need, though he said nothing, not even when his robe slithered from his shoulders and fell like a stole into the crooks of his arms. He shook it loose, so that it dropped to the floor.

Darleston pressed him backwards until his bottom hit the table, and then held him trapped there, just looking and skimming his hands lightly over his upper body. New skin, shiny and pink, stretched over the site of the wound in his upper arm. The indentation of the ball remained at the centre of the scar. Darleston examined the exit wound too, discovering its contours with his fingertips. He bent and kissed the scar, then briefly rested his head there upon Lyle's shoulder.

'Don't grow maudlin on me, I'm fine.'

'Not maudlin, relieved. I thought I'd lost you.'

Lyle's good hand caught in Darleston's hair. 'I'm here. Nothing need separate us.'

'There'll always be obstacles.'

'That's not cause to surrender.'

Darleston held onto Lyle harder then, encircling Lyle's waist so that they were linked together chest to skin, Lyle naked, him clothed. They stayed that way for several minutes, both breathing hard, until their lips sought one another again.

This time the kisses made them groan. Lyle gave everything, affording Darleston no chance to pull away. Not that he wanted to, except perhaps to extend a hand to Emma.

Together, all three of them. That's how it had to be now.

'Upstairs,' he whispered to Lyle.

Up they went, tugging Emma along too. She seemed determined to hang back and let them have their moment first, but that's not how Darleston wanted it to be. This had to be correct from the start. The bond between them might be triangular, but he intended that to be its strength; exclusion was not going to be part of the arrangement. It didn't matter if Lyle and Emma chose not to touch, as long as they were comfortable with one another and understood he wouldn't play at taking turns or having favourites.

They stumbled into the first bedroom, the one he'd given Emma for the night. It was a cheerful, sunny room, a mix of gold and lavender, with frilly feminine drapery. He and Lyle took time getting to the bed, content to drift while they kissed and explored one another's bodies. Lyle's tongue stabbed between Darleston's lips, striking him like a lance in the guts, but overwhelming him with arousal rather than pain. Years had flown by but nothing had ever really changed between them. The desire to be with one another, the hunger to meld their bodies into a single shape, remained as insistent and sharp as the first time Darleston had felt it. Lyle had always been and ever would be his greatest invitation to sin. Those eyes, that wicked grin, they were like an offer of gin to a sot. He couldn't resist. That this man had somehow stumbled upon a wife whose appeal Darleston equally relished was nothing short of a miracle.

'I need this, Robert.' Lyle turned in his arms. He slithered briefly from Darleston's grasp to spread himself out over the flowery eiderdown. 'I've had nothing but my own hand to take the edge off for so long, and that was not so easy to accomplish with two maidens sitting by my bedside.'

Darleston ducked his head to bring his nose close to the

cotton tented over Lyle's erection. 'You could have asked Emma to perform her duty.' He remembered the feel of her lips around his cock and how pleasing her sucking had been. She would have given swift satisfaction.

Lyle shot him a look of distaste. 'I'd never ask her for that. We both know it would be a lie. Nothing has changed in that regard.'

That was as he suspected, but was glad of the confirmation. 'I know your desire doesn't extend in that regard.' He tickled the root of Lyle's cock with his tongue, making the entire length of his shaft grow doubly stiff before he plucked open the drawstring around Lyle's waist and tugged down the plain cotton fabric. Lyle's prick rose, hard, seeking urgent relief. His fingers twisted in Darleston's hair, communicating urgency as Darleston aligned his mouth. 'But that doesn't mean I can't entertain myself with the thought of it.'

Lyle made a croaking noise in the back of his throat that complemented Emma's gasp of surprise. He almost laughed at them both. He'd never really understand how they could be happy sharing him but not want to love one another in the same way. Still, he wasn't about to bemoan it.

Lyle tasted both salty and tart. He wanted to linger, but sometimes swift worship usurped a more lengthy exploration, and this was one of those occasions. Lyle's nails bit into his scalp, entwining pain with the pleasure Darleston gleaned from the rhythmic thrusts into his mouth. His lover had not been lying when he'd claimed that he needed this. Lyle was wound incredibly tight. Unrestrained sighs spilled from his mouth. He burned too hot, too quickly, so that the act came to an altogether bitter-sweet ending. He jerked, giving an almighty cry. Darleston swallowed the gift and rose to cover Lyle with his body afterwards. They lay pressed tight, breathing hard, he clothed, Lyle undressed, exchanging kisses until his jaw ached.

Emma had waited patiently throughout, and her eyes gleamed when he sat and turned to her. She came and lay beside him on the bed with her head propped upon her hand. A passionate warmth filled her eyes. A hereto unremarked dimple flashed briefly in her cheek as she curled her legs behind her and rose to her knees.

Lyle held on to him, seemingly unwilling to release his grasp. Darleston didn't mind the tug upon his buttons. He gave a gasp when Lyle's hands found his cock and began to knead. Still his gaze remained steadfastly on Emma.

She unfastened her hair first, allowing the chestnut strands to cascade down her back. Following that she poured into his hand a sea of pins, which he promptly deposited on the floor. The front of her gown gaped as she moved, revealing a glimpse of the creamy skin beneath. She seemed not to notice, though the buttoned-up woman he'd met back in June would have been mortified by such exposure.

Following a nod from Lyle, Emma shrugged off the dress and at least one petticoat. She knelt before them in nothing but her stays. Her chest rose and fell with each breath. Darleston released the uppermost clasp, then a second, which exposed her breasts with their darker areolas. Playfully, she circled a finger around one nipple until it peaked. Then she twisted it, making her breath catch and grow quicker.

Darleston watched her, unable to mask his delight. Her cunny grew moist and he inhaled the scent of her arousal. 'I see you've mastered your lessons in self-pleasure.'

If he circulated the tale of her awakening amongst the beaus in town, no one would believe it. Not that he had any intention of doing so.

Lord, she was an absolute delight, but he had not forgotten their last encounter, or the promises he'd made. He wanted to stroke her cunt. To wet his fingers there and know her heat, then be able to slide his prick inside her and ride them both to fulfilment.

They sat on either side of him, watching him, beseeching him. Darleston raced through the buttons of his waistcoat, not caring if he dislodged one or two or tore the fabric in his haste. His shirt and breeches were easier as the fastenings were fewer, and Lyle had already dealt with his placket. He stepped free of boots, breeches and stockings all in one go. Then he stood before them for inspection, his long lean body flatteringly bronzed by the candlelight. His cock reared straight and proud. It bucked, seeking again the comfort of Lyle's hand.

Darleston covered the brand upon his stomach, only for Lyle to peel his hand away and trace the raised lines with his tongue.

'You shouldn't be ashamed of it. We each of us have our scars.'

True enough, though he still didn't care for this one. It was the only gift Lucy had given him that he couldn't be rid of. Still, Lyle's kisses soon chased away the painful memories associated with the ugly blemish, particularly when his mouth closed over his cock and began to suck.

Darleston pumped his hips a little. Lyle's attentions were too skilful for him not to respond. But he reached out over Lyle's back to where Emma still knelt.

A more riveting sight he'd never seen. He knew her nervousness, the fears that crippled her, but she came willingly enough into his arms, her hand shooting out to greet him in the place he needed to feel her touch most. My God, he hadn't realised how much he'd craved this. He'd shut off so many of his emotions in order to deal with Lucy. Now Emma's tongue, the brief, precious, brush of her lips, cast wide the floodgates. He didn't hear or see for several minutes. He only felt.

Felt both of his lovers, their movements perfectly complementing one another.

Lyle shimmied out from between them, allowing him to enfold Emma in his arms at last. When his thoughts next reawakened, she lay prone beneath him with one leg hooked around his hip. Somehow he'd always known her to be a sensual, sexual being – a fact she seemed determined to prove to him now as she offered herself up.

He put his mouth to her puss and supped her down. He laved her clitoris with his tongue, until she moaned so loudly that she bit on her own hands to muffle herself.

Lyle lay alongside them. Darleston's heart danced every time Lyle's palm settled over his arse. His lovers had been talking. If they'd compared notes they'd have easily worked out what he'd been wishing for all this time. Hell, he'd virtually spelled it out to Lyle several times in the past.

Only he knew what it would cost Emma to perform it. She'd been so worried about the possibility of conceiving a child. There were means of preventing that, but he had not thought to prepare a sheath.

'Do it, Robert. Let me see you pleasure her. Your prick's so stiff you're going to walk bow-legged for a week if you don't do something with it.' Lyle's tongue traced the shell of his ear.

'I can't.'

No matter how slick and welcoming her body was, no matter how much he wanted it. It didn't matter that he ached from root to tip.

'What do you mean, you can't?'

'I know she doesn't wish to conceive.'

Lyle pinched him tight around the base of his shaft, which was just as well, for he thought he might actually come.

'You could withdraw.'

'That's hardly reliable.' That, and he knew he'd never manage it.

'Don't you know any other way? What have you done all these years past?'

His first instinct was to shake his head. 'Well, there is one thing. But only if Emma consents.'

'Anything,' she agreed immediately. 'What is it?'

'I'll have to go to the kitchen.'

Both his lovers groaned.

'I'll be quick,' he promised. 'Just wait right there.' Pausing only to scoop up Lyle's robe and throw it over his own nakedness, Darleston ran down to the kitchen. He ignored the squeals of the maids and his cook and had them fetch and prepare what he needed. Then he scrambled back upstairs, tripping over the hem of the robe.

'What is it?' Emma sat up as he approached the bed. They had both done as instructed and stayed exactly as he'd left them.

Darleston shed the robe and crawled back onto the bed. He held out the little cap of lemon peel on the tip of his finger for her to inspect.

'What do you do with it?'

'Lie back. It goes inside you.'

'Is that safe?' Lyle asked.

'It's a piece of lemon, what harm could it do?'

Emma lay back. She hissed as he pushed the little cap inside of her and made sure it was seated right. When he lay over

349

her once more, he saw his own relief mirrored in her gaze. They both needed this. Nay, not just them, but Lyle too.

Lyle guided him into place. The tip of his cock slipped and slid against her wetness. In his excitement he was probably a little hasty, but Emma was slick and welcoming, and they'd all waited far too long for this. He lifted her hips, pulled her onto his cock and she enveloped him like a soft kid glove. Perfect. Magnificent. Glorious.

They duelled together horizontally, panting with exertion, until sweat slicked all the points where their bodies met, and ran down his back in rivulets.

Lyle nibbled at his shoulder. His hot hands traced circles over Darleston's back and buttocks, raising shivers with their promise of future pleasure. The headboard banged against the chamber wall each time he thrust, and he sighed in time with Emma each time he withdrew. At some point, he wasn't sure when, Lyle was no longer lying beside them but rose behind them instead. Thick, sweet fragrance filled the air. Something liquid but warm splashed against his rear. Darleston turned his head while still wrapped in Emma's embrace. Lyle knelt behind him, stroking the slim white wand of his cock. The splashes he'd felt against his arse weren't the eruption of Lyle's pleasure, as he first thought, but a means of attaining it.

'Let me join you in this.' With his palms, Lyle spread wide Darleston's cheeks. The rude press of his middle digit followed. Slowly, Lyle wormed the tip of his finger inside Darleston's arse, an act that brought such feverish heat to his whole body that it felt as if streams of sparks were encircling his shaft.

The pleasure from both front and back wrecked his ability to reason or exert any kind of control. Thankfully, his instincts took over.

'This is what you wanted, isn't it? To be fucked both ways at once.' Lyle lapped at the sweat covering his back.

'Do it,' he commanded. The press of Lyle's digit simply wasn't enough. 'Don't toy with me. Fuck me.'

'I think you'll spill right away if I so much as touch you with my prick.'

Likely he wasn't wrong, but that didn't lessen his need.

'Stop offering me platitudes and deliver.'

'You're sure? I've no intention of riding you gently.'

'Perfectly sure. If Emma agrees.'

'Do it,' she gasped. Her eyes were alight with fever as she watched Lyle slide into position. Darleston held himself still, or at least as still as his body would allow, for his hips had taken up the rhythm of love and rocked without regard for what the rest of him wanted. Beneath him, Emma lifted to meet each downward thrust. Her soft curves encompassed him. He held tight to her, stared into her eyes.

Lyle's hands seemed all-encompassing as he guided his prick home. 'That's it. Push back. Slide on to me.'

It wasn't so much a slide as a rapid jerk. The intense pressure of Lyle's cock penetrating his arse was more than enough to make him jolt. He'd been over and over this scenario, never truly believing it would happen. There had been so many obstacles to attaining it, and yet here they were, naked, writhing, moving together as one, Lyle guiding them – or maybe goading them – while Emma breathed in shallow little gasps beneath him. To his surprise, she reached out and stroked her husband's leg, the only part of him she could reach. Lyle accepted it. He didn't balk at her touch. Instead he buried himself a little deeper, and then increased the pace.

So beautiful – yet Darleston couldn't hold onto the feeling.

He knew pleasure, but it was diffuse, formless, like a breath of air. It filled him with life, but he couldn't pin it down.

He didn't grasp it. With that realisation he came.

The fizz started somewhere behind his bollocks. Each time Lyle hit him there, the light it caused burned a little brighter, until the sensation enveloped the whole of him, and his body released its gift in a single vast outpouring. He held still in that moment, not really conscious of anything other than his own skin. As reality began to reassert itself, he felt the pulse of Lyle's climax deep in his rear, while Emma's muscles fluttered around his shaft in a rhythmic grip.

He couldn't speak in the aftermath, so he just held Emma tight and let Lyle hold him. He dwelt for a while in that state of peace. Eventually, Lyle's cock slipped from his arse and he slipped from Emma.

They gazed at one another, knowing that they'd become lovers in the truest sense of the word.

'Will it serve for more than one round?' Lyle asked of the little cap. He lounged back against the mound of feather pillows and gave a contented yawn.

Laughter crinkled the corners of Emma's eyes.

'I've no idea,' Darleston said. He'd never thought to ask.

'Well, if you're not sure, you'll just have to run down to the kitchen again.'

Darleston tentatively put a foot out of bed. At this rate, they'd have no breakfast, for he'd have frightened all his servants away.

'Come here, lemon tart.' Lyle snuggled his wife to his side. 'I'll keep you warm while Robert raids the larder. Better be quick though, or else you never know – I might start getting ideas.' And, with a grin, he tweaked one of Emma's nipples.

CPSIA information can be obtained
at www.ICGtesting.com
Printed in the USA
LVOW07s1908200117
521696LV00006B/34/P